THE DEATHMASTER

A HISTORICAL THRILLER

A NOVEL BY

HUGO N. GERSTL

THE DEATHMASTER

A HISTORICAL THRILLER

A NOVEL BY

HUGO N. GERSTL

PANGÆA
Publishing Group

THE DEATHMASTER

ISBN 978-1-950134-33-5
Pangæa Publishing Group
www.PangaeaPublishing.com

Editors: Joyce Krieg; Paul Karrer; Katharine Ball; Donna Young

Cover images:
Brick wall, Court hammer,
Court hammer bitting the base @Freepik.com
Open chapter fleuron images from
@Truemitra - FreeVector.com

Cover design and typesetting by
DesignPeaks@gmail.com

For information contact:

PANGÆA PUBLISHING GROUP
25579 Carmel Knolls Drive, Carmel, CA 93923 – USA
Telephone: 831-624-3508/831-649-0668 –Fax: 831-649-8007
Email: info@pangaeapublishing.com

To:
Laurie Harper, who started this ball rolling;
Lisa and Richard, who put up with me and shepherded it along;

Jane Bednar, Vanessa Vallarta, Barry Dolowich,
Andy Swartz, Erica Gamecho,
Colleen Miller, Herb & Sharon Chelner,
Dick & Claire Gorman,
Harry & Margaret Klompas, Tom and Jill Green,
Ted Gerstl & Candy Schwartz,
Margie & Harmon Glantz, our children and grandchildren,

And, of course and eternally, for my
LORRAINE

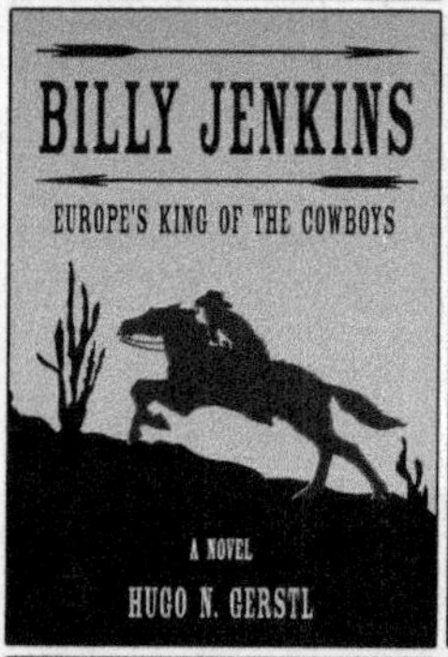

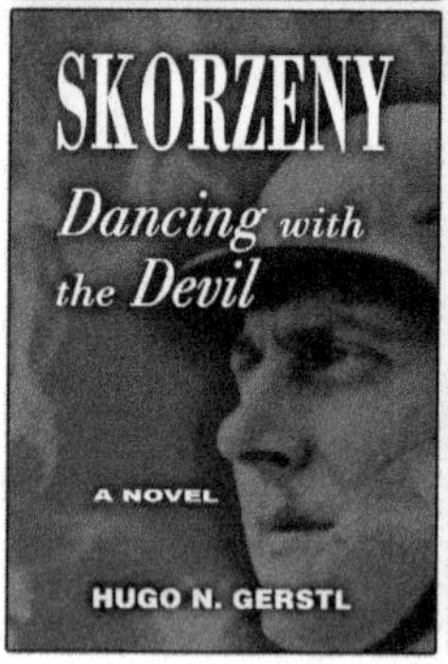

This novel is based on a true story.

The trial is a matter of public record.

FOREWORD AND
GEOGRAPHICAL APOLOGIA

Cluj, known today as Cluj-Napoca, is in Northern Transylvania –
Romania. It has been contested by Hungary and Romania for centuries.
In 1940, Germany and Italy compelled what was then known as Ruma-
nia, to cede a substantial part of Transylvania, including Cluj-Napoca,
to Hungary. That land was reclaimed by Romania at the end of World
War II.

Jews have occupied Romania for hundreds of years – always at the
uncomfortable sufferance of the Romanian populace, always with anti-
Semitic problems. Yet, in 1954, Romania was the only country in the
world that featured a *Yiddish* broadcast over its short wave radio service.

I have used the name *Romania* instead of the old name *Rumania*
throughout this book.

APRIL – JUNE, 1944

BUDAPEST
APRIL – MAY, 1944

"Blood for cargo, cargo for blood!" the tall man barked, his thin, cruel lips spitting out the words. "Tell me who you want to salvage – women who can bear children? Men in their prime? The aged? The young? Speak up!"

The stocky, round-faced blond man sat listening nervously. A young woman sat behind the desk in the German's luxurious hotel suite, pencil in hand, ready to take notes.

After a few moments, the man answered carefully. "It's not for me to decide whom you are to murder, Colonel Eichmann. I would like to save everybody. I don't understand this deal. Where are we to get the cargo? You have confiscated everything. The local Jews and our friends abroad may perhaps gather some money if lives are to be saved."

"Go to Switzerland, Turkey, Spain, wherever you please, so long as you can produce the cargo."

"What sort of cargo do you want?" the blond man asked.

"Ten thousand trucks and one thousand tons each of tea, coffee, and soap are worth a million Jews to me," the taller man replied.

"I haven't the vaguest idea where to get all of these cargoes. Who on earth do you think will treat this offer seriously?"

"I am willing to offer your people one hundred thousand Jews in advance," Eichmann said. "On receiving the consideration, I will release the remainder in the same proportion as I receive what I want. Pick any-one you want, anywhere you want — Hungary, Poland, Slovakia. To show my good faith, I will cease the deportations and exterminations while the negotiations are being carried out."

"Have you talked to the Chairman of the Jewish Agency Rescue Committee about this, Colonel?"

"I trust that since you work hand-in-glove with him, you will bring this to his immediate attention. I have found him to be most cooperative."

"When do you expect me to accomplish all of this?"

"You are to set out no later than May eighteenth, one month from today. On that date, we will begin to deport twelve thousand Hungarian Jews a day. None of them will be exterminated during the negotiations, but you, Herr Brand, must return within two weeks after you leave. I can't put your Jews on ice and preserve them forever. If the negotiations demand more time, we'll be considerate. You, however, must come back quickly. Your return, coupled with the verbal acceptance of my offer, will inspire me to cease the gassing and lay down the advance payment of one hundred thousand Jews immediately."

JERUSALEM
JUNE, 1944

The three men sat around a table perspiring in the sweltering heat of the Jerusalem summer. The large electric fan noisily thrumming at the other end of the room furnished barely enough circulating air to keep the place from being oppressive. Several strips of flypaper hung from the ceiling, filled with pestiferous insects in varying forms of decay.

The eldest of the three men spoke first.

"I agree we are placed in a difficult situation. The British have wisely placed restrictions on immigration to Palestine. After all, why should we offend our Arab hosts any more than necessary? If we want a state of Israel that has any meaning in today's world, we must encourage only the right kind of Jews to come. How could we hope to survive as a nation of pushcart peddlers and Torah scholars living five hundred years in the past?"

The young man sitting across from him was obviously agitated. "That's monstrous, Doctor Weizmann!" he said tightly. "I'm told we've already lost five million Jews in the Nazi ovens. Five million! My God, there'll be no remnant left. We've got no choice! If we allow the rest to perish, we're no better than the Germans."

Weizmann looked over at the younger man, who wore a blue and white arm patch depicting the Biblical State of Israel, an arm raised, its hand bearing a rifle, and the words "Only Thus!" emblazoned on it.

"Ah, Menachem," he said, nodding his head sagely. "To you everything is black and white. Every man starts his life believing he's on the side of good. When you're young, it's easy to know exactly what's right and what's wrong. But as you grow older, the borders of good and evil start to blur. That may be hard for you to comprehend. I only ask that you think back to what I say when you're twenty or thirty years older. When I was young, I was no different from you. I saw a political system rotten with corruption. I believed I was God's chosen, the hero who would single-handedly bring justice to Israel and the world, but in the end I didn't.

"The real world is a place where you do what you must to survive as best you can. You learn not ask certain questions. Otherwise you wake to find your entire people destroyed, with no remnant at all. Then you start to ask different questions, the kind it never occurred to you to ask when you were young. Do you understand what I'm saying?"

"That what our eyes show us is wrong is not. That if enough people tell you black is white you start to believe it."

"On the contrary, you come to understand right and wrong more deeply. You understand your own shortcomings the better. Then, one day you realize your somedays are past."

"Must it always be that way, Doctor Weizmann?"

"That's the most difficult question, Menachem. We all grow older. Perhaps you may realize the dreams of youth. Only time will answer that. Now that you know I'm not a god, that I'm simply a man, perhaps we can talk as friends, even though I realize your Irgun wants everything right now."

"No matter what you say, it is absolutely immoral to stand by and do nothing when we have the opportunity to save a million of our own human beings!" Now, the odor of the younger man's nervous perspiration added to the discomfort of the room.

Chaim Weizmann and Moshe Sharett, who had formerly been known as Moishe Shertok, sipped calmly at their glasses of tea. Finally Weizmann spoke, his eyes betraying the sadness he felt. "Our first loyalty is to England, which has stood by the promise it made to us in 1917. It is indeed a tragedy that so many must die, but remember, in days of old, Moses led the people out of Egypt and they wandered in the desert for forty years until all of the older generation had died out and a young, vigorous Israel could be reborn. Who is to question God's ways, blessed be to Him? Perhaps it is His intent that we be left with only the strongest buds on the tree of life."

"Gentlemen," Sharett addressed them, slicking back his pomaded hair. He was a head shorter than either of them, with a smooth, urbane look. "I think we have to take a hardheaded look at reality. First, how do we know this offer is even real? Second, assuming it is real, what do we do now? The British are holding Brand in Cairo. The two weeks Eichmann gave him are past. Third, where and how could we even obtain the cargo he says he needs? Finally, now that the Allies have invaded Normandy and the Germans appear to have lost the war, what's in it for us?"

"The ability to save God knows how many hundred thousands of our brothers and sisters," the Irgun man said. "There are nearly a million Jews in Hungary. God knows how they've survived so far, but they have survived. Those Jews could be the backbone of a strong, new Israel. There are sons, daughters —"

"Yes, but who needs them?" Sharett responded. "We've got enough difficulties with those we have. And assuming we are somehow able to save these Jews, exactly where do you propose to put them? The English —"

"You and your damned English!" the Irgun man spluttered in disgust. "We fought for the Balfour Declaration – a National Home for Jews – and where has it gotten us? If the English have their way, they'll hold on to this little bit of Empire until the last Jew rots or walks away in frustration."

"Or until your terrorists force them to expel us altogether," Weizmann said mildly.

"Enough," Sharett said. "I suggest we vote on the issue."

"I think," Chaim Weizmann said, "a vote may be unnecessary. I, for one, do not believe the offer is genuine, nor do I believe it is made in good faith. I salute Mister Brand for his courage, although I find it somewhat naïve and foolhardy. I suggest such a Jew is the kind we need in the new Israel. We should make every effort to have the British release him so he might return to Palestine."

"What about the Jewish Agency Rescue Committee chief?" Sharett asked. "Has anyone asked him out about Eichmann's supposed offer?"

"No," Weizmann answered. "My understanding is he's traveling everywhere he can, seeking the release of as many Jews as possible through proper diplomatic channels. I suggest he has shown great restraint and maturity."

"And I suggest he may be showing something very different," said the Irgun man. "Gentlemen, if you'll excuse me," he said, rising. "One day we may all live to be sorry for the way we acted this morning. And I, for one, will not have the death of even one Jew on my hands."

DECEMBER, 1953 –

JERUSALEM, ISRAEL

1

"Do you see this – this – garbage? How dare they allow this piece of swill to be published in the State of Israel?" The tall, stocky man fumed as he shoved the three page mimeographed letter under the Prime Minister's nose. "Absolute shit!" he shouted, as if the power of his voice would topple Sharett from his seat.

"Easy, easy, Rudy," the Prime Minister replied. "Everyone speaks his piece in Israel. You know the old joke – when you get two Jews together between them they'll have three opinions."

"Not funny, Moshe." He looked out the window at the bare trees. In half a year, the heat would be oppressive, even at the seashore, but now, in mid-December, it was blustery and frigid.

His mood, however, vacillated between cold disgust and heated anger. "For God's sake, it's been five years since independence. You'd think we'd have laws like any civilized nation. Some controls on what a scandal-monger can do. Think what this could do to my career, let alone yours."

The Prime Minister rose to his full five-foot-four height and paced about the room, trying to calm his visitor. "Rudy, this is a smudgy, cheap little letter. It's probably got a readership of fifty people. Harmless drivel. Leave it be."

"Easy enough for you to say," the taller man said, removing his glasses, extracting a handkerchief from the breast pocket of his perfectly tailored blue serge suit, and wiping the thick lenses. "You were safely in Palestine during the troubles. Lest you forget, I was the one who risked my life. Would you rather have been in my place?"

Sharett averted the other's glance. There were many things best left unsaid.

"I'm sorry, Moshe," the first man said. "I overstepped my bounds. It was a hard time for us all. Thank God we were there at the creation. Where is Ben Gurion, if I may ask?"

"Sde Boker."

"Ah, yes, the great man in retirement."

"You should see him," the Prime Minister, Moshe Sharett, said, chuckling. "The man of the soil, home on the kibbutz, cradling a lamb in his arms, his white hair blowing in all directions. That photograph appeared in *Life* magazine last week. What a joke! Can you imagine David Ben Gurion being gentle with anyone or anything? And a farmer?"

"He seems as comfortable as you and Weizmann with our good friends the British."

"Yes, Rudy, and there was a time when the company you kept wasn't so great either." Sharett returned to his swivel chair and sat down. "What do you have in mind concerning this article? Do you know the man?"

"A worthless old Hungarian scum, a pensioner. He fancies himself a newspaperman because he wrote a few articles in the thirties while he was in Vienna."

"Pity you never thought to hire him for *A Jovo*, eh?" the Prime Minister remarked mildly, mentioning the ruling Mapai Party's leading Hungarian weekly journal. "You might have nipped this in the bud. Would you like some tea, Doctor Kasztner?" Sharett asked, trying to stem the rising tide of tension he felt in the room as the two political veterans edged closer to discussing some of the nastier secrets of their success.

"Moshe, I know you're a busy man with little time to waste. I'm making a formal request of my Party leader."

Sharett sat in silence, waiting for Kasztner to go on.

"I want justice. I want this man silenced."

"What do you know about him, Rudy?"

"His son was killed in the War of Independence. His daughter worked with the Irgun as a nurse. She's a junior officer in the Information Ministry. You should see the looks she gave me after this hate letter was published."

"So fire her. Do you own dirty work."

"With a Labor Government in power?" He laughed, without humor. "Who do you think would outlast whom if she made a stink?"

The Prime Minister read through the mimeographed sheet. He bit his knuckles.

Kasztner lit a cigarette and smoked it underhand, in the East European manner, waiting patiently for his colleague to say something.

"Is any of this true?"

"Not a word of it. You've known me since my days in Cluj. How could you even think to ask?"

"I don't for a moment doubt your word, Rudy. I simply need to know because if we succeed in making this *really* public, we'd damn well better be sure we're completely in the right."

"Moshe, trust me. Would I have come to you if I didn't know that? You of all people know the irresponsibility of the press."

"Present company excluded, of course?" The smaller man raised his eyebrows. Kasztner not only edited the *Mapai's* weekly, but he also owned the largest Hungarian language newspaper in the country.

"They're referring to you as Ben Gurion's lesser shadow," Kasztner said, ignoring Sharett's barbed jibe. "Perhaps this would show them you mean business: a warning shot that will make every editor in the land sit up and take notice. What's more, you're not risking your own political neck at all."

"What do you suggest?"

"A criminal libel action."

Sharett mulled Kasztner's proposition over in his mind. Whoever this Greenwald was, he meant nothing to Sharett and could do him no harm. An old man, a pensioner, Kasztner had said. Hungarian scum. And by the looks of the mimeographed letter, probably without funds even to hire a lawyer. A little nothing who would probably plead guilty the moment the bailiff knocked on his door. Still, Sharett thought, the man must have something in him to have survived the Holocaust. A son killed in the Great War, a daughter. The public adopted strange heroes these days. Perhaps the promise of a light sentence? If it were done carefully, diplomatically, no matter how small the case, it would set good precedent.

He looked at the man seated across from him. Doctor Rudolf Israel Kasztner was a true Israeli hero, with impeccable credentials and all the right connections. He was forty-seven years old, an ardent Zionist, a man for all seasons — lawyer, publisher, diplomat, party mainstay — and he had a proven track record during the Holocaust. Kasztner had arranged for two shipments of Jews to escape the Nazis' death net as it descended over Hungary. On August 18, 1944, he'd secured the release of more than three hundred of his compatriots. Another 1,368 Jews, most of them Hungarian and Transylvanian, were spared nearly four months later, on December 6, 1944, due to his efforts. Some party historians even suggested that Kasztner had ensured the survival of the Jews in the Budapest ghetto and influenced Himmler's decision to put an end to the mass murder of the Jews in the camps. As spokesman for the Ministry of Trade and Information, he was one of Sharett's strongest supporters. Who knew how far such a man could go, given the present political climate?

"Is there some reason you can't — or don't want to — simply bring a civil suit in your own name?"

"There are two reasons. First, I find it a sign of low breeding to blow my own horn. More important, a civil action will not sound a warning to the general Israeli press. The longer they think they can get away with anything they say, the bolder they'll get until it leads to anarchy. I am a government officer. If the government itself files this action, it will send the appropriate message to the press."

"The lawyer in you speaking up?"

As if prodding him on, Kasztner said, in a confidential tone, "Moshe, have you ever known me to counsel anything imprudent?"

"No, Rudy. You have survived admirably, as we Jews always have, by the use of your brain. I only question whether your judgment may be affected by your anger at this apparent smear tactic, coming as it does from a man you don't even know, a man old enough to be your father."

"I don't say it has to be a large case. You don't have to use one of the higher-ups. A good, solid government lawyer, say Amnon Tell, who's got a strong record of convictions. It's just that a lesson must be taught."

"I don't doubt your anger, Rudy — and you've every right to it — but I can't help but think you may be crossing a dangerous river and asking me to be your boatman."

"I'm only asking you to do justice, Mister Prime Minister."

Sharett lit a Turkish cigarette, puffed at it a few moments, read the article once again. When he spoke, his tones were measured. "You've left the *quid pro-quo* up in the air, of course. I trust there may come a time when the favor will be returned?"

"Would I have sought you out if that were not implied?"

"Very well, Rudy, I'll ask Cohen to press charges."

"You won't be sorry, Moshe. That I can safely promise you."

2

Snow in Jerusalem was not unusual during this season, but somehow this winter of 1953-54 seemed more frigid than he could remember. Drifts and eddies of wet slush whirled at his feet as a stiff wind from the north batted them about the gray light poles and garbage bins that lined Ben Yehuda Street. This snow was not light and powdery like the flakes he remembered from his youth.

Jerusalem the Golden, he thought. Even with the colorless sky that hid the sun and dulled the day, the city's golden sandstone buildings shimmered. His Jerusalem, his home. He crossed the road briskly, and moved into Jaffa Street, entering the blocky, modern building that housed his — and a dozen other attorneys' — offices. He was the first one in today, nothing unusual. He removed his hat and gloves and rubbed his hands together vigorously.

Samuel Tamir had passed his thirty-second birthday a month ago. He had sand-colored hair, blue eyes, and a bony face, hung in a lean, five-foot ten-inch frame. He looked like nothing so much as an extra in an American cowboy movie. As was his habit, he perused Jerusalem's two largest daily newspapers, as well as one from Tel Aviv. As usual, the journals concerned themselves with Arab violence, Arab threats, government scandals, personal scandals, and the poor management of the scarce water supply.

His eye barely caught a small snippet on page six of *Ha'Aretz* about the government issuing an indictment about some kind of criminal libel trial. That piqued his interest somewhat, because, like many countries in the Middle East, the relationship between the press and the politicians was never a comfortable one. The article contained virtually no details except the name of the accused, one Malchiel Greenwald, seventy-two. *Now, what in the devil was the government doing chasing an old man for criminal libel,* he thought? The State always talked about shortages in the budget, yet they spent money on something like this? How absurd!

"Tea, darling?"

"*Nu*, what else, my love?" Tamir grinned boyishly at his wife, a short, slender woman, who served as his office manager as well as the mother of his children and the center of his universe. The outer office was filled with trophies — not his trophies, but Ruth's, for she was one of Israel's most renowned running champions.

Ruth returned momentarily with two tulip glasses of tea, set one down in front of her husband, and plopped herself into one of the two stuffed, wingback chairs that faced his large desk.

"Files and folders, folders and files," she remarked. "Are we never to see the bottom of your desk?"

"Good thing we don't," he replied. "We make a good living from these folders and files, and if they ever stop coming —. By the way, what's on our morning calendar?"

"Nothing much. A man who called just before we closed yesterday. His name was Greenwald, and he said it was certain to be one of the most important cases you ever had."

Samuel Tamir sighed. "Everyone has the largest, most important, most pressing case I've ever had. It seems that the ones with the 'largest, most pressing, most important' cases are the ones with no money — the ones who want me to work for nothing, for the glory the case is sure to bring me, and for the good of the practice of law. God knows I've represented enough of those kind."

"True," his wife replied. "But you know as well as I that someone has to do it. Thank God the practice is thriving and there are those who pay quite handsomely. Of course, it doesn't hurt to have a mother who's a Senator."

"Greenwald?" He'd seen that name before, and recently. Of course, there were hundreds, perhaps thousands of Greenwalds living in the Jerusalem-Tel Aviv-Haifa triangle. "Did he mention anything about his case?"

"Only that he felt you'd be proud to represent his interests against the Government."

"That could mean anything and nothing," Tamir replied.

"He seemed in a hurry to get the earliest appointment possible. Asked what time you got in in the morning. Spoke rather rapidly, as though he were very nervous about something."

"Most people who see a lawyer are." Tamir sighed. "Well, block out my time for an hour. That should be more than enough. What do you want to bet he'll pay the fee with a bag of pistachio nuts or some *baklava*?"

Malchiel Greenwald, for that was the old man's name, looked almost comic with his neatly trimmed goatee, tilted fedora, a bright muffler with mittens to match, and a cigar stub threatening to ignite the tip of his nose. On closer examination, Tamir could see that his overcoat was seedy and threadbare, and there were holes in his shoes. Nevertheless, he strode into the office confidently, his walking stick swinging briskly in his right hand.

Malchiel's daughter, Ariana, who accompanied her father, was, as the American movies liked to say, a "show stopper." She was twenty-three and, although not a sabra —born and bred in Israel — Ariana Greenwald combined a bewitching blend of strength and sensuality — a young woman possessed of a God-designed body that made her the perfect model for travel posters displaying the new Israel. She had an open, intelligent face, clear blue eyes, and straight, shoulder-length hair the color of cornsilk. She used no makeup and her tanned skin, long, sleek legs and light freckles were a legacy of her fifteen year sojourn, first in Palestine, then, when the land became independent, Eretz Israel.

"I know you," Tamir began when they were introduced. "You were a nurse in the Irgun. I was an Irgunik as well."

"Your name was Shmuel Katznelson back then."

"Mm-hmm. You were married to Gabriel Alaknar at the time."

"The operative word, Mr. Tamir, is *was*. The divorce was final a year ago." He looked questioningly at her. "There was just one too many of his beautiful Sabra girlfriends. There comes a time when one can't look the other way and pretend not to see. Of course, you weren't that way. You were an honorable man even then. You and Hanna —"

Tamir's face whitened momentarily, as the young woman continued. — "which is the reason my papa is here to see you this morning."

Ruth brought in two more tulip cups of tea, which the Greenwalds accepted with thanks.

"He's here because you're having troubles with the ex-husband?" Tamir asked.

"No, he's here because he's having troubles with our great and good government."

Tamir glanced at his wristwatch. The quick look was not lost on the old man.

"Not to worry," the elder Greenwald said. "I have a small stamp collection with which I am pleased to pay you for your time."

How many times had Tamir heard this before? The pride of the very poor. No matter how strapped they were, they did not want to take charity from anyone. Still, he had committed an hour to this man, and Malchiel Greenwald was on time — actually fifteen minutes early — for his nine o'clock appointment. He escorted the Greenwalds into his office and bade Ruth come in as well.

"Mr. Greenwald, your daughter said you are having a bit of a problem with the government. I understand you're probably nervous about it."

"What's to be nervous about, Mr. Tamir? I'm giving you the opportunity of a lifetime. I only hope you realize how important I am. After all, how many lawyers get the chance to defend a seventy-two-year-old retiree who can't even write Hebrew, who's being sued for criminal libel by the government of Israel itself? Why, this morning's *Ha'Aretz* even wrote a few lines about me on page six, at the bottom. I may not be as illustrious as President Weizmann, but at least I'm not ignored altogether. Who knows what will happen, eh?" The man was, beneath the bombast, uniquely charming. He knew his place in life's pecking order, but was not above pricking the balloon of posturing pretentiousness.

"Counselor, my daughter tells me you are a good man, a kind man, and that there are considerations more important than money to you. I must tell you, I don't consider myself a prophet. I'm not even very important. But there are times when even a poor man must stand up for the truth."

3

"Mister Greenwald, what are you supposed to have done?"

"It's in the indictment, Mister Tamir," he said, withdrawing a thick sheaf of papers from his greatcoat and handing them to the lawyer.

Tamir read quickly through the preliminary allegations. His eyes widened as he carefully read the offending article, attached as an exhibit, a smudged, badly mimeographed three-page document printed on cheap, white paper, entitled "Letter to my Friends in the Mizrahi."

I have waited a long time to expose this careerist whom I consider, because of his collaboration with the Nazis, an indirect murderer of my dear people. Who is this spokesman for the Ministry of Trade and Industry? Who is this big shot leader of Mapai? Who is this boaster of great achievements in the rescue of Hungarian Jews? Who is this fellow who has been put high on the list of candidates for Israel's parliament by the government party, Mapai?

This character is Dr. Rudolf Kasztner, a political adventurer, driven on by a sick megalomania!

For whom, on whose account, Dr. Kasztner, did you go like a thief in the night to Nuremberg to become a witness for the defense of S.S.

Colonel Kurt Becher, the murderer of Jews, the man who wallowed in the blood of our brothers in Hungary? Kurt Becher – Economic Administrator of the Gestapo! Why did you save him from the death penalty, which he had so richly earned? You flew to Nuremberg to save a mass murderer of the Jews. What induced you to do that? What kind of gentleman's agreement was there between this murderer Becher and this man whom I accuse as a collaborator with the Nazis?

It is this same Kasztner that the Mapai party has taken to its bosom and placed high on the list of officials.

My God! Kasztner's deeds in Budapest cost us the lives of eight hundred thousand Jews!

We demand an impartial public committee to investigate. Kasztner must be removed from the politics and from the society of this land. We shall keep this on our agenda until the evil is ended!

Tamir sat staring at the smudged type. There was no misreading its accusation and its objective, neither subtlety nor ambiguity in the message. Tamir knew that in Israel there was only one crime that merited the death penalty — collaboration with the Nazis to bring about their extermination of Europe's Jews.

"Do you know how serious these charges are, Mister Greenwald?"

"I do, Mister Tamir. That's why I'm here. I could as easily have requested the Public Defender, but I see no reason to spend the rest of my life in prison for telling the truth."

"The truth?" The lawyer read through the charging allegations once again, slowly and carefully this time. He scribbled a few notes on his yellow legal pad. "Doctor Kasztner's reputation is beyond reproach. He's Deputy Minister for Trade and Industry of the State of Israel, a *Mapai* candidate for the *Knesset*. During the War, he was head of the Jewish Agency Rescue Committee in Hungary. You dare accuse him of collaborating with the Nazis and implicate him in the murder of eight hundred thousand Jews?"

"I do," Greenwald replied quietly.

"My God, man," the lawyer continued. "You know of the anticollaborationist law?"

"Yes. Our attorney general himself was instrumental in passing it through the Knesset."

"Why didn't you go to the Attorney General's office and request that Doctor Kasztner be tried?"

"Doctor Kasztner? He's one of *them*, a big shot in Israel's ruling political party. How do you think I'd be treated if I, Malchiel Greenwald, a little pensioner, went into the halls of the high and mighty and said, 'I insist that you press capital charges against the former head of the Jewish Agency Rescue Committee for collaboration with the Nazis. I insist that you try a High Minister of Israel on charges that carry the mandatory death penalty?'"

"Mister Greenwald, as a journalist you must have had some factual basis to make these allegations."

"Of course."

"What was your evidence?"

The old man reached into his pocket and withdrew a crumpled envelope. "Read for yourself."

The lawyer reached out for the envelope as though it were a lifeline. Moments later, he looked across the desk at Malchiel Greenwald as if trying to take the measure of the man.

"But this is unsigned. There is no name anywhere, no identification. It is anonymous."

"I know that."

"Surely you must know the identity of this mystery author."

Greenwald wagged his finger. "I do not, and if I did, why would I reveal it? A journalist always protects his sources."

But for the gravity of the situation, Samuel Tamir might have laughed out loud. It seemed more and more apparent to Tamir that he was not dealing with a journalist; he was dealing with a lunatic.

"Mister Greenwald," he said. "Surely you are aware that there must be admissible evidence if you wish to defend a libel suit. Granted, if you have good faith belief that what you say is true —"

"As indeed he does, Mister Tamir," Ariana broke in. Tamir stared appreciatively at Greenwald's attractive daughter. "My father would not have published anything but the truth. I work in the Ministry of Trade and Information. Things are said —"

"Yes," the advocate said, clearing his throat. "But there must be more than just your father's hearsay statement, an unsigned, anonymous letter, and office gossip."

"There is," Greenwald continued. "There was a discussion in the Cafe Vienna a month ago —"

"Yes?"

"The talk was about how it was time that rascal got his comeuppance."

"Very good," Tamir said, brightening. "Would you be able to convince these witnesses to speak with me?"

"No."

"Why not?" the advocate asked, his face slackening.

"Because I don't know their names. They came to the coffee house two or three times. I haven't seen them since."

Tamir stood up, walked over to a window to the left of his desk, and looked into the street. The clock on the building across the way read nine-fifteen. He'd been with Greenwald and his daughter for thirty minutes. Cars, mostly prewar Fords, Chevrolets, here and there a Mercedes, drove up and down Jaffa Street. He remembered when the streets were bare except for tanks and clandestine irregulars throwing Molotov cocktails into one and two-story buildings from time to time. *Could it have been only seven years ago?*

Tamir looked squarely into Malchiel Greenwald's face for several moments. The old man's face was neither malicious nor cunning, merely old and wizened.

The attorney looked toward his own desk stacked high with papers. Behind it, on the hardwood floor, lay five similar stacks. He didn't want for paying clients. He'd just opened his new office in Jerusalem last month and already he had a surfeit of business. There was no earthly reason why he should take on the case. Greenwald was nothing more than a down-at-the-mouth pensioner with a remarkably attractive daughter. In the time they'd been talking, Malchiel Greenwald had not produced one shred of viable evidence in his defense. Suppositions, speculation, hearsay, the imaginings of a doddering old man. The target of Greenwald's attacks was a pillar of government integrity, a man with no known vices or enemies. A charter member of the Establishment. How dare this old fool question his background of such as Rudolf Kasztner?

Yet there was something about the way the old man and his daughter held themselves, about the way they spoke. The quiet refusal of the perpetually downtrodden to acknowledge defeat. What if there was a shred of truth in what the old man said?

Tamir returned to his chair and sat down. He considered himself a shrewd judge of character. He had to be to have survived Kenya, where he'd been held prisoner by the British while his contemporaries were either being turned to ashes in Hitler's ovens or enjoying a university education in Johannesburg, the London School of Economics, or in Cambridge, Massachusetts. Samuel Tamir was not a pillar of the Establishment. Very few members of the *Irgun Zvai Leumi* were. *Hanna had not been ...*

No, the Establishment were the Chaim Weizmanns, David Ben Gurions and Chaim Cohens of Israel — those who had played the game of appeasing the British to gain their own ends. The Establishment consisted of smooth, urbane, flawlessly faultless characters. Like Rudolf Kasztner.

Tamir frowned. There was not a scintilla of evidence to back the most defamatory attack ever made on an Israeli government official. An anonymous letter and some nameless cafe chatterers. It was sheer nonsense even to think of trying to defend such a case. A hundred-to-one shot. But Israel was a land that regularly exported miracles.

His job was not to judge truth or falsehood. He had been called to the Bar so that he might tenaciously search out and establish the truth. And if — God forbid! — what this old man hinted at in his home-mimeographed throwaway letter was the truth, what then?

"Mister Greenwald, perhaps I may be missing something, or perhaps I may be underestimating you."

"So you'll take my case then?"

"I don't promise anything at all. Perhaps if I knew more about you —"

MARCH 1938 - VIENNA

4

The ten-year-old Steyr XX wheezed once, backfired as it slowed, and turned into the circular driveway. Malchiel enjoyed the sound of the rhythmic shoosh-shoosh of the wiper blades and the soft crunch of the tires as they rolled over the wet pebbles. For some reason, he felt happiest when the soft, misty rain bathed his adopted city in its moist, gray cloak. Despite the recent troubles, he still believed Vienna was like nothing so much as a beautiful woman, a feast for the senses, something to be held, savored, and loved.

He remembered when he'd first moved to their third story flat at one hundred twelve Zirkusgasse at the beginning of nineteen thirty-one. The three-story brownstone, with its large, graceful windows, had clearly seen better days, as had this District, the third *bezirk,* eight miles from the circle of streets that belted the city's center, the *Ringstrasse.*

"Ah, well," he'd told his young wife, Leah. "Better a splintery park bench in Vienna than a mansion in Cluj. Besides, we've far more than a park bench. We have the entire floor to ourselves. A bedroom for Itzhak, a nursery for baby Ariana, two bathrooms, a large bedroom for us, and room to spare throughout." That had been seven years ago.

Greenwald alighted from his car, entered the apartment house, and started to climb the staircase immediately to his right. Walking what he considered his beat, and his daily climb up four flights of stairs kept him spry enough that even at fifty-six he was able to take the stairs two at a time.

When he got to the top of the last flight, Malchiel opened the door. "Leah, I'm home!" he said, extending his arm in a sweeping gesture. He handed her a small bouquet of winter flowers, then looked at her downcast face. "Problems, darling?"

"Of course there are problems. Every day they grow worse. You fancy yourself a journalist, yet you don't see the world beyond your cigar," she said, more in resignation than in anger.

"What do you mean?"

His wife shivered. "It's chilly in here."

"We'll cure that in a few moments." He walked over to the huge fireplace, tossed some large logs on the grate, inserted kindling between the logs, reached into his coat pocket and brought forth a silver-colored lighter. As his wife watched, he flicked the wheeled wick several times before it eventually erupted into a small flame, then carefully held it to the smallest, narrowest piece of pine kindling.

"Now, my dear, what is so terrible that you're wearing such a long face at four o'clock in the afternoon?"

"Malchiel, how could you bring your family to a place like this?" She handed him a copy of the *Tageblatt,* Vienna's largest paper.

The dateline was March 10, the day before, and the headline blared, "PLEBISCITE!" Malchiel read the story quickly, scanning for the main point with a practiced eye.

"Last Wednesday night, Chancellor Schuschnigg, speaking at Innsbruck, ordered a national vote to take place March 13. The single question to be determined is, 'Are you for an *independent,* social, Christian, united Austria? Yes or No?' Schuschnigg announced he had the support of the workers and was certain he would win in the coming vote."

"So?" Malchiel said. "He wants to show the world that Austria remains safe for everyone. I'm sure the vast majority will vote with our government."

"Do you really believe that Austria will remain safe for Jews?" Leah said, her voice rising, her face flushed.

"I believe all this anti-Jewish talk will blow over. Storm clouds have always blown over the house of Israel. Don't forget, Leah, we've kept the mercantile life of Europe going since the Middle Ages. Where would the universities, the law courts, the great orchestras be without us? How could Vienna have become the world center it is without Mahler, Freud, Einstein, Karoli?"

"Please don't humor me with that drivel," Leah said, pulling up a straight-backed chair and sitting across from him. "Beneath its veneer of *Gemütlichkeit* Vienna is the most anti-Semitic city on the Continent. When Hitler annexes 'poor little Austria' —"

"Don't say that, darling," Malchiel said, trying to calm her. "There's no way the government will let them in. That's why Schuschnigg's holding the plebiscite."

"Malchiel Greenwald," she said, in exasperation. "You are my husband and I swore to obey and follow you everywhere, but you have responsibilities, too. Twice a week you travel between Vienna and Budapest in a car so old it can barely make the trip. Each week you hope you'll see your byline in one of the newspapers and you think your fortune's made. You're an intelligent man, Malchele," she said, softening when she saw his hangdog look. "Yet, you had to take a job managing a fourth class hotel to support us. Why do you insist you must be a journalist? Vienna's got more of them even than Budapest. Ask your friends Strothness, Hamilton, Lavalier. Better yet, ask those who didn't make it, Sandor, Tetzel, a hundred more. You're a little fish trying to fight your way upstream."

"But my readers —"

"Your readers?" She laughed bitterly. "You have precisely fifty-two relatives who buy newspapers every day to see if the name Malchiel Greenwald is signed to anything."

"It's a question of connections, and connections I do not have, Leah. Perhaps it's because I'm Jewish."

Leah looked up at him, the briefest hint of a smile playing around her lips, though her eyes remained frightened. "I know several Jews who have already left Austria."

"Yes, but many are staying."

"Those who are incredibly naïve and shortsighted."

"Sshh," he said, putting his fingers to his lips as he heard footsteps coming up the stairs. "We'll talk about this later."

The door swung open and their two children, Itzhak, fourteen, who, at five-foot-nine was already taller than his father, and Ariana, their youngest, who, at eight, was in a particularly cute, pudgy stage, entered the room. Würstl, their elderly dachshund, yipped excitedly as he smelled the familiar scent of the children, and trundled happily toward them, shedding long brown hair in his wake.

"'Good evening, children," Greenwald said, rising to take them both in his arms. "Did you have a good day?"

Brother and sister looked sideways at one another, then away.

"Not so bad," Ariana said solemnly.

"It could have been worse," Itzhak added.

"That bad?" their mother asked.

Tears came to Ariana's eyes. She ran to her mother and buried her face in Leah's apron.

"What happened?" Malchiel asked.

"We passed by Friedmann's Department Store," Itzhak said. "A bunch of brown-shirts had cordoned off the area around the store. They were carrying signs that read, 'Austrians! Arm yourselves against Jewish atrocity propaganda! Buy only at Christian shops!' The brown shirts were smashing at the iron bars with sledge hammers."

"That's it, Malchiel!" Leah said sharply. "We must leave this place now! If you don't leave Vienna, I will, and I'm taking the children with me!"

Greenwald moved his hands, palms open, up and down in a gesture meant to quieten her. "We'll be all right, darling. We're clear out in the third district. The Turkish Synagogue's right down the street. We'll be safe. Where did you see this, children?" he asked.

"Mariahilferstrasse, right near the Opernring," Ariana said, sniffling.

"Just as I thought, downtown," he said. "You see, Leah, there's really nothing to worry about."

"What do you mean, 'nothing to worry about'? The children ride the tram through town to attend the Talmud-Torah each day, now that they're not allowed to attend public school anymore. There have been attacks on buses, streetcars —"

"But not on conveyances carrying children, darling."

"Not yet."

"But the plebiscite — "

"Damn Schuschnigg and his stupid plebiscite! It will never happen!"

"But he's in control."

"You think he's in control. How long do you think it will be before the Nazis come across the Austrian frontier? Hitler was born in Austria. He's made noises about a Greater Reich since Dolfuss was assassinated four years ago."

"Why can't we move, Papa?" Ariana asked.

"I didn't say we can't, Ariana," he said, drawing her close to him. "It's just not time yet."

"When will it be time, Papa?" Itzhak asked. "Kids down the street call me 'filthy Yid' to my face. I heard that last month Schuschnigg and Hitler met secretly at Berchtesgaden and the führer demanded that Schushnigg grant amnesty for all Nazi prisoners or the Reichswehr would invade Austria. Is Seyss-Inquart really the new Interior Minister?"

"Yes, Itzhak. Why?"

"Because he's the biggest anti-Semite of all," Leah said, angrily.

"Leah, for God's sake, calm down. You are a cultured, intelligent Hungarian citizen."

"You're wrong, Malchiel," she said, quietly furious at his insensitivity. "I'm a Hungarian *Jewish* citizen. That makes a rather significant difference. We are doomed if we stay in Austria. Don't you realize what it means to be an outcast simply because of an accident of birth?"

"Let me tell you something, Malchiel. The Germans have always been very meticulous. They work together like cogs in a well-oiled machine. They are the sons and daughters of the gods. They pay minute attention to detail. When they come here, they'll do exactly what they've done in Berlin. Every rose in our municipal gardens will be perfect. Every tree will be just so. The führer wishes to purify the German race along the same lines."

"Maybe I should stop by the *Weissenhof* for a while," he said. "I might be able to find some new leads on the Plebiscite."

"I warn you husband, if we don't leave here permanently within the next few weeks it will be too late. At least in Budapest, things are quiet."

"Yes, but who knows how long Admiral Horthy will remain in power? Don't worry, children," he called after the two youngsters who were trudging disconsolately down the hall to their rooms. "I'll be back in a couple of hours."

As he pulled the door shut behind him, he realized he was trembling, more in anger than in fear, an anger born of the guilty awareness that Leah was probably right. Maybe it was time to pack up and get out. Still, he thought, as he drove into the main part of town, even in its worst days, Vienna was the graceful, charming capital of all Europe, much more cosmopolitan than Budapest, a universe away from his hometown of Cluj on the Romanian border.

His thoughts turned to the Plebiscite, which was set for the week's end. *Would Hitler really accept an affirmative vote? He had already broken a dozen solemn promises, pledges and treaties to everyone else. Why should the vote of a weak Austrian state make a difference?*

After he parked in a side street off the Ringstrasse, he walked three blocks to Café *Weissenhof*, his favorite coffee house, long the haunt of Vienna's resident foreign correspondent community. As he entered the L-shaped place, he glanced at the clock. As usual, it was ten minutes behind time. His own watch told him it was four thirty-five. Good, he thought. The *Tageblatt* would be delivered in half an hour. He removed the *Manchester Guardian*, which was wrapped in a rattan frame, from its rack near the door.

Malchiel walked down the familiar bay to a small, circular booth under high, bullet-shaped windows. He sat at the small, gray marble, circular table, on a moth-eaten black, buff, and orange vertical-striped upholstered chair. Josef, the swarthy, middle-aged waiter, who always looked as if he needed a shave, approached him moments later. Josef, an ardent

Social Democrat, could be counted on to speak of the detestable Nazis in the strongest language.

"The usual, Herr Doktor Greenwald?" he asked solicitously, knowing Malchiel's preference for coffee with cream.

"Thank you, yes, Josef. What news about the Plebiscite?"

Josef shrugged his shoulders. "I haven't seen any of the usual crowd all afternoon. You know the gossip from last night?"

"Of course. My wife says the same thing, the Nazis won't let it happen."

"Ach, those thugs," he nearly spat. "I'll be back in a moment, Herr Doktor."

He returned momentarily, bringing Malchiel his coffee and the obligatory two glasses of water that always came with it. There were many reasons why Malchiel Greenwald loved Vienna, but the most compelling were its ubiquitous coffee houses, where obsequious white-jacketed waiters invariably addressed you as "Herr Doktor," no matter your station; where, for the price of a cup of coffee, you could read newspapers in a dozen languages from all over the world for hours without being asked to order anything else.

Each group frequented its own café. Malchiel, who wanted to learn all he could about almost everything, had spent time in most of them: the Café Freyung, where medical students discussed everything from the latest dissection of a cadaver (and there were more of them in Vienna than anywhere else) to Freud's latest works on psychotherapy; the Vindobona, one of his favorites, where he traded stamps from all over the world with other philatelists; the Herrenhof, where he'd watched chess games for days at a time; the Schubert, where every musician in town traded gossip; and the Pucher, where all the deals were made.

Greenwald glanced down at the *Guardian*. There was little news about the plebiscite. His eye was drawn to an article on the third page. The British foreign office was concerned over Arab complaints that too many Jews from Europe were flowing into the territory of the Palestinian Mandate. Ministry officials had promised they would confer with Doctor Weizmann about ways to curb the uncontrolled influx. The newspaper suggested that perhaps a quota system would be appropriate.

He was interrupted less than half an hour after he'd entered the café. Shortly after five in the afternoon, he heard a loud commotion coming from a block away. When he stepped outside to investigate, there were more than a thousand people wearing Swastika armbands. Since the police appeared to be in control, he thought nothing of it and returned to his table at Café Weissenhof. An hour later, Theodor Blohrer, the disheveled-looking stringer from the Yugoslav press, burst through the door. Looking nervously around the bay, he spotted Greenwald, the only other familiar face, and motioned Greenwald to follow him.

Two blocks away, an unruly mob of another thousand Nazis swarmed toward them. Malchiel felt a cold stab of fear as the horde approached. He heard shouts of *"Sieg Heil! Heil Hitler! Schuschnigg 'Raus! Ein Volk, Ein Reich, Ein Führer!"* The police looked on, doing nothing.

Greenwald ducked into a nearby telephone kiosk and attempted to call home. The lines were not working. He muttered to Blohrer that he must return to his flat, then walked toward his car. When he asked the nearest policeman what had happened, the officer answered, "The plebiscite has been called off."

He walked rapidly through side alleys, found the Steyr mercifully untouched, got in, and turned the engine over. As he drove slowly toward the outskirts, he turned on the radio. Within two minutes, the Strauss waltz playing on the air was interrupted by a male voice. "Attention! Attention! In a few moments you will hear an important announcement!"

Greenwald pulled to the side of the road, as he saw many others doing, and stopped. He left the motor running so as not to deplete the battery while he listened to *Radio Wien*. Chancellor Schuschnigg came on without introduction. His voice almost broke several times during the brief speech, but he somehow held it under control. Malchiel's face paled as he listened to Schuschnigg's words.

"My fellow citizens. This day has placed us in a tragic and decisive situation. The German government today handed President Miklas an ultimatum, ordering him to nominate a chancellor and cabinet designated by the Reich. He was told that if he did not do so within twelve hours, German troops would invade Austria. I declare before the world that German reports concerning disorders by the workers, the shedding of streams of blood, and the creation of a situation beyond the control of the Austrian government are all lies. Austria has yielded to force. We are not prepared, even in this terrible situation, to shed blood. It is with a broken heart that we have decided to advise our troops to stand down. I take leave of the Austrian people with a word of farewell uttered from the depth of my heart. May God protect Austria."

The radio played a recording of a tune originally composed by Josef Haydn, which now, given the words *"Deutschland Über Alles,"* had a sinister ring. Doctor Seyss-Inquart came on the air. He announced that he considered himself responsible for order, and commanded the Austrian army not to offer resistance. Greenwald stared at the receiver dumbfounded. Resistance to what? Schuschnigg had said the German ultimatum was capitulation *or* invasion. Had the Nazis already broken the terms of their own ultimatum?

Greenwald attempted to telephone his apartment again. The lines were still down. He'd have to fight his way through the crowds. As he drove slowly toward the Kärntnerstrasse, one of Vienna's main streets, there were mobs everywhere on the street, singing Nazi songs. The few policemen who stood around now wore Swastika armbands.

As he approached the Graben, the center of town, he saw young toughs heaving bricks through the windows of Jewish shops. The crowd applauded their efforts and hurled stones and garbage through the broken plate glass. In less than an hour, Vienna had been transformed into a Reich city. The red, white, and black swastika flag draped every public building. It took Greenwald two hours to drive home. He decided to pack the family's goods, leave Vienna permanently, and return to Budapest within the month.

On March 18th, Malchiel Greenwald paid a visit to the Café Weissenhof. As he entered what had been the central focus of his professional existence, he was immediately struck by the fact that all the international newspapers were gone from the racks. The *Kronen Zeitung* was still in its accustomed place, but it had clearly and swiftly submitted to *Gleichschaltung*, Nazification. The double-sized headline read *Jews Fined 550,000 Reichsmarks for Supporting Schuschnigg's toppled government! Every piece of Jew-owned property in Austria will be seized if the fine is not paid immediately.*

Greenwald turned and was about to leave his former haunt, when he noticed that the atmosphere in the Weissenhof had changed, and not subtly. Josef and the other waiters, all conspicuously wearing swastika lapel pins, almost fell over themselves soliciting the custom of three men in SS uniforms, who had aimlessly wandered in.

Fortunately, he'd found parking less than a block away and was in process of leaving the center of the city, the First District, when he came upon a series of detour signs redirecting traffic around the Kärntnerstrasse. As he stole a sidewise glance onto Vienna's main street, he saw more than a hundred men wearing badges with yellow six-pointed stars and the word *Jude* pinned to the front of their shirts, on their hands and knees, using toothbrushes, soap, and water to scrub the street. Moments later, Greenwald watched in horror as two hundred "honorable, upstanding Aryan citizens" urinated, defecated, and poured garbage where the Jewish crews had just finished cleaning.

As he was about to turn into a sidestreet, Blohrer, his friend from the Yugoslav press, flagged him down and jumped into the Steyr.

"You don't want to go there," he warned Greenwald.

"Why not?" Malchiel asked.

"Reserve work crews,'" Blohrer replied. In response to Greenwald's inquisitive stare, the Slav continued, "I was lucky enough to escape when I produced papers showing I wasn't a *Yid*. The authorities round up the first two hundred Jewish men they can find in different neighborhoods each morning at six. They tell them they're going to a work detail. Then they make them stand all day in a fenced-in schoolyard. There are no toilet facilities, so they have no opportunity to relieve themselves. If they can't hold it in and have to piss or shit their pants, they better damn well pray that not so much as one drop spills on the ground. If they 'despoil' so much as one inch of precious Reich land, the offending Jew is ordered to lick the urine or eat their own shit, and if they don't, they're beaten until they can no longer stand."

"How long do they stand?" Greenwald asked, feeling a wave of nausea come over him."

"From six in the morning 'til eight at night. Nothing to eat or drink during that time."

Greenwald, turned the Steyr away from the sidestreet and drove another two miles as unobtrusively as he could toward the city's outskirts. Along the way, he endured even more sickening sights. As he passed Friedmann's Department Store, its windows now covered by iron bars, he saw Nazi thugs in broad daylight breaking down the front door and spraying different colored paint over everything they could find.

"No sense in trying to clean it," Blohrer said. "The 'paint' contains sulfuric acid."

Greenwald's elderly Steyr slowed to a crawl as automobiles traveling in both directions jammed the road leading into and out of the city, its drivers and passengers laughing, jeering, and pointing to children painting the windows of every fourth business building with the words, "This business is owned by a filthy Jew, an enemy of the State and a Christ killer. Please do not patronize this store." The children, some as young as five years old, were signing their names under these, and similar, slogans.

Three days later, Malchiel Greenwald had all his exit papers in order. Frau Gruber, the elderly Jewish widow who lived on the ground floor and who had been their landlady and friend for the past seven years, was distressed to seem them leave, but she was punctilious to a fault. "If you wait until the end of the month, that will give you time to clean up the flat and I can inspect it. I will, of course, restore your deposit to you immediately you depart. The electricity is paid until the end of the month? The telephone?"

"Yes, Madame."

"And your position at the hotel?"

"Herr Gmeinde was not displeased. His business is down by half since the Nazis came to power. He'll be saving money."

"What about you, Herr Greenwald?" She had a maternal fondness for the man who'd invited her to take dinner with them several times in the past.

"I have, God be thanked, managed to put away a small savings."

"In the Austrian State Bank?" she asked.

"In Hungary. At least that's a safe place."

"For the present."

"We live from day to day, Frau Gruber. What about you? It won't be safe for you to stay here much longer."

"That is true, but what could I get for this house now?" She sighed. "You know, when my late husband, the *Rechtsanwalt,* was still alive, we occupied the entire house. We had servants, galas. Vienna really was the world's most beautiful and cosmopolitan city back then, before the War."

"I know," he responded gently. How could this lovely, frail old woman hope to survive the coming onslaught? "Ernst is in England, is he not?"

"Oh, yes," she said, brightening at the mention of her youngest and only surviving son. "He's managing Richard Tauber."

"Ah, *Komn Zigane, Wien, Wien, nur Du Alein,*" Greenwald said, mentioning two of the most popular melodies in Vienna which, even now, were standard fare in the wine houses of Grinzing. "Before Tauber left, he was the most popular singer in Austria. The king of the operetta, the darling of Vienna!"

"Also half Jewish," Frau Gruber said. "Why else do you think he left Vienna? He'd amassed enough money for a lifetime."

"Could you move to London to be with your son?"

"If I chose to abandon my home, all my belongings, leave like a gypsy with nothing but the clothes on my back, letting seventy-nine years' worth of memories sit here and rot. But no one, not even the Nazis, are going to disturb an old lady who can be of no harm or use to them."

"You should consider it, Frau Gruber. There's still time."

"Have you done anything about the children's school?"

"Good heavens!" Greenwald exclaimed, looking at pocket watch. "It's two thirty. I've only forty minutes to pick them up. Please excuse me, Gnädige Frau."

As he drove toward the inner city, Malchiel realized that the red, white, and black Swastika now hung from every public building and a majority of private ones as well. The small Talmud-Torah school was tucked into a nondescript side street in one of Vienna's poorer areas. There were cage bars around the front of the two-story building.

He made it into town by three o'clock, where cars were parked on both sides of the street, waiting for the children to emerge. Since the demise of the Schuschnigg government, no Jew dared ride the city's public transportation. Malchiel parked the Steyr two blocks away and started walking toward the school.

He had just about made it to the front door, when the children started streaming out. As their parents held open the doors to their automobiles to accommodate their youngsters, Malchiel heard the eruption of screams behind him.

He turned just in time to see an ocean of thugs, bearing guns and heavy clubs, in black shirts and Swastika armbands, charging toward the school. As he looked toward the school, Ariana walked out the gate toward him.

"Ariana! Get back into the building!" he shouted as the toughs bore down on him.

The girl turned, white-faced, and scampered back into the school edifice.

The four huge men nearest Malchiel seized him and threw him roughly to the ground. One of them grabbed his right arm, forced it up into a vicious hammerlock. "Yid scum!" he snarled. "Rotten piece of shit! Why do you want to warn the little Heebies? Nits grow into lice, just like you, you fucking Christ-killer!"

Malchiel felt an intense pain and heard a snap as his right arm splintered. Someone turned him on his back and started clubbing him. He felt his mouth bleeding. As he spat blood, he felt most of his teeth rattle around, then leave his mouth along with the viscous red liquid.

Now, they started kicking him in his stomach, his ribs, his face, and the back of his neck. Groaning, Malchiel rolled himself into a fetal position, his hands covering his groin.

One of the toughs sneered, "As if you have something left to protect, you old fart. You probably can't even get it up anymore except to fuck a good Christian cunt!" With that, he kicked Malchiel hard, breaking his chin. As Malchiel brought his left hand up to grab his face, the brute cracked his club against Malchiel's thigh, aiming for the testicles. Malchiel's eyes were tearing. Within a few minutes at most, they'd be swollen shut.

A rough voice panted, "I'll teach you to insult the Führer, you race polluter!"

Amazed that he was still conscious, Malchiel felt rather than saw a hand reach into his mouth and grab his tongue. He felt a searing pain as the jagged edge of a knife sliced his tongue so it was hanging by a thread.

At that moment, Malchiel heard an furious growl as a tall man wearing a caftan and yarmulke, the Jewish skullcap, grabbed the tormentor and threw him to the ground. "Don't you dare harm another human being, you abominable pervert!" Malchiel's unknown savior shouted.

Half a dozen bullies immediately grabbed the tall man. One of them ripped his caftan from throat to knee, exposing the man's thin, pale body. Another pulled a polished, silver-colored knife from a scabbard. "All right, Jesus-killer, this'll show you not to mess with your betters!" He slashed the knife horizontally across the tall man's throat, severing the jugular. While the Jew gurgled in his death throes, the Nazi brute pulled the knife in a downward motion, from the man's forehead to his groin, slashing him open in the shape of a cross.

Malchiel felt a gush of warm liquid and raised his eyes. The tall man's blood streamed onto his head and face. He gagged as the dead man's body, relieved of muscular control, voided its bowels. The smell of feces mingled with that of sour sweat, half-digested food and death. The man's intestines and organs, cut loose by the knife, dropped onto Malchiel's head and tumbled onto the concrete where he lay. Malchiel screamed until he felt himself being kicked in the face once again. Then, everything went black.

DECEMBER, 1953 – JERUSALEM

5

"What happened then?" an ashen-faced, obviously shaken Tamir asked.

"I was lucky. They believed I was dead and lost interest in me."

"What about the children?"

"Almost all of them made it back into the school that day. Ariana and Itzhak were all right. The police made no apologies, but they were able to get them safely home"

"And you?"

"I survived, thank God. All my teeth were knocked out. Fortunately, they were able to sew my tongue back on, so I never lost my ability to talk. My arms and legs were broken, but I was in good shape and they mended nicely."

"And the rest?" Tamir carefully avoided the direct question.

"They never got any part of my manhood. The police took me straight to Mariahilf Hospital."

"How long were you unconscious?"

"Only a day. The moment Leah came to visit, I told her to leave for Budapest immediately. Frau Gruber was most helpful."

"How long were you in hospital?"

"A week. One of the newspapers I worked for in Budapest got one of their staffers to transport me to Hungary. I stayed in bed at home for another five weeks while we made plans. Herr Gmeinde was a gem. He sent me my entire retirement and vacation pay — illegally I'm sure — without waiting to clear authorities."

"What ever became of Frau Gruber?"

"Praise God, she got out in time. She sold her apartment house and moved to England. I was shocked to receive four thousand schillings in the post while I was convalescing. She insisted I take it and make a new life for Leah and the children. She said to pay it back when I could. Ultimately I did. She died five years ago, a very old lady. We remained in contact until the end."

"With the vacation pay, the retirement, and papa's small savings, that was more money than he'd ever seen in his life," Ariana added.

"Within six months, it became clear that Europe was no place for a Jew to be," Greenwald continued. "During the last weeks of summer, 1938, Hitler and Neville Chamberlain met at Munich. On September 30, Chamberlain, and Daladier turned the Czech Sudetenland over to Germany.

"A month later, a Jewish exile shot Ernst vom Rath, a legation secretary in the German embassy in Paris. Within twenty-four hours, synagogues all over Germany went up in flames, Jewish homes were devastated, stores pillaged and destroyed. More than a hundred people were killed. Twenty-five thousand were arrested. By the next sunset, *Kristallnacht,* Crystal Night, had spread to Vienna. Five large synagogues in the city were burned to the ground. Not one major Jewish-owned business was left intact. By that time, we had emigrated. You could still go to Palestine without being shot or drowned by the British exclusionary policy."

"Would you like a bit more tea?" Tamir asked.

"Please."

"Ruth, would you please get the Greenwalds some tea?"

Ariana smiled gratefully at Tamir, who had anticipated her own thirst. She knew that once a busy lawyer kept you in his office for nearly two hours, particularly when he knew in advance that there was little or no money, he was being more than courteous.

Ruth Tamir entered the room, served each of them a tulip glass of tea and a small, plastic cup of orange juice, and took a wooden seat to her right. "How did you manage to live?" Tamir asked.

"We moved to Jerusalem," Ariana said. "Father put up a few hundred pounds — his life's savings — and bought a small hotel, the Hotel Austria. It wasn't much. We could accommodate twenty guests a night if you put three or four in one room. We charged one dollar a head. We all made beds, swept floors, filled kerosene stoves, did what we had to do. When the killings started in Europe, the British closed down Palestine's ports. You and I remember that, don't we, Sam?"

"Ah yes, the perfidious White Paper," Tamir said, his face a sneer.

"So now we had to outwit not only the Germans but the British authorities guarding the shores of Empire," Greenwald said. "I helped organize illegal immigrant runs to Palestine. I stopped when my relatives were shipped off to Auschwitz and killed in the German ovens."

"Itzhak and I joined the Irgun," Ariana said. "My brother was killed fighting in the battle of Mount Zion."

Ruth Tamir spoke for the first time. Greenwald saw that the lawyer's wife and his own daughter were two beautiful sides of the same coin, one blonde and freckled, the other slender, dark-haired. "Thank God the British were finally forced to show good grace and leave, and we established Eretz Israel," she said.

"And I grew a goatee, bought a walking stick, and decided to become a journalist again," Greenwald said, a humorous glint in his eye. "But who would hire a seventy-two year old man unable to write Hebrew? So, every week I composed an article, had it translated into Hebrew, and had it mimeographed. 'Letters to My Friends in the Mizrachi.'"

He stood, emptied out his pockets, and placed a piaster, the smallest Israeli coin, on the advocate's desk. "I spent my last piasters mailing out one thousand copies of each issue. The pamphlet was free. All I asked was that somebody read it. I published fifty pamphlets and nothing happened, except that most of my Letters ended up in trash barrels. Then came Pamphlet 51, the one you have in your hands, and here we are, the State of Israel versus Malchiel Greenwald. Is there anything else you wish to know, Counselor?"

Tamir looked at his wife, who rose from her chair and nodded. His intense look softened.

"What do you know about my husband?" Ruth Tamir asked.

"That he was in the Irgun and was at detention camp at Gilgil, Kenya."

"Samuel was born Shmuel Katznelson. He joined the Irgun when he was fifteen years old. They nicknamed him 'Tamir' — tall and straight — and he later adopted his nickname as his family name. At twenty-three, he was an Irgun Commander in Jerusalem.

"We weren't equally matched by any means," Ruth continued, her eyes losing their focus, returning to another world. "We had a handful of irregulars with some stolen guns hidden in a few basements. The British had more than one hundred thousand seasoned soldiers equipped with tanks, cannon, and machine guns.

"We all led double lives back then," she said, smiling. "Sam worked as a broadcaster on the British radio while he took up the study of law at the British Government Law School in Jerusalem. It took them three years to catch him."

"There were two-hundred sixty of us behind the barbed wire in Kenya," Tamir said. "Every one of us was Irgun. Not one detainee was Haganah." Tamir rose from his desk and came toward them. He half stood, half sat in the edge of the desk as he continued. "Mister Greenwald, it seems we've both changed careers. When I was released from Gilgil, I bought myself a black gown, rented a law office in Tel Aviv, and within five years I've been able, with God's help, to open an office in Jerusalem as well."

He was silent for a moment as if pondering a heavy question. "There's something very strange here," he finally said. "Why would the government sue you for libel? Why wouldn't Kasztner sue you himself?"

"To get what?" Greenwald responded. "My stamp collection? My pension? I own nothing. Now that I've told you this, Mister Tamir, I must apologize for wasting so much of your time. I can't afford lawyer's fees. I realize there's a hundred-to-one chance, a thousand-to-one chance —"

"They said that about the Irgun," Tamir mused. "Please excuse my saying so Mister Greenwald, but I do not believe the government would have brought this charge against you unless they had something larger on their minds. With all respect, sir, you are one of the smallest fish in the Israeli pond. Sharett and his Mapai must have a different agenda, a need to establish a legal precedent that goes beyond Malchiel Greenwald's 'Letter to My Friends in the Mizrahi'..."

"Perhaps a need to hide something?" Ruth asked quietly.

In that moment, Tamir made his decision. "If I take the case, Mister Greenwald, will you agree to one thing?"

"Anything," Greenwald said, barely believing his ears.

"Will you agree to let me handle your defense any way I see fit and not interfere with any direction I may take?"

"I will be behind you in anything you do."

"So be it, Mister Greenwald," Tamir said, rising and shaking the dry, trembling hand that reached out to him. "You have just found yourself a lawyer. God help us both."

6

"Good morning, Doctor Kasztner, my name is Amnon Tell. It's my privilege to tell you I've been appointed trial counsel to try the State's case against Malchiel Greenwald. Needless to say, sir, I've heard all about your efforts on behalf of the Jews in Hungary and I'm honored to make your acquaintance."

Kasztner looked about the state prosecutor's office. It was small, ten by twelve feet, sparsely furnished, a steel case, government issue desk, and dark green metal chairs covered with red plastic. On the wall behind Tell's desk were black-and-white photographs of Prime Minister Sharett and Attorney General Chaim Cohen.

Kasztner sized up the lawyer who was to represent him. He'd suggested Tell to Sharett because of the prosecutor's reputation, not because he personally knew the man. Now he'd find out more. The man who stood facing him was narrow-faced, thin bodied, short, about fifty years of age. Kasztner gathered from the man's opening greeting that he was a stickler for formality of speech and manner. Good. The type of underling Kasztner liked.

"The honor is mine."

"Frankly, Doctor Kasztner, I had not expected that the matter would go this far. It appears to be an open-and-shut case."

"What do you mean you did not expect it to go this far?" Kasztner asked. Tell noticed the slightest look of unease cross Doctor Kasztner's face. *Probably he's nervous because this is his first experience with the criminal system,* the lawyer thought.

"Usually in a situation such as this, a little old man like Greenwald is terrified the moment he's served with legal papers, and wants to do everything he can to minimize the damage: a visit to the State Prosecutor's office to beg for mercy, perhaps contact from the Public Defender."

Kasztner looked at his LeCoultre wristwatch. "Perhaps we'd better talk, counselor. Is that what happened in this case?"

"Not at all, Doctor Kasztner. I received a response from Greenwald's lawyer, which was why I requested we meet this morning."

"You mean to say Greenwald managed to find himself some shyster lawyer?"

"I'd hardly call Samuel Tamir a shyster," Tell responded. "He's a very shrewd, very successful barrister with offices in Tel Aviv and Jerusalem."

Kasztner looked about Tell's office once again. He'd heard you could tell how good a lawyer was by the appearance of his surroundings. By that measure, Amnon Tell wasn't all that successful. How could a pensioner like Greenwald afford a lawyer with two offices, one in each of the two largest cities in Israel?

"What do you know about Tamir?" Kasztner asked.

"He was born thirty-two years ago, Shmuel Katznelson. Married, three children."

"I don't mean that, Mister Tell. I mean what do you know of his professional reputation ... his ... his ethics?"

"If you mean is he someone who haphazardly stirs up trouble, the answer is no. He defends a lot of people, even Arabs."

"My God, man! Arabs? How could he? What kind of ethics is that?"

"He's claimed publicly that everyone in our society is entitled to the best representation possible. He's become rather an important nuisance insofar as our government is concerned."

"Have you come up against him before?"

"I have."

"And?"

"If you mean what is my success record, Doctor Kasztner," the lawyer said, lighting a cigarette, "I must tell you that for the most part he and I have settled differences between his client and the State without the need of trial. On any given day, given the specific circumstances and the precise facts of any case, either lawyer will win or lose a case. We all make appropriate noises in front of a judge and hope for the best."

"Not exactly a ringing endorsement, is it, Mister Tell?"

"Doctor Kasztner, I am only a human being, as is Samuel Tamir. We do the best we can given the facts we have. I suggest your case is not one of my more difficult challenges. There is no truth to anything Greenwald says, is there?"

"Of course not."

"I thought as much."

"You said Tamir has two offices. That means law clerks, investigators — "

"Correct."

"And our side?"

"The same. Plus, as the State, we command a great deal more authority. As you may have noticed, we don't devote our budget to fancy offices. Would you like coffee or tea, Doctor Kasztner?"

"Coffee please. What did Tamir's response say? Did he deny the allegations?"

"As a matter of fact, Greenwald admitted he wrote and published the pamphlet."

"So there should be no trouble in gaining a quick conviction. What defense could he offer?"

"Doctor Kasztner, he used the one defense that places everything at issue. He claims that what he wrote was the absolute truth."

"But that's ... that's perjury!" Kasztner spluttered.

"No, Doctor Kasztner, these are pleadings, not sworn affidavits. All he is saying is, 'You've made allegations, now it's up to you to prove them.' Of course you're aware that the burden of proof is on the State. I've asked you here to find out the names of the witnesses you'll be able to produce."

A young woman came in, poured two cups of freshly brewed coffee for them, offered them cream and sugar, and left.

"I don't understand why it's necessary for me to provide you with your witnesses, Mister Tell." Kasztner seemed nonplussed. "I thought when the state brought this action, it had made sufficient investigation to produce its own witnesses."

"Don't get me wrong, Minister Kasztner," Tell replied equably. "The State of Israel is fully prepared to subpoena witnesses and interview them. All we're asking for is your help in giving us names, last known addresses, the substance of their testimony." Tell was mildly surprised that Kasztner seemed so upset by his request. Generally, a complaining witness was adamant about providing all the help he could for the prosecution — usually too much so and a good deal of it irrelevant. Could there be any truth to Greenwald's allegations? Samuel Tamir might be a nuisance, but he was by no means a fool.

"Are we limited to witnesses who live in Israel?"

"That depends on the numbers, Doctor Kasztner."

"I can name at least three hundred fifty witnesses. Given sufficient time, my staff could search the records of the Joint Agency and find another fifteen hundred. Would that be sufficient for your purposes?"

Tell whistled softly. Clearly he had misinterpreted his client's nervousness. Anyone able to produce so large a number of witnesses, here and abroad, was well connected, a man to be reckoned with. "Doctor Kasztner," he said respectfully. "Absent especially compelling circumstances, you would need five or six witnesses at most to make the State's case. I suggest that you and I adjourn to our conference room and evaluate the most appropriate witnesses for our cause."

The next two hours passed rapidly. Several times, Amnon Tell found himself blinking in astonishment at the scope and breadth of Kasztner's list. Even without notes to prod him, his client's memory was phenomenal. Names, dates, events poured out of Kasztner's mouth as though he were an encyclopedia of who was who, and who did what during the Jewish efforts to salvage what few of the six million they could. Government dignitaries, men and women of worldwide repute now living in Switzerland, England, the United States, and, to give balance, several simple Hungarians, Poles, Romanians, Czechs and Slovaks — men, women, young people, Jews, Catholics, Gypsies — all of whom Kasztner was confident would testify to the saintliness of the man who had been responsible for saving their lives.

"And Greenwald?" Tell asked. "What, if any, evidence will be muster?"

"I hate to sound skeptical Mister Tell, but I do not believe that any of his so-called 'witnesses' are alive today. We lost millions in the camps during the last war. I don't say I could — or did — save more than the smallest remnant of our people, perhaps a couple thousand at most."

Suddenly, uncharacteristically, Kasztner started to weep. "God, I should have done more. If only I could have done more — "

The state's counselor rose, came around the table at which they had been sitting, and patted the larger man on the shoulder until the weeping subsided.

"Doctor Kasztner, our Bible says he who saves one life, has saved the whole world."

"But if one lets go of a life he could have saved, is it not as if he had destroyed the universe?"

"We need not debate such a tragic thing, Doctor Kasztner. I am only saddened that a man such as you must even dirty his hands with the prospect of such a trial. Perhaps you might convince the Attorney General, or even the Prime Minister, to abandon this whole embarrassment. Let the old fool go to his grave with his own guilty conscience. It would be so much easier for you."

"I've thought about that, Mister Tell," Kasztner said. "It would be the easy route to take, but it would be wrong. You see, if I, as a government official, were to avoid my own civic duties, hard though they may be, then why bother to have such a thing as libel laws? We would revert to a nation of savages, where irresponsible men and women, using the press as a shield, could spread the most scandalous lies imaginable with complete impunity. How safe would anyone's reputation be in such a society? No, Mister Tell, while I appreciate your compassion, I have chosen to become a public servant, and if the State has decided to protect order within its frontiers, then who am I to challenge it, to destroy from within the government to whom I owe my very life?"

The prosecutor's eyes brightened with unshed tears and he felt choked. "I respect your sacrifice more than I can tell you, Doctor Kasztner. I can well see why you've attained your position. I feel ashamed in forcing a man of your obvious integrity and character into the witness box."

"I don't see any need to do that," Kasztner said smoothly. "With the witness list I've given you, it's such a complete case that perhaps I should simply observe the proceedings."

"The only thing is that if you did not take the stand voluntarily, Tamir would undoubtedly subpoena you on his client's behalf."

"Can he do that? I thought there were laws against self-incrimination … that you could not be compelled to testify against yourself."

Had Kasztner made a grave slip of the tongue or was Prosecutor Tell simply being paranoid, overprotective? No, Tell thought, it was a simple thing for a layman to assume that just because someone was involved in a criminal trial, regardless of whether he or she were being charged with anything, that person could somehow refuse to testify if there was something damaging that might come up.

"That's not quite the way the law works," Tell said. "You see, you're not on trial in this case. Although Mister Greenwald has accused you of certain despicable and outrageous acts, the State has not. The State of Israel is bringing this as a criminal case, not a civil case, so you're not seeking damages. It is the State, not you, that has the burden of proof."

"So I'm not really a necessary party at all."

"To the contrary. The action is being brought on your behalf, which means, it would be far better for us were we to introduce you and tell your story to the Judge than to have it brought out by Tamir on cross examination."

Kasztner lit another cigarette. Tell could not help noticing that his hand was shaking visibly. "Is something the matter, Doctor Kasztner?"

"No, of course not. It's just that I've seen one too many movies where a crafty lawyer twists things around, makes black look white and white look black, confounds and confuses even the most innocent of witnesses."

Again a reference to "innocence," Tell thought. *From a man who was the state's nominal plaintiff. Strange indeed. I must have our investigators obtain sworn affidavits immediately. Perhaps show them to Tamir, suggest a guilty plea in exchange for a very light sentence, a few days in jail, a thousand pounds' fine, payable over time, of course. Maybe even a suspended sentence.*

"What do you know of Tamir's cross-examination techniques, Mister Tell?"

"I don't mean to cause any undue concern, Mister Minister, but Samuel Tamir is one of the boldest, most effective advocates practicing today. You must never be taken in by his courtesy, his boyish looks, or his ready smile. The man's as dangerous as a dynamite dump. You're sure you won't reconsider? I'd be happy to assist you in requesting that the Attorney General drop the case."

"You sound as if you have doubts about this case," Kasztner said.

"Not at all, Minister Kasztner. I'm convinced of three things. One, that you're an extraordinarily courageous man; two, that you're committed to the rule of law in Israel, regardless of the personal inconvenience to you; and three, that your reputation must be vindicated against this scurrilous attack on your character. I only thought to give you an opportunity to escape the unpleasantness."

"Once again, no thank you, counselor. Let us press on together."

"Indeed, Doctor Kasztner. I'm certain God will bless our efforts. Something a little stronger than tea to seal our bond? Perhaps schnapps or brandy?"

"Schnapps would be fine, Mister Tell. Then let us begin our work."

7

"Ariana, I'm delighted you could get time off to work with the 'Greenwald Defense Forces,'" Ruth Tamir said. "How were you able to work it out?"

"I'm used to long hours, Ruth," Ariana said, embracing Tamir's wife and alter ego. "Not that I could ever hope to compete with you. One day I'm going to learn the secret of how a girl only five years my senior and a good twenty pounds lighter than me manages to get three kids ready for school in Tel Aviv each morning, drives an hour-and-a-half to Jerusalem four days a week, runs a law office, teaches a Bible class, climbs mountains, and still remains the fastest woman mile runner in Israel."

"Aren't all Israelis given to that sort of life?" Ruth replied, smiling. "What'd you tell Jacob Nussbaum?"

"The truth. That I'd start at six in the morning and work straight through if he'd let me off at noon."

"No argument from you-know-who?"

"Kasztner's out of the office buttering his political bread most of the time. His job's largely ceremonial. Jacob's no great admirer of Kasztner. I don't know whether it was to impress me or just because he thinks Kasztner's an arrogant ass, but he said he hopes Sam trounces the good doctor in court."

"At least one of the public in our corner. Tell me, Ariana, every time I've met Nussbaum he's making cow eyes at you. I don't mean to pry but?"

"Ruth, there's nothing there and I'm afraid there never will be. I guess I never acknowledged in my heart that Gabriel and I really were divorced until December of last year."

"Don't tell me you and Sam —?"

"No, Ruth, you don't have to worry about that, not that I haven't fantasized from time to time. He's the perfect man, and I thought to myself, 'Some women have all the luck,' but when I met you, I said, 'God, if only I could be as lucky as the two of them.' Then I realized I could be that lucky if only I stopped living in the past. It's been almost two years."

Ruth Tamir did not look askance at the beautiful younger woman. In Israel it had been a normal, everyday occurrence since the pioneer days that if a healthy young man and a healthy young woman had perfectly natural feelings, it was not always necessary that a Rabbi be there to solemnize what was going to happen. Even so, she adored her husband with every fiber of her being.

"Come into the library and I'll introduce you to the rest of the 'Greenwald Defense Forces.' You'll probably find yourself the center of attention. They'll fight to be here when you are."

Ariana groaned in mock indignation and followed Ruth into a fifteen-by-eighteen foot room, packed floor to ceiling with law books on each of its walls. As she entered the room, four men, the oldest of whom couldn't have been more than thirty-five, rose to their feet.

"Ariana, I'd like to formally introduce you to our team. This," she said, pointing to the oldest of the four, a short man, five foot six inches tall with a slightly thickening waistline and a somewhat bookish look, "is Dov Levin. Dov was in Sam's Irgun unit in Jerusalem. He's now the 'lawyer's lawyer,' my husband's chief legal assistant. Dov's got an entire law library in his head. If a precedent exists anywhere in the civilized world, he'll find it faster than anyone I know."

"Miss Greenwald," he said, bowing slightly.

"Arieh Marinsky," Ruth said, tapping a blond, slightly built man about Samuel Tamir's height. "He comes from Shanghai, fought in the

Irgun, was kidnapped by the Haganah, but released. He fought with the Palmach against the Arabs. When the shooting stopped, he studied law."

"Ah, a lion in our midst," Ariana said, noting that his name was the Hebrew for lion.

"Delighted to have you aboard. May I call you Ariana?" he asked, pumping her hand. Ariana felt an immediate comradeship with Marinsky.

"Of course, if I might call you Arieh."

"And I'm Dan von Weisl," a third man said, stepping forward and gripping Ariana's hand. He was in his late twenties, dressed in casual slacks, an open-necked white shirt, and tan pullover sweater. *Enchanté jolie mademoiselle.*"

"Don't be bowled over by his showoff ways," Ruth said, laughing. "Dan's our official translator. He's fluent in English, French, German, and Hebrew, a graduate of at least two universities in England with fancy names, and he still hasn't found himself a wife. You'd think at twenty-eight someone would have snapped him up by now."

Ariana's eyes locked on the fourth man and his piercing brown eyes locked on hers. She felt a sudden thrill of excitement course through her body, an electricity she hadn't felt since Gabriel. He appeared to be quite young, twenty-three at most, and stood six feet tall. His black hair was stylishly long and his complexion was swarthy.

"And this," she heard Ruth say through a fog, "is Ephraim Biran, a law student at Hebrew University. Ephraim's the youngest member of our team, but don't let his age fool you. He's experienced more in his twenty-one years than most of us go through in a lifetime. When he heard we were taking on your father's case, Ephraim appeared on our doorstep one morning and volunteered to help us find witnesses or do anything else. His background gives him a personal stake in the outcome of this case."

"Miss Greenwald." He took her hand, squeezed it firmly, held on a little longer than was necessary. As she looked into his eyes, she felt naked. It had been two years ... He was an incredibly handsome young man.

"All right," Ruth said. "Now that we've all met, let's go over where we are and what we have to do. It's now January 18, 1954. We have two months before the trial gets under way. Ariana, how much help can we really expect from your father?"

"Papa's the kindest, most loving father than ever lived. He's not embittered in any way, but Papa, God love him, will be totally ineffective in assisting us." Ariana was a realist.

"I gathered as much when I listened to him the first time he was here. Does he know the names of any Hungarian survivors? Any at all?"

"Probably a few."

"That's a beginning. You and Ephraim will start looking for witnesses. Arieh will tell you exactly what we're searching for and what information we need to know from each of these witnesses, provided we can find any."

"Shmulik, you really bit off a big one this time, eh?"

"That's nothing new, is it Ema?"

"I suppose not. What do you know about this fellow Kasztner?"

"Not much. That's why I called on my mother the Senator to help," he said, hugging her affectionately.

"And I thought it was just because you needed a place to stay while you're in Jerusalem."

"That, too."

"I thought as much," she said. Bat-Sheva Katznelson was not a large woman, but her presence was commanding. She had iron gray hair, warm blue eyes, and, when she wasn't on the Knesset floor, liked to wear loose-fitting, comfortable clothes. She was one of the few women Senators in the Knesset, the political superior of Rudolf Kasztner, and a woman of strong moral conviction. "I suppose you'll want everyone to stay here as well?" she said, grinning. "God was good to give your father and me the foresight to build a large house."

"Ema, are you sure it's all right? It'll be a long trial and I don't think it'll be a popular one. You may find angry picketers surrounding the place."

"It wouldn't be the first time this family's taken on unpopular causes. When did we ever teach you to run in fear from anything?"

"Never."

"Good. Consider the house yours as long as you need it. Now, tell me more about this Kasztner. The little I've seen of him, he seems to me to be one of those political climbers who knows exactly whose boots to lick and when. I can't say I'm partial to those oily types, although I've really heard nothing one way or the other. Shmulik?"

"Yes, Ema."

"Is this another of your do-it-for-no-money crusades?"

"I'm afraid so, Ema," he said without embarrassment. "But business has been good enough that I can afford to take it on."

"How long will the trial take?" she called out, as she walked into her capacious kitchen.

"With the witnesses I have right now, a day-and-a-half."

Mrs. Katznelson returned from the kitchen with a tray full of sweet rolls and two mugs filled with black coffee. She beckoned her son to sit on the veranda overlooking the new part of Jerusalem.

"What are your chances?"

"Right now, given the state of the evidence? A hundred to one or less."

"Then why did you take it?"

"Because I feel there's something very strange about the whole thing. A seventy-two-year-old nobody, who doesn't have a mean bone in his body, and who is not certifiably crazy, suddenly publishes an absolutely scathing indictment about a man who's not running for any office, who's a friend of the Mapai Party higher-ups, and whom he's never even personally met. He's shown me an anonymous letter which I've confirmed is not in his handwriting, and he tells me there's all kinds of coffeehouse gossip about it.

"The owner of the Cafe Vienna told me he's heard similar gossip, although he never paid it much mind. He couldn't identify any specific customers who actually said anything that would be admissible in evidence, but he confirmed that stories about Kasztner have been circulating for over a year and, unlike the smug glee that usually attends gossip, there's a real sense of bitterness whenever Kasztner's name comes up."

"What do you think, Samuel?"

"On paper, Kasztner is unassailable. His credentials rival those of Ben Gurion or Weizmann and it never appears that he's a political climber. It's just that whenever an appointment is available, he usually gets it, quietly and efficiently. Libel laws require malice. I don't believe Greenwald is capable of malice. Strangest of all, and probably the one thing that tipped the scales in favor of my taking on this case, is why the government of Israel — not Kasztner himself — is pressing this case in the criminal courts. What does Kasztner himself have to gain?"

Bat-Sheva Katznelson pondered the question a little while. Then she answered carefully. "From what I gather, Kasztner has his eye on the foreign ministry. A courtroom gives him a public rostrum from which, if he acquits himself well, he comes off as an international hero. The government benefits, for this kind of case tempers the irresponsibility of an absolutely free press with a signal that liberty is not license."

"And if the government loses, Ema?"

"An interesting concept, my son. You, yourself don't seem to believe you'll win."

"I didn't say that, Ema. I said a hundred to one shot. What would you have said the odds were when we declared independence and the Arab legions threatened to throw us into the sea?"

"As I said, Shmulik, an interesting concept."

8

The *shouk* bordering the Hebrew and Arab quarters of Jerusalem is a huge marketplace where the animosities of the Middle East give way to commerce. The smells of garlic, onions, fried falafel and grilled lamb pervade the area, and one can hear shouted encouragement in all the languages of the Levant as well as most European languages. Bedouins regularly sweep into the area, offering camel rides and occasionally offering pretty girls — only half in jest — huge dowries to become one of their wives.

The Bosphorous Restaurant, a reminder that less than four decades ago the entire area had been under Turkish control, was a popular meeting place for businessmen and lawyers. One could exchange the latest news in the semi privacy of curtained booths while dining on succulent lamb kebabs, shashlik, and wonderful lamb-and-vegetable stews.

Samuel Tamir and Amnon Tell sat contentedly toward the rear of the restaurant, nursing cups of thick Turkish coffee.

"Good of you to meet me here, Sam," Tell said. "It seems we can still spot a potentially troublesome little case and have the good sense to discuss it away from the participants."

"I agree, Amnon. Why in heaven's name is the government pushing this one so hard? Surely Greenwald's too small a fish for anyone to worry about. Why don't you boys play in a bigger pond, search for more important things to do?"

"I almost wish I could. The government's putting an awful lot of effort into this one. Almost as if the Prime Minister himself is treating this as a personal affront." A swarthy, mustachioed waiter approached them quietly, his apron stained with many kinds of food.

"Baklava, please," Tell said to him.

"The same," Tamir said.

When the waiter had left, Tell continued, "I realize we've got discovery fights ahead of us, but I thought as a friend I'd give you a bit of a free look at what we've got." He withdrew a thick sheaf of papers from his briefcase. "We've taken more than twenty witness statements. We have a dozen sworn affidavits attesting to Kasztner's character. D'you know, he personally saved over sixteen hundred people?"

"Mmm-hmmm, so he says."

Tell's eyebrows lifted. "These affidavits are not from him and, so far as we can make out, they're not from his cronies or from people he paid or threatened. The records seem to bear out everything he says."

"So what do you want me to do, Amnon?"

"Plead your guy in. Look, if he issues an apology — Sit down, Sam, you needn't get upset about my offer, please listen to it first, OK?"

Tamir, who'd started to rise, sat down again, remembering his manners.

"I'm not saying it has to be an abject, humiliating *mea culpa* type apology. It can be carefully worded and neutral, 'If I said something I shouldn't have said that might conceivably have offended someone, I regret it,' that kind of thing. No damning admission, so to speak. And a plea of no contest so there's no civil repercussions."

"He'd still be found guilty and sentenced."

"We could work out a little bit of jail time for show, a thousand pound fine —"

"Amnon, Malchiel Greenwald has nothing. He can't afford to pay *attention*, let alone money."

"Don't tell me you're doing this for free?" Tell asked, his eyes widening. "You don't get two offices in nice buildings by giving your brain away. Someone's got to be paying for this — the Communists, Kasztner's personal enemies, the press?"

"If they are, it will come as a wonderful surprise to me. So far as I know, I'm not only not getting paid, I'm out of pocket three pounds for this lunch."

"Not to worry, the State will pay for it," Tell said, his face relaxing into a rare grin which showed tobacco-stained teeth. "You're serious, he's not paying you?"

"Absolutely. The man has a small stamp collection and a pretty but virtuous daughter."

"Ah-ha, I knew there'd be something there."

"Not what you're thinking, you would-be dirty old man," Tamir said. His own grin was open. "She and Ruth hit it off immediately. Ariana Greenwald worked in the Irgun. But a Haganah man like you wouldn't know of such things would you?"

"Samuel, you and your type are one gigantic pain in the ass, but thank God we had you around back when the British were mucking things up. Seriously, what do we do about Greenwald?"

"Have we been assigned a judge yet?" Tamir asked.

"Benjamin Halevi."

"Mr. Stickler-for-details. As strict a jurist as ever sat on the bench. He's an arch conservative but he's fair. Do you think he'd go along with a deal?"

"Depends on what the deal is," Tell replied. "They usually do. Judges are just like the rest of us. They like to avoid difficult decisions or, if they're forced into it, they make decisions on the narrowest grounds possible. If they can work a quiet plea bargain, they've managed their calendars and can go home at night believing they've done justice."

"You said the government is pushing this one hard, Amnon. Do you think they might be quietly pushing the judge, too?"

"Our incorruptible judiciary? I won't say there are those who can't be influenced. Since the Mapai Party appointed them all, I'd be less than candid if I said they don't respond to the hand that feeds them. But from what I've heard, Halevi's an independent sort who's made some unpopular decisions. You never can tell where his sympathies will lie. Your client's a poor old man."

"Which leads us back to the money. A thousand pounds would bankrupt him."

"Five hundred then? Spread out over ten years. Fifty pounds a year?"

"If he lives that long. I don't think he'd ever go for the jail time."

"Come on, Sam, five days of home detention?"

The men sat for a few moments, thoughtfully mulling over the options as they ate the last of their honeyed confection. Tamir caught the waiter's eye. "Two more cups of *bohtz*, please," he said, using the word "mud" the universal Hebrew slang for Turkish coffee.

"Amnon," Tamir began at last. "Greenwald seems awfully sure of himself. It's almost as if he and God made a pact and he feels God's on his side. Did you ever think what would happen if the old man was telling the truth?"

"Truth depends on what point of the earth you're standing on, doesn't it?" Tell replied. "Why don't you read some of the affidavits?"

The defense lawyer went through the documents carefully, mentally noting names, occupations and the substance of what each witness had to say.

"I knew where we were bound, but I felt I could not tell my wife. At the last possible moment before the train left the station, I saw Doctor Kasztner, well dressed and immaculate as always, personally walk up and speak to the guard and show him a paper. Next thing I know, my wife, our two children, and I were taken out of the cattle car into which we'd been stuffed and returned to the Budapest ghetto. There isn't a day in my life I don't remember Doctor Kasztner in my prayers."

. . .

"As Doctor Kasztner's secretary, I knew he was indefatigable in his efforts. He told me he often worked eighteen hours a day, seven days a week, trying to get Jews released wherever and whenever he could. I had no reason to doubt his word. Kasztner lived better than most of us did. I knew he met with the Germans several times a week, but in the end his diplomacy saved lives. This was what we were trying to achieve."

The encomia went on and on. Jewish Agency executives, bakers, engineers, widows, rich, poor. The meaning of their declarations couldn't be clearer: Kasztner was a tireless worker, a savior, a saint. The underlying between-the-lines message was that none of these good people could understand how anyone would have the temerity to question Doctor Kasztner's good works.

Tamir's raptor mind pecked at the weak underbelly of the affidavits ... "Kasztner lived better than most of us." "Kasztner told me he worked seven days a week." "Kasztner was well-dressed and immaculate as always."

If Doctor Kasztner had been a saint, he had not taken a vow of poverty or deprivation, even during the worst days of the Holocaust. No one asks that a man in high position, even a Jew in high position, be one with the common people. Yet, there was not one declaration that ever showed him being part of the crowd. He was always a leader apart.

Tell's words echoed in his mind. "The government's putting an awful lot of effort into this one. Almost as if the Prime Minister himself is taking this as a personal affront." Could Moshe Sharett somehow be involved in Kasztner's machinations, God forbid?

Samuel Tamir had seen the danger of an all-powerful government struggling to stay in power to the very last moment. He had come to the conclusion that all governments were the same. Why should Israel's be any different? A party in power wanted to consolidate its authority. As hubris set in, that government became ever more entrenched and, paradoxically, ever more paranoid, ever more repressive. And always the first thing to go was freedom of speech, freedom of the press. *Freedom of the press! By God, that was it!* Moshe Sharett's government was pushing this puny little case to set a precedent. If Greenwald's *Letter to My Friends in the Mizrahi* could be shut down for what it said, then even the *Jerusalem Post* wasn't safe. This case was nothing more than a power grab!

Samuel Tamir could look authority in the eye and take its measure. He could see the ignoble reality of Jewish nobles — they were human beings, neither better nor worse than anyone else — and he did not fear the consequences of defending any worthy person at any time in any court. To do less than give the very best he' had was to shun his own moral burden, his own spiritual task.

When he spoke again, it was quietly, but Amnon Tell could not miss the change that had come over his adversary. "I'll speak with Malchiel Greenwald, Amnon. I cannot give you my answer now. But I think I know what it will be."

"Mister Greenwald, Ariana," Tamir said, escorting them into his office. "I appreciate your coming on such short notice."

"What more would I have to do this morning?" Greenwald said. "Watch the flowers blooming in my neighbor's garden? Schedule a hundred appointments for all my well-wishers?" His attempt at sarcasm was veiled by the gentle, humble pride of the little man who knew his place in the social hierarchy and had accommodated to it.

"I had a long meeting yesterday afternoon with Prosecutor Tell." Tamir went on to describe the evidence he'd seen, the offer Tell had made. "Judge Halevi, who'll be trying this case, is a stern man, one who would undoubtedly give you a much stiffer sentence were he to find you guilty. I've appeared before him. He finds defendants guilty more than ninety percent of the time."

"Can you challenge his right to try the case?" Ariana asked.

"I could, but in this case I wouldn't."

"Why not?"

"Because although I may disagree with the way Benjamin Halevi runs his courtroom, and although I'd like to stand before a more liberal jurist, I believe you won't find a fairer-minded judge in the whole of Israel."

Tamir walked around his desk to where his clients sat. He took the old man's leathery hands between his own and looked Greenwald directly in the eye. "Their offer is a half-apology, four or five days in home detention, and fifty pounds a year for the next ten years. Although I don't want to influence your decision in any way, I would be happy to loan you the entire five hundred pounds at no interest, pay it to the government and get them off your back. You can pay me back as, when, and if you can. I promise you I'll never press you for repayment. Although I told you when we started that one of the conditions of my representing you was that you would follow my instructions to the letter and let me try the case my way, this is one decision that rests with you. Think about it for a while, Mister Greenwald. You can call me in a couple days and give me your decision."

The old man smiled, a grim, determined smile, puffed himself up in his chair, and said, "Mister Tamir, I don't need time to consider my decision. I thank you for your extreme courtesy and your patience with an old man. But to concede even the smallest point, to accept the government's offer, would be tantamount to admitting my guilt. And I am not guilty, Mister Tamir, regardless if Kasztner brings five witnesses or five thousand, regardless if I have not one witness to speak for me at present. I have you as my counsel, Mister Tamir. I trust you. I trust Judge Halevi. And I trust in my own innocence in the eyes of God and in the eyes of the world. Therefore you must understand, Mister Tamir, that I shall never plead guilty."

"Thank God," Tamir said warmly. "I respect your decision, Mister Greenwald. Now let us go forward and never look back."

9

As the sun set over the Judean hills, Ariana Greenwald and Ephraim Biran trudged back toward Tamir's office to report their findings.

"Six possible witnesses this afternoon, five deceased, the sixth slams the door in our face. Not a very good beginning," Ephraim said.

"An understatement. What time are we supposed to be back at the office?"

"Tomorrow morning," he said.

They'd worked together for half a month. Ephraim had never been anything but scrupulously polite. Still —

"Can I treat you to dinner for your efforts?" she asked.

"I'd appreciate that, Miss Greenwald. It would sure beat student cafeteria meals or left-over spaghetti." It was the first time Ariana had seen him smile, and it made him handsomer still, for it came from his depths and he did not smile frequently.

"I'll do it on one condition, Ephraim."

"What's that?"

"You stop with the 'Miss Greenwald' already. Good heavens, how old do you think I am?"

"I've no idea. Twenty-five, twenty-six maybe?"

"Do I look so old?" she asked, smiling flirtatiously.

"Nn ... no .... uh, I really don't know. He blushed furiously. "It's just that you seem so ... so worldly and competent in the face of all this."

"Ephraim Biran, I'm twenty-three. Now that we've settled that, will you please call me Ariana in future?"

"O.K.," he smiled again, "Ariana."

She chose a restaurant where she'd been many times before, inexpensive, but with excellent food. As always, it was crowded, but she spotted a small table for two in the back. She signaled Ephraim to follow her.

"'Evening, Ariana," Aaron, a big, burly bear of a man her own age said. "The usual?"

"Not tonight. Aaron, I'd like you to meet Ephraim Biran from Mister Tamir's office." The waiter nodded politely. "Ephraim and I have been walking our feet off all afternoon looking for witnesses. We deserve something better than falafel and tabouli. I'd like your roast chicken dinner, chips, salad and Coca-Cola to drink. How about you, Ephraim?"

"The same, please."

"Two roast chicken dinners, Aaron." The waiter departed. "Now, Ephraim, you've obviously read Tamir's dossier, so you know almost all there is to know about me. I know nothing about you except you're a third year law student at Hebrew University, that you seem to survive on thin air, and that in the time I've known you I've seen you smile only once, a very handsome smile I might add."

Biran blushed. "I've always had trouble talking about myself with anyone," he said. "I read somewhere that women get very bored when all a man wants to do is talk about himself. I thought if I listened more, learned more, it might somehow make me a more interesting person. They say God gave man two ears and one mouth so he could listen twice as much as talk."

Ariana laughed, then momentarily choked up at his innocent sweetness.

"I don't know about other girls you've talked to, but I'd like to hear about your life."

"It's not a pretty story, Ariana."

"Ah-ha!" she said, trying to lighten the conversation. "A love affair gone sour? Three children no one knows about? Hey, I'm joking, Ephraim. You don't need to look so glum."

"It's not that way at all, Ariana. No children, no wives, not even a girlfriend."

"Better I don't ask, then."

"Well, you wanted to hear about me, so here goes. I was born in a small village in Ukraine, a few miles from the Polish border. My father had a small dry goods store and my mother helped out in the shop, which would have been unheard of a few years before I was born, but times were changing for all of us. I had an older sister, Sarah, who would have been your age —she and I were always best friends — and another sister, Rebekah, who was four years younger than me.

"One day, when I was ten, some German troops came through our village. I'd finished my studies early that day and was out in the fields beyond our village, lying in the warm sun, watching the clouds go by overhead, inventing shapes for them in my mind, when I heard a loud commotion coming from the village.

"I followed the sound, keeping my distance, because sudden loud sounds had always frightened me — thunder, the sound of many horses' hooves, that kind of thing. I watched, horror-struck, as the Germans rounded up every Jew in our village, my father, my mother, Sarah and Rebekah, among them. They took them to a place outside the village —." Ephraim started to weep. "My family went to their deaths with dignity. No begging, no weeping. Sarah was beautiful, like you. I thought they were going to rape her at first, but they were just too damned tired, I guess. Excuse me for a few moments. Is there a men's room nearby?"

Ariana pointed wordlessly. She gulped down a drink of water, blew her nose, and was somewhat more composed when he returned, ashen faced.

"I... I didn't know," she stammered. "I'm so sorry ..."

"Don't be," he replied. "I've held this inside me so long, relived that day a thousand times. I've never allowed myself to get close enough to another human being to let them know this. Believe it or not, I feel better than I've felt in eleven years. Would you mind terribly if I went on?"

"Are you sure you want to?" she asked gently.

"More than ever. Somehow, I managed to escape the slaughter. I knew where there was a small cave, a mile beyond the village. I stayed there for a week, sneaking back to the village at night to pore through the garbage cans. The pickings were very lean. Since the village was under German control, I knew I'd be shot if I showed my face in the village, and I knew I'd starve if I didn't get some food and fresh water soon.

"Somehow, I made my way west to a forest near the Polish border, it may even have been in Poland for all I knew. I hid there for the next few months, eating berries, leaves, whatever it took to stay alive.

"One night, I heard men speaking Yiddish nearby. When I investigated, I found they'd camped near where I'd hidden. I didn't reveal myself to them for several nights. Finally, when I couldn't stand the loneliness any longer, I came out of the brush in broad daylight. My hair was a greasy, rotted tangle. What clothes I had were in tatters. I probably stank worse than they. I hadn't had a bath since the day my family was slaughtered.

"But I was tall for my age and stronger than most. My first assignment was to carry messages to some partisans in Bratislava on the Slovakian frontier. I had successfully delivered those messages and was about to recross the border into Poland when I was seized by Hungarian gendarmes on charges of smuggling. Next thing I knew, I was taken to Budapest, where I was thrown into a jail cell. There were two others in that small cell, a girl perhaps two years younger than me, and an older woman, who must have been in her early twenties, but looked much older. Her front teeth were broken, and she must have been beaten very badly."

Ariana's eyes started to tear up as she listened to Ephraim's story of his season in hell. The young man opposite her stopped, took a long draught of water, wiped his lips with a paper napkin, took a deep breath and continued.

"I thought for certain I'd either be killed or starve to death, but somehow my case never went to trial. That woman was probably the reason I'm alive today. She made the days go by quickly, teaching us

Hebrew and constantly talking about Palestine, the new home for Jews. There were times when I simply wanted to give up, but that lady, I don't even remember her name, convinced the other little girl — her name was D'vora — that we had to survive, that we were the future of what she called Israel.

"She told me I had to keep on living, one day at a time, until my Bar Mitzvah, and then one day at a time after that, and another day after that."

Ephraim stopped for another moment, blew his nose into the napkin, and continued.

"One morning I woke up and she wasn't there anymore. I thought my last day had come, but later that same morning, D'vora and I were taken by a car, not a police car, driven by a much older man, who dropped us off somewhere in the High Tatras. D'vora was met by the remnants of her family and I was introduced to a small group of the partisans who'd sent me to Bratislava several months before. I never saw D'vora again.

"For the next year, I learned to kill, to deliver messages, to do whatever the partisans wanted me to do. I ran weapons to the outskirts of Warsaw. Occasionally they sent me to visit one of their Polish or Russian informants. The Germans had already destroyed the life I'd known. I vowed to repay them any way I could.

"Baruch Levy, one of our freedom fighters, took pity on me when he heard my story. He knew of a woman in eastern Poland who helped refugees get through Ukraine. The woman got me as far as Kovalevskiy. A Russian farmer introduced me to a butcher, who helped me move ten miles farther south. Men and women, Jews and *goyim*, helped me. Each night, I slept on a different pile of straw, in a different barn.

"Finally I got to Odessa, where I was crammed aboard a coal barge bound for Istanbul, among a herd of scrawny cattle. I didn't eat for four days. I still remember the first meal I had in Istanbul. A raw onion fell off a truck rolling down the wharf. I grabbed it before the next truck had a chance to run over it, and devoured it nearly whole. I've had many meals in my life, but if I live to become a rich man and dine with heads of state, nothing will ever taste as good as that onion. After I'd eaten that incredible feast, I returned to the dock where I'd landed. A man named Turhan

Türkoğlu picked me up at the dock and took me to a safe house in the Belgrade Forest. I stayed there for fifteen days, then slowly made my way south to Mersin, where I met a small group of Jewish blockade runners.

"The rickety, old boat I was on made it to a point ten miles south of Cyprus when we were picked up by a British patrol. I was sent to a refugee camp near Nicosia where I remained until the war ended.

"A friend of mine in the camps knew the Katznelson family. When they heard my story, they took pity on me. Mrs. Katznelson has a lot of influence. They got me to Israel, illegally I'm sure, in 1946, and arranged for me to go to Selah Shalom Kibbutz in the Negev. My school marks were such that I was selected to attend law school. Although I have no proof, I'm certain the Katznelsons were instrumental in getting me accepted."

Ariana looked directly into his eyes, took his hand in hers, and smiled at him. At that moment, he felt she was the most beautiful human being he'd ever seen. He felt lighthearted, clean, for the first time in his memory.

"Ariana, how can I ever thank you for letting me unload all this on you?"

"Sssh," she said, putting her right forefinger to his lips. "It's over, Ephraim. We can't bring your family back, but it is Jewish tradition that they will continue to live through you. I'm sure they would have been — they are — prouder of you than if you had been the first President of Israel. You can thank me by accepting this evening as a rebirth, a new beginning for the rest of your life."

She was about to say more, but at that moment the burly Aaron reappeared, bearing two huge plates filled with food. The chicken was done to perfection, with a healthy brown color and crispy skin. Surprisingly for Israel, the French fries were not greasy, and the salad, a concoction made of chopped onions, tomatoes, green peppers, cucumber and parsley, sweetened with lemon and sugar, smelled fresh and delicious.

They dived into their food, using it to dilute the rising tide of conflicting emotions they felt – hunger, pain, sadness, death – and the life force which pulls all human beings away from death, and which has been called everything from lust to the beginnings of love. They were not yet lovers, but they were more than friends.

After the meal, over American-style coffee, they discussed child-hood memories of different places they'd been and seen. Ariana told Ephraim about her unfortunate early marriage to Gabriel — thank God there were no children. He seemed to take it in stride. People adapt to hard times in any situation.

Their conversation was interrupted when an attractive dark-haired young woman with a guitar sat on a stool in the opposite corner of the room and started singing. Her voice was throaty, husky, strident as she sang songs of unrequited love, or love lost. Ariana and Ephraim were about to leave when Aaron told them, "Alisa Fineman, unquestionably Israel's best undiscovered singer. Stay for the next song. I think you'll appreciate it."

The singer stood up, nodded to the audience, and said, "Eli, Eli." She started strumming her guitar very gently, and in a voice possessed of almost spiritual tenderness she sang the powerful words to one of the most beautiful melodies Ariana had ever heard.

> "Oh Lord, my God ....
> I pray that these things never end ...
> The sand and the sea ...
> The rush of the waters ...
> The crash of the heavens ...
> The prayer of the heart.
> The sand and the sea,
> The rush of the waters
> The crash of the heavens
> The prayer of the heart."

At the end of the song, there was complete silence in the restaurant, punctuated by quiet sobs. The plain, simple song had that effect on its hearers, whether they'd heard it once or a hundred times, for it summed up not only the innermost thoughts of a happy soul, but the memory of Israel's greatest modern heroine.

"'A Walk to Caesarea,' Ariana said softly to Ephraim. Hanna Senesh wrote it when she was eighteen. She and Sam … By the time she was twenty-three she was dead, cut down by Nazi torturers in Hungary after she had parachuted into the occupied country."

"Odd you should mention that," Aaron interrupted them. "She was Hungarian, like you. Her mother lives in Israel now."

"I didn't know that," Ariana said, obviously surprised.

"Hanna was killed in the late fall of 1944, just about the time Doctor Kasztner was doing all his rescue work in Hungary. You might want to ask her mother if she was familiar with his work," he said inscrutably.

"Do you know where we might locate her?" Ariana asked.

"One of our regulars, the old man playing chess over there, is a friend of hers"

Ariana waited until the old man turned away from the chessboard and the other player left. She approached him. "Excuse me, sir," she said.. "Might I speak with you a moment?"

The man mumbled something in Hungarian. Ariana immediately switched to her native tongue. "I'm sorry to interrupt, sir," she began again. "My name is Ariana Greenwald, and …"

"Greenwald?" the man said, as if trying to remember something. "Greenwald? Are you related to Malchiel Greenwald, young lady? The one Kasztner is suing?"

"I'm his daughter."

"My name is Imre Plotkin. I changed it to Henri when I escaped to France in the summer of 'forty-four, then to Chaim when I made it to Israel. I come from Cluj, same as Kasztner. Ah, young man, sit down, sit down."

"Thank you, sir," Ephraim said in passable Hungarian. "My name is Ephraim Biran. I come from Ukraine." Ariana's eyes widened. Biran had not told her he was fluent in Magyar, although given his background, she should have guessed it. "Aaron told me you're friends with Mrs. Senesh, Hanna's mother?"

"I am, and I can tell you she's no friend of Kasztner's either."

"Did you say 'either,' Mister Plotkin?" Biran asked, picking up the implication immediately.

"I did. Rudolf Kasztner has no friends among the 'little Jews' of

Hungary, or at least among the pitiful remnant who survived."

Hardly daring to believe the blind luck that had brought her to this place at this moment, Ariana managed to keep her voice calm. "What do you mean?"

"Kasztner was the darling of the Nazis, the hero of the 'prominenti,' those Jews in Switzerland, England, the United States and Palestine who wanted to present a calm, civilized face to the world. He was so busy meeting with his German friends at the Majestic Hotel, traveling to and from Switzerland during 1944, that he had very little time for the likes of us."

"Us?" Biran interrupted.

"Those of us who weren't in a position to advance his career or his status with the international power clique. We were beneath his concern."

"You know this for a fact, sir?" Ariana asked.

"Well, now, if I'm asked under oath whether I saw any of this, I would have to say no," he said, watching their faces drop with disappointment. "But there is a small, tightly-knit Hungarian survivor community. I'm sure that among them there may be a very few, probably no more than three or four, who saw, who knew."

"Is there any chance, Mister Plotkin, any chance at all, that you might be able to help us find them, maybe talk to them?" Ariana asked. "My father's life may be at stake. The trial is supposed to start in two weeks. So far we've had no luck at all finding witnesses."

"Does your father have a lawyer, child?"

"Samuel Tamir," she said.

"Ah-ha! The lawyer for the damned. You've made a fortunate choice, Miss Greenwald."

"Not I, Mister Plotkin. My father, as you may have gathered, is one of your 'little people.' He has no money. Tamir's taken this case on for, I believe they call it the public good."

"Let me tell you, miss, he may be doing the public far more good than he thinks. It's getting late. Why don't you and your young man meet me at my home tomorrow afternoon, say three o'clock? My address is —"

10

Imre Plotkin lived in a walk-up flat, three floors above the crowded street. The place was tiny, a postage-stamp sized living room and dining area, a bedroom with hardly enough room for Plotkin's single bed, a desk and chair, a bathroom so small that its shower was a spigot that hung from the ceiling and poured water into the middle of the room, from whence it escaped from a drain in the floor, and a minuscule kitchen.

Ariana guessed Plotkin was about her father's age. Like her father, he had the wispy grayish hair of any number of old men. His eyes were a bright, intelligent brown, and he was eager to greet them. Without waiting, he poured them tea in half-cracked mugs, and showed them a handwritten list he'd prepared earlier that morning.

"I've spoken with three witnesses, two men and a woman, who'll be happy to talk to you. I tried to get in touch with Catherina Senesh, but she's out of the country at the moment. She's not expected back for a month."

"But the trial could be over by that time," Ephraim said.

"Not if Samuel Tamir lives up to his reputation. Did you know that the estimable Doctor Kasztner was tried in absentia in Cluj by the survivors?"

"What?" Ariana almost shouted as the magnitude of this disclosure slammed into her with the force of a railway locomotive.

"Well, it may not exactly have been a trial in the sense that lawyers know it, but there were brief, secret meetings during the spring of 1945, and I'm told that Kasztner was found guilty of conspiring with the enemy."

"But that's the *only* capital crime in Israel, Mister Plotkin," Ephraim said. "The only one that carries the death penalty."

"As it was in Cluj, Mister Biran. But how can those whose destiny is death sentence someone far above them to die, eh?"

"When can we speak with these survivors?" Ariana asked.

"I've arranged for them to come here within the hour."

Late that evening, after dinner at a falafel stand, too intoxicated with the excitement of their discovery to be exhausted, Ariana and Ephraim walked the mile from Plotkin's apartment to the Hebrew University bus stop.

Neither of them knew how it began. One moment she took his hand in hers. The next moment, they were kissing and embracing.

"Ariana…" he started to say.

"Sssh. Words only get in the way. How far do you live from here?"

"Half a kilometer."

"Well," she said, regaining her composure. "A public street is no place for a man and woman to do serious cuddling. What are we waiting for?"

Ephraim's lodgings were minute, a small room in a block of student dormitories. There was a single bed, a student desk and chair, a small lamp, and a table radio. They'd hardly gotten in the door when Ariana turned on the lamp and shut off the ceiling light. …

Afterward, they lay still for several minutes. Then, they reached over toward one another, alternately stroking and holding each other. As she reached up to touch his face, Ariana felt, then tasted, a salty wetness.

"Darling, you're crying," she said tenderly.

"I think I love you, Ariana."

"Mmmmm," she said, sighing.

"Did you hear what I said? I love you, Ariana."

But she did not hear. By that time, she had drifted off into a soft, blissfully contented slumber.

11

The courtroom of Department Five of the Jerusalem District Court was sixteen feet square, smaller than Tamir's waiting room, with no windows. There were three rows of benches for spectators. Ariana Greenwald, sitting in the first row, estimated twenty-five people at most could jam into those benches. There was no jury seating, no jury. There was only room for the judge, his bailiff, two counsel's tables, and a witness box.

Her father, dressed in the most conservative suit he owned, albeit a dozen years old, sat proudly next to his advocate. He turned, winked at his daughter, and flashed her a small victory sign. Samuel Tamir's face did not betray anything. He sat at counsel's table in his black lawyer's gown, staring intently at the wall.

She involuntarily sat up straighter when the prosecutor, Amnon Tell, entered. Despite his impeccable black robe, he wore yellow socks. In her nervousness, she felt like laughing out loud, but restrained herself. Tamir had told her Tell was one of the best "convicting" barristers in Israel, that he had a hot temper, and that sneers, invective, and righteousness could pour out of this sliver of a man. Even though her father did not face anything near the death penalty, she realized that his reputation was on the line. Ariana was surprised that she did not see Rudolf Kasztner anywhere in the courtroom.

Tell smiled at Tamir and chatted amiably with the defense counsel.

"I'm sorry your client didn't see fit to accept our offer, Sam. It's still open, you know."

"Thanks, Amnon, but we're ready to go at this point. How long do you think it will take?"

"Normally, it would run two or three days, but with you in it, it may run a full week."

Their conversation was interrupted as Shlomo, Judge Halevi's bailiff, entered the room from a side door. "Gentlemen, the Court."

Judge Halevi entered the room, wearing a black robe and a black *yarmulke*, the Jewish skullcap. Ariana was immediately taken by the magnetism of the man. He was in his late forties, a commanding, handsome, consummately dignified presence.

Benjamin Halevi had read over the papers in the case two nights before. He had thought about them last night, while he and his wife attended a concert of the Israel Philharmonic. Music was one of Halevi's great passions. Justice was the other.

Halevi had been among the first Jewish judges appointed by the British during their Palestine mandate. Later, the Ben Gurion government appointed him President of the Jerusalem District Court, a lifetime job. Halevi's dignity and his strict attention to detail were reminders of his German upbringing. He had graduated from the universities of Freiburg, Göttingen, and Berlin, left for Palestine in 1933, and spent one year in an agricultural settlement. The judge studiously picked up a pen and wrote a few words in a thick notebook. Since there was a lack of trained court stenographers in Israel, Judge Halevi would be taking down all the questions and answers himself. His face betrayed no emotion, his body exhibited no gestures. He had twin faiths, one in God, the other in the State of Israel.

"The District Court for the District of Jerusalem is now in session," he intoned. "Case Number 124-53, the State of Israel, Plaintiff, versus Malchiel Greenwald, Defendant. Counsel please state your appearances."

Tell rose. "Ready for the Plaintiff, Your Honor. Chaim Cohen, Attorney General of the State of Israel, by Amnon Tell, Assistant Attorney General for the State."

"Mr. Tell." The judge nodded.

"Ready for the Defendant, Malchiel Greenwald, Your Honor. Samuel Tamir."

"Mr. Tamir," the judge intoned, precisely as he had acknowledged Tell's presence.

"May I see both counsel in my chambers for a few moments? Court stands in recess."

Judge Halevi's offices were crowded floor-to-ceiling with law books. A photograph of his wife and three children sat on his desk, facing outward. Tamir was quick to observe a Guarneri violin, which he knew was Judge Halevi's pride and joy, in a velvet-lined violin case on the credenza behind the desk.

Halevi removed his judge's robe and wig. He smiled and beckoned the two counsel to sit in the chairs before him. "Tea, Amnon? Sam?"

"Yes, thank you," Tell said.

"The same for me, Your Honor," Tamir replied.

The judge pressed a buzzer, requested that the clerk bring in three glasses of tea, and made small talk while waiting for the refreshments. His clerk, a nondescript woman of thirty-five, brought glasses of tea and lumps of sugar on a silver serving tray, placed the tray on the Judge's desk in front of all three men, and left.

"Now, then, fellows," Halevi began in earnest. "I've read through the letter that Greenwald sent to his friends in the Mizrahi. Pretty strong stuff."

"I agree, Your Honor," said Tamir.

"And your man admits he wrote it?"

"He does, Your Honor."

"Then what's to argue about? We talked about Amnon's offer at the pretrial conference. It sounds like a pretty good deal to me, Sam. Your client's facing five to ten years and a pretty stiff fine which, I understand, he'll probably never be able to pay. You're sure he won't accept."

"Positive, Your Honor."

"His defense is that what he said was the truth. Yet in reading your list of witnesses and what they propose to say, it doesn't look like you have anything at all to offer. Hearsay, which you know is inadmissible. Character references for Mister Greenwald, which don't mean much when he's not the one who was libeled. Chances are good that I might entertain a motion severely limiting all of the evidence you propose to introduce. What about you, Amnon? Can you sweeten the offer at all?"

"How, Your Honor?"

"Completely suspend the sentence, put Greenwald on nonreporting probation?"

"What about the fine, Your Honor?"

"On a guilty plea, I'd be willing to go along with a five hundred pound fine. Given the apparent intemperance of the writing, I hardly think a lesser fine would be appropriate."

"I'd be willing to consider it, Your Honor," Tell said.

"Sam?"

"I'm afraid it's still no deal, Your Honor. My client is absolutely convinced of his innocence."

"That means you're pinning all your hopes on your ability to cross-examine the prosecution's chief witness. You know his reputation?"

"I do, Your Honor."

"I don't mean his reputation as a rescuer, Sam. I mean his reputation as a smooth, cagey survivor who's spent a good part of his life dealing with very difficult people. His life has hung in the balance many times and the answer he gave often determined whether or not he lived to see the next sunset. That does not mean that I intend to believe or disbelieve him more or less than any other witness who takes the stand in my courtroom. It simply means I don't think he'll be an easy witness to trap or trick."

"I don't intend to trap or trick him, Your Honor," Tamir said. "Truth is not a relative thing. It either is or it isn't. It's that simple. And my study of his record leads me to believe I might be able to establish that truth through his mouth."

Judge Halevi lifted his eyebrows. "Sam, I don't mean to tell you how to run your case, and you know as well as I that whatever you say in court is immune from defamation laws, but I suggest your last remark may have been somewhat intemperate."

"I'm sorry, Your Honor. I apologize. It's just that emotions may tend to run rather high in this case."

"Not if you count the number of observers in the benches. Will there be any pretrial motions?"

"I don't envision any, Your Honor," Tell said. "It looks like a clean, quick case to me."

"Sam?" '

"No, Your Honor."

"I trust your first witness will be Doctor Kasztner, Amnon? How long do you anticipate you'll have him on the stand?"

"Three days at most."

"Cross-examination, Samuel?"

"I truly don't know, Your Honor. It depends on how he answers my questions."

"I reserve the right to cut you off if the questions become repetitive or irrelevant. I'd like to see this case conducted in an orderly manner. Looks like a week or two at most."

"But you will listen to the evidence before you make your rulings, Your Honor?" Tamir asked.

The judge glared at Tamir. "Have you ever known me not to listen to all relevant evidence, counsel?"

"No, Your Honor. No offense meant."

"None taken. Now, gentlemen, a few ground rules. Any objections to evidence will be clearly stated. No lectures. Nor do I anticipate that any objections you make will be framed in such a manner that it will lead the witness to answer in a given manner. If that happens once, I will advise you at side bar. If it becomes a habit, I will let you know my displeasure and will, perhaps, impose other sanctions as well.

"Finally, I expect you to ask relevant questions, proving material facts. If either of you wanders off the path too often, I will have the offender submit questions to me and I will ask them of the witness. Understood, gentlemen?"

"Yes, Your Honor," both lawyers answered.

"Good. This is not a jury trial, so we're not faced with the endless rhetoric that goes on in such a trial. At least that's one thing we can be thankful for, eh, fellows?"

"Yes, Your Honor," they answered, once again in unison.

"Very well, then. Trial will commence in two hours. I trust that will give you ample time to have your first witness ready to testify."

"I believe so, Your Honor. I advised Doctor Kasztner to be here at beginning of trial. I've no idea why he wasn't here when you first took the bench, but I'm certain it wasn't deliberate."

"No matter, Amnon. He's a witness. I don't see him as being on trial in this case. Two hours it is, gentlemen."

12

"Opening argument, Mister Tell?"

"Waived, Your Honor."

"Mister Tamir?"

"Defendant reserves opening argument until the beginning of his case, Your Honor."

"Very well. Are there any stipulations before we start taking evidence?"

"Yes, Your Honor," prosecutor Tell said. "The parties stipulate that Pamphlet Number 51 of a publication entitled, 'Letter to My Friends in the Mizrahi,' may be admitted into evidence without further foundation, and that this pamphlet was authored, published and distributed by the defendant, Malchiel Greenwald. Further, the parties stipulate that the Rudolf Kasztner to whom the pamphlet refers is the same Doctor Kasztner who will testify here in a few moments."

"So stipulated, Your Honor," said Tamir.

"Thank you, gentlemen. The pamphlet is admitted as Exhibit One and the stipulations are accepted. Proceed with your first witness, Mister Tell."

"Thank you, Your Honor. The State calls the Honorable Doctor Rudolf Kasztner, Deputy Minister for Trade and Information of the State of Israel."

Doctor Kasztner's entrance produced a stir of the type that surround important men. As he entered the room, a dark-haired, cleverlooking man in his late forties, smiling, wearing horn-rimmed glasses, immaculately dressed, the half-dozen reporters who had entered the courtroom within the past hour, had only one attitude toward Doctor Kasztner, respect. Kasztner bowed slightly to Judge Halevi, acknowledging the judge's importance. Halevi nodded back at Kasztner. Tell smiled. Tamir sat with an impassive look on his face.

Tell had rehearsed his star witness for the past two months and had become more impressed with Kasztner each time they met. The Minister had personal mannerisms which made him unique, and, thought Tell, highly credible. He tipped slightly forward when he spoke. When he argued, always in respectful if somewhat magisterial tones, he steepled his fingers together. Doctor Kasztner was suave, worldly and sophisticated, politically solid. Tell had heard him deliver monologues in five languages. When the prosecutor had practiced a dry run cross-examination of Kasztner within the past week, the Minister was easily able to confuse his would-be cross-examiner. He was a born statesman and diplomat.

"Good morning, Doctor Kasztner. My first question concerns your background. I would like to ask my learned colleague for his consent that you be allowed to answer in the narrative."

"No objection, Your Honor."

"Go ahead, then, Doctor."

CLUJ, ROMANIA –

BUDAPEST, HUNGARY

FEBRUARY 1940 – SPRING 1943

13

FEBRUARY 1940

The three passengers, two men and a woman, talked animatedly as Marko, József Fisher's chauffeur maneuvered the lawyer's 1934 Chevrolet Master sedan toward the entrance of Cluj-Napoca Railway Station. The terminal, built seventy years before, when *Kloiznburg* was part of the Austro-Hungarian Empire, had been instrumental in propelling Cluj from a backwater of twenty thousand in the year it was built, to its present population, nearly six times that many. More than four out of every five inhabitants were Hungarian, even though Cluj was still part of Romania. Of those, nearly forty percent were Jews.

The mood in the car was a mixture of fear and vaguely optimistic hope, a microcosm of the ambiguous feelings throughout Europe.

"Poland's gone," Fisher said. "Now that the Reich has shown what they're all about, every Jew wants out. "Nine months ago, the Saint Louis proved what the Nazis have been saying all along: no matter how much everyone sympathizes with our plight, no one in the world wants Jews."

"God help me for saying this, but I almost can't blame them," the younger man said. "One only has to look around this city. Fifteen thou-

---

sand Jews in Kloiznburg. Three quarters of them still live in the eighteenth century. Torah scholars waiting for the Messiah to come. Clothed
head to foot in caftans that haven't been washed in years. They condemn
the Christians as heretics and anaethematize anybody who associates with
one. They're totally unreceptive to any ideas that developed during the
last two hundred years, and if they feel one drop of water a year on their
smelly bodies, it only happens when they can't duck out of the rain."

"Aren't you being a bit harsh on our coreligionists?" Fisher said,
raising his eyebrows.

"Perhaps, Doctor Fisher, but we're trying to build a Jewish homeland in Palestine and we need new blood, vigorous young blood to ensure
that we survive. God Himself understood that at the time of the Exodus."

"You raise an interesting point, Rezső," the older man replied.

"What are you men talking about?" the woman asked. "The Saint
Louis? The Exodus?" At that moment, Marko swerved to avoid a pothole
in the street.

Fisher explained to his daughter Greta, the younger man's wife,
"Last May, Goebbels announced to the world, 'We mean the Jews no
harm. To prove it, we're sending 937 Jews on one of our luxury liners, the
Saint Louis, to any port they want, with no restrictions.' All the passengers held landing certificates permitting them to enter Cuba, but when
the Saint Louis reached Havana, the Cuban President refused to honor
the documents and forced the ship to leave."

"After the ship left Havana harbor, it sailed so close to the Florida
coast that the passengers could see the lights of Miami. The captain appealed to the American authorities for refuge, but the U.S. refused to
allow the Saint Louis to land and the Coast Guard ships patrolled the
waters off Florida to make sure no one jumped to freedom. The ship had
to return to Germany. Not a single passenger made it out of Germany."

"God knew about the need for new blood thousands of years ago,
when the Jews left Egypt," Rezső Kasztner took up his father-in-law's
narrative. "Have you any idea how far it is from the Egyptian frontier to
Palestine?"

"Of course," the young woman replied. "About five hundred kilometers."

"A little over three hundred miles. Yet, it took the Jews *forty years*
to reach the Promised Land. Do the calculation, darling. If those people

walked ten miles a day, not at all far by today's standards, it would have taken thirty *days* to make the journey. Why do you think it took them four hundred-eighty times that long to get to Canaan?"

Doctor Fisher took out a pack of Carpaṭi cigarettes and passed it around. His daughter and son-in-law declined, but Marko extracted a steel lighter and flicked the wheel to light his employer's cigarette. "According to today's Torah scholars, God wanted to make sure that the old generation died out before they entered the Promised Land. Even Moses was not allowed to set foot in what became Israel. That's because He didn't want anyone to come to the Jews' new home who'd known the sting of slavery. He wanted only those young, vigorous men and women who'd been born free."

"You've made my point," Kasztner said.

"And you, Rezső?" Fisher asked. "Now that the authorities have banned *Új Kelet*, you've got to find work. No one's looking for a Yiddish journalist in today's Europe."

"Fortunately, I've made Zionist contacts as far away as Palestine. If things continue the way they seem to be going, they'll need all the rescuers they can get, which is where I fit in. I know how to negotiate, who to bribe, how much they want, and my fifteen years writing for *Új Kelet* has given me valuable connections in the underground."

"You expect Transylvania will be returned to Hungary?" Marko interjected.

"I do," Fisher said.

"As do I," Kasztner joined in. "The Viennese have been absorbed into the Reich, and before the war it was Austria-Hungary. Blood runs thicker than water, and Hitler dearly wants Hungary in his pocket."

"But Admiral Horthy may not want that," Greta said.

"He might not have that option," her husband said. "There are ninety million citizens of the Reich. Less than a tenth that number in Hungary. Poland has thirty-five million inhabitants. It took Germany four weeks to annihilate that country." He looked at his Benrus wristwatch. "Seven o'clock. The Budapest express should be leaving within the half hour."

"Do you have your tickets, Darling?"

"Of course," Kasztner said, reaching in the inside breast pocket of his pearl grey jacket. "Oh, and I almost forgot my hat," he said as Greta leaned to her right and handed it to him.

"How long will you be gone?" she asked.

"No more than a month or two."

"So long?"

"I'd like to get the lay of the land before I start a serious job search at the Jewish Agency."

"I'll miss you, Darling."

"And I you, Greta."

"If only we'd started on a baby."

Kasztner glanced sharply at his wife. "Greta, you know we've discussed this before. I can't think of a worse time to bring a new child, particularly a Jewish child, into the world." He softened momentarily when he saw her hurt look. "It'll be only a few years, Darling. This war can't last forever and Palestine is the safest place for Jews."

"Then why can't we move there now, Rezső?"

"Too much work to do laying the groundwork for a new Palestine. Too many to rescue."

"Why couldn't you do your rescue work from Palestine? Bring our own child up in the new land?"

"We'll discuss that when I get back," he said brusquely.

He opened the rear door, leaned over and gave his wife a hurried kiss on the cheek, and headed toward the inside of the terminal.

The 7:30 train from Cluj to Budapest was delayed forty minutes, which gave Kasztner a chance to purchase two cinnamon-laced sweet rolls and a cup of strong coffee at the station buffet. The first-class compartment was half full when he boarded. Kasztner took a seat by the window. It was actually eight-thirty by the time the train's whistle blew two sharp blasts, signaling its departure. The chuff-chuff of the steam locomotive had always been a siren song to him: off to a new adventure somewhere beyond the next mountain, the far valley.

The train gathered speed, and the gray morning soon produced a slow rain over the February countryside, where narrow, sandy roads led away into the forest, and, beyond his sight, into the Carpathian mountains.

As the train clattered across northwestern Romania, Kasztner felt ill at ease. Perhaps he'd been too arch in expressing his views about "the right kind of Jews" to his father-in-law. Jozsef Fisher, a pillar of Cluj's Jewish community and an esteemed member of the city council, represented *all* of its Jews. *But,* Kasztner thought, *any intelligent man would see that he was right. When the war ends — and it will end sooner or later — we'll be dealing with modern, educated world leaders. It would be ludicrous to send pushcart peddlers and Torah scholars immersed in the eighteenth century to deal with the likes of Churchill, Roosevelt, and, yes, even Joseph Vissarionovich Dzhugashvili, the upraised Georgian peasant who nowadays called himself Stalin.*

Kasztner stared at the droplets sliding across the window, his mind consumed by what he anticipated would be a new life in a new place. Budapest, nearly fifteen times the size of his home town. Budapest, home to the *right* kind of Jews, habitués of the cabarets and nightclubs, *Gundel's* Restaurant, Vaci Utca, and the fabled Gellert Baths. Civilization.

The woman in the seat across from him spread a newspaper over her lap, cut slices of apple with a paring knife, then chewed them, slowly, deliberately. The man with a long, gloomy face sitting next to her stared out into space in a trancelike state, obviously lulled by the rhythmic clickety-clack of the train's wheels passing over the seamed tracks.

Half an hour after they'd started, the train pulled into the station at Gârbău, marked in both its Romanian name and in its Hungarian, *Magyargorbó.* Less than five minutes later, the train continued westward, passing through *Aghireşu-Egeres,* before it entered the mountain country near Huedin, an hour's ride from Cluj.

At Huedin, Kasztner disembarked to relieve himself, for the W.C. inside the station was considerably cleaner than the ones in the train. Back in his first-class accommodations, he found that the gloomy-looking man had gotten off at Huedin and had not returned when the train departed the station.

The locomotive remained at the platform for the better part of a quarter-hour. The stationmaster stood by the first class carriage and smoked a cigarette until, after what seemed the slowest fifteen minutes in Kasztner's memory, he drew a pocket watch from his vest and waited as the second hand swept around the dial. As he started to raise his flag, a family of Orthodox Hasidic Jews, two men dressed in gabardine and wearing *payess*, earlocks, and heavy *yarmulkes*, Jewish skullcaps, and a woman and her two daughters wearing clothing the covered every inch of their bodies, hurried along the platform and entered the third-class compartment in the car immediately ahead of Kasztner's.

The stationmaster signaled to the engineer and the engine jerked as the train began to move. Moments later, two men dressed in identical gray flannel trousers and matching shirts, one of them wiping the rain from his eyeglasses with a handkerchief, came down the corridor and peered through the window into Kasztner's compartment. They took a moment, then, noticing that the woman who'd earlier been slicing the apple had placed a large canvas bag on the seat next to her and she was not going to move that container for anyone, went off to find seats elsewhere.

The next large station, Oradea, was two hours' distance from Huedin. Sensing he had nothing in common with the woman, Kasztner lay back and dozed in his comfortable seat as the train hurtled through the mountain country. Oradea, the last large city in Romania, lay only eight kilometers east of the the Hungarian frontier. There'd be an hour layover here, time to grab a quick lunch.

Slightly smaller than Cluj, Kasztner knew that Oradea would be one of the first targets of the Nazis, should they ascend to power here, and also one of the most important communities that must be saved, since fully one out of every three residents of the city, which his coreligionists called *Groysvardeyn*, was Jewish.

As he prepared to disembark, the five *Hasidic* Jews who'd boarded the train at Huedin, rushed by in front of them. They were met by a dozen similarly-garbed local Jews. Men hugged men, women hugged women, but there was absolutely no hugging between the sexes. Kasztner felt a shudder of revulsion. Exactly what did they have to add to civilized society, save several extra unwashed bodies?

For that matter, what did *any* of the provincials on the platform, Jew or Gentile, have in common with the educated, civilized people with whom he associated? Louts, peasants, bumpkins. But they outnumbered the Jews by a factor of two to one in Oradea, and in Germany, Poland, Romania, and Hungary that numerical superiority was ten to one. It would not be hard to see which group would survive, given those odds.

But there would be time to digest all this later. Maybe not at all.

After a lunch of cheese-and-tomato sandwich on țară pâine — country-style cornmeal bread — and an apple, Kasztner reboarded the Budapest-bound train. While the woman who'd sat opposite with him was nowhere to be seen, all four seats in his compartment were filled by junior SS officers, *Untersturmführers* by their collar badges. He nodded perfunctorily at them and they at him, before he walked down the corridor to the first compartment with available seating.

Less than ten minutes later, the train stopped at Borş, the last community on the Romanian side of the frontier, for only so long as it took the customs control flagman to wave the engine on. After another few minutes, the train stopped at tiny Ártánd, just over the Hungarian border, where the formalities were more pronounced. As the conductor ambled by, checking and punching the passengers' tickets, Kasztner asked, "How much longer 'til we get to Keleti terminal?"

"Four-and-a-half hours. It'd be a good time to take a nap until we get to Szolnok." He yawned and put his hand over his mouth.

While they were stopped, a man a few years younger than Kasztner, dressed in a natty suit and wearing an alpine hat, entered the compartment. "Do you mind if I sit here?" he asked politely.

"Not at all," Kasztner replied. "I've had no one to talk to for the past four hours and the conductor just told me it'll be another four-and-a-half."

"That's correct," the newcomer said. As the train departed the passport control area, he introduced himself. "David Grossman," he said, reaching out his hand.

"Rezső Kasztner. You're Jewish?"

"Uh-huh. Originally from *Wien.* Not such a comfortable place nowadays."

"You might not be alive if you'd stayed there."

"You got that right," the younger man said.

Kasztner nodded. "When did you leave *Wien*?"

"Two months before the *Anschluss*. My family got out in 'thirty-six. I stayed on 'til the end of the following year, when I took my engineering degree. Of course, by then I'd have had to be deaf, dumb, blind, and just plain stupid not to see the handwriting on the wall. Hitler's *kinder* were already camped on the border. Fortunately, the Schuschnigg government gave me an exit visa in January. I packed everything I owned, two suitcases and a thousand *schillings,* and took the next train down to Salonika."

"Cigarette?" Kasztner said, holding out a pack of Carpaţis.

"Thank you, don't mind if I do," the younger man said.

For the next few minutes, each man smoked in silence, relaxing as the engine chugged through the countryside. Apropos nothing, Grossman remarked, "This has got to be most monotonous landscape on earth."

"You're right about that," Kasztner replied. "The peasants call this werewolf country. They have almost as many *bubbe meises*, old wives' tales, as we do in Transylvania."

"Your home?"

"The big city of Cluj, actually. But close enough to Dracula country to breed legends and other such hocus-pocus."

"Lots of our *landsmen* there," Grossman said, using the communal word for one's fellow Jews.

"Yes and no," Kasztner replied. "About a third of them like you and me, but two-thirds of them would prefer life under the *Baal Shem Tov*," he said, referring back to the founder of the Hasidic movement in the 1700s.

"Nothing necessarily wrong with that," Grossman said, taking off his shoes and sighing with pleasure as he wiggled his toes. "The Viennese Jews were the most modern assimilated Jews outside of Berlin, and look where it's gotten them."

Kasztner felt a cold prickle as he heard those words, but there was no sense in causing his short-term companion discomfort, so he smoothly changed the subject.

"Any reason why you've left the safety of Metaxas' Greece to come back to Admiral Horthy's shaky domain?"

"Yep," David Grossman replied.

When he saw that his compartment mate said no more, Kasztner did not press the issue. He closed eyes, not to be rude, but to give the other man space and privacy. It took several moments before Grossman spoke again.

"I'm actually up here to help rescue Jews."

"No, really? What a remarkable coincidence! It seems we're in the same game."

"Oh?"

"Yes. I've worked with the Cluj Rescue Committee, but now it's time to expand my horizons."

"Komoly's bunch."

"You know him?"

"I know *of* him. His group works with the Establishment Jews in Palestine."

At that moment, he heard a whine as the locomotive slowed down. When Kasztner looked out his window to see why, he noticed there were heavy snowdrifts and a howling wind, which whipped from the front to the back of the train, impeding its progress.

"You don't seem to think much of the Jewish Agency," he said to Grossman, his tone neutral, but a trifle cool.

"I'm not saying their way is the wrong way. It's just *different*."

"Different? How?"

"They seem to have more patience. They're much more selective in who gets entry permits from the Brits. It's like, if you speak the King's English and have a university degree, and if you're a dyed-in-the-wool Zionist, step to the front of the line."

"I trust you don't feel that way?"

"Mister Kasztner, to me a Jew is a Jew. I saw how it was in Vienna, the most cosmopolitan city in the world and the most anti-Semitic. I believe Hitler and his allies don't separate the educated, cultured, modern Jew from the *Hasidim*. The only good Jew is a dead Jew. I believe they're out to annihilate as many Jews as they can, regardless of what kind of Jew they are. My people want to save as many Jews as we can, without asking what kind of Jew they are."

"An interest concept. Mister Grossman," Kasztner replied. "You know, you're quite right. It is the most boring landscape I've seen and I'm feeling a bit tired at the moment. Would you mind if I dozed for awhile?"

"Of course not, Mister Kasztner. It's been nice chatting with you."

"Yes, your ideas are … interesting."

Grossman noticed that as Kasztner fell asleep, he kept his shoes on.

14

Friday, 27 September 1940

My Dearest Jozsef,

The weather in Budapest has finally turned a bit cooler. Summer was sweltering. I cannot count the number of times I wanted to return to Cluj just to walk in the Turda Gorge and feel the mountain breeze. The best thing I can say about the two-room apartment I rent in Váci utca is that it's on the most famous and accessible street in central Budapest.

It's been that way since the Middle Ages, when its length, just under a mile, paralleled the entire length of Pest. For the past hundred-fifty years, it's been the address for anyone of consequence in the City. Váci starts at Vörösmarty Square and runs down to the Great Market Hall. It's divided by Erzsébet Boulevard. The two separate parts, to the north and the south of Erzsébet are totally different. The northern part is overcrowded with tourists and shop windows in every building, while the southern part, where I live, is much quieter and, because of the run-down condition of the apartments, much cheaper.

I've been able to keep a roof over my head and food in my belly by sending dispatches to the newspapers in Kolozsvár, the official name of Cluj now that it's been restored to Hungary by the Vienna award last month. At first, I believed the annexation augured well for the Jews, but Germany has brought pressure to bear. Gömbös was anti-Semitic, but he was tolerable as long as Budapest's Jews assimilated. The Nazis and the Fascists were able to get him removed as Prime Minister, and now the Diet has passed a number of so-called "Jewish laws."

I imagine there'll be changes in Romania which will squeeze the vise even tighter. King Carol's abdication in favor of his son Michael I, an 18-year-old kid, means that the real power is now vested in General Antonescu, who's in bed with Germany, Italy, and Japan.

All of this means I need to get started sooner than ever on moving up the Zionist Federation ladder. Could you possibly find a way for me to meet Komoly. A word from you would be much appreciated. I remain indebted to you as my mentor, my guide, and my friend.

With deep affection, Rezső

"Thank you for your patience, Doctor Kasztner. Chairman Komoly will see you now." She knocked once on the wooden door between the reception area and Komoly's office, then opened it and escorted 35-year-old Rezső Kasztner into the office of the Chairman of the Zionist Federation of Hungary *Rather unimpressive office,* Kasztner thought. Although the Federation's offices were on fashionable Erzsébet Boulevard, one of Pest's main streets, one block off the Danube, Ottó Komoly's small office was disorderly, with file folders stacked in no apparent order, in piles on the floor, on Komoly's rather pedestrian desk, and on an unmatching table behind the desk.

Komoly appeared somewhat younger than his forty-nine years: moderate height, thinning, dark brown hair combed back to reveal a "widow's peak," and wide-set blue eyes. Komoly shook hands with the younger man, then signaled him to sit in the single wooden chair in front of his desk. He put down a dossier he'd been reading and held out a pack of Juno cigarettes. Kasztner took one. Komoly lit it from a steel lighter on his desk.

"Rezső Kasztner, late of Kloiznburg," he said, using the Yiddish name for Cluj, "although for the last month, after the Vienna Award, it's back to its Hungarian name, Kolozsvár, for the time being. How long have you been in our fair city?"

"Nearly eight months. I trust you've read my resumé?"

"Of course. Doctor Fisher's a wonderful man," Komoly said emphatically. "Lawyer, member of Parliament, president of the Jewish Community of Kolozsvár, leader of the National Jewish Party. It didn't hurt your fortunes that you married his daughter. I understand you're a lawyer as well?"

"Yes, sir." *As if you didn't know.* "My father-in-law encouraged me to go to work at *Új Kelet*. I spent ten years there until the government shut it down. During that time, I practiced law in Romanian Cluj. I was not surprised when the anti-Semites came to power. About 1936, I realized the German octopus was spreading its tentacles throughout central Europe."

"What have you been doing since that time, Doctor Kasztner? Undoubtedly you've had to engage in bribery, threats, cozying up to some rather unpleasant people," Komoly said, with not a hint of censure in his voice.

As if you haven't done the same things, Kasztner thought. Out loud he said, "Whatever it took to help Jews survive. I'm not ashamed of what I've done if it helped our people. Knowing whom to bribe, how much to pay, whom to flatter, knowing when to pay off police so that charges against my clients would be dropped—"

"An opportunist who's managed to survive shark-infested waters," Komoly said, holding his own cigarette underhand in the eastern European style. "So why are you approaching me?"

"I need Zionist Agency help so I can provide Jewish refugees with safe passage. I've been able to obtain exit visas from the Romanian government. Unfortunately, not much help from the Jewish Agency's leadership in Tel Aviv. Our 'friends,' the Brits have imposed strict quotas on the number of Jewish refugees allowed into Palestine."

"So you need entry visas?"

"Yes."

"You've got paper hangers?" Komoly said, using the common word for forgers."

"True," Kasztner replied, "but the limeys have sharpened their eyesight." Komoly, seeing that the younger man had crushed out the remains of his cigarette, held out the pack once again. "Thank you, I will have another one. I need a higher number of legitimate entry visas to Palestine."

"I'm afraid I can't help you directly in that department. You need to see Moshe Krausz, the Jewish Agency's Budapest representative, who controls the Palestine entry visas. Same building as me, one floor up."

"That sonofabitch was less than no help at all," Kasztner blustered when he returned to Komoly's office three hours later. "I had to wait in line two hours in the reception area. There were at least forty Jewish refugees ahead of me. You'd think Krausz would have known of me the minute I told his secretary who I was, and she should have known that for every one of those refugees waiting in line, my work would have saved ten, maybe even a hundred of them. She wouldn't budge, so I barged past her into his office."

"Not the kind of thing that would endear you to Krausz," Komoly remarked mildly.

"That may be, Chairman Komoly, but I don't have time for niceties. Hundreds of Jews are sent to the death camps every day. For every minute I had to wait in line, God knows how many Jews may have died."

"And you don't think that a refugee who'd risked his life to get from Poland to Slovakia to Hungary had the same right as you to see Mister Krausz in the order prescribed?"

"I don't deny that they had the right to see Mister Krausz, but he could certainly have chosen to see some earlier than others based on the importance of their mission."

"An interesting concept, Doctor Kastzner. So, did you get to see him ahead of those waiting in line?"

"Fortunately, I took matters into my own hands. I'm sure after I explained to Krausz why I was entitled to speak to him ahead of some of the others, he understood."

"He spoke to you, then?" Komoly asked.

"If you want to call it that. I got the same doubletalk I'd heard from Palestine. He didn't want to alienate the British; every entry visa had to be legitimate and properly processed, which consumed all his time. I offered to help, but apparently Mister Krausz had more important things on his mind than processing as many Jews as he could get out of Eastern Europe in the minimum amount of time possible."

"Did you get anything out of your meeting with him?"

"If you want to say we took an instant dislike to one another, that's all that came out of it."

"Doctor Kasztner, I'm sure you would not be surprised to know that Moshe said much the same about you. 'Loud, pushy, and arrogant' were the words he used."

"I'm sure I can survive one more petty bureaucrat in my life. I'm only sorry he has to be one of *us,* and that things will go worse for so many Jews who need to get out of death's way and into friendlier conditions. All I want to know is do you think you can use my help."

"Now that you mention it, Doctor Kasztner, the vice-chairman of the Jewish Agency Relief Committee in your home town of Kolozsvar— Kloiznburg, Cluj, whatever you want to call it — retired last month. Unquestionably, we'd like to infuse that position with fresh, new blood, and if the vice chairman's replacement is 'young, brash, pushy, and arrogant,' so much the better."

SEPTEMBER 1941

"Gentlemen, thank you for coming here on such short notice." There were four of them gathered in the Agency's conference room, which, while significantly larger than Komoly's office, was equally spartan.

The two younger men, Joel Brand, blond, chunky, and pleasant-faced, and Kasztner, the same age as Brand but more austere looking, had met earlier that week through Samuel Springmann, the third man sitting around the table. Springmann, a jeweler by trade, had been bribing officials, in part with money from the Jewish Agency, to carry messages and food parcels into Łódź and other ghettos in Poland.

"The reason I asked you here is to discuss the current political climate in the Generalgouvernement —"

"Poland," Springmann remarked.

"Östmark, Rumania, France, and elsewhere," Komoly continued. "You've no doubt heard rumors about the construction of new kinds of camps in Poland and Czechoslovakia. For the most part, Hungary is still safe for Jews."

"For the most part," Kastner echoed. "But two years ago the 'Jew eaters,' the Arrow Cross, bombed the Great Synagogue. Last month they rounded up twenty thousand Jews from the smaller towns and villages, deported them to Galicia, and shot them."

"The Kamianets-Podilskyi Massacre, " Brand joined in. "Thank God for Admiral Horthy."

"Yes, but for how long? There are more than twenty thousand Jews in Kolozsvar, twice as many as two years ago," Kasztner said. "In Budapest, Jews consider themselves Hungarians first. Last year, Horthy wrote prime minister Teleki that he felt they controlled everything, every factory, bank, business, theater, and the press, and that the Jew was the image of Hungary abroad. It's absolutely the opposite in Kolozsvar. The Cluj Jews are 'eastern' Jews. They're Jews first. Their lives are devoted to their religion and their culture."

"I've been thinking that very thing," Komoly said. "'Your' Jews and Budapest's Jews hardly seem to inhabit the same planet. Meanwhile, both sets of our *landsmen* ignore that Germany is tightening the noose."

"There are over eight hundred thousand Jews in Hungary. What we need is a single, coordinated effort to aid and rescue as many of our worthy brothers as we can," Kasztner said. From the looks of the other men, Kasztner knew they had grasped his meaning when he used the word "worthy."

"What about Poland?" Springmann asked.

"Poland's gone. We need to get as many as we can *out* of *that* god-forsaken hellhole."

Ottó Komoly placed his chin between the thumb and forefinger of his left hand and tapped on the table with a pencil for several moments. "*Va'ada Ezra ve'Hatzalah*," he said, almost to himself. "An Aid and Rescue Committee, under the auspices of the Zionist Federation of Hungary. But who would chair such a committee?"

Kasztner was the first to reply. "Ottó, you're the obvious choice for chairman. Your name alone gives the committee the national credibility and prestige it needs."

Komoly sighed audibly. "Doctor Kasztner, are you implying that I'm not busy enough with everything I'm already doing? You'll work me so hard you'll have me in my grave before the Nazis ever make it to Hungary." He chuckled mirthlessly.

"I don't mean that at all, Mister Chairman," Kasztner replied, lighting up a *Carpați*, a brown Romanian cigarette. "I propose that you be the public face of the Committee, the titular head. Unless either of you," he said, turning to Springmann and Brand, "would like to be the workhorses, I'm prepared to act as vice chairman and serve as the overall manager of operations."

There was no opposition to Kasztner's offer. During the next hour, the four men discussed the preliminary details of how the committee would operate. Each put forth the names of those they felt would benefit the committee. Although Kasztner was less than enthusiastic about the nomination of Moshe Krausz to the committee, his objection was over-ruled, first because of Krausz's position with the federation, and second because he was known to have connections throughout Budapest's Jewish community.

The men were unanimous in their goals: the *Va'ada* would raise money, forge documents, maintain contacts with intelligence agencies, run safe houses throughout Hungary, and coordinate with similar agencies in Romania, Bulgaria, Turkey, and way stations from the Soviet Union to Palestine.

After the meeting adjourned, Joel Brand and Kasztner walked for ten minutes to the Dohany Street Synagogue, the largest Jewish temple in Europe, where they became better acquainted with one another in a coffee house adjacent to the Great *Shul*.

"So here we are, two 'foreigners' in the big city," Brand ventured, trying to start an amicable conversation.

"I'd hardly call a five hour drive from Cluj 'foreign.' Of course, there's three hundred years' difference between the two places. You were born near there?"

"Naszód, but my family moved to Erfurt, Germany when I was four."

"Time to do away with the formalities if we're going to work together? Joel and Rezső is fine with me," Kasztner said.

"Sounds good to me. My father founded the Budapest telephone company and prospered. Money hasn't been an object, but I've never considered myself a slave to wealth."

Of course not. It's never an object when you've got enough to live like a rich man anywhere you want, Kastner thought.

Brand continued, "When I was nineteen, I worked my way across the United States, washed dishes, worked on roads and in mines. I joined the Communist Party, worked for the Comintern as a sailor, and sailed to Hawaii, the Philippines, South America, China, and Japan. What about you, Rezső?"

Sure, moneybags. Kasztner extracted a pack of Carpaţi cigarettes from his jacket pocket and held it out to Brand, who took one, struck a match, and lit both his and Kasztner's.

"My dad spent most of his day in the synagogue, while mom ran the family store," Kasztner said. "We weren't destitute, but we were by no means wealthy enough to travel, so my trips were limited: fom Cluj to Budapest and back. I went to the local schools, earned my law degree, and studied a bunch of languages."

"I didn't become involved with the Zionists until '34," Brand said. "A year before, just after Hitler was sworn in as Chancellor and, thank God, just *before* the Reichstag fire, I was arrested as a communist. When I was released, I left the Reich as quickly as I could and took a job at my father's telephone company in Budapest."

"And found a girl and got married and lived happily ever after?" Kasztner asked, removing his horn-rimmed glasses and wiping the lenses with a napkin he'd dipped in water before he put them back on.

"Pretty much. When I got here, I joined a group of Jews preparing to move to Palestine to work on a *kibbutz*. That's where I met Hansi. We married six years ago. Our plans changed when my mother and sisters fled to Budapest and we had to support them."

Why couldn't daddy have supported them just fine and you could have gone, had you wanted to? "So you're still working for your father's company?" Kasztner asked.

"No, after we got married, Hansi and I opened a knitwear and glove factory on Rozsa Street. Today, we've got over a hundred employees."

"With your father's wealth and connections, I'm not surprised."

Joel Brand had a fleeting feeling that his companion seemed envious of the wealth and position into which he'd been born. He'd noticed the same thing during the meeting in Komoly's conference room. Kasztner seemed attracted to power and had a tendency to cozy up to Komoly, the senior man in the room. That feeling was confirmed shortly afterward, when he asked Kasztner about his background.

"I started working for Doctor Jozsef Fisher in '28. Six years later I married the boss's daughter, Margarethe."

"So we've become *prominenti*, although by different routes."

"I've earned the right to call myself one. More than three quarters of the Jews in Cluj are provincials living in the seventeenth century: caftans and earlocks, clothing covering every centimeter of their bodies, go to *shul* once an hour, and bathe once a month."

"Your people?" Brand said, raising his eyebrows at Kasztner's elitist comment.

"Eastern cousins," Kasztner replied, not batting an eye. "In our business, it really doesn't matter. We're playing a numbers game. The more we can count, the better our chances of survival, eh?"

The newly elected vice chairman of the Hungarian Jewish Rescue Committee glanced at his Jaeger LeCoultre watch. "Time for me to get back to Cluj and give Greta the news that we'll be moving to Budapest within the month. I look forward to our working together, Brand."

His companion noticed that Kasztner had ceased using his first name. So much for informality.

15

MAY 1943

"Chairman Komoly, are you all right?"

"Just a little more tired and frustrated than normal, Rezső."

"Frustrated, sir?"

"For three months I've been sending daily cables to the Jewish Agency and the 'Joint' representatives in Switzerland, Istanbul, and Tel Aviv about the slaughter of our people in Poland and the new camps the Germans have been building there."

As Komoly picked up a glass of water, Kasztner noticed that his hand was visibly shaking, but he said nothing. *And you look like shit*, he thought to himself. "No answer, sir?"

"None. You'd have thought the Agency and the 'Joint' would have gone screaming to the press in England, the United States, everywhere they could find a listening ear, but my cables have never been published anywhere; since England, America, and the Soviet Union had become allies, they'd publicize what was happening if for no other reason than to alert the rest of the world."

Komoly flinched as the water spilled over his glass. Kasztner quickly stood up. Without a word, he wiped the water from the chairman's desk and refilled it from a nearby pitcher.

"Any other news, Mister Chairman?"

"There is, Rezső. At the beginning of the year, Premier Kalai officially declared that any Jew who could obtain a visa to Palestine would be permitted to leave Hungary with his family. That sounded like the answer to our prayers, but because of the British immigration policy we've only been able to send out nine Jews a week. *Nine Jews out of eight hundred thousand!* What a ghastly joke that's become! Döme Sztójay and his Arrow Cross are gaining more power every day."

"Admiral Horthy's still holding power."

"Yes, but for how long? Horthy refused Hitler's orders that Hungary slaughter its Jews, but he has no force to back up that refusal."

"Chairman Komoly, there must be half a million Jews in Budapest alone. Surely they'd sent messages to relatives overseas, friends —?"

"That's the biggest problem of all, Rezső. Budapest's Jews believe everything will be all right. They think that since the tide has turned against the Germans, and Hungary's been safe up to now, if the Germans have to devote their resources to the war effort, they'll have less time and inclination to bother with the Jews."

Time for me to make my move. I must be careful how I do it, though. "Do you think, Doctor Komoly," Kasztner suggested, elevating Komoly's rank several notches, "that heading up the Chair of the Zionist Federation of Hungary *and* serving as Chairman of the Hungarian Jewish Rescue Committee at the same time might be too much for one man, even one as efficient and talented as you?"

"You've been doing most of the work for the Rescue Committee …"

"Still, the stress of being chairman still falls on your shoulders. You're the one who signs the cables no one answers. You're the one who worries about every Jew we lose, every one sent to the 'resettlement camps,' which we both know means the death camps."

"Do you have any suggestions, Doctor Kasztner?"

"I might, Ottó. What if you were to withdraw from your position as Chairman of the Hungarian Jewish Rescue Committee. Turn the day-to-day chairmanship over to someone else, Krausz, Shamu Stern, Pinchas von Freudiger, so the burden would fall on them," Kasztner said, mentioning names of rivals he neither liked nor trusted.

"Neither Stern nor von Freudiger is strong enough. You and Krausz would be at each other's throats in a minute, so putting him in charge of you would only destroy your effectiveness. Would you consider accepting the Chairmanship of the Rescue Committee, Rezső?" Komoly asked. "After all, that's been your bailiwick for almost two years?"

"I would consider it a supreme honor, Doctor Komoly. As long as we both know I would always turn to you for guidance and counsel, and in my heart you will always be the chairman."

16

MAY 1944

At 10:00 a.m. on Saturday morning, May 20, 1944, Kasztner, who was well aware that this was *Shabbos*, but really didn't care, drove his DKW F8 sedan up to the barbed wire checkpoint surrounding the Majestic Hotel on Swabian Hill. The bright sunshine and late-spring morning breeze made the view of the Danube and the buildings fronting it breathtaking. S.S. sentries checked his identity and that of his passenger, a dark-haired woman in her early thirties. The captain of the guard radioed the hotel's front desk.

"There's a Jew named Kasztner at the perimeter. No yellow star, the registration papers for the car are in his name. There's a woman with him, a Jewess, identified as Haynalka Hartmann Brand, also no Jewish star. He claims he's here to see *Obersturmbahnführer* Eichmann."

In less than a minute, the two-way radio squawked back, "Approved. Send them to the main entrance."

"*Jawohl, Heil Hitler!*"

When the car came to a stop, one S.S. sentry held the driver's door open for Kastzner and the other held the passenger's door open for Hansi

Brand. They alighted, took the elevator to the second floor, and were immediately shown into Eichmann's office.

But for the large swastika flag and the de rigeur photograph of Hitler staring into the middle distance, his right hand raised in the Nazi salute, this room resembles the chambers of a middle manager in any central European bank, Kasztner thought.

Eichmann, who looked so plain and banal to Kasztner, despite the reputation which had preceded him, remained seated, his left arm resting on a stack of bound papers. Without waiting for an invitation to do so, Kasztner took a seat in the chair directly in front of his host. *Typical,* he thought. *My chair is conspicuously lower than his.* Hansi positioned herself in a similar chair, a few feet behind Kasztner. A stenographer sat to the left and slightly behind Eichmann, ready to take notes.

"Thank you for seeing me on such short notice, Obersturmbahnführer," Kasztner began."

"Do you wish to discuss the Vrba-Wetzler report or the errand on which I sent Mister Brand?" His voice was cold, businesslike.

Doctor Kasztner was equally direct. If Eichman had expected him to come sniveling, hat-in-hand, he seemed surprised that this Jew seemed to treat him as an equal, nothing more, nothing less. "I am willing to discuss both of them and other matters of mutual interest."

"You know who I am?"

"Of course. I also know the reason you were sent to Budapest and your position of power over the, ummm, Jewish situation."

"You've heard that from Brand?"

"Among others. I was surprised that you chose to entrust what I hope was a *bona fide* offer to my subordinate, before discussing it with me."

"Mister Kasztner, you are a Jew. I suggest you might want to mind your manners and consider carefully the tone of voice in which you address me."

"Obersturmbahnführer Eichman, I have no doubt that you exercise the power of life and death over every Jew in Hungary, myself included, if the Vrba-Wetzler report is true. But I think at bottom line, you and I, regardless of our respective stations, are businessmen first. You would not have approached Mister Brand if you didn't want —dare I say need? — to cut a deal."

Adolf Eichmann raised his head and glared coldly at his visitor, as if to stare him into submission. Kasztner's gaze never wavered. Eichmann said nothing as Kasztner continued. "Permit me to set forth some facts as I see them. First, a *Judenfrei* world would not benefit the führer. If there were no Jews left, whom could he blame for losing the war?"

"You dare say such a thing?"

"I do." *You've undoubtedly thought the same thing. If the Reich is so powerful and dominant, and if killing off Jews is at the top of Hitler's list, why would he sanction the mention of trading a million Jewish lives for ten thousand trucks and one thousand tons of tea, coffee, and soap?* "Do you think I'm not aware that Germany no longer has access to Ploieşti since the Americans bombed the oilfields last August, or that Germany is now using coal to fuel its trucks, as well as to make margarine?"

"Doctor Kasztner, you're aware that I could send you to the camps with a snap of my fingers," Eichman said. Kasztner noticed a subtle change of tone in the usually arrogant lieutenant colonel. With a wave of his hand, he dismissed the stenographer, who left the room quickly, without a word. "If you want to talk, just you and me, perhaps the young lady might excuse us?"

Kasztner whispered something to Hansi, who nodded and departed.

When they were alone, Eichmann asked Kasztner, "May I offer you wine? Brandy?"

"Cognac, if you please." Kasztner stood up and moved his chair closer to Eichmann. "Tell me, Colonel, do you really believe Joel Brand can get anywhere near what you asked?"

"Probably not."

"The deal you offered him comes to a thousand dollars per Jew?"

"Maybe a bit less."

"What if we couldn't raise that kind of money or find a place to get the goods? You know as well as I that the British would be the first to throw roadblocks in our way. They're fighting a war for their national survival. Their winning the war trumps their desire to help Jews. Since they're kissing the Arabs' arses, they're not pleased that the Jewish agencies are pushing them for a homeland in the exact same place the Arabs consider *their* territory."

"And your point is?"

"Is there a possibility of negotiating separate pieces of a deal."

"Such as?"

"Suppose we start with my figure of $1,000 per Jew. Let's say I can raise enough to save two thousand Jews, but I can't find more. At least I'd be saving *some* Jews, which is better than none at all. Would you be willing to sell as many Jewish lives as I can buy?"

Eichmann stroked his chin thoughtfully and poured Kasztner another draught of cognac. "Possibly. But that would lead to another problem. Brand told you the shipments of 12,000 Jews a day would start momentarily. If the Vrba-Wetzler report about the camps gets out to the foreign press, we'd have another Warsaw uprising on our hands. We can't afford to spend our war resources fighting a *three* front war, Eastern, Western, and the Jews."

"What I'm hearing," Kasztner said, "is that the *quid pro quo* is we get to save Jews, provided that the Jews who aren't saved must not know *their* destination."

"The *Mishna* says that he who saves one life saves the whole world. The trade-off is you get to save any number of worlds you can afford — you get to play God and choose the ones you want to save. You'll be a true hero in Israel. In exchange, we have a gentleman's agreement that the Jewish Agency Rescue Committee will assist us in, shall we say, diverting the remaining Jews' attention away from things which, at the end of the day, will be of no real importance to them."

"An interesting concept, Herr Obersturmbahnführer. I'll need some time to think about it. Thank you for this very … enlightening … conversation."

Kasztner was pleased as they drove back to the city center. When he replayed the conversation to Hansi, she gave him a warm look.

"From what I saw, you really stood up to him."

"I hope I said the right things, Hansi. You never can tell, you know."

"Oh, Rezső," she said. "How could you think otherwise? Everyone adores you."

Kasztner laughed it off, but the way Hansi moved her breast against his arm clearly signaled that *someone* adored him.

"What have you heard from our traveling emissary?" he asked.

"Joel's been gone three days. He phoned from the Agency in Istanbul and told me there was some mixup in who was supposed to accompany him to the Syrian border, and it'll take a few days to straighten it out."

"So the whole thing's up in the air for now? It seems there are delays everywhere."

"Everywhere?"

"Margarethe's parents are hesitant to leave Cluj and come to Budapest. Something about Doctor Fisher losing his law practice. So my wife is staying in Cluj for the time being, waiting for her father to decide."

He glanced at his watch. "One o'clock. Neither of us have had anything to eat since breakfast. I think a celebratory lunch is in order."

"I'm not crazy about the idea of a crowd right now. Why don't we go back to my flat? I'll warm up some gulyás and spaetzle. A good solid midday meal for a good solid man," she said. "After this morning's episode, you can probably use a little extra strength." She gazed meaningfully at him, as if to underscore her words.

On the way to the Brands' apartment, they stopped at a state-run liquor dispensary, where Rezső bought a bottle of expensive 1937 vintage Szekszárdi L12 Cuvée. During lunch, he uncorked the wine and they drank to the success of Brand's adventure. Then they drank to Kasztner's success with Eichmann that morning. They stood and walked over to the window overlooking the street, but not for long.

They turned toward one another and kissed. "Might as well get a little cooler," she said, unbuttoning her blouse.

Taking a signal from her, while they were kissing and embracing, he reached around behind her and unhooked her bra. She sighed with anticipated pleasure …

"You're a bad boy, Rezső Kasztner," she said, huskily.

JERUSALEM – FEBRUARY 1954

17

The next day, Kasztner's testimony brought the Germans into Budapest in the spring of 1944. Warriors had captured cities before, cut off thousands of adult heads, slit open thousands of children. But these diversions always climaxed a battle lust.

Prosecutor Tell asked, "Doctor Kasztner, are you saying there was no immediate blood lust, no rape, or anything like that?"

"No, counsel," Doctor Kasztner answered. "It wasn't like that in Hungary. There was no fighting, no resistance. The Arrow Cross had already come to power legally. The Germans were invited in as welcome guests. They entered calmly, almost like sightseers. They organized the slaughter of the last million Jews as if they were opening a meat packing business rather than conducting a war."

Kasztner gave his testimony quietly and factually. Everyone who heard him already knew what had happened to Jews. Yet he held the small audience in the courtroom spellbound. "Mister Tell, it would not assist the trier of fact in this case to see six million gaunt dead ones in all their postures, oozing skulls, interlaced pipe-stem arms and legs, torn breasts, and hunger-hollowed bellies. All we need to is go to the archives and look at the photographs.

"But the other part of this story – the one I must tell – is not known too well. The other side of the coin was the spectacled German high officers in their long military overcoats and polished boots who gave the orders, these superior Germans, proud, educated men who supervised the Jewish slaughter."

Judge Halevi shuffled nervously about on his high bench, clasping and unclasping his hands.

"Go ahead, Doctor Kasztner."

"I spoke with these S.S. officers first-hand on many occasions. It was as if they let me into their inner sanctum so they could say at the end of the war that a Jew was actually invited to watch them as they sat in fine offices, drank, smoked, played cards, listened to phonograph records, went horseback riding, made love to girls – and sometimes to one another. When I saw them, there was no hint of remorse, and I met them all. Himmler, Becher, Eichmann, Krumey, Hoess, Klages, von Wisliczeny."

"Did you see any orders, hear any telephone conversations?"

"I did. The German high officers seemed almost proud that I was listening as they issued orders to German industrialists for bigger Jew-burning ovens, for new types of trains to carry the new kind of cattle going to Auschwitz. These men were cold-blooded and efficient, counselor. They never displayed any hint of shame. To the contrary, they were full of triumph and congratulations to one another for a job well done."

"Pardon me for saying so, Doctor Kasztner," Tell said, his hands trembling, "but these people sound like medieval ghouls."

"To see them, Mister Tell, you would think they were anything but that. Their uniforms were always neatly pressed, they were scrupulously correct, precise, polite in whatever they did. The stereotypes we see in the American cinema do not portray them accurately at all. As we know all too well, many former Nazis have become the best friends Israel has had. They were the ones who dutifully voted for reparations, large interest-free loans to Israel, the ones who stand on the front lines in the war against Russian communism. You see, Mister Tell, Christians forgive very well. It is the thing they do best, and the Germans, after all, are a Christian nation."

As he sat comfortably in the witness box, Doctor Kasztner told the court how he sat equally comfortably in the nicely furnished German headquarters offices, looked into the Germans' eyes without fear as they discussed rescue deals, and offered them money and a correct business attitude as he bargained for Jewish lives.

As the third day of Kasztner's direct testimony began, Tamir's eyes and ears remained intent on this noble rescuer of Jews. There was something about his voice. It smacked of egomania, smug political terminology that veiled every fact. But Tamir could catch no proof, nor could he hear any evidence of a lie.

"Yes, Mister Tell, I served as head of the Jewish Agency Rescue Committee for the eight hundred thousand Jews of Hungary."

"How did you become the Chairman of the Committee, Doctor Kasztner?"

"The great bulk of Hungary's Jews were without organization, totally unprepared to speak with one voice. Fortunately, the Germans recognized the Jewish Agency Rescue Committee as the only legitimate voice of our people, the only organ that could talk straight business in the language they wanted to hear."

"'Business', Doctor Kasztner?"

"Yes, counselor. The Germans were by no means idiots. They were well aware of that without materiel, the war effort would collapse much sooner than it ultimately did."

"Doctor Kasztner, was there ever an offer made for the abandonment of the extermination plan?"

"There was. Eichmann offered us the idea of sending somebody out of Hungary to arrange for materials in exchange for Jews. I wanted to go as the emissary but Eichmann picked a lesser member of the Rescue Committee, Joel Brand, for the errand,"

Tamir busily took down this name and circled it in red.

"On May 20, 1944, I went with Mrs. Hansi Brand to meet Eichmann. The deportation had started on an enormous scale and at a shocking pace. We demanded that Eichmann stop the deportations, otherwise Brand's mission would fail. Eichmann answered me that this couldn't be done."

"Was this the first time you personally met Adolf Eichmann?"

"Yes."

"Go on, Doctor Kasztner."

"I told him a hundred human beings were being jammed into a single train compartment under unbearable conditions. He answered, 'In Ukraine, the Jews have innumerable little children. It will be possible there to jam even larger numbers into the compartments.'"

"Were you able to come to any agreement with Eichmann?"

"Not at first. Eichmann talked to me constantly about Brand's failure to return, or to send back any word to him. By June 3, Eichmann gave me an ultimatum: 'If I don't get an answer from Brand in a few days, I'll let the mills of Auschwitz start grinding.' Later, after lengthy negotiations, I made a deal with Eichmann to increase the number in the group to 1,300 people. The number later increased to 1,680."

"Did the Hungarian government do anything to stop the deportations?"

"Yes, Mister Tell. After the Allied invasion of Europe and the new Russian offensive, Admiral Horthy instructed his government to stop the deportations."

"Did that stop the Germans?"

"For the time being, but, of course, we didn't feel secure. We made an additional agreement with Eichmann in case the Germans managed to overcome Horthy's will."

"How did that agreement eventuate?"

Kasztner took off his glasses, wiped them, put them back on. He steepled his forefingers under his chin, then answered in slower, more measured tones than before. "I traveled from Budapest to Switzerland, Vienna, Bratislava, Berlin, and Hamburg, always in the company of S.S. Nazi leaders, chiefly Kurt Becher. Becher told me that Himmler had given him clear instructions not to harm the remaining Jews in any way. He told me Himmler wanted no more money from the Jews, and that all the money previously accepted from the Jews would be paid back to them. 'You must come with me to Berlin,' Becher said to me, 'and hear all this from Himmler's own lips.'"

"Did you go to Berlin?"

"I did. I went to Berlin with Becher. The meeting with Himmler failed to materialize, but the trip was not wasted, because Becher and I decided to go to the Nazi concentration camps and take the necessary steps to bring about the plan on which we had agreed."

At this low point in trial, Tamir detected the first possible break in Kasztner's heroic armor. It was not anything the great man said. Rather, it was a matter of sound. Kasztner's voice had changed ever so subtly. It had become almost overfriendly. Was there the slightest hint of an apologetic note in it?

Kasztner continued. "From August 1944 to May 1945, the Nazi leadership suddenly realized the war effort was lost and they had best make friends among the surviving Jews, when and where they could."

"So you stayed in the same hotels they did?"

"Yes, counselor. I ate and drank with them, took walks with them, discussed philosophy. I couldn't simply talk rescue with them every day, all day. That would have been counterproductive. As it was, we were always on pleasant social terms."

And while telling of these matters, Tamir noticed a new quality in Kasztner's story. He boasted of his Nazi companions. He wanted everybody to hear how he had spoken with Himmler, Hoess, and Eichmann, on equal terms, not as a supplicant.

Yet, in the midst of his testimony, Tamir detected an unboastful sound come into his voice, the sound of apology. Tamir, sensing that Doctor Kasztner, in an Israeli witness box, was apologizing for something, kept a friendly look on his face. He did not want to alarm the witness. Doctor Kasztner went on at great length about the exhilarating time after August, 1944, when he gallivanted through Germany and Nazi occupied Europe as a companion of high S.S. officers.

The questions became clearer in Tamir's head. *Why did the Nazis favor Kasztner so much? Why should these mass killers be so considerate of the Jew, Kasztner? Why did they allow him to be the only Jew in Budapest to live in a house unmarked as Jewish? Why was he exempted from wearing the yellow Star of David on his coat front? Why did they allow him the special privilege of having a telephone, after all the phones had been ripped out of Jewish houses to prevent communication? Why was he the only Jew in*

Budapest allowed to ride in an automobile and to own his own car? Why was he allowed to travel alone and freely to Vienna, Bratislava and even Berlin? Why this unique favoritism? Why did the S.S. elite treat Kasztner as if he were the representative of a great national power instead of a powerless Jew? Of what possible use could Jewish Agency Official Kasztner have been to the exterminators of Jews?

Then, like a frightening ghoul in the night, the grim answer grabbed Tamir so hard that he begged the court's indulgence and asked for a fifteen minute recess. He hurried to the bathroom, where he bathed his face and neck with cold water just in time to avoid being overcome with nausea. It was the answer he had been searching for and had secretly been terrified of discovering.

Rudolf Kasztner was dear and valuable to the Nazis because he helped them slaughter Jews.

After Tamir returned from his brief break, still ashen faced, Greenwald passed him another note: "Are you all right?" Tamir nodded, took a deep breath, and resumed writing in his own trial book as Kasztner went on.

The witness continued. "I went to Nuremberg from Switzerland at the beginning of 1947 at General Taylor's request. He was the Chief Prosecutor of the International Court and I was his advisor in matters pertaining to Jewish extermination."

"How long did you remain in Nuremberg, Doctor Kasztner?" Tell asked.

"Eight months. Then I returned to Switzerland in order to emigrate to Israel. I received a cable from General Taylor guaranteeing my expenses and a fee if I would return to Nuremberg to assist him. I showed the cable to Ben-Gurion, who advised me to go. After a conference with the top officials of the Political Department of the Jewish Agency, it was agreed that I join General Taylor. The Jewish Agency paid for the trip."

"Doctor Kasztner, in his 'Letter to My Friends in the Mizrahi' the defendant Greenwald accuses you of aiding Kurt Becher after the war. Is this true?"

Here it comes, Tamir thought as Kasztner raised his voice, showing emotion for the first time in the trial.

"I state categorically and without reservation that I gave no testimony in Nuremberg in favor of Becher. Greenwald's statement in his pamphlet that I went to Nuremberg to save Becher is a total lie. The German Court of de-Nazification invited me to give testimony about Becher when I was in Nuremberg. I refused. I'd had enough of Germans during the war."

"Did you assist the court in any way, Doctor Kasztner?"

"I sent them a sworn affidavit. It is a total lie that I helped Kurt Becher escape punishment in Nuremberg. I repeat, and I re-emphasize, that I gave no testimony or affidavit in Becher's favor."

Suddenly, the courtroom erupted as several of the reporters spontaneously applauded. Judge Halevi sat for about ten seconds, smiling benignly, then brought his hammer down gently.

"Gentlemen of the press," he intoned. "I think each of you respects the rules of court enough to know that such an outburst is inappropriate. In ordinary circumstances, I would chastise you more severely, but since you have conducted yourselves with remarkable restraint and decorum so far, I request that you continue to do so. I would appreciate if there were no more outbursts, spontaneous or otherwise."

There was silence in the Court.

Tamir wrote a one word message which he passed to his wife, Ruth. "*Bingo!*"

"I have no further questions, Your Honor," Amnon Tell said. "Perhaps this might be a good time to adjourn for the day."

"I think that's a good idea, Mister Tell," the judge replied. "Mister Tamir, would you and the prosecuting attorney remain in court after the rest leave. I'd like to speak with you for a few moments."

"In Chambers, Your Honor?" Tamir asked.

"No, I think we can do what we have to right here. You may leave, Doctor Kasztner, but I'd prefer if Mister Greenwald remains."

The courtroom was cleared except for the two lawyers, Greenwald, and the judge.

"Gentlemen," the judge said, not unkindly. "I think the evidence at this point is pretty convincing. The prosecution has clearly made out a prima facie case. Mister Greenwald, I know you probably have evidence you'd like to present, and I understand that emotions are running very high in this case. But my job is simply to ascertain the facts and try to see that justice is done. Your counsel is an admirable young man who's appeared in my court before. I respect him and I respect your position, but I feel that in this case he's bitten off a bit too much. Defending Arabs on petty charges may be one thing. Attacking so invulnerable figure as Doctor Kasztner, a national Jewish hero, is something quite different. There could be threats, perhaps more than that.

"Having said this, Mister Greenwald, I ask again, not in any way condemning you, whether nor your counsel would consider a change of plea to 'no contest' and trust the court to determine the proper sentence?" There was no anger in Judge Halevi's voice, simply a tired sort of resignation.

Tamir was silent for several moments. It would take months of hunting for facts, digging into records all over the world, tracking the globe for witnesses. And all this without money on hand. He turned to his client. "Mister Greenwald, you've heard what the judge said. It's likely that if you plead guilty now, the judge won't be too severe. Judge Halevi may be less pleasantly disposed if his offer is rejected."

Greenwald gave a one word response: "Never!"

Tamir turned back to the Court. "Your Honor, we remain with our original plea, not guilty. However, given the beginnings of evidence we've recently discovered and the absence of some of our witnesses, we respectfully request a ninety day continuance."

"I beg your pardon, counsel?" the judge said, aghast.

"Your Honor, during the past three months, I have completed five trials in Tel Aviv. My staff has been working day and night on this case to ensure that we provide Mister Greenwald with an adequate defense. I do not want to insult this court or my brother at the bar by commencing my cross-examination of Doctor Kasztner without some pretty solid evidence to back it up."

"Mister Tamir," the judge said, raising his voice to betray his impatience. "You tell me this now, when Doctor Kasztner has already completed his testimony on direct examination, when this case is virtually over as far as I can see? At the beginning of this case, I asked if both counsel were ready. You said you were and I took you at your word. This request borders on contempt."

"Your Honor," Tamir said, "I mean this Honorable Court no contempt. At the time this trial commenced, I had no idea of certain things that would he brought to my attention, and they directly affect the defense of this case."

"Mister Tamir," the court said sternly. "This is a relatively simple case. You admit you've had this case for three months. Now, you come to court at the end of the third day of trial and state that you are not ready to proceed. I can take this to mean one of several things. First, you should never have taken on this case if you felt you could not handle it. Second, if you knew that your schedule did not permit, you should have turned the trial management of this case over to one of your associates, whom I know to be competent barristers. Third, you are testing the patience of this Court very severely, whether for publicity or other purposes I don't know. Fourth, and least likely, you might possibly have stumbled on some evidence that might conceivably have some minimal relevance or weight in this case.

"I am strongly inclined to deny your request. I am strongly inclined to hold you in contempt of court. You have five minutes to convince me that I'm wrong."

"Very well, Your Honor," Tamir said, rising and facing the court directly. Greenwald noticed that his lawyer was completely unafraid of the court's inclination.

"As you may or may not know, Your Honor, defense counsel is working *pro bono publico,* without fees, in this case. We have precious little money to mount any type of defense. But, Your Honor, at the beginning of my association with Mister Greenwald, I believed him when he said he was telling the truth. After listening to the prosecution's chief witness, I am more than ever convinced he is telling the truth.

"We started with nothing, Your Honor. In the past two days, I have received word from unexpected sources in England, Switzerland, the United States, Hungary, and Germany that there are documents we neither knew nor suspected to exist when we started this trial. One of the witnesses we believe the defense will call, Catherina Senesh, is abroad at the present time."

"Catherina Senesh?" the Court asked, expressing interest for the first time in what Tamir had to say. "Hanna Senesh's —?"

"Hanna's mother, Your Honor. A woman who was in Hungary at the same time her daughter was incarcerated and brutally abused. A woman who was in Hungary at the same time Doctor Kasztner was traveling all over Europe while serving as the Chairman of the Jewish Agency Rescue Committee."

"Has she committed to testify in this case?"

"Not yet, Your Honor."

"Do you have any inkling whatsoever of what she would say were she summoned to testify?"

"Yes, Your Honor."

"Would you be willing to make an offer of proof?"

If I don't show the court what I intend to prove through this witness — hell, I haven't even spoken with her yet — the game's over. I'm at the top of the high diving board. The line behind me's crowded. It's 'shit or get off the pot' time. God, give me strength. If Halevi catches me lying …

Tamir took a deep breath, faced the judge squarely and answered, "Your Honor, we believe Mrs. Catherina Senesh will testify that she tried to bring Hanna's plight to Doctor Kasztner at a time when he could have saved her life, and that Doctor Kasztner coldly, callously, and with conscious disregard for Hanna Senesh's rights, turned a deaf ear, ignored Catherina Senesh's pleas, and refused to see her until after it was too late."

"You're certain she'll say this, counsel? You had best be sure of your facts."

In for a penny, in for a fortune. "I am certain, Your Honor," Tamir said quietly.

"How long until she's available for trial?"

"At least two months, Your Honor."

"And the rest of your evidence?"

"I intend to travel to the United States to meet with members of Jewish organizations. I must try to get certain records, which I may not be able to obtain. But I've got to try to do it."

"How do you intend to do so if, as you say, there is no money available to try this case?"

"Your Honor, I am prepared to borrow money from my parents, if necessary."

The Court considered this bold statement. *Tamir's parents are wealthy, well connected. Reuven Katznelson's been a primary contributor to the development of the Hadassah Hospital. Tamir's mother, Senator Bat-Sheva Katznelson is powerful. If his parents are willing to stake their son, can there possibly be something to what he says?*

"Mister Tell, what is your response to this sudden request for continuance?"

"I agree with Your Honor's inclination in this matter. The State has rights too, Judge Halevi. Doctor Kasztner has been seriously libeled. He has the right to vindicate his name. A delay would certainly prejudice those rights, Your Honor."

"How would a continuance prejudice you? Be specific, Mister Tell."

"Mister Tamir is not the only lawyer who has a multitude of cases awaiting. He is not the only one in this case who has witnesses waiting to go forward. He is not the only one who has calendars to meet, people to see."

"I understand your point, counsel."

Judge Halevi battled with his conscience. He was committed to managing his calendar. On the other hand, his sworn duty was to uphold truth and justice.

Judge Halevi stared down at his notes for several moments. When he spoke, it was in calm, deliberate tones. "Counsel, I have considered the defense request for a ninety-day continuance. This request is most unusual as well as untimely. Defense counsel has candidly admitted that because of the press of time, he has been unable adequately to prepare his case. The court does not consider this to be a satisfactory excuse for continuance."

Tamir bit down hard on his lip. He knew what was coming. Without the continuance, the chances of victory in this case increased from a hundred-to-one to ten thousand to one.

Halevi had listened with respectful attention as a politically popular, highly respected hero had given testimony. The defendant was a little man, a nobody, a nothing. Then Judge Halevi thought of a small sign his wife had given him as a gift early in their marriage, "A society is not judged on how it treats its best citizens, but on how it treats its least citizens."

Judge Halevi continued. "By the same token, the prosecutor's objection to a continuance is not extraordinary. The court hears such objections every day. The prejudice inherent in the request is not a specific prejudice to the prosecution in any but a general sense. It is prejudice to the order of this Court. The Court has a calendar. There are litigants waiting in line to go to trial every day. They are prejudiced by the request for continuance because their rights are at least equal to those of Doctor Kasztner and Mister Greenwald: they have a right to their day in court, too.

"I am not overly impressed by Mister Tamir's desire to go to the four corners of the earth at this late moment to gather new evidence, although I respect his loyalty to his client in wanting to do so. But I am concerned that Catherina Senesh is not presently available to testify. Mister Tamir is a member of the Bar, an officer of the Court, and the Court must take him at his word. Mister Tamir has made a rather specific offer of proof. If Mrs. Senesh says what Mister Tamir claims she is going to say, there is no question that such testimony will carry great weight with this Court. On the other hand, if the Court finds that Mister Tamir's statement is willfully false, then this Court would be inclined not only to hold Mister Tamir in contempt and impose very severe sanctions, but would also report this matter to the Bar and request disciplinary action.

"The Court is not convinced that Mister Tamir has treated contemptuously with this Court, but the Court is convinced that Mister Tamir was delinquent in failing to attend to his duties to his client and this Court in the timely preparation of this case.

"Thus, Samuel Tamir is fined two hundred pounds for dereliction of his duties, the defense's request for a ninety day continuance is denied. But the defense's further request for a continuance is reluctantly granted for a period of sixty days."

18

The mood was anything but defeatist in Tamir's office that evening. He was already in his law library, reading a letter from his father when the meeting convened. Ruth had given him the letter an hour earlier, and he was digesting it again.

Tamir's father, Reuven Katznelson, one of the leading dignitaries of Jerusalem, had been away from home when the trial started. After reading the press reports of the Kasztner's three days of heroic testimony, he had written his son a letter from Tiberias.

"Dear Shmuel:

"As you know, when we last spoke, I questioned you about the wisdom of taking this case on. Now, as I read what the papers have to say, I am convinced you did the right thing.

"This Kasztner story is very strange. Go into it. What does it mean when he says 'They picked the prominent ones for rescue, the masses were left behind?' Uncle Joseph gave his life putting the masses of Jews on ships and smuggling them to Eretz-Israel. He didn't look for the prominent ones. He was unable to save all he wanted.

"Knowing you as I do, I know you've been studying Kasztner quietly, carefully, looking to spot the signs of a lie. Sometimes the truth itself is disguised to look like a lie and sometimes vice versa. I know this sounds like confused logic, but perhaps if you look at what Kasztner calls 'the truth,' from a different perspective, you might better fathom my meaning.

"If you simply say, 'Why should there be a lie in this moving tale of Jewish heroism and rescue?' you have not asked the basic questions: *What heroism? What rescue?* The Jewish rescuer and his Jewish Agency aides are all alive. But where are the eight-hundred thousand Jews of Hungary?

"You owe the eight hundred thousand the duty to speak for them in court, those who became the ashes of Europe. You have embarked on one of the most important missions of your life. Don't give up!

Love, *Abba*."

"Thank God Halevi gave us sixty days. Now we go into high gear."

"We'd better," Arieh said. "What on earth possessed you to blindside all of us with that offer about Catherina Senesh? We haven't even talked to the woman and you're prepared to lay your license on the line."

"True," Tamir replied. "But I was given some preview of what she might say if we can somehow get her on the stand."

"How so?" Dov asked.

"Ariana and I befriended a Jewish immigrant from Hungary, Imre Plotkin," Ephraim said. "The man who sat in the courtroom on the first day of trial, the one nobody recognized. He told us Catherina Senesh talked to him many times about how she tried to get Kasztner to intervene when Hanna was taken prisoner. She tried for days on end to see him, left messages, even had a telegram sent to his office. The great man was unavailable. His aide promised Mrs. Senesh that Kasztner knew all about Hanna's predicament and would contact her as soon as he had something to report."

"Which, according to Plotkin, was never," Ariana added.

"But how do we know she'll testify in court, Sam?" Ruth asked.

"We don't. However, they say the apple never falls far from the tree. We all know how the daughter acted. I would hope the mother is similarly courageous and has the same belief in truth. Ariana, Ephraim, Catherina Senesh will be your first objective. Don't be surprised if she won't see you right away. Now that I've revealed her name in court, you can be certain the prosecution will try to get to her before we do. I'm sure they'll try everything possible to convince her to stay as far as possible from Judge Halevi's courtroom.

"Dov, Dan, Arieh, I've already given you your assignments. You're big boys, used to playing hardball with the other big boys. You've got the names of witnesses I want you to interview, the questions that need to be briefed, and the scheduling of witnesses. Ruth, you'll continue to manage both offices."

"And you, Sam?"

"For the first thirty days I'll be traveling. My parents have loaned me the money for the trip. Members of our international defense committee have agreed to put me up in their homes. They have access to certain critical documents I'll need when I cross-examine Kasztner. As soon as I get back, I intend to devote most of the rest of my time seeking out and speaking to a key witness, Joel Brand, Kasztner's closest associate. He was involved in a mission so bizarre and impossible even I find it hard to believe."

The mood was considerably darker in Attorney General Chaim Cohen's capacious and richly furnished office, which stood in unmistakable contrast to the spartan surrounding of his subordinate.

"How in hell did he manage to get a continuance, Tell? You know I wanted this case over with quick and clean. God, what a botch job."

"I did the best I could, Chaim. Even you as Attorney General could not have forced Halevi to rule otherwise. Sixty days is not a big deal. Tamir tipped his hand, said he was going to use Catherina Senesh."

"Sharett's fuming. He wanted this over with by Passover. Kasztner's nervous as hell, and they're blaming me."

"You act like this Kasztner trial is the biggest thing in the world. I've got a desk full of work that will keep me busy for months, and you're calling me on the carpet because some politician got the State to file an action against a seventy-two-year-old man who, for some unknown reason, gets a pain-in-the-ass like Tamir to represent him. Get serious, Chaim, if you want me off this case, just let me know."

"I'm sorry I raised my voice, Amnon. It's just that Sharett's pushing this. Kasztner's the sweetheart of the higher-ups. I'm carping at you because Sharett chewed my ass. I suppose we can tell Sharett there's some good to be found in this."

"Of course," Tell said. "We order a transcript. That way the good doctor knows exactly what he said. He can review his testimony until he can repeat it in his sleep. We make sure our witnesses know what they're up against when Tamir cross-examines them."

"What about Catherina Senesh? Kasztner seemed particularly upset about the mention of her name," the Attorney General said. "Between you and me, Amnon, and not to go farther than these four walls, do you think there's a shred of truth anywhere in what the old man said in his newsletter?"

"Kasztner swore there wasn't a thing to what Greenwald said."

Cohen changed the subject. "So, my friend, what else have you got to do in the next sixty days?"

"I told you," Tell said. "One look at my desk and —"

"Come on, Amnon, you're not trying to impress me. Your job's secure."

"In that case," Tell said, relaxing, "I thought maybe a few days at Tiberias, away from all this political pressure …"

"Good," said Cohen. "Before you go, would you mind meeting with Sharett, Kasztner and me? Sort of a hand-holding exercise."

"Not a problem, Chaim."

Kasztner paced around the living room of his immaculately furnished upper-class, two-story home at Six Emmanuel Street in Jerusalem.. The excellent herbed chicken and fresh garden vegetables his chef had prepared had not changed his mood.

"Dammit, David," he said to his nephew, also a lawyer. "I don't need this delay, not when the Mapai leaders are caucusing to choose the next Knesset candidate from our district. I don't know why Sharett ever got this fool idea to make this a criminal case in the first place."

"Uncle," David Dubovitz said. "I don't see why you're upset. The newspapers and the radio are all over you. If you ran for Prime Minister today, you'd have a serious chance of unseating our present leader."

"That's just it," Kasztner said, lighting a cigarette and inhaling it. "The press is not out to glorify Rudolf Kasztner, they're out to sell newspapers. Today's hero can be tomorrow's sacrificial goat. That's why I wanted this case to be over with quickly."

"Surely you're not afraid of a little nothing like Greenwald."

Kasztner walked over to a cabinet and extracted a bottle of brandy. He poured a snifter for himself and one for his nephew. "No, David, I don't fear Greenwald. But there will always be those who are envious of a successful man. Jealous troublemakers can always find ways to bring down honorable men. They can always find obstreperous lawyers to take on their cause. What do you know about this fellow Tamir? You, as a lawyer, must have seen him, heard things at Bar meetings?"

"They say he's like a pit bull. Once he bites your leg, he'll never let go."

"What are you, working for him or something?" Kasztner snapped angrily. "I meant the dirt. Every man has his vulnerable spot. Does he have a sharp temper? A lady friend?"

"The man's defended Arabs. He's may not be popular in government circles, but he's got friends in high places. His mother's a senator."

"A friend of the Arabs, eh? David, who do you know in the press that would be willing to explore this man's past dealings? Who might be willing to put Tamir on trial?"

"Uncle, surely you don't mean to suggest —?"

"David, I simply asked you a question. If I were somehow to be found guilty …"

"Uncle Rudolf!" Dubovitz said, shocked. "You're not on trial! You're acting like you're the defendant, and all you've done the past three days is tell the truth. Why even think of trying to conduct yourself in anything but the cleanest manner possible? You are not the accused, you're the victim."

"Ah, yes," Kasztner said, regaining his composure. "I fear I may have lost my perspective. Forgive my outburst, David. I just felt when I saw that smug little man in court, when I caught the hateful glare in his lawyer's eyes, when I looked at that pretty little daughter of his, an underling, a nothing just like him, and knew she thought I was somehow lower than she was, I let my temper get the better of me."

He sipped his brandy thoughtfully. "You're right, of course, nephew. I have nothing to lose in this case, particularly since I have truth on my side and sixteen hundred people that are alive today solely because I was there to rescue them."

19

Tamir was exhausted when the BOAC DC-6 touched down at Idlewild Airport. He'd had a grueling journey, from London to Shannon, then to Gander, Newfoundland, and finally to New York. His only memories of the fourteen-hour trip were of seeing a floodlit blanket of the green hills when the plane landed in Ireland at one in the morning to refuel, and of watching bright red and yellow flames pouring over the wings of the large aircraft as the four noisy engines belched fire into the night. He'd slept fitfully, three hours at most. The adrenalin was pumping, but he knew he'd need rest because of the merciless schedule in the fifteen days he'd budgeted to work in the United States.

The customs inspector looked cursorily through his grip, then motioned him out a door with barely a nod. When Tamir alighted into the passenger reception area, he saw a familiar face. "Ben?" he called out. "Ben Hecht?"

"Himself," the man answered. "All one-hundred-ninety pounds and fifty-six years of me. So, you decided to take on the Mapai and the great, good Fathers of Israel, those sanctimonious bastards."

"I see you're your usual sweet self," Tamir said, hugging the older man. "It was wonderful of you to come fetch me. Even better that you'd let me stay a couple of nights with you and the famous bandleader."

"Oh, Billy doesn't mind for a moment. Our beloved Mister Rose is presently going through his third — or is it his fourth? — divorce. 'Til death do us part, and all that."

The two men chuckled. For all his personal foibles, Billy Rose had been a faithful and long-term hero in the birth of Israel.

"You still writing, Ben?"

"Mostly out in Hollywood, but there's little work nowadays. Mc-Carthy and his witch-hunters are trying to paint every Jew they can find a lovely Communist red, or at least pink. I'm about halfway through my magnum opus, *Child of the Century*. Why? Are you looking for a publicist?"

"No, mostly a friend. I don't have many in Israel if we're to believe the papers."

"Aww, screw the papers and screw the Establishment, Sam. You know as well as I that we could put a man on the moon and the Weizmanns, Ben Gurions, and Sharetts of the world would say it never happened."

Tamir shivered as he got into Hecht's black Cadillac. He'd left the warmth of a balmy Israeli spring. While London had been misty, the cold was somehow not as biting as the wind rolling off Jamaica Bay.

"You remember how well I was treated?" Hecht continued, once he'd started driving and turned the heater to its highest setting.

"I remember the full-page ad you and Billy and your Congressman friend took out in 'forty-three," Tamir said. "You were trying to raise thousands of dollars to buy Jews their freedom. Did the Romanians really say they'd get the Jews to safety for fifty dollars a head?"

"Yep," Hecht replied. "If you can get them as far as the Romanian frontier, we'll feed them and make sure they get through Bulgaria and over the border to Turkey. Fifty dollars a head."

"Was the deal in writing?"

"Of course not," Hecht said. "They weren't fools. They knew it was only a matter of time before Hitler's S.S. came over their border. But I trusted them. For once in their anti-semitic existence, they felt some compassion, or guilt, for the way they'd treated Jews for the past few hundred years. Of course, the Hungarian Jews thought they were safe at the time, as long as Horthy was there to protect them. I suppose they were safe, after a fashion, but there were thousands in Slovakia, in Poland, even a few in Austria who trusted us."

"But not the Jewish establishment?"

"Sam," Hecht replied. "Between the Jewish godheads and the great and noble governments of England and the United States, we — and those people we wanted to save — were royally fucked over. Stephen Wise, the great and good American Jewish leader, denounced our effort as a hoax. Weizmann and Ben Gurion pooh-poohed it to the American State Department. Only our friends in Treasury listened to us, but even Harry Hopkins and Morgenthau couldn't tell Roosevelt it was for real, so we lost our one great opportunity to really save Jews. It was left to the Joint and to smooth talkers like your friend Kasztner to save the Jews. Fat lot of good that did."

"Could you really blame them?"

"I could, I did, and I do," Hecht replied. "Fucking British bombed the *Ben Hecht*, can you believe it? An Irgun 'warship' named after me."

Tamir had been forewarned that Ben Hecht was what the Americans called a "loose cannon." Hecht had been a right-wing Jewish militant, an American with some clout in Hollywood, but Tamir feared that in recent years, the man had gone a little bit "over the edge" and had to be handled carefully. The older man thought every government leader was corrupt, not to be trusted, and Israeli leaders were the worst because they had shown they were neither better nor worse than any other politicians.

Still, Tamir knew that Hecht, Rose, and their "American Irgun" had friends in high places. Hecht demonstrated this as he pointed out where Tamir would be staying. As used as he was to the Israeli concept of a palace, having attended many dinners at Jerusalem's King David Hotel, Tamir gaped in amazement as they approached the Pierre from Upper Manhattan.

Among the grandest of New York City's grand hotels, the Pierre rose forty-one stories on the site of the Gerry mansion at the corner of Fifth Avenue and 61st Street. Tamir's eyes followed the skyscraper tower up over five hundred feet, as it rose in a blond-brick shaft from a limestone-fronted Louis XVI base. Its topmost floors, modeled after the Royal Chapel at Versailles — Corinthian pilasters and arch-headed windows, with octagonal ends, under a tall, slanted, copper roof pierced with bronze-finished bull's-eye dormers, made it a landmark he'd seen in motion picture travelogues of Gotham before he'd ever visited the United States.

As Hecht's Cadillac pulled up to the front entrance of the Pierre, the doorman snapped his fingers. Immediately, two underlings gathered up Tamir's suitcases and, accompanied by Hecht, escorted the Israeli lawyer to his luxurious room on the twenty-first floor. As Tamir looked out the window, he beheld the whole of vast Central Park and beyond, all the way to the northern end of Manhattan Island.

"Sam, I know you need your rest, but I want to introduce you to a few of our friends who I think will be most helpful to you. I've arranged for a small breakfast at nine tomorrow morning. Think you can handle it?"

"What else have I got to do in America?" Tamir answered wearily.

Next morning, after the longest and most restful sleep he'd enjoyed since the trial began, Samuel Tamir took the swift, silent elevator, which, he noticed, was operated by a liveried attendant, who turned the gold-plated wheel to the right or to the left, to start or stop the gilded cage on its descent to the third floor dining room.

As he entered, he heard the strains of Tony Martin's recorded voice singing an ode to the city, the same song he'd heard when he;d alighted at Idlewild the day before:

"The great big city's a wondrous toy ... just made for a girl and boy ... We'll turn Manhattan into an isle of joy."

"Yeah, yeah, yeah, great Rodgers and Hart song, but RKO made a musical a couple of years ago, *Two Tickets to Broadway*, Howard Hughes spent a shitload of money on Busby Berkeley, Tony Martin and Janet Leigh, and still lost over a million bucks. Now if I'd have written the script ..."

"Mister Hecht," the maître d' said politely, "we've set up *Chez Escoffier,* a private dining room, for you and your friends. The others are already waiting. Follow me, please."

When Ben Hecht and Samuel Tamir entered the private salon, the first thing Tamir noticed was an elegant lead crystal chandelier and a sideboard loaded with warm croissants, cinnamon pastries, heaping bowls of fresh, out-of-season fruit, and large urns of Robusta and Arabica coffees and green and black teas.

Hecht introduced the Israeli to the "few of our friends" before Tamir had a chance to sit down. "Sam, I'd like you to meet the tall, dark, and handsome lawyers of our group. Captain Richard Gutman's the tall one." The two shook hands. Gutman stood a head taller than Tamir.

"God knows what mixed blood this one has," Hecht said, pointing to the next man in line.

"Sol Jaari," the man said, smiling. "A Middle East mongrel, or so my parents told me." He was swarthy, with an open face. "And the Nazi poster boy standing next to me is Dick Sonnenfeldt. Each of us got a turn to question General Kurt Becher in March 1946."

"Junior attack dogs," Hecht broke in. "Moving right up the ladder, this guy, who obviously looks younger than his age because he bathes his head in the best hair dye money can buy, is Lieutenant Colonel Walter Rapp from the State Department, who was head of the evidence subcommittee of the War Crimes Council in Nuremberg." Rapp, a short man who stood ramrod straight, nodded formally, but Tamir noted a mischievous glint in his blue eyes.

"Finally, Sam, the big guy carrying the dossier, is Brigadier General Telford Taylor, chief of the War Crimes Council." Taylor's name had already come up at the trial and Tamir had been most eager to meet him. A robust-looking, exceedingly handsome man, he could not have been more than forty-five. Tamir was instantly drawn to his commanding presence.

"General," he said, "what do I call the Chief Prosecutor at the Nuremberg trials?"

"Retired," the older man said, grinning."

Tamir, who felt immediate warmth for a kindred spirit, rejoined, "And trying to shoot 'Tailgunner Joe' in the ass."

"You got it," Taylor responded. "One of these days, hopefully sooner rather than later, that witch-hunter sonofabitch senator will get his comeuppance. Let's you and I sit together at this overpriced feed."

"Sounds good to me," Greenwald's defense counsel said. The two men moved over to the sideboard, where each grabbed a tray, poured himself an oversized cup of coffee, ladled a generous serving of fruit into a bowl, and put some rolls onto a plate.

"Don't overload yourself, Sam," General Taylor said. "The good stuff's coming in a few minutes."

While they were waiting for the main course to be served, Taylor opened his manila folder and handed the younger lawyer a sheaf of documents. Tamir started reading them, frowned, slowed down, and read three or four of them over very carefully.

"Are you sure these are genuine?"

"I am. Duplicate originals are kept in the National Military Archives in the Pentagon."

"Is there some way I can get into the Archives?"

"There is. I've arranged for you and Colonel Rapp to have the run of the place for as long as you need to be there. You'll have two secretaries at your disposal."

"General Taylor," Tamir said. "I don't know what to say or how to thank you. I'm involved in 'the longest of long shots.' I came to New York with a round-trip plane ticket and ten dollars to my name. I've always heard Americans were an open people with hearts as big as their country, but I never dreamed I could count on such kindness."

"Mister Tamir, we've got a commercial for a pretty good American wristwatch over here. Reminds me of your people. 'Takes a lickin' and keeps on tickin'. You folks took one helluva lickin' during the last war, but you sure kept on tickin' after the Ay-rabs tried to kick your butts in this last go-round. I think your case is about to keep on tickin'.'"

A phalanx of waiters approached the table bearing platters heaped with eggs cooked three different ways, rashers of bacon, potatoes and onions, and the *pièce de résistance*.

"Kippered herring and onions fried in butter," Taylor remarked. "You can't get enough of them. Afterward, you can't get enough water and you pee all night," he said, using a spartula and spoon to amass a large portion, disdaining most of the rest of the food.

Breakfast lasted two hours, during which time Tamir pumped all of the information he could out of the men sitting around the table.

"How in the world can I authenticate these documents, Colonel Rapp?"

"No problem," his host replied. "I was there, I took the statements, I know the handwriting, and I'd be willing to testify if necessary. I'll give you an affidavit which you can take back with you to Israel."

"But a large part of it is hearsay."

"There are exceptions to the hearsay rule, Mister Tamir, and they're as valid in Israel as they are in the U.S. They're an official record of a proceeding in a duly constituted court. They're a business record. They are part of immediate past recollection recorded. They are not being used to prove the truth of what was said, only that those things were said by certain people. And most important, I think you have the best witness in the world to identify some of these documents right in your own court in Jerusalem. Let's go to it."

For the next ten days, they did.

On the plane back to Lod Airport, Samuel Tamir felt an electric excitement. The valuable papers were locked in his briefcase. He took time once more to review some of his background notes, which laid out a grisly scenario.

Kurt Becher distinguished himself as a Jew slaughterer in Poland and Russia. An important liaison figure between Hitler and Heinrich Himmler, the S.S. Reichsführer appointed the former wheat broker to the post of Commissar of all German concentration camps and Chief of the Economic Department of S.S., the section that removed gold fillings from the millions of teeth of the dead Jews, cut off the hair of millions of Jewesses before killing them, and shipped these bales of hair to German mattress factories; in converting the fat of dead Jews into bath soap; and in figuring out effective methods of torture to induce the Jews awaiting death to reveal where they had hidden their last possessions.

As Himmler's overall aide, Becher was top man in Budapest from 1944 on. In 1945, Hitler rewarded Becher with the rank of Lieutenant General of the S.S. Waffen Command. Tamir reread the copy he had made of Colonel Rapp's sworn affidavit:

"Kasztner approached me as an official of various prominent international Jewish Agencies. To the best of my knowledge, he arrived in Nuremberg as a voluntary witness on behalf of S.S. Colonel Kurt Becher. I believe his visit was aimed solely to help Becher. Until Kasztner's arrival, it was highly probable we would try Becher.

"As a result of Kasztner's pleadings and endeavors on behalf of Becher, many of my staff came to regard Becher with increasing sympathy and personally went out of their way to assist him in every possible manner. On numerous occasions, I observed interrogators in friendly, if not warm, conversations with Becher. This conduct on the part of my staff was unprecedented and contrary to our rules insofar as S.S. members were concerned. When I asked about this conduct, I was told this case was an exception to the normal rule. It was the first and only time we were furnished proof that a high-ranking S.S. officer, Becher, was personally instrumental in saving the lives of tens of thousand of Jews at a great personal risk to himself.

"Becher's ultimate release was solely the result of Kasztner's pleadings and the contents of his sworn testimony. His affidavit regarding Becher was the main, if not the sole reason underlying our decision to free him."

Tamir was now certain his impression of Kasztner, a feeling which flew in the teeth of popular opinion, had been correct.

"So far we've gotten statements from Jacob Freifeld and Leon Blum."

"Damned good statements. This evening we'll see Imre again. What a godsend he's been. Anything on Mrs. Senesh?"

"She's due home in three days. Imre says the government is putting heavy pressure on her not to testify or say anything to anyone; they've made not-so-veiled threats that her job is not as secure as she thinks."

"Bastards," Ephraim said. "How do you tell the world that the government is trying to block evidence?"

"You don't," Ariana said. "You just work a little harder, a little smarter than they do and hope that Mrs. Senesh will react like most honest people: when confronted with the power of a court subpoena, she'll tell the truth."

20

Trial recommenced at the conclusion of the sixty day recess. "Your witness, Mister Tamir," Judge Halevi intoned.

Most of the spectators who filled the courtroom were Kasztner supporters, prepared to see Tamir make a fool of himself as he assaulted the great man. Kasztner strode to the witness box, fully prepared for the expected onslaught, trained by Attorney General Cohen and Prosecutor Tell to speak his piece, not to get easily excited, to think about each question the defense counsel asked and take his time answering.

"Good morning, Doctor Kasztner," Tamir began respectfully, smiling at the witness. "Are you somewhat nervous?"

"A little, Mister Tamir," the witness replied.

"You needn't be, sir. We're all engaged in a search for truth. We are simply trying to ascertain facts. If you can help us in this search, so much the better for us all. Are you comfortable, Doctor Kasztner? Not too hot or too cold?"

"I'm fine, thank you, counselor. I'd feel better if we just got on with it."

"Indeed, Doctor Kasztner. On that we agree. Let's begin then."

"Doctor, correct me if I'm wrong, please, but records from that time seem to show that a man named Komoly was the head of the committee."

"Yes, counselor, but after a while he seemed to lose his energy and effectiveness. The Hungarians and later the Germans refused to take him seriously."

"But they took you seriously, sir?"

"They did, Mister Tamir. After some time, the committee shouldered me with most of Doctor Komoly's responsibility, even though we agreed to allow him to retain his title."

"So, although he was the titular head, you were the one actually charged with leadership responsibility?"

"Yes, by the committee, of course. No one man made these decisions."

"And Chairman Komoly didn't object to being elbowed out?"

"To the contrary, Mister Tamir. I think he was relieved to be out of the line of fire."

"I see. Now, you said the Hungarians and Germans did not want to deal with Komoly, but they dealt with you?"

"That's correct, counselor. For some reason, whether it was my dress, my manner, or the fact that I spoke easily to them in their own languages, they seemed to like me."

"Particularly General Becher?"

"Colonel Becher at that time, counselor, but yes, we did get along. I never pretended I didn't know he was the cat and I the mouse, and that he could end my life at any time. If that was what you call a 'particular' relationship, I defer to your definition."

"I see. Now, Doctor Kasztner, once again I wish to remind you that simply because I say something, you need not defer to it unless it's the truth. I want us to understand one another from the outset."

"I understand fully, Mister Tamir. Thank you for your concern."

At the midday break, over a lunch of falafel at a stand-up counter, Arieh asked Tamir, "Why the kid glove treatment, Sam? You've spent the whole morning trading pleasantries. Judge Halevi almost fell asleep after the eleven o'clock break."

"Because he's very smooth, very eager to parrot his script. If I know Tell and his boss, they've rehearsed Kasztner for everything except polite, innocuous questions. He's probably read the transcript more times than I have and can probably recite it by rote."

"So, what happens next?"

"I keep the questioning light, inconsequential. I'm trying to watch how long he takes to get impatient, to want to get this charade over with. It's going to be a matter of who's got the most patience, who's got the staying power."

"Gentlemen," Kasztner said. "I think you've misread Tamir. He's had me on the witness stand an entire day. I doubt if he's drawn enough blood to spot my fingernail."

"You did very well with his questions," Tell admitted.

"It seems as though Tamir's sleeping through this trial. Perhaps he's lost confidence in his 'case' after all and just wants to give the old man a show before he caves in."

"I wouldn't be too sure," Chaim Cohen said. "I've never seen Samuel Tamir lay down for anybody. He's had two extra months to prepare. We know he's been trying to get to Catherina Senesh, although when Mrs. Senesh thinks about what our investigator said she may conveniently be unavailable to testify."

"I'm told his people have talked to some Cluj survivors," David Dubovitz said, pouring himself a cup of coffee from a stale pot that had been sitting on the hot plate for three hours.

"Doing his own leg work?" Cohen asked, raising his eyebrows. "I can't see why he'd do that. He's got Dov Levin who's forgotten more than most law professors ever knew. Tamir likes to have his case all prepared for him so he can just march in and try it."

"Gentlemen," Kasztner said. "Did any of you ever stop to think that maybe Mister Tamir understands the truth of what I said? I wouldn't be the least bit surprised if, after he questions me, he'll try to get me to drop charges as a matter of charity."

"I don't think that at all," Tell cautioned. "And Doctor Kasztner, I think it best that you don't feel that way either. At least not until his cross-examination is completed. Let's be thankful that the court admitted all of our documentary exhibits this afternoon. That will go a long way toward hammering the nails in the coffin of this case."

21

An amicable Dr. Kasztner returned to the witness box on the second day of cross-examination, eager for more fencing. The newspapers had reported his witty answers of the first day and Attorney Tamir's inept efforts to shake him.

"Good morning, Mister Tamir," Kasztner said. "Time for today's little chat?" He smiled benignly at the defense counsel.

"I guess it is, Doctor Kasztner," Tamir responded, smiling back. Tamir's smile faded and Kasztner felt a slight chill as Tamir started his cross-examination.

"Yesterday afternoon, you told us of your relationship with Kurt Becher?"

"That's correct. He the cat, me the mouse." Kasztner smiled and winked at one of the reporters in the first row.

"You indicated in your direct testimony that you never gave evidence in support of Kurt Becher, is that correct?"

"That's what I said, counsel."

"By that, you mean you never gave testimony on Becher's behalf?"

"That's correct."

"Or gave him any other assistance?"

"Also correct."

"Tell me, Doctor Kasztner, after the war, did you ever give an affidavit of any kind to anyone which in any way mentioned or had anything to do with Kurt Becher?"

"Object," the saturnine Tell said. "Asked and answered."

"Overruled," Judge Halevi said neutrally. "This is cross-examination counsel, and the questions are preliminary. The witness may answer."

"Repeat the question, please," Kasztner said. For the first time during the trial he seemed ill at ease.

"After the war, did you ever give an affidavit of any kind to anyone which in any way mentioned or had anything to do with Kurt Becher?"

"I ... I don't know. I may have, but I'm not sure."

"Doctor Kasztner, did you give an affidavit to German investigators concerning Becher's Nazi status."

"Yes, I believe I did."

"Have you a copy of that affidavit with you?"

"I don't know. I may have. But I'm not sure."

"You brought in a briefcase bulging with documents. How is it you did not keep a document of such historical importance?"

Before Tell was on his feet, objecting to the argumentative nature of the question, Kasztner blurted out, "I don't have to keep every scrap of paper."

"Was it a long or short affidavit?"

"I don't recall how many pages. I think it was short."

Arieh winked at Dan von Weisl, his translator. He knew what was coming. Judge Halevi's eyes were wide open.

Tamir continued. "Was it in favor of Becher or against him?"

The witness paused, looking like man searching for the exact truth. Tamir caught the sudden caution that came into Kasztner's eyes. *The bastard's trying to figure out how much I know about the affidavit, about Becher, about everything. He's still trying to make it a sparring match.*

Kasztner answered slowly and adroitly, as he'd been schooled to do. "The affidavit was neither in favor of nor against Becher. I tried only to tell the truth, neither to help nor to damage him."

There were the first mild sounds of a gasp here and there in the courtroom. A first wondering look at Rudolf Kasztner. What kind of Jewish Agency leader would possibly try "not to damage" Kurt Becher of the Death Corps?

Tamir continued in a friendly voice. "Am I correct in my assumption, Doctor Kasztner, that your only aim in Nuremberg was to serve truth and justice?"

"That is true."

"Is it also true that you had no reason, personal or otherwise, to help Becher?"

"That's true."

"Would you agree with me that the most you would do for this man Becher would be to tell the truth about him without offering any personal opinion in his behalf?"

"Yes."

"By the way, when was Becher released by the International Authorities in Nuremberg?"

"December 1947."

"And your testimony in Nuremberg had nothing in any way to do with securing his release?"

"None at all."

Tamir suddenly dropped all pretense of friendliness and his voice was savage with accusation. "I tell you now that owing to your personal intervention, Kurt Becher was released from prison at Nuremberg!"

Kasztner lost his calm demeanor. His eyes blazed, his fist shook, and he shouted at Tamir, "*That's a dirty lie!*"

Tamir addressed Judge Halevi quietly. "May I have Exhibit 22, Your Honor?"

The clerk passed Tamir Exhibit 22, which had been admitted only the previous day on motion by the prosecution. "Doctor Kasztner," Tamir continued. "Do you recognize your signature on this document?"

"Yes. It's my signature."

"Would you please describe Exhibit 22 to the Court."

"It is a letter I wrote to Eleazar Kaplan of the Jewish Agency dated July 26, 1948."

"It's a long letter full of facts and figures about the money deals between Becher, Eichmann and yourself, correct?"

"Yes."

"In this letter, you explain in meticulous detail what became of the Jewish rescue money."

"That is correct."

"And you wrote this letter? All of it?"

"I dictated it to my secretary, yes."

"Doctor Kasztner, would you read the second and third sentence in paragraph three out loud."

"Objection," Tell said, jumping up. "The document speaks for itself."

"Your Honor," Tamir responded, "it is critically important to this court that the author of the letter read these two sentences into the record."

"It would seem that Mister Tell's point is well taken, counsel. The letter does speak for itself and this Court is somewhat literate. Why is it necessary that you have the witness read these sentences out loud as part of his testimony?"

"Impeachment, Your Honor."

"Please explain how it will impeach his testimony, Mister Tamir."

"Your Honor," Tamir said, "I believe if you let the witness read the two sentences, the impeachment will speak eloquently for itself."

"Very well, Mister Tamir. I don't see what harm it will do. I will give you some latitude. This is cross-examination, after all. The objection is overruled. You may read the two sentences, Doctor Kasztner."

Kasztner glanced at the letter. He looked nervously at his lawyer, awaiting further instructions. After a few moments, Judge Halevi repeated in the same monotone, "You may read the two sentences out loud, Doctor Kasztner."

"'Kurt Becher was an ex-S.S. Colonel who served as liaison officer between me and Himmler during our rescue work. He was released from prison in Nuremberg by the occupation forces of the Allies owing to my personal intervention.'"

The courtroom was silent except for the furious scribbling of a phalanx of newspaper reporters.

After a suitable period, Tamir asked, "Doctor Kasztner, you wrote in this letter that Becher was released owing to your personal intervention?"

"Yes."

"And you cried out a few minutes ago that when I said the same thing to you it was a dirty lie."

"Yes."

Arieh knew the next question. The judge knew the next question. Prosecutor Tell felt, rather than heard the next question, knowing there was nothing he could do to stop it. The reporters paused, some smiling to one another as the headline story of the day rode on Tamir's next words.

"Doctor Kasztner, I give you your choice. Pick out which answer you prefer now."

"I wish to emphasize what I said before, that it is a lie!"

"In your letter to the Ministers of Israel did you write the truth?"

"Only the truth!"

"And to this honorable court, do you tell the truth?"

"Only the truth!"

"Will you try to explain yourself for the record, Dr. Kasztner?"

Tamir turned from the witness. For the moment, Kasztner's flushed face was evidence enough. The judge, the journalists, indeed everyone in the courtroom stared at the witness. *How could a man call a statement a dirty lie, then admit that the statement was true, then call it a dirty lie again?*

Kasztner looked about the room, coughed into his handkerchief, wiped his glasses as though thinking carefully, and finally answered. "I have no doubt in my mind that what I did in Nuremberg about Becher was favorable for him. When I wrote about Colonel Becher's offer to hand over certain Jewish money to the State of Israel, I wished to explain the reason for such an offer so that the minister would believe in its reality. For this reason, I phrased the letter somewhat boastfully, hoping to make it easier for Mr. Kaplan to realize that Becher's statement about the money was worth his attention. So if I'm guilty of an uncautious phrasing of a letter, I am willing to admit it."

"How did you have the nerve to say I was telling a dirty lie when I used your own words that Becher was released through your personal intervention?"

"It is a lie!"

At this point, Prosecutor Tell, seeing his witness on the ropes, hyperventilating under the hammering questions by Tamir, finally jumped up. "I object, Your Honor. It is unethical for a lawyer to torture a witness."

Judge Halevi allowed himself the shadow of a smile for the first time as he replied, "Mr. Tell, it is unethical for a lawyer to interrupt cross-examination when the opposing counsel has cornered your witness. Sit down."

Tell started to splutter something, thought better of it, glared at Doctor Kasztner as if to say, "*How dare you put me in this position?*" and sat down.

Tamir, knowing he was drawing blood, and lots of it, continued chipping at Kasztner. "I tell you further, Doctor Kasztner, that you not only saved Becher from the International Court in Nuremberg, but that you gave a sworn affidavit to the German de-Nazification Court and also saved him from their punishment."

"No! That's untrue!"

"Doctor Kasztner, I see from the large pile of documents you have introduced into evidence that you have a tendency to collect things. Would you give us a copy of that sworn affidavit?"

"I don't think I have it."

At this point, Judge Halevi interjected. "Can you obtain a copy?"

The witness, obedient to authority, answered, "I can, but it will take some time."

Prosecutor Tell again jumped to his feet, trying vainly to run interference for his badly stumbling client. "Your Honor, why is this a matter of any importance? Greenwald's libel doesn't mention any affidavit given to the German court."

"It is important to me as the trier of facts in this case," Judge Halevi said. "I trust you get my drift, Mister Tell."

Tamir immediately followed up the Judge's point. "Doctor Kasztner, did you recommend leniency for Becher in your affidavit?"

"No, I don't think so."

"Doctor Kasztner, will you agree with me that to intervene in favor of a high S.S. Nazi officer and bring about his release is a criminal act from our national point of view?"

"Positively. It is a crime from a national point of view."

When court adjourned for the weekend, the Becher story spread through Israel.

The mood in the government prosecutor's was grim as the three men glared at one another.

"How could you dare let him make a monkey of me with that questioning?" Kasztner demanded angrily. His face was flushed red again, this time with rage, not embarrassment. "You must immediately demand a mistrial, get a new judge, do something now!"

"What do propose, Minister Kasztner?" Tell asked quietly.

"Anything. Withdraw the documents you put into evidence! How in the world did you let those things get in without reading them?"

"I read them, Doctor Kasztner. Not as carefully as I might have, but I was relying on the fact that you had read them all, that you knew them all by heart before you brought a briefcase full of them into the courtroom. May I remind you that Tamir tried to keep them out, but you and I insisted that they go in."

"You and I?" Kasztner fumed. "I don't remember that I played any part in it."

"Gentlemen," David Dubovitz interrupted. "If each of you is trying to blame the other for what happened this afternoon, that will accomplish exactly what Tamir's forces want. A classic case of divide and conquer."

"How would you have answered Tamir's questions?" Tell asked sarcastically, finally giving vent to his own hot temper.

"Actually, not too much differently than Uncle Rudolf did. Perhaps a bit more coolly, perhaps more generally, like during the first day of questioning."

"Nice idea theoretically," Tell answered, "but it's pretty hard to think that fast when opposing counsel is throwing specific daggers instead of open-hand slaps to the face."

"We've got forty-eight hours before the next court session," Dubovitz continued. "I suggest we use a good part of that time reviewing every single document, sentence by sentence, word by word. After that, you and I – and I suggest maybe Attorney General Cohen – put our witness through a grilling such as he's never had in his life, one that will make Tamir's cross-examination seem like a cakewalk."

"I don't know that I like that idea at all," Kasztner replied, clearly ill at ease. "Tonight's the Sabbath. Israel is completely closed down all day tomorrow. Isn't it God's desire that we all rest?"

"I suggest, Uncle, that it's God's desire that if you want to save your ass, you'd damn well better spend the time cramming and sweating. Unless you want to walk straight into Tamir's buzz-saw as ill-prepared as you were this morning."

After a warm, relaxing Sabbath dinner at Reuven and Bat-Sheva Katznelson's spacious house in Jerusalem, the assembled crowd celebrated a brief prayer service. Then the Israelis sang pioneer songs. Afterward, Malchiel Greenwald, who proved quite adept on the clarinet, and Ariana, an accomplished guitarist, played *czardas, k'satzkes, and freylachs*. As a surprise for Ephraim, Ariana played and sang a particularly poignant Ukrainian song that brought tears to his eyes.

Samuel Tamir reminisced about the War of Independence. "We had so few tanks, so few arms, we were such a David against the massed Goliath of the Arab world that, as always, we had to use our brains rather than brawn. The battle for Hebron was a classic example."

"I remember that well," Dan said, chuckling. "We had five tanks and a few hundred men. The Arabs had ten times that many. Dayan's idea that day was sheer brilliance."

In answer to Ariana's questioning glance, Ruth said, "There was a large hill between our forces and the city. Dayan sent the five tanks toward the city, but very widely spaced, so that one tank disappeared around the south side of the hill just as another tank was coming around the north side of the hill. The tanks did not go directly into the city, but continued going around and around the hill. The Arabs did not think to look to the back side of the hill. They assumed that we were simply massing a large number of tanks on the south side preparatory to an all-out attack on the city.

"Several of our supporters spoke the local Arab dialect fluently. They spread word throughout the marketplace that the Jews had sent hundreds of tanks and ten thousand troops to attack the city. The Arabs never thought to climb the hill and look. They simply watched as the tanks kept coming for two hours. Ultimately, they surrendered without a shot ever being fired."

"Well," Tamir interjected laconically, "they really didn't have much of a chance to climb the hill, since our entire force of a few hundred had set up a chain from one end of the rise to the other. The Israeli Air Force, such as it was, learned a lesson from Hebron and did the same thing over the skies of Jerusalem. Sortie after sortie, wave after wave of aircraft. All ten of them," he said, laughing.

The Sabbath candles burned lower. Glasses of Sabbath wine were passed about. Not one word was uttered about the trial until Samuel's mother, the Senator, proudly brought in a copy of the evening Likud party paper, which celebrated Tamir's legal brilliance of that afternoon.

"Let's not discuss work tonight, *Ema*," he said. "It's *Shabbat*. God has declared this a day of rest.

"I suggest we're all getting a bit tired," Reuven Katznelson said. "The hour is late, the wine is warm, and this week has taken its toll on all of us."

"One more song," Dov suggested. "We can stay up for five more minutes. Which one will it be, Ariana?"

In response, and to universal approbation, Greenwald's daughter played what was to become the theme song for them all, Hanna Senesh's *Eli, Eli*. The mingled voices were soft, harmonious, and loving.

22

The following Monday, Kasztner's step had lost its spring. He studiously ignored Tamir as he marched to the witness box. For the first time, a grim-faced Kasztner accepted the chair proffered by the bailiff. Tamir resumed his cross-examination without preamble.

The judge noted there were two new men sitting next to Prosecutor Tell at counsel's table. Judge Halevi did not recognize the younger man, but the face and body sitting on Tell's right was very familiar to him, the Honorable Chaim Cohen, Attorney General of the State of Israel. The judge glanced at his watch and stifled a yawn as Tamir continued his questioning.

"In 1944, Becher was placed in charge of the Economic Department of the S.S. Command in Hungary, correct?"

"Yes."

"March 1944, he was transferred to Hungary?"

"Yes."

"In January 1945, Becher became a lieutenant general?"

"Yes."

"In the same year he was appointed Special Reichs Commissar for Himmler and placed in charge of all concentration camps in German occupied territory?"

"Yes."

Kasztner wiped his glasses. *"Keep your answers brief, direct, to the point, don't let them trap you,"* Cohen had warned him *"Keep your cool,"* his nephew, Dubovitz, had counseled.

Still, Kasztner noticed he was breaking into a light sweat. *That fucking Tamir is playing cat-and-mouse with me again. Well, let him try. I've played this same game before, with more vicious players, with much more at stake, and I survived.*

Tamir continued his dry-as-bones questioning. "Becher was arrested immediately after the war and kept imprisoned for two years?"

"Yes."

"He was released in December, 1947?"

"Yes."

"On page 108 of your testimony before this court you stated, 'When I was in Nuremberg I gave no testimony concerning Becher to the International Court or any of its officials. No testimony or affidavit.' Did you said that?"

Kasztner began to fidget. "Let me see. ... Yes, I did."

"I show you this affidavit. Is it your sworn affidavit?"

Kasztner felt a grabbing in his stomach. He felt powerless to stop what was coming and started to hyperventilate. "Yes."

"Is that a true and correct copy of your signature?"

"Yes."

"On page 241 of this court's record, you said, 'Every German was a robber when he had any chance to be one, and Kurt Becher was definitely no exception.' Did you say that?"

"Yes."

"On page 291 of this court record you agreed with me that to intercede on behalf of any high S.S. officer, including Becher, would be a crime from our national point of view?"

"Yes."

"I will read to you your sworn affidavit:

'I, the undersigned, Doctor Rudolf Kasztner, wish to make the following statement in addition to my affidavit submitted to the Inter-

national Military Tribunal, Document 2605 P.S., concerning former Lieutenant-General Kurt Becher. There can be no doubt that Becher belongs to the very few S.S. leaders having the courage to oppose the program of annihilation of the Jews, and trying to rescue human lives. Having been in personal contact with Becher from June, 1944 to April, 1945, I emphasize on the basis of my personal observations that Kurt Becher did everything within the realm of possibilities to save innocent human beings from the blind fury of the Nazi leaders. Therefore, even if the form and basis of our negotiations may have been highly objectionable, I never doubted for one moment the good intentions of Kurt Becher ... In my opinion, whether his case is judged by Allied or German authorities, Kurt Becher deserves the fullest possible consideration ... I make this statement not only in my name but also on behalf of the Jewish Agency and the Jewish World Congress. Signed, Doctor Rudolf Kasztner, Official, Jewish Agency in Geneva, former Chairman of Zionist Organization in Hungary, 1943-1945, Representative of the Joint Distribution Committee in Budapest.'"

Judge Halevi stared open-mouthed at the witness. Prosecutor Tell looked studiously at the floor as if the secrets of the universe were to be found there. Every reporter in the courtroom glared at Kasztner. It was unheard-of, unimaginable that a Jew, particularly a sophisticated, high-ranking Jew, would dare to make such an affidavit. How dare this same high-ranking Jew lie about it in a high Israeli court?

Kasztner's face turned scarlet under the Court's withering stare. "Who gave you permission to offer this affidavit in the name of the Jewish Agency?" Judge Halevi asked.

"Dobkin and Barlas gave me permission to speak in the name of the Jewish Agency," Kasztner replied in an undertone. "Mister Perlzweig, chief of the political department of the World Jewish Congress, gave me permission, and Mister Riegener, European representatives of the World Jewish Congress gave me permission."

The judge continued his own cross-examination, "Did they permit you to intervene for Becher and recommend leniency?"

Kasztner paused for a long moment and stared out at the Attorney General, the highest legal mind in the land, his lawyer, his savior. In response to the silent request for some kind of help, a lifeline to rescue him, Chaim Cohen sat writing notes on a yellow legal pad. Finally, Kasztner ran out of time.

"Did you hear me, Doctor Kasztner? Did these men permit you to intervene for Becher and recommend leniency?"

"From my talks with these officials, I understood I was permitted to make the statements I made."

The judge wrote several lines on his own legal pad, then nodded at Tamir to continue.

"When you told this court that you never gave any testimony or affidavit to the International Court of Nuremberg or any of its institutions, you knowingly and willfully lied."

At this point, Kasztner lost all control and screamed, "*I deny that! What you are doing is a national crime!*"

Tamir continued very quietly. "Well, let us consider this matter of national crime, Doctor Kasztner. You have agreed with me that any intervention by a Jewish official on behalf of a high S.S. officer, including Becher, is a national crime. Now that it has been revealed that you did exactly that, do you agree with me that you are a national criminal?"

Kasztner's voice was barely a hoarse whisper. "That is your version."

"Your witness, counsel," Tamir said, returning to his seat.

"Have you more cross-examination, Mister Tamir?" the court asked, openly respectful, clearly interested in what new facts were going to be forthcoming.

"I do, Your Honor, but I feel that at this point Mister Tell or his associate, Mister Cohen, may want to try to rehabilitate their witness."

"There is nothing to rehabilitate, Your Honor!" Tell shouted, caustically pointing his finger at the defense counsel. His face was as red as Kasztner's had been moments before. "I repeat, nothing at all to rehabilitate. The witness has been truthful, he has been entirely consistent to the degree that any human being can be consistent. I challenge Mister Tamir to tell me what he ate for dinner three nights ago. The Court has erred grievously in allowing this scurrilous brutalizing of an honorable man to continue unabated. I object and I move to strike all of this testimony."

"Mister Tamir?"

"Thank you, Your Honor. I know of no law that says the Prosecutor has the right to insist that the court admit all evidence that proves his case, but to throw out and disregard any evidence, no matter how relevant, that tends to prove the contrary."

"Thank you, Mister Tell, Mister Tamir. The Prosecution's objection is overruled. The motion to strike Doctor Kasztner's testimony on cross-examination is denied. The evidence is clearly relevant, material, and, I might add, it has certainly raised serious issues of fact in the court's mind. I ask you again, Mister Tell, do you wish to examine your witness at this time, for whatever reason you may desire?"

"No, Your Honor," Tell said, barely concealing his anger. "But at this point, the prosecution moves for a mistrial."

"For what reason, counsel?"

"To ask the court to recuse itself from presiding at this trial."

"On what grounds, Mister Tell?" the judge said equably.

"It appears from the Court's last statement that this Court is prejudiced against the interests of my client."

"Mister Tell," Judge Halevi said quietly. "May I remind you that your client is the State of Israel. How could I possibly be prejudiced against the very government which elevated me to this position?"

"With respect, Your Honor, you know very well what I mean. Doctor Kasztner's interests are coextensive with those of the State in this case. He has suffered a grievous calumny. The State has an obligation to protect its citizens from such outrageous libel."

"Well, now, counsel, that's the question the court is supposed to determine, isn't it?"

"Yes, but Your Honor, this motion is based upon what the State respectfully feels is an unconscious predisposition to rule in a manner inconsistent with the evidence."

Judge Halevi reddened, but he preserved his decorum as he addressed the Prosecutor. "Thank you, Mister Tell. Your motion for a mistrial is denied. The trial of a lawsuit is a search for truth. That can best be accomplished through competent evidence, not vitriolic posturing. If you can point out anything I have done that will in any way deter us from finding out the truth through the development of evidence, I will be happy to reconsider my ruling. If you feel that the court is guilty of abuse of discretion, feel free to appeal to the Supreme Court."

"But, Your Honor, an appeal could take years, and depending on the Court's verdict, Doctor Kasztner could suffer unwarranted shame and humiliation by virtue of a completely unfair ruling."

"All appeals take time, Mister Tell. All the court is advising you is that you have not presented any grounds for a mistrial "

"Judge Halevi," Tell fumed. "I insist that all of these comments be reported for the record. If I am deprived of the right to try my case as I see fit, why bother to have trials in the first place? Why have lawyers if the judge is going to do everything? We are trying a serious, heinous crime, a claim so substantial that it sends a message to irresponsible press through-out the state of Israel. Your Honor, you are sworn to uphold justice. Yet you do a grave injustice by shackling counsel who seeks only to emphasize the truth. Let that be reported."

Judge Halevi was keenly aware that newspaper reporters in the courtroom were busily transcribing everything they could. He chose his words carefully, to defend the record, but spoke them in icy tones so there would be no doubt as to his meaning.

"Mister Tell, no one is more aware than I of the great honor done me by the governing body of this land which selected me to be a Judge. Nor does anyone challenge the sanctity of the state to be free from unlawful interference with its duties by an irresponsible press.

"However, under the law which the Attorney General himself helped to draft, the Judge is vested with discretion to preside over the conduct of trials. If that discretion is abused, that is a matter for the higher court on appeal. But how can there be order if there is chaos in these proceedings? How can justice best be served? By rule of law or by rule of the mob? I am bound to uphold our precious heritage. I intend to do so in the best way I know how. Mister Tell, the court has made its ruling. Accept this ruling with good grace and please conduct yourself with decorum commensurate with the seriousness of this case, is that clear?"

"But, Your Honor ..."

"I repeat, *is that clear?* One cannot support a Court if one has contempt for it."

"Yes, Your Honor," Tell said. He glanced over at his superior, then back to the court and stated, "Your Honor, I sincerely apologize to the Court for my outburst. I pray the Court won't hold it against my client."

"Your apology is accepted, counsel. Perhaps I became a bit testy myself. I assure you that this small interchange between us has not affected my view of this case one iota."

"In the interests of justice, Your Honor, the prosecution requests a brief continuance of two weeks."

"For what reason, Mister Tell?" the Court asked patiently.

"I have a murder trial due to start Monday, Your Honor. It's been continued three times and ..."

"But you are actively involved in trial in this case, Mister Tell. I believe that constitutes a bullet-proof excuse. Mister Tamir?"

Greenwald's attorney conferred very briefly with his client and his associates. "No objection, Your Honor," Tamir responded. "Although I note with some concern that the Court imposed sanctions against defense counsel when I asked for a continuance previously."

"I noticed that myself, counsel. Mister Tell, if I grant this motion, I can either impose a similar sanction against the Prosecution or I can vacate the Court's earlier imposition of sanctions against the defense. Which do you prefer?"

"That, Your Honor, is a matter of the Court's discretion, and I will abide by it," the prosecutor said smoothly.

"Very well. The motion for continuance is granted. This court is not a traffic policeman who wants to give out traffic fines like candy. In fact," he smiled ruefully, "the Court's wife felt the sting of such a sweet last week." There was genuine laughter throughout the courtroom, the laughter of comic relief in a situation fraught with tension.

"In lieu of imposing a fine against the Prosecution, the Court vacates the fine previously imposed against Mister Tamir. I would like to see counsel in my Chambers in ten minutes. Mister Cohen, you are invited to attend as well. Court stands adjourned."

"First thing, Your Honor, I apologize for my outburst. I simply got caught up in the passions of the moment."

"Amnon, your temper is somewhat legendary in the Court system," the Judge chuckled. "It hasn't stopped you from being a fine advocate. Your apology is accepted and I ask you to accept mine. The reason I called the three of you into my Chambers was to see if we can explore some way of settling this case without going farther. The last couple of days have been 'interesting' to say the least. Chaim, Amnon, in your eyes your client may walk on water, but he seems to have stumbled on some pretty sharp rocks."

"I admit he didn't cover himself with glory today, Ben," Chaim Cohen replied.

"But there's still a lot of water in the river. Sam, I congratulate you, by the way. You are truly one of the most brilliant pests I know. You're sure you wouldn't consider coming over to the State's side once this little brouhaha is over?"

"Coming from you, that's high praise, Chaim. Many thanks, but like all of us I just try to do my homework and see what the evidence says."

"Gentlemen," Halevi interrupted. "I'd like to get back on track. I'm not prejudging this case, but I seem to remember a time estimate of three days to one week. We've already more than doubled that, not counting the sixty day delay I gave Sam and the two week delay I've just given the prosecution. I recognize both of you feel this is a very important case, but I do have one or two other trials pending. Is there any room for negotiation?"

"I don't think so, Your Honor. Doctor Kasztner now feels it imperative to prove his innocence," Tell replied.

"Innocence?" The judge arched his eyebrows. "But he isn't even on trial, Amnon. Which raises a very interesting point. If, for whatever reason, the defense develops any specific evidence that might implicate Doctor Kasztner in acts of collaboration with the Nazis ..." Judge Halevi glanced meaningfully at Attorney General Cohen. "As I recall, Chaim, you were the author of the only law on the Israeli books authorizing the death penalty, collaboration with the Nazis."

"Benjamin," Cohen shot back. "Surely you would never expect the government to try one of its own Ministers for such a crime in the face of such weak evidence as Sam has presented. Effective cross-examination is one thing, but it hardly establishes a prima facie case."

"Calm down, Chaim," Halevi said. He looked at the tall, bald man, like himself German by birth, a famed orator who'd emigrated to Israel from Frankfurt in the nineteen thirties. "If, I said, if… I realize it's Greenwald, not Kasztner, who's on trial here. I just think it should not be beyond the foresight of the prosecution to sense that such a possibility exists, and if this matter were somehow to be settled this afternoon …?"

"What do you suggest, Ben?"

"A civil compromise. Mister Greenwald issues an innocuous statement like 'If there was any harm done, I regret such harm.' Kasztner issues a statement such as, 'I regret any inconvenience caused by court proceedings.' The lawsuit would be dismissed and the two men would simply go on about their lives."

The lawyers were silent. "Gentlemen, why don't we break for an hour? I suggest each of you speak with your clients in private rooms. If you feel you're making progress and you need more time, I'll give you whatever extra time you need. I'm certainly willing to remain here into the evening hours. I'll speak with your respective clients if you think that will help. I'll see each of you back here after you've spoken with your clients."

23

"I will not even consider it," Kasztner said. He had recovered from the morning's events after a long talk with his nephew. "I hope I don't need to convince my own lawyers that I have not done anything wrong. I saved Jews, plain and simple. Whether it was one or two thousand is not the question. I did what I had to do and I did it successfully."

"Rudy," Cohen said. "Please consider carefully what Judge Halevi said about the anti-collaborationist law."

"Chaim, you know full well I did not collaborate with anyone unless you want to call my pre-Independence dealings with the Founding Fathers of this country 'collaboration.'" Cohen's eyes narrowed. Tell stared at his fingernails.

"Might I ask what the Honorable Deputy Minister is inferring?" Cohen asked carefully.

"You may, indeed, counselor. Since we're within the confines of a room together and I can always invoke the attorney-client privilege, I will tell you directly what I mean. The American president referred to a domino theory. I am that domino."

"What do you mean?" Cohen said, unwilling to believe what he was hearing.

"Everyone cut deals and kissed our enemy's ass. When Brand had the opportunity to save one million Jews at a high, but affordable cost, who was it that handed him over to the British at the Syrian border? Chaim Weizmann, David Ben Gurion and Moshe Sharett, that's who! The Haganah, the so called 'legitimate' Jewish defense force, that's who!"

"And you're inferring that if we 'abandon' you as you put it, you take the Israeli government down with you?" the Attorney General asled. "As long as we're behind closed doors, Rudolf, I would say that almost smacks of blackmail."

"It may at that," Kasztner retorted. "But the leaders of all the civilized countries of the world are in a situation of mutual blackmail with one another, even as we speak. So, Chaim, please spare me your moralistic views and those of the judge on the anti-collaborationist laws. The government can't try me, and it knows it can't try me, because I'm a survivor. If the government tries to take me down, I, like Samson, will pull the temple down around me."

There was silence in the small room, except for the muted ticking of the clock on the wall above them. To Amnon Tell, the room suddenly seemed warm, stuffy, oppressive.

"Gentlemen," he said. "I'm not of the same caliber as you two. I work on small questions, such as this trial. Judge Halevi's suggestion avoids embarrassment for everyone; we all simply walk away from this one."

"Mister Tell, you miss my entire point," Kasztner said. "For the prosecution to walk away from this case would be tantamount to defeat. Rudolf Kasztner would either be condemned as a liar or the government would be seen to have thrown in the towel and to have told the press they could print anything they wanted, This case must go forward. My good name must be exonerated. I am depending on the two of you to do it."

"And you're willing to take more abuse from Tamir to salvage your good name?"

"Of course. I'm certain you'll be there to rehabilitate me completely."

❧

Across town, Tamir and his client, Malchiel Greenwald, were engaged in a remarkably similar discussion, albeit concerning different sides of the same coin.

"The judge is offering you the opportunity to walk away. No apology, no fine, no jail time, and since I've been doing this for nothing, no attorneys' fees or costs."

"Mister Tamir, I appreciate everything you have done for me thus far. But that is not the point. Eight hundred thousand Jews went to their deaths because of Rudolf Kasztner. If we do not go forward, the world will forget what Kasztner did, just as the world has always forgotten the Jews in the past.

"I am almost seventy-three years old. In my time on earth, I have seen that Jews are generally 'Not Welcome' in the world's polite society. As a result, Jews have always aspired to become 'members of the club,' even if it meant turning their backs on their own.

"Rudolf Kasztner stepped over the bodies of eight hundred thousand Jews to do that. Oh, he saved a few: token Jews, 'good' Jews, relatives and friends. But I am willing to risk any punishment the court might ultimately mete out to me because someone must speak for the eight hundred thousand who have no voices left to speak, no ears left to hear, no bodies with which to live. I cannot rest until the matter of Kasztner's guilt has been addressed, I meant it.

"Until this whole thing came up, I was one of those little people whose lives have meaning only to them. I don't flatter myself that I've accomplished much of anything, or that my words will necessarily live beyond my death. But for once in my life, I have the opportunity to speak for so many, for so many ....

"To say 'If there was any harm done to Doctor Kasztner, I regret such harm' would be to lie to myself, to lie to the bones of those who perished in the ovens. The sin of ignoring the man who needs help is as bad as taking out a gun and shooting him, for the end is the same. For me to turn my back on those who gave their lives is tantamount to my being party to their annihilation, and that I will not – I cannot – do. I do not regret the harm done to Doctor Kasztner. I do not regret that I have an advocate to whom truth is more important than money. I do not regret a thing that has happened during this trial, or that will happen during this trial. And if I am convicted and sentenced, the friendships I have made, the privilege of being a part of your life, will well be worth anything I have risked."

"Gentlemen?" Judge Halevi asked the lawyers, in his chambers.

"My client says 'Absolutely no deal,'" Amnon Tell responded.

"Sam?"

"The same, Your Honor."

The judge gazed at a picture of his wife, his three children. The present and the future, God willing, of Eretz Israel. "I suppose my talking with Mister Greenwald and Doctor Kasztner won't help?"

"It won't, Your Honor," the lawyers replied in unison.

"Very well, then," Halevi said wearily. "Sam, I've remitted a goodly sum of money to you, enough for a round trip to Europe."

"I congratulate the court on its prescience," Tamir said, smiling. "That's where I intend to be during most of the next couple of weeks."

"Am I to speculate that this will not be a vacation?"

"Let's say it will be a working holiday."

24

The land on both banks of the Danube rose into high, richly forested hills. South of the hilltop towns of Visegrad and Szentendre, the first displaying many castle towers, the second displaying an equal number of church steeples, the greenery gave way to riverside workshops and forges, then to big industrial buildings. Ruth Tamir held her nose as the air became heavily tainted with the yeasty smell of breweries and the moldy stench of tanneries.

They'd had a most successful meeting with Simon Wiesenthal, who'd given them extensive background information on Kasztner's primary Nazi associates, as well as two names to look up in Budapest once they'd left Vienna. On impulse, they'd decided to take a boat downriver from Austria to Hungary. Wiesenthal had been kind enough to send one of his Hungarian associates, a young lawyer named Ferenci Makai, with them to make the introductions.

Makai, a bright-eyed, eager young man, one of the 'assimilated Budapest sophisticates' Kasztner had talked about, proved himself to be a well-informed river guide.

"Ah, the signs of civilization," said Makai. "But at least the Hungarians have the good sense to locate their smelliest industries well away from the city and downwind of it."

"Are we in Budapest?" Ruth asked.

"Sort of. There are actually three cities. We are now passing Obuda, old Buda, on the right. We'll shortly be coming to Buda itself, also on the right bank and we'll land there briefly for immigration formalities. It's made up of rolling hills, unlike Pest, which is on a flat plain."

As the three of them alighted, they found themselves in a huge, flagstoned square with a church at one end and government buildings are the other. The landward length of the square was occupied by a long, three-story inn. A big, white-painted wooden cross hung above its central door.

"The White Cross Inn," Makai said. "For years, it was the eastern terminus of the Vienna-Budapest stage, as well as the destination for river travelers."

Above them and a little to the south, rose a high hill, with stone stairs and bastion walls zigzagging from the bottom to a massive castle on top. A graceful suspension bridge forded the river from the base of the hill to Pest. Beyond the bridge, on this side of the river, rose another high hill topped with a sprawling walled fort.

After a restful evening at their hotel, just the other side of the Chain Bridge, they awoke and went deep into the rabbit warren of narrow streets in the old section of Pest.

Just off Revolution Square, Makai rang the bell to the third floor flat in an old, gray stone building which, from its appearance, had been standing in this place for the last two centuries. A small sign announced that the resident of flat 3-D was one Antonin Peretz. The man who answered the door was short, about sixty-five, and barrel-chested with a pugnacious face and close cropped, brush-cut hair.

"Mister Peretz? My name is Ferenci Makai."

"Ah, yes. Wiesenthal called and told me to expect you. And this must be the Israeli advocate Tamir, ach, such a young man, and his wife, the runner."

"A pleasure, Mister Peretz," Ruth said. "Are you, by chance, any relation to the famous writer?"

"Alas, no. In my younger days I was a *shochet*, a butcher, which, praise God, managed to keep me strong. I was able to jump out of one of the trains on the way to Auschwitz and make it to a partisan camp in the forest. Coffee? Tea?"

"Whichever you prefer, Mister Peretz," said Tamir. "Thank you so much for seeing us on such short notice. You've heard about the trial?"

"Yes. You're defending this fellow Greenwald against the great snake, Kasztner. I knew very well of his activities during the War," Peretz said. "Not first hand, mind you, but I have two witnesses with whom I think you'd be most interested in speaking, Joseph Katz, who came from Nodvarod and survived Auschwitz, and David Rozner, also a survivor, who came from Cluj and went back after the War."

"Do you know Catherina Senesh, Mister Peretz?"

"Certainly," replied the former butcher. "Who doesn't? Now there's a witness against your Doctor Kasztner," he said. "After Hanna was killed, there wasn't a person in our circle to whom she didn't complain about that arrogant bastard."

"What was his reputation in Hungary, Mister Peretz?"

"Depends on who you ask," Peretz replied. "Most of the Jews of Cluj didn't survive the war. Rozner and Katz told me that Kasztner sold the Jews a bill of goods, told them they were being resettled to a farming community and that they'd be safe if they moved to the ghetto. Of course, they all got shipped to the Polish ovens. Katz says Kasztner knew they were being shipped out and hid it from the Jews. But I suppose you'd like to hear the evidence from the horses' mouths?"

"I would, Mister Peretz."

"Very well, I'll arrange for you to speak with them."

"What progress on stopping Catherina Senesh?"

"None. She wouldn't budge an inch when we told her she could lose her job. She told us that the minute any more pressure was exerted on her, she'd speak with Bat-Sheva Katznelson and that would be that."

"Shit!" Kasztner exploded. "Should I try to contact her?"

"That's the last thing you should do," Cohen replied. "I have news that could possibly be worse."

"Oh?"

"The defense has been speaking to Joel Brand."

"Joel? But he and Hansi were my closest associates. Surely there are laws concerning privileged communications?"

"There are several types of privilege: husband and wife, lawyer and client, physician and patient, clergyman and penitent. But there's no privilege between friends or associates. Why? Is there something we should know about Brand's testimony?"

"Nothing I think Sharett doesn't know about already. Brand and I haven't spoken in some years."

"Any reason for that? I thought you were the closest of associates."

"We were .... for a time ...." Kasztner replied. "But we haven't seen each other since the .... mission."

"I see," Cohen replied. "Amnon, perhaps a pre-emptive strike by calling him as our witness?" Cohen said.

"Probably a good idea," the prosecuting attorney replied. "A question or two at most."

"You are indeed perceptive."

"Doctor Kasztner, you're sure you don't want to avail yourself of the Judge's offer?"

"Does Greenwald?"

"No."

"Then you have my answer as well. If this is war, let it be an all-out war to the finish. His reputation against mine. Whatever Senesh says, whatever Brand says, I have the right answers."

"You think so, Rudy?" the Attorney General asked. "Somehow, I don't think Sam Tamir would cower in fear at the specter of going face-to-face with you in the courtroom."

Tell lifted his eyebrows. The look on his face was anything but respectful.

"Then you must convince the judge to give us a brief delay."

"That would signal Judge Halevi that some kind of chicanery was going on. I certainly couldn't justify a delay on legal grounds, and it would be unseemly for the Attorney General of Israel to be held in contempt of court. "

"But ... but —" Kasztner spluttered, his arrogant confidence of a few moments ago obviously spent.

"But what?" Chaim Cohen asked.

"You're the Attorney General, you're — *we're* the government."

"I suppose you could check into a mental clinic, claiming an emotional breakdown," Tell ventured.

"Are you suggesting I tell the media that I'm crazy?"

Neither of the lawyers responded.

When trial resumed the following week, Judge Halevi asked, "Mister Cohen, I notice your client is not in the courtroom this morning. My recollection is Mister Tamir was to resume his cross-examination. Is there some reason why Doctor Kasztner is absent?"

"Unfortunately, Your Honor, Doctor Kasztner has been summoned on government business to Buenos Aires, Havana, Washington and thence to New York."

"Regardless of government business, his priority was to be here this morning. I could, of course, hold counsel in contempt of court. I won't do so only because I know both of you would never condone such reckless actions, and I accept Mister Cohen's statement that he only found out about this ludicrous behavior on someone's part last night, but I am sorely tempted to declare a mistrial and grant the defendant all costs of trial incurred to date. Do either of you know of any reason why I should not do so?"

The prosecution lawyers, exercising discretion, said nothing.

"Mister Tamir?"

"Your Honor, while I concur that there is no reason to further delay the trial, I would be willing to stipulate that in the interests of orderly justice, the prosecution may call other witnesses and I be given the opportunity to resume my cross-examination of Doctor Kasztner when he returns from abroad."

"Gentlemen, this seems like a gracious concession," the Court said. "Mister Cohen, Mister Tell?"

"So stipulated, Your Honor."

"Very well, Court will reconvene tomorrow morning at nine o'clock."

25

Promptly at nine the following morning, the Court said, "Call your next witness, Mister Tell."

"The prosecution calls Chaim Jacobs to the witness stand, Your Honor."

The witness, a tall, distinguished-looking man of sixty, with white hair, moustache and goatee, approached the podium. Prosecutor Tell began his direct questioning.

"What is your current occupation, Doctor Jacobs?"

"I am a professor of history and political science at the University of Jerusalem."

"How long have you been so employed?"

"From 1950 to the present."

"Would you state your education, please?"

Tamir rose. "We will stipulate that Doctor Jacobs occupies the Chaim Weizmann Chair at the University of Jerusalem."

"Doctor Jacobs, what was your occupation from 1935 to 1950?"

"I was Vice Chairman of the Joint Distribution Agency for World Judaism."

"That organization is commonly known as the 'Joint?'"

"Correct, Mister Tell. That is a shorthand term that has come into use throughout the world."

"Did the Joint exercise supervisory authority over other Jewish agencies throughout the western world during World War II?"

"It did. "

"Doctor Jacobs, do you know Doctor Rudolf Kasztner?"

"I do."

"How long have you known him?"

"I met him in 1937."

"Are you aware of his work in Hungary during the Second World War?"

"I am. Regardless of the difficulties he faced, Doctor Kasztner never gave up his attempts to rescue Jews. On August 18, 1944, the Germans sent a contingent of three hundred eighteen Jews to Geneva. On December 6, 1944, another one thousand, three hundred sixty-eight Jews were transferred from Bergen-Belsen to Switzerland."

"So one thousand, six hundred eighty-six Jews were saved directly due to Doctor Kasztner's efforts?"

"At least that many, Mister Tell. We believe Doctor Kasztner was instrumental in Himmler's decision to put an end to the killing of the Jews in the concentration camps."

"What is Doctor Kasztner's reputation in the hierarchy of the Joint Agency?"

"It is impeccable, Mister Tell."

"Have you seen the 'Letter to My Friends in the Mizrahi' published by the defendant?"

"I have."

"Do you have an opinion as to whether or not it defames Doctor Kasztner?"

"I object, Your Honor." Tamir was on his feet. "Calls for an opinion which the witness is not empowered to make."

"Mister Tell?" the Judge asked. "Isn't this matter within the province of the Court?"

"Ultimately yes, Your Honor," the prosecutor replied. "However, Doctor Jacobs, who knows Doctor Kasztner intimately, who worked with him for an extended period of time, who knows of his good works, and who has read the article is entitled to his opinion as to whether or not this article damaged Doctor Kasztner."

Judge Halevi pondered the matter for several seconds. Finally, he looked over at Jacobs and said, "Doctor Jacobs, has reading this article in any way changed your opinion of Doctor Rudolf Kasztner?"

"Not at all, Your Honor."

"Objection is sustained. Anything else, Mister Tell?"

"No, Your Honor."

The cafeteria occupied a large room that could fit two hundred people at eighty tables in the center. At each side of the room, there was a track on which courtroom personnel, lawyers, litigants, witnesses, and anyone else who happened to be in the building that day pushed their trays, selected watered-down stews, limp salads, overcooked vegetables, and tired-looking breads, pastries and cakes toward a cashier's stand. At the end of the line, one could pick watery coffee, tea, or the ubiquitous Coca Cola. The meals were cheap, filling, and generally produced an abundance of gas and a feeling of heavy sleepiness by mid-afternoon.

Tamir and Ruth had brought a fresh fruit salad from home. He watched as members of his staff, Malchiel and Ariana Greenwald, made their unspectacular choices from the carte de cuisine. "I'll pay for everything," he told the cashier.

Amnon Tell and his witness, Chaim Jacobs, paid for their lunches at the cashier's stand adjoining the line at the other end of the room, and walked to a far corner of the room.

Suddenly, Tamir's eyes widened. A familiar-looking, pugnaciously handsome man with a cynical smile, wispy hair, a light moustache, and a large wen on his lower left cheek entered the room. Tamir rapidly left the line and headed toward the newcomer.

"Ben!" he said, grinning. "What in the world are you doing in Jerusalem?"

"I thought I'd come by and observe the trial. Maybe help if I can."

"You're joking!"

"Never more serious in my life, Sam. I think your client's getting a royal screw job from the press. I want to see if I can even things out."

"But you write for an American paper. They haven't even taken notice of this trial over there."

"That's not entirely accurate," Hecht replied. He withdrew a small press clipping from his pocket. "Page thirty-seven, *New York Times*, just after your last session with the eminent Doctor Kasztner."

Tamir scanned the article. It was a small article, perhaps two column inches, that simply reported the fact that a libel trial was going on in Israel that pitted the State against well-known renegade defense lawyer Samuel Tamir.

"I repeat," Hecht said. "That's not the real reason I came over."

"What is?"

"Like I just said, I feel your client's getting screwed over by the Establishment and I'm here to help you see that his rights don't get trampled in the process."

"And you think you can help?"

"I do. Listen, Sam, I know your mom's a big-shot senator and your dad's a high muckamuck with the Hadassah Hospital, but there are places an old reporter, even an unpopular one like me, can go that they can't. One learns things in the gutters that those who dine with the classes don't know and *don't want to know*. Understand?"

"Uh-huh," Tamir nodded. Hecht was a loose cannon, paranoid with an axe to grind. Still, this man had many admirers as well. Regardless of the fact that those who were helping Tamir mount a defense were increasing, there were never enough hands. Whatever else Hecht might be, he was intelligent, perceptive, and, Tamir had been told, absolutely relentless when it came to mining a lode of information.

"Very well, Ben," he said. "I accept your most generous and needed offer on condition you let me spring for the lunches while you're here."

"At this five-star restaurant?" Hecht snorted. "I'll make more than the usual number of enemies when I belch all afternoon."

"What choice do I have?"

"What choice do *you* have, lawyer boy?" Hecht laughed. "OK, you've got yourself a deal," he said, walking toward the line. He grabbed three rolls, a large bowl of chicken soup, four pieces of greasy-looking fried chicken, a pile of fried potatoes, and a slice of apple pie.

"Watching your waistline, are you?" Tamir said, winking at the older man.

"Yep. Watching it get larger by the day. Who's the guy chatting with your opponent? He looks familiar."

"Chaim Jacobs, Jewish Agency."

"The Joint? I remember him. Vice Chairman or something like that."

"Uh-huh. He's now an endowed professor at University of Jerusalem."

"Figures."

"What do you mean?"

"The right hand washes the left hand. He's always been Mister Establishment. I wasn't here this morning. What'd he testify to?"

"They all trusted the Nazis. Kasztner tried to warn them. Kasztner was responsible for saving thousands of lives. Kasztner this, Kasztner that. What a great guy Kasztner was."

"Self-righteous hypocrite," Hecht growled. "He knew what was going on."

"How do you know?"

"Remember the article I showed you?"

"Uh - huh."

"Ask him whether or not he ever saw it."

"How will that help our case?"

"Knowing your mind, I think you'll be able to spring forward from there. As I said, Sam. It's time they got a little of their own."

26

"Your witness, Mister Tamir."

"Thank you, Your Honor. Good afternoon, Doctor Jacobs."

"Afternoon, Mister Tamir."

"Doctor Jacobs, you are presently an endowed professor at the University of Jerusalem, correct?"

"Correct, Mister Tamir."

"Prior to your appointment to this chair, Doctor Jacobs, what was your experience as a university professor?"

"I had none."

During the next quarter hour, Tamir established that Jacobs, a member of the ruling Mapai Party, owed his appointment to the Board of Regents which, itself, had been appointed by the party, and that the Mapai Party had constituted the government of Israel since the inception of the State.

"Doctor Jacobs," Tamir continued. "While you were with the Joint Distribution Agency, did you communicate with Zionist organizations?"

"Constantly, on a daily basis, in Israel, England, and the United States. We communicated through the American embassy in Geneva. We made transatlantic telephone calls about twice a week."

"Doctor Jacobs, were you unaware of the mass genocide going on in the Nazi ovens at the time you met with Kasztner in April, 1944?"

"Not entirely, Mister Tamir," the witness answered carefully. "The evidence was such that we felt it would be irresponsible to accept the word of a few people from the fringe element when we were negotiating directly with the German government itself."

"Does the name Peter Bergson mean anything to you?"

"He was a member of the Irgun, a terrorist organization which demanded the immediate declaration of an independent state of Israel in the late thirties and early forties."

"Did you consider him on the fringe?"

"I did."

"How about Samuel Merlin?"

"The same."

"Does the name Ben Hecht mean anything to you?"

"Yes, he was an American newspaperman and playwright of some repute."

"Did you ever meet Mister Hecht?"

"No, I did not."

"Do you know of his reputation?"

"Only from what I've been told."

"Do you know of Mister Hecht's reputation for honesty?"

"No, only of his reputation in general, and on that I'd prefer not to comment."

Tamir glanced down at his notes, made some check marks, and went on.

"Doctor Jacobs, have you ever heard of Guy Gillette?"

"Yes, he was an American Senator from California who was in league with Mister Hecht, Mister Bergson, Mister Merlin and a novelist named Louis Bromfield."

"How did you hear of them?"

"In 1943, they staged a number of public meetings in the United States aimed at convincing the world that the Germans were guilty of mass genocide."

"Did you receive any correspondence from these people?"

"Yes.

"Did you receive any newspaper ads from these people?"

"Yes."

"When was that?"

"January of 1943."

Tamir took the full page advertisement from the *New York Times* that Ben Hecht had handed him during the lunch break, showed it to prosecutor Tell, and asked that it be marked for identification.

"Doctor Jacobs," he continued. "Have you ever seen this advertisement?"

"I have. I received a copy from the Bergson-Merlin group early in 1943."

Tamir asked that the advertisement be admitted as evidence.

"Object, irrelevant," Tell said.

"What is the relevance, Mister Tamir?" Judge Halevi asked, not unkindly.

"To impeach the witness when he says he did not have knowledge of the annihilation of the Jewish people in the German ovens, Your Honor."

The judge considered the ad for a moment. It occupied a full page and there was no mistaking its content:

FOR SALE
70,000 JEWS AT $50 APIECE
GUARANTEED HUMAN BEINGS!

The ad stated that the Romanian government had offered the American and British governments to allow seventy thousand Jews to leave Romania at the cost of fifty dollars each for transport to the border. The ad stressed that the offer would be void as soon as the Germans entered Romania. They were due any week. The ad explained that $3,500,000 would rescue the seventy thousand Romanian Jews from murder by the Germans.

Judge Halevi scratched his head thoughtfully. He was shocked by what he read, but was it really relevant to this case? Still, in order to give a complete judgment based on a total transcript, he knew the defense had a right to cross-examine the witness for impeachment purposes, even though the prosecution had not brought the matter to the court's attention on direct examination. "Counsel," he said slowly. "On the supposition that this document may be used to impeach the witness, or help amplify his testimony, I am going to admit this document into evidence. The objection is overruled."

"Thank you, Your Honor," Tamir said sincerely. *Thank you, Ben Hecht.*

"Doctor Jacobs, were you aware of similar advertisements in the London papers?"

"Yes, we received copies of those ads."

"Did you ever investigate whether or not the Romanian government had, in fact, made such an offer to the American and British governments?"

"We did. We specifically asked the American Jewish Congress in New York and the Jewish Agency in London to investigate the *bona fides* of this advertisement."

"Did you obtain responses?"

"Yes. Rabbi Stephen Wise in New York issued a statement to the effect that no confirmation had been received regarding an alleged offer by the Romanian government to allow seventy thousand Jews to leave Romania, and thus no allocation of funds was justified. The Jewish Agency in London also denied the Romanian offer."

"You were in contact with the British Foreign Office during that time?"

"We were."

"And you were in contact with the American State Department during that time?"

"We were."

"Doctor Jacobs, did the Joint Agency, of which you were Vice Chairman, ever inquire of either the British Foreign Office or the American State Department if they had, in fact, received an offer from the Romanians to transport seventy thousand Jews to the Romanian border at fifty dollars a head?"

"Not to my knowledge."

"Why not?"

A light sheen of perspiration broke out on the professor's face. He glanced from Tamir to Tell to the Court, then looked down at his fingernails. After the passage of more than a minute, the Judge said, "Did you hear the question, Doctor Jacobs?"

"I did, Your Honor."

"Why didn't the Joint Agency make any attempt to obtain verification or denial of the Romanian offer from the American or British government?"

"We were in very sensitive, very involved negotiations with our American and English friends at that time, and concurrently, we were trying to open discussions with German representatives in Geneva."

"*In other words, you didn't want to make waves?*" Tamir almost shouted.

"Objection, argumentative!" stormed Tell.

"Sustained," said the court.

Not according to the press, Tamir thought, as he heard loud scratching behind him.

"Doctor Jacobs, did you ever determine whether the Romanian offer was genuine?"

The witness sat in numb silence, waiting for the prosecuting lawyer to object. Tell did not say a word. "You may answer the question, Doctor Jacobs," the judge said.

"Yes. We learned from the American Undersecretary of State, Adolph A. Berle, Junior, in June 1945, that the offer had been genuine."

"Did you ever determine what happened to the seventy thousand Romanian Jews?"

"Yes, after the war," Jacobs said, almost in a whisper.

"What happened to them?"

"They were herded into barns by the Germanized Romanians under General Antonescu, hosed with gasoline, ignited, and shot down when they came blazing and screaming out of the barns."

"Herded into barns, hosed with gasoline, ignited, and shot down. *Do you still maintain, Doctor Jacobs, that you had no inkling of what the*

Germans were doing to the Jews as of the time you met with the Germans in Hungary?"

"I never said that," the witness mumbled.

"In your direct testimony, Doctor Jacobs, you said that at the time of the first meeting in the Hotel Majestic you had heard rumors of 're-settlement to camps,' mostly in Poland and Czecho-Slovakia."

"Your Honor, may I step down from the witness stand for a few moments, please?"

"Of course, Doctor Jacobs. There will be a fifteen minute break. Court is in recess."

During the brief intermission on the proceedings, Samuel Tamir studied some additional documents, made a few notes, and sat back in his chair, eyes closed. His reverie was interrupted by a tap on the shoulder from his associate, Arieh Marinsky.

"I think you've got him on the ropes, Chief."

"What do you mean?"

"I followed Jacobs into the restroom. No sooner he got there, he closed the stall and I heard pretty violent retching going on. When he emerged five minutes later, he looked awfully haggard and he used paper towels to bathe his face in cold water."

Tamir nodded, but otherwise said nothing.

Chaim Jacobs returned to the witness stand, his face pale white. He looked five years older than he had when he'd ascended the stand that morning. He asked the court if he could continue his testimony sitting in a chair rather than standing. The court consented. Shlomo the bailiff brought Doctor Jacobs a straight-backed chair.

"Are you all right, Doctor Jacobs?" Tamir asked solicitously.

"I am fine," the man answered in a quavering voice.

"You said there was a problem concerning Jews who were not ac-counted for."

"That's correct."

"How did you find out that these Jews were not accounted for?"

"Letters from family members."

"Where were these family members?"

"Primarily in the United States, England, Israel, and Turkey."

"How many inquiries did you receive between nineteen forty-two and nineteen forty-four when you met with the Germans in Budapest?"

"Several."

"More than a hundred?"

"Could have been —"

"More than a thousand?"

"I don't recall."

"Do you have any recollection whatsoever how many inquiries you received?"

"No, there were several."

"Did the Joint Agency ever respond to these inquiries?"

"We were busy investigating."

"Not my question. Did the Joint Agency ever respond to these inquiries?"

"Counselor, we had no news to report."

"*Doctor Jacobs, that is not my question. Sir, did the Jewish Agency, of which you were the Vice Chairman, ever respond to the inquiries, whether there were two, a hundred, a thousand, ten thousand, whatever — did the Jewish Agency ever respond to so much as one inquiry?*"

"I don't ... I don't recall whether we did or not," the witness stammered.

"Did you know anything about the background of any of the S.S. men you met with in Budapest in 1944?"

"Not at that time."

"Did Eichmann tell you he was used to dealing with Jewish affairs?"

"Yes."

"Had you ever met Adolf Eichmann before?"

"No."

"Did you ask him during your meeting in April, 1944 what he meant when he said he was used to dealing with Jewish affairs?"

"No."

"Why not?"

Tamir let the question hang in the air. The witness asked the bailiff for a glass of water, took several sips, and stared down.

"I repeat, Doctor Jacobs, why not?"

"I.... I have no answer," Jacobs finally blurted out.

"After April, 1944, you knew Adolf Eichmann personally, did you not?"

"Yes."

"At the conclusion of the meeting, you had no reason to believe Eichmann was not a man of his word, did you?"

"I had no reason to disbelieve him at that time."

"Have you ever heard of Joel Brand?"

"Yes. Until May of nineteen forty-four he was Doctor Kasztner's chief assistant."

"Did you ever receive knowledge from any source that Adolf Eichmann had offered Joel Brand to spare one million Jews in exchange for trucks, coffee, tea, and soap?"

"Objection, irrelevant," Tell shouted, jumping to his feet.

"Overruled. Sit down, Mister Tell," Judge Halevi said sharply.

"I heard that such an offer was made."

"From whom did you hear that such an offer was made?"

"Your Honor, I'd rather not say. I believe it would interfere with national security."

"There is no such objection in my court, Doctor Jacobs," the judge said. "You may answer the question."

"I'd rather not, Your Honor."

"Doctor Jacobs, the court does not mean to cause you unnecessary consternation, but unless Mister Tamir withdraws his question, you must answer. If you do not answer, you could be cited for contempt of court. Mister Tamir, what say you?"

"Your Honor, it is quite important that I receive the answer to this question, although I think I already know it. May we have a sidebar conference?"

"Yes, you may. Come forward Mister Tamir, Mister Tell."

When they were gathered very close to the Judge, within his, but no one else's hearing, Judge Halevi whispered, "Mister Tamir, what is this all about?"

"Judge," Tamir whispered back. "I think the witness received a call from Moshe Sharett, our Prime Minister, in the summer of 1944 asking

Jacobs his opinion of the Joel Brand mission. If he did, then Jacobs was put on notice, and if that happened, the defense wants to find out if Jacobs told Kasztner about the Joel Brand mission and whether he, Jacobs, questioned Eichmann about it."

"That's going pretty far afield," Tell whispered.

"Not if it implicates Kasztner," Tamir shot back, still whispering.

"Mister Tamir, I think you've already done a remarkable job of neutralizing this witness. I don't see anything to be gained by implicating a sitting Prime Minister in this situation. Surely you don't intend to call Prime Minister Sharett to the stand, do you? I probably wouldn't allow it anyway, since Kasztner is the main prosecution witness and I have no information that Moshe Sharett had any part in this."

Tell, well aware that Prime Minister Sharett was, indeed, the moving force behind the entire trial, said nothing.

"Sam, have pity on the old man, will you? How about going on with the questions tying Kasztner into this situation? I'll take your point about Moshe Sharett instituting the call as an offer of proof, all right?"

"If you say so, Your Honor," Tamir said softly.

After Tamir walked back to defense counsel's table, the court announced, "Doctor Jacobs, Mister Tamir has agreed to withdraw the question."

"Doctor Jacobs, did you ever ask Rudolf Kasztner if he knew anything about the Joel Brand mission?"

"Yes," the witness, by now emasculated and reduced to a shell, said hoarsely.

"What did he say?"

"That he knew of no such mission."

"Did you ask him where Brand was at that moment?"

"I did not."

"Why not?"

"I have no answer to that question."

"Did you ever ask Eichmann about the offer?"

"No."

"Why not?"

"Because I never had occasion to talk to him after the April meeting in Budapest."

"Doctor Jacobs, in your earlier testimony you stated that Rudolf Kasztner was directly responsible for the rescue of one thousand, six hundred eighty-six Jews."

"That's correct."

"Do you know this of your own personal knowledge?"

"Yes."

"You heard from all of these Jews that Doctor Kasztner was directly responsible for saving them?"

"No. Not all of them."

"Any of them?"

"I'm not sure. Perhaps a few of them."

"How many?"

"I don't recall."

"You didn't speak with any of the S.S. men to see whether or not they felt Kasztner was responsible for saving this many Jews?"

"That's correct."

"If those who were rescued didn't tell you Kasztner rescued them and the Germans did not tell you Kasztner rescued them, how do you know that Kasztner rescued them?"

"He told me himself, in December, 1944."

"I have nothing further."

The witness got up from his chair very slowly. The man who had strode into the courtroom full of strength and vitality that morning trembled and tottered as he slunk out of the room late in the afternoon. He said not a word to the reporters who followed him to request an interview.

27

The two men walked arm-in-arm through the Old City's *shouk*. As they passed through the narrow, unbearably crowded alleys, their ears picked up the sounds of this rowdy inland piece of the Levant, a noisy, polyglot mixture of all the peoples of the Earth. Egyptians selling bolts of cotton cloth were shouted down by Chinese hawking ginseng herbs guaranteed to increase sexual performance. Greek fisherman promised the freshest fish in the Mediterranean. Persian merchants displayed piles of colorful carpets stacked higher than Tamir was tall.

Houses leaned against one another. Merchants and beggars congregated in narrow alleys. Urine ran down gutters in the middle of these commercial "boulevards," mingling with odors of fried fish, onions, cabbage and khari peppers. One shout was indistinguishable from another. Tamir and the older man were pushed and shoved anywhere they walked. They ignored the entreaties of the clamoring hawkers, but enjoyed listening to the voices tempting whatever tourists had risked their safety to come here after sundown.

"Woman, sah? Nubian. Very black, very hot. You evah been with black woman, sah? My seestah. She is virgin, sah." This from a greasy-looking, brown boy of ten.

"A horse, perhaps, My Lord? From the sands of Arabia. Very strong, very cheap."

"Alms, patron. Dispossessed of my fortune and my feet, look here Your Kindliness, I have only to beg."

"Come with me, young man. I want to show you some interesting drugs, guaranteed to give you the potency of a lion. You can lie with twelve women in one night!"

Street musicians, jangled, piped, and beat drums, each clashing with and trying to outdo the other. The Old City was a mixture of Cairo, Baghdad, Teheran, Beirut, all the exotic names that conjured up the mysteries of the Middle East.

Tamir knew there was order in this apparent chaos. Jewel merchants, usually Persian or Lebanese, sometimes Syrian, camped on the east side of town. Brown-skinned hindus from farther East congregated in spice bazaars north of the jewelers. Food purveyors were strung through the center of the market; to the extreme south there was a very special 'commercial' part where one with sufficient money or curiosity could buy everything from soft little boys to the most potent drugs. The Jewish inhabitants of the New City rarely, if ever, strolled into this part of Jerusalem.

Within ten minutes, Tamir and the older man had left the stuffy confines of the marketplace and the heavy air of the alley and ascended a slight rise beyond the city. As they walked through a high field, lit by a slender crescent moon and a million stars, the old man was the first to speak.

"You're disturbed?"

"Yes, Rashid. You knew right away? You're right, as always." They walked a while farther, silently soaking in the eternal myriad stars that hung suspended in a stone-black sky. It amazed Samuel how simply being in the presence of this ancient Bedouin soothed him.

"The trial?"

"Yes. I carry a great burden of guilt on my heart."

Rashid al Sharif ibn Fahd was seventy-six years old. He carried his years with fierce pride and great dignity, his six foot tall frame lean and spare. In years past, he'd been a caravan master, one of the last to ply the route between Diyarbakir in Eastern Turkey and the Yemeni coast. For the past few years, well past his prime, but willing to change with the times, he'd posed for pictures as a "Tourist Sheikh," a faintly sinister Bedouin chief, who gave Israeli and Western visitors rides on tame camels, usually as ancient as he.

Tamir's father had introduced him to Rashid when Samuel was eight years old. An instant affinity had grown between man and boy. The schism between Arab and Jew had never disturbed that relationship. A talk with Rashid always refreshed his soul.

"The deputy minister?"

"No, an old man. Chaim Jacobs."

"Ah, the esteemed professor of history."

Somewhere below them, a small rivulet rushed over a pile of rocks, making gentle splashing sounds in the night. The old man patiently waited for his younger friend to go on.

"I humiliated him this afternoon. He'd aged several years by the time I was through."

"And you blame yourself." It was a statement, not a question.

"He was a simple man, not a bad man. Jacobs' sole function was to report on what he knew, meetings he'd had with the Germans. He did not start out meaning to harm anyone."

"No one does. Did he not voluntarily come forth to testify?"

"He was called as a witness by the government." The lawyer picked up a handful of small stones and threw them, one at a time, toward the sound of the water.

"Do you think Professor Jacobs didn't know he would subject himself to cross-examination? He'd read the newspapers before he came to court and I'm sure he'd spoken with the State's experienced lawyers."

"Yes, but somehow it seems so immoral to pick a fight with a defenseless old man."

Rashid thought about this for several moments before he gave his answer. "Samuel, do you have faith in the justness of your cause?"

"Yes, I do. I truly harbor deep suspicions about Doctor Kasztner."

"If you didn't have faith in your cause would you have taken the case?"

"I.... I don't know. Lawyers are supposed to hold themselves out as public advocates. We're not paid to be the judge or the prosecutor. I make my living by accepting cases, not all of them just, not all of them winners."

"And your opposing counsel?"

"Amnon Tell's doing the same thing I do, only he's limited to one client and he can't turn that client down."

"Shmulik," the old man said gently, using the diminutive he'd used since Tamir was a small boy. "You are not the cause of Professor Jacobs' torment. When you chose to take up the law, you vowed to search for truth. Do you believe that truth is a relative thing, something that changes with the moment or the political party in power?"

"Absolutely not," Tamir said resolutely. "Truth is the same if you're Mapai, Likud, Haganah, or Irgun."

"Oh?" Rashid hesitated a moment. "Was truth the same in Nazi Germany, Samuel?"

"The truth was prostituted to the ends of the state."

"What about Israel? Do you believe the Jewish view of truth differs from that of the Palestinian Arabs, my friend?"

Tamir stopped throwing his stones. He felt his jaw tightening as he wrestled with the question, unable to lie, unable to give his old mentor a pat answer.

"But surely there must be certain basic truths?"

"Do you think an Arab receives the same justice as a Jew in an Israeli courtroom?"

"Theoretically."

"Practically?"

"No," Tamir answered. "Rashid, I wanted to talk with you this evening so I might feel better. I feel more agitated now than when we started talking."

"Only for a moment. I intended it to be that way, my young friend."

"You intended that?" Tamir said sharply.

"Yes. Samuel. What makes a human being different from any being?"

"We think. We reason."

"Do you believe a lion killing a gazelle ever thinks about truth or goodness? Or that Hitler's dog Blondi ever wondered whether the Fuhrer was telling the truth or had embarked on a humane course?"

"No."

"Why, then, is a lion or a dog necessary if neither is interested in truth?"

"I've never thought about it that way."

"According to your Bible, Sam, man was created a little lower than the angels, He was given dominion over the animals of the earth. He can use that dominion for good or evil."

"Theoretically."

"Hitler's ovens proved that even in the twentieth century man had not come very far since the slaughter of Biblical days."

"So?"

"But in every civilization, there are those few individuals who move their society forward. Perhaps their individual accomplishments are not remembered after their deaths, but the world is a slightly better place because they lived in it for however brief a period."

"What does that have to do with my cross-examination of Professor Jacobs?"

"You momentarily hurt, but did not kill, a single man. The fact that you feel guilty about your mental examination of one witness is what makes you different from Rudolf Kasztner or Adolf Eichmann. People like Kasztner are proud they saved a few. By your searching the souls of witnesses, who knows to how many others, you are exposing the truth that they turned their backs on the many to save the few. Kasztner sacrificed eight hundred thousand human beings to save less than two thousand. Which of you is the more moral human being in terms of your 'absolute truth?'"

Tamir thought for a few moments. Rashid didn't wait for a reply before he continued. "Those who turn their heads away because they do not want to witness evil contribute to that very evil by condoning it."

"Yes."

"Did Chaim Jacobs turn his back on what was going on?"

"Yes, but ..."

"But what, my friend? Weren't you the one that said 'Truth is absolute or it isn't?'"

"I did, Rashid."

"So Chaim Jacobs, as good a human being as he was, turned his back because he did not want to know about the evil he suspected was going on."

Tamir looked up to the stars, as if for an answer. A shooting star fell from the sky.

"Must he be punished now because he turned his back?"

"Yes. But his punishment comes from within himself, not because you started it."

"What do you mean?"

"Sam, when you get to be as old as me, you realize we are put on earth to go through a learning experience. The victory of life is not in looking at all the major victories we claim we've won in our lives. Rather it is looking back at how far we've come. If we survive defeat after defeat after defeat, if we suffer our last days in constant pain, but we still stand with our heads and our souls unbowed, then we have fulfilled your God's, my Prophet's, definition of a successful life. Shmulik, how many lessons have you learned from pain?"

"More than I care to count."

"Can you look back on any single event that caused you a tremendous amount of pain, but from which you learned a critical lesson in your life?"

Suddenly, without warning, Samuel Tamir put his head in his hands and wept as he thought back to an evening early in nineteen forty-four …

He held her hand. She stroked his face, very gently.

"Samuel, Samuel," she sighed. "So strong, so innocent."

"Must you go, Hanna? There is so much you could do here. Your poems, your songs, your writings —"

"Ah, sweet little Shmulik," she said. "How could we ever truly be happy, knowing that millions have perished in the ovens of Europe while we stood by and did nothing?"

"But what you propose is so dangerous. You could be captured ... or worse." He shuddered as he thought about what a man could do with her delicate, milky-white body.

The young woman was calm, her voice soothing, her words quiet. "If that is God's will, I'm willing to accept it, Sam. You'll find a wonderful woman of your own some day. Someone who'll be able to give you the love you need, the love you deserve."

"But Hanna ... ?"

"Some day you might realize, perhaps you already realize, that the most important thing he or she can to is to be true to himself or herself, not to compromise one's ideals."

"You sound like a martyr."

"I'm not a martyr, Samuel, and God knows I'm not a heroine. I'm a simple girl who sees a light of hope through the tunnel of this horribly dark night of Jewish despair. If I die, the name Hanna Senesh will never mean a thing. If I live without doing something to try to help my people, it will mean even less."

"Hanna ..."

She placed her fingers to his lips, and stroked gently from just beneath his nose to his chin. "I really have no fear, Samuel. Or maybe I do, I don't know. What I do know is that I'm one of the lucky ones. God has shown me the beauty of the Negev, the running stream, the flowers that come after the spring rain. I have known true freedom. Promise me one thing, Samuel?"

"Anything, Hanna."

"Pursue truth. Defend those who have no defenders, even if you're one battling a thousand. And if, for some reason, I do not return, remember me when you fight for justice."

❧

"Are you all right, Shmulik?"

"I am now, Rashid."

"You did not destroy Chaim Jacobs this afternoon. You taught him that a man must always look inside himself, that he must always measure by his own yardstick whether he did the right thing. If Professor Jacobs can find pain in what he did wrong and strive to make up for the fact that he missed the mark, then you will have done a great good deed."

"Thank you, Rashid. I think it's time to go home now."

"Perhaps you don't feel better, yet, young Tamir. But the healing has begun."

28

Menachem Bader a short, stocky man in his late fifties, with a full shock of black hair, who was neither old nor frail, strode aggressively to the witness stand. Amnon Tell knew calling Bader was a calculated risk. Bader's testimony might exonerate Kasztner, but, conversely, it might open up the entire government of the State of Israel to serious question.

"Mister Bader, what is your present position?

"Deputy secretary in the foreign ministry."

"What position did you occupy during World War II?"

"I served as liaison between the Jewish Agency and David Ben Gurion, Chaim Weizmann, and Moshe Sharett. I shuttled between Turkey, Syria, Palestine and Egypt."

"Do you know Joel Brand?"

"Yes."

"How did you first meet him?"

"On May 19, 1944, we received a cable from Vienna informing us that Brand, a member of the Budapest Rescue Committee, was on his way to Turkey. He arrived on the appointed day and told us exactly what was going on in Nazi Europe."

"Have you ever heard the term *'Blut fuer ware?'*'

"Yes, I heard about it from Mister Brand. He told us about a deal Adolf Eichmann had proposed."

"Who was 'us' Mister Bader?"

"The Agency committee in Istanbul."

"What was your first impression?"

"The Agency thought the offer was a malicious swindle, but Brand told the us that Eichmann had agreed to postpone killing twelve thousand Jews a day for two weeks in order to get some kind of commitment. The Agency did not meet Eichmann's deadline. Brand's delay brought letters pouring in from the Jews of Hungary, pleading for Brand's immediate return, warning that the extermination of the Jews would start up if Brand failed to come back to Budapest."

"What was the Agency's position?"

"We felt cooperation with our British allies was the surest way to ensure the establishment of a Jewish state after the War, so we told the British representatives in Turkey about the Eichmann offer. The Brits told the Jewish Agency representatives they wouldn't stand in Brand's way if he wished to go to Palestine to report personally to the Jewish Agency."

"Did you tell all this to Brand?" Tell continued.

"Yes."

"What was his response?"

"Brand was nervous about the further delay. When he arrived at the Syrian border, he was arrested and confined by the British."

"Did the Agency take any action to assist Brand?"

"Yes. After Brand's arrest, Moshe Sharett went to the Syrian border and spoke with Brand in the presence of a British Intelligence Officer. Unfortunately, Brand's arrest in Aleppo led to the collapse of his mission. He was detained by the British for four and one half months. During that time, the Eichmann offer fell through."

"Your witness, Mister Tamir."

"Mister Bader, who was the Agency official who informed the British of Joel Brand's arrival in Istanbul?"

"Ehud Avriel."

"Who accompanied Brand to the Syrian border?"

"A Turkish Jew. I don't recall his name."

"When did the news of Brand's arrest reach the Jewish Agency in Jerusalem?"

"Immediately after the arrest."

"When did Sharett contact Brand?"

"Twenty-four hours later."

"Mister Bader, I challenge you that your entire story is a malicious distortion of the truth! I challenge you to deny that Sharett and you knowingly trapped Brand and induced him to set out for the Syrian border. Sharett knew all along of the impending arrest and was waiting for Brand at the border in a nearby British military camp before the train pulled in!"

Bader was caught off guard. His face reddened, but he controlled his anger and said, in a quiet voice, "You're wrong. You know you're wrong."

"Isn't it a fact that Sharett was waiting at the border before Brand's arrival?"

"I don't know."

"Isn't it a fact that it was Ehud Avriel who accompanied Brand to the Syrian border? That the Turkish Jew was nonexistent?"

Bader blushed furiously. He knew he was caught in Tamir's trap. If he lied and was found out, he could find himself in the defendant's chair within a few months.

"That is correct, Mister Tamir. Avriel did accompany him."

"Did Ehud Avriel witness Brand's arrest?"

"Yes."

"But Avriel was not arrested?"

"That's correct."

"Avriel was in the service of the British Intelligence, was he not?"

"I don't think so."

"Is it not true that at least some of you thought the British were planning to trap Brand and that's why they allowed him to travel to Syria?"

"That is true."

"Did you inform Brand that his journey to Syria was possibly a British trap?"

Now Bader started to perspire freely. He asked the clerk for a napkin, wiped his forehead, licked his lips nervously. "We did not inform him."

"Why not?"

"Out of awe and respect for the emissary of the doomed."

Tamir asked for a momentary break in the questioning. He huddled with his staff. "How sure are you that we've got Brand available?"

"As of last night, he was ready," Arieh said.

"Does the prosecution know we've been in touch with him?"

"I'm not sure, but I think so."

"Any chance he's 'gone south' on us?"

"I hope not. It's been known to happen."

"I've got enough out of Bader on the Joel Brand story. Obviously Brand is going to be an important witness if nothing happens to him."

"You think the government — ?" Ephraim asked.

"Depends on how desperate they get, or how much they feel they'll be embarrassed if the truth comes out," Tamir replied.

After the brief recess, Tamir made a tangential shift in the questioning.

"Mister Bader, have you ever heard of Michael Dov Weissmandel?"

"I believe I did."

"Who was he?"

"He called himself a mystic. He lived in a cave outside Bratislava."

"Isn't it a fact that he physically rescued over a thousand Jews with his own hands and got them out from under the Nazis' noses."

"He told us he was rescuing Jews."

"Did you believe him?"

"We got so many letters we didn't know whom to believe."

"Your Honor," Tamir said, "the defense requests this letter be marked next in order."

"So marked," the court clerk replied.

"Mister Bader, have you seen this letter before?"

Bader scanned the letter carefully. "I have seen this letter, yes."

"Isn't it a fact that you received many such letters from Rabbi Weissmandel?"

"I don't deny that. So did a number of us in Turkey, Switzerland and Palestine."

"Did you take these letters seriously?"

"We received so many letters we didn't know which ones were legitimate."

"May I read this letter into the record, Your Honor?"

"What does it tend to prove, counsel" the Court asked. "A public reading will only consume more time."

Tamir thought for a moment, then asked, "Would the Court read the letter before I begin my next questions?"

"Very well. Court is in recess."

Judge Halevi felt a heaviness as he walked slowly into his chambers. Once out of the presence of the participants in the courtroom, he picked up his precious Guarneri violin, something he did when he was about to tackle a particularly onerous task. The instrument was made of beautifully aged wood, and Judge Halevi felt at one with his forbears, Jewish and Christian, as he stroked the warm rosewood.

The instrument had been made by hand a good three hundred years ago. It had withstood the test of time and the deaths of a dozen former owners. Halevi was aware that this magnificent creation would delight ears other than his own long after the Greenwald trial, long after the present government of Israel had passed into history, long after he himself had been gathered to his Maker.

He plucked the A string, then carefully brought it into tune with the high E string, the D string, and the rich, low tones of the G string. Without thinking, he started playing *Oif in Pripitchek,* a Chasidic melody which had graced the Pale of Settlement everywhere in Europe where Jews had lived before the Holocaust. The violin wept, almost as if it knew what Weissmandel's letter would say. It was the soft, caressing voice of the bearded, caftaned father proudly taking his young son in hand and leading him to *cheder,* to school, for the first time. Its words were in Yiddish, a language that had practically died with the six million, a moribund language of a people destined to meet a tragic fate, and they were simple, childishly simple, and conveyed the aura of another time.

> "Off in Pripitchek, burns a little fire, and the room is hot
> and the Rabbi teaches the little children their alphabet—"

Nothing. Nothing and everything. For to the observant Jew of the shtetl, there was nothing more important than learning. These were the roots from which Benjamin Halevi had sprung. The Judge put down the violin, turned on his Victrola, and placed the needle on a 78-RPM recording of Pachelbel's *Canon.* He read the letter which had been written on May 15, 1944, the day after the Nazis started deporting the Hungarian Jews to the ovens at Auschwitz.

"May 15, 1944 -- in a cave near Lublin.

"Shalom and greetings.

"Yesterday the Germans began deporting Jews from Hungary. Every day, 12,000 souls are being taken away. Four deportations of 45 such trainloads move daily out of Hungary. Within 26 days, everyone in that area will have been deported. The deported ones go to Auschwitz to be put to death by cyanide gas. A great number are dead on arrival.

"The Germans allow a few of the strongest to stay alive. They are branded with a number burned into their arm and the Star of David burned into their chest. Most of these privileged ones die within a month. Others take their place.

"Each of the transports goes directly from the train to the gas chambers. They are completely consumed in the ovens and leave no evidence behind. The dead bodies are burned in specially made ovens. Each oven burns 12 bodies an hour. In February, there were 36 ovens burning. We have learned that more have been built. A few eyewitnesses told us that in February there were four disposal buildings. More have been built since then.

"Formerly, the Germans killed and burned the Jews in the forest of Birkenau, near Auschwitz. Now the killing and burning take place in the buildings shown on the enclosed map. In December, the Germans built special trains to transport Hungary's Jews to their extermination. This is the schedule of Auschwitz, from yesterday to the end: 12,000 Jews are to be suffocated daily and their bones and ashes are to be used to fertilize the German fields.

"And you, our brothers in Palestine, in all the countries of freedom, how do you keep silent in the face of this great murder while five million Jews have been murdered? And silent now while tens of thousands are still waiting to be murdered?

"Their destroyed hearts cry to you for help as they bewail your cruelty. You are brutal, you are murderers because you watch in cold-blooded silence. Because you sit with folded arms and you do nothing, though you could stop or delay the murder of Jews at this very hour. In the name of those who have been murdered, we beg, we plead, we cry out and demand you take action, that you do deeds now, at once!

"The ministers of all lands must raise a loud and piercing outcry that must enter the ears of the world, the ears of the German people, the ears of the Hungarian people. Let them cry out a warning to the German murderers! Let them proclaim they know all that has been done in the past, and that which is still being done. And should join in this outcry of outrage against the German murderers.

"Let this outcry be heard over all the radios and read in all the newspapers of the world: that unless they stop at once the deportations of Hungary's Jews, Germany will forever be exiled from civilization. We ask that the crematoria in Auschwitz be bombed from the air. They are sharply visible as shown on the enclosed map. Such bombing will delay the work of the German murderers. Bomb all roads leading from Eastern Hungary to Poland. Bomb the bridges near Karpatus. Drop all other business to get this done. *Remember, one day of your idleness kills 12,000 souls!*

"You, our brothers, sons of Israel, are you insane? Don't you know the hell around us? For whom are you saving your money? How is it that all our pleadings affect you less than the whimpering of a beggar standing in your doorway?

"Murderers! Madmen! Who is it that gives charity? You who toss a few pennies from your safe homes? Or we who give our blood in the depths of Hell? There is only one thing that may be said in your exoneration: that you do not know the truth. This is possible. The villain does his job so shrewdly that only a few guess the truth.

"We have told you the truth several times. Is it possible you believe our murderers more than you believe us? May God open your eyes and give you heart to rescue in these last hours the remainder. Most important, bomb the Auschwitz Crematoria and the bridges leading to them. Such bombing can vitally delay the evil work of our slaughterers. God who keeps alive the last remnant of Israel will show His mercy for which I pray. We await God's help – and yours."

The judge pondered the message for several minutes. He had eyes. He could see. He had ears. He could hear. And what he saw in the depths of his own soul during those several minutes were film clips he had seen several times. Stark black and white pictures of naked living cadavers. Men nearly six feet tall who weighed less than seventy-five pounds. Women whose breasts had become shrunken to nonexistence, yet who held dead babies to those breasts as if, by giving suck, they could somehow grasp back from Satan the young lives which he had so bitterly snatched away.

Open mouths, haunted eyes, black circles. Shriveled skin, the spark of mortality almost extinguished. What did those poor beings think as the cameras were taking these photographs? Is this the kind of souvenir they would have chosen to send to a wife, a husband, a mother? *Having a lovely time, wish you were here.* Judge Halevi suddenly felt very cold.

"*My God,*" he said softly. "*I was in Palestine at the time. Safe and warm and dispensing British justice. What did I do to help those whose destiny was the ovens? Could I have done more? Al cheyts shechetanu l'fanecha,*" he said under his breath. *The public confession he, and all Jews, made every Yom Kippur, the Day of Atonement. "And now I must judge another human being who is accused of doing even more than I did? A human being hounded by the same guilt that hounds me, that hounds all of us? And what is worse is that Greenwald's accusation may be true. If it is, God help us, it extends not only to Kasztner but to all of us, myself included. God help us all.*"

The judge went into his private bathroom. He turned on the hot water tap. When the water was sufficiently warm for his purpose, he soaked a towel with water and placed it over his face while he sat down on the toilet seat. He remained that way for a long time. Then he looked at his wristwatch. More than an hour had passed. He must not keep the litigants waiting.

The judge cracked the door to the courtroom open without pushing the usual buzzer to signal his arrival. He looked out into the courtroom without being seen. Crowds of reporters had gathered in two separate groups, one surrounding Tell and another, larger group engaged in animated conversation with Samuel Tamir.

Halevi thought about his own children. His eldest son had married properly and was now interning at the Hadassah Hospital on Mount Scopus. He'd always been the thoughtful one, and Halevi thought, for a sliver of an instant, of calling Yaakov.

He thought about his daughter Bat'ya, pregnant now with what, the Lord willing, would be Halevi's first grandson. God's in His heaven, all's right with the world. She'd married into one of the first families in Israel a *prominenti*. A dagger of discomfort sliced into him. He was thinking like the defense counsel, Tamir, and wondered if there was any truth to what could be a horrible reality: the Jews wanted settlers to come to

Israel all right, and the British didn't mind if Jews resettled in Palestine, *provided they were the right kind of Jews;* erudite like himself, clean, hard-working, *civilized* in the sense that the English considered themselves civilized.

Civilized like his youngest daughter, Irena, who was secretly dating a Christian man. There'd been terrible arguments at home, anguished tears, rage, but in the end he knew it would be useless to shout, to forbid, to issue edicts. He, a high judge in Israel, knew there was one law he couldn't hope to enforce, the simple law of nature. He buzzed, signaling his formal re-entry into the courtroom. The groups around the lawyers scattered instantly to their seats.

Tamir continued his cross-examination of Menachem Bader, not so much to implicate Kasztner in the single-handed murder of eight hundred thousand Jews, but to paint a larger, more horrifying picture of brother betraying brother, Jew betraying Jew, ally abandoning ally, and whole nations taking the path of least resistance, even if it meant the death of countless innocent people. Tamir's tactic was to guide Menachem Bader, who was now eager to be his friend, through a history of what happened after Weissmandel's letter.

"What ever became of Rabbi Weissmandel, Mister Bader?"

"He survived and eventually moved to a small town in New York."

"Did the Germans ever find out that he was writing letters?"

"Yes. Apparently one of the letters fell into their hands."

"How do you know this?"

"We received a letter from him in November of 1944, relating that in August he had been captured by S.S. troops and put on board a train headed for Auschwitz. The Germans allowed him to keep the stale crust of bread he had in his hands when he boarded the train. Fortunately, they didn't inspect it because inside the bread he had planted a coil of emery thread that could saw through steel. At night, he cut a hole in the sealed car and leaped out into the darkness."

"Do you know if he continued his rescue work after he escaped?"

"I'm told he did."

"Did the Jewish Agency ever learn about the British response to Weissmandel's plea for bombing the concentration camps and the roads leading to them?"

"We did."

"What was that response?"

"I don't know."

Tamir extracted a letter from a pile of papers on his table.

"Have you ever seen this letter before, Mister Bader?"

The witness nodded, but did not respond verbally.

"This letter is from Richard Law of the British Foreign Office, addressed to the Jewish Agency and dated September 1, 1944, correct?"

"That is true."

"The letter says, and I quote, 'The matter of bombing the crematoria received the most careful consideration of the air staff. I am sorry to have to tell you that in view of the very technical difficulties involved we have no option but to refrain from pursuing the proposal in present circumstances.' Do you recall receiving that message?"

"Yes."

"What did the Jewish Agency do when they got that letter?"

"We considered it and discussed it among ourselves."

"And?"

"What do you mean, 'and,' Mister Tamir? There was nothing we could do. We didn't have planes, ordnance, or troops. We had no standing to do anything except thank the British for considering our request."

"Mister Bader, only two more questions. Did you, or any member of the Jewish Agency to your knowledge ever respond to any of Rabbi Weissmandel's letters?"

"I don't think so."

"Why not, Sir?"

"Because many letters like this came to us every. We could not answer them all."

Tamir let the answer hang in the air, looked down at his papers, shuffled them for a few seconds, looked at the judge, then at the witness.

"Because many letters like this came to us every day. We simply could not answer them all," he said softly. "I have nothing further of this witness, Your Honor."

29

The courtroom was silent for several moments. Chaim Cohen finally rose ponderously to his feet. "Your Honor, the prosecution respectfully moves to strike the entire last portion of Mister Bader's testimony, including the letter from Rabbi Weissmandel."

"On what grounds, Mister Cohen?" the Judge asked.

"Your Honor, in order properly to frame this motion, I ask that the courtroom be cleared."

A hefty, late-middle-aged man with thinning hair and a burgeoning midriff, who had been sitting in the first row of spectator's seats, rose. "Your Honor, might I be heard on this matter?" he asked in American-accented English.

The judge, who'd been conducting the proceeding in Hebrew but who was fluent in the intruder's language, looked sternly down at the man. No one spoke in Judge Halevi's court unless asked or given permission to do so in the ordinary course of trial.

"Are you a lawyer, sir? I don't recall your appearing before me in the past."

"No. Your Honor," the man replied. "I am not and I have not."

"Then why do you interrupt the proceedings in this courtroom?" Judge Halevi asked sharply. "You are not a party to these proceedings?"

"I am not."

"You are not expected to testify as a witness?"

"I may well be called as a witness."

"Your name, sir?"

"Ben Hecht, Your Honor."

The judge was taken aback. The name Ben Hecht was not unknown in Israel. Judge Halevi had never met the American, but he knew that some years ago the British had sunk an old munitions ship named the *Ben Hecht*. The advertisement authored by Hecht in 1943 had been introduced in evidence at trial.

"Mister Hecht," the judge said. "Normally this court would not tolerate interruption of the orderly course of its business, not even by a foreign dignitary such as yourself. But I am the first to admit this has not been a normal trial. You may address the court from where you stand."

"Your Honor," Hecht said. "I object to Attorney General Cohen's request that his objection be heard *in camera*. This is a public trial."

"Motions are not necessarily public, Mister Hecht," Halevi replied. "We are not taking evidence. This is simply a motion to strike prior testimony."

"That's precisely why it is so important that this argument be public, Your Honor," Hecht responded. "If the court decides to strike this evidence, it will be as if the testimony had never taken place, as if Rabbi Weissmandel had never written his plea. Your Honor, by your ruling, you yourself could be part of the organized state seeking to cover up everything that went on during that time."

"Mister Hecht!" the judge fairly shouted, "I find such a statement intolerable and contemptuous! How dare you accuse this court of complicity in what went on!" The judge suddenly froze in the midst of his speech, his anger suddenly defused by a shocking realization. *The reason I'm so furious with this man's outrageous charge is because it is true! If I cover up this evidence, I could be called to account as a co-conspirator to willfully ignoring the shouting of the millions.*

"I'm sorry for my outburst, Mister Hecht," the jurist said. "This court has always considered itself fair and just to all concerned. To have a non-lawyer impugn the court's integrity is shocking."

"I humbly apologize," Hecht said, in a tone that was anything but humble. "But you, yourself said only a moment ago that this was not a normal trial. In this trial, we are talking about a time in man's history that was anything but normal. Your Honor, I may be presumptuous, but I believe the prosecutor's objection is going to be that none of Mister Bader's testimony is relevant to whether Malchiel Greenwald libeled Rudolf Kasztner, and this assertion is technically correct."

"That is for me to decide, isn't it, Mister Hecht?"

"Yes, Judge Halevi, but I believe the next part of his objection is going to be based on a claim of 'national security.' I'd wager he's going to argue that Mister Bader's unfortunate responses to Mister Tamir's cross-examination would humiliate and indict the Founding Fathers of the State."

"Are you claiming prescience, Mister Hecht?"

"No, Your Honor," he said, grinning. "Call it newspaperman's intuition."

"Which, I surmise, will be part of the dispatch you file with your newspaper this evening?" the judge said.

"If I may respectfully comment, it seems Your Honor pretends to prescience."

"Mister Hecht, I am not here to debate with what you feel you must write, although I advise you that you risk a contempt of court citation if you attempt to prejudice public opinion by writing anything other than what actually occurred during the public segments of this trial. Whatever you write will not affect my opinion one way or the other. You have raised an interesting point, which I will certainly consider when I rule on the prosecution's motion. I find your manners lacking, but I suppose that type of thing goes on in America. The Attorney General's request to clear is granted. The bailiff is instructed to insure that everyone except counsel removes from the courtroom."

"Mister Cohen, state in detail the reasons supporting your motion to strike Mister Bader's testimony."

"It is unlikely to have any probative value for either party in this case," Cohen said.

"Mister Tamir?"

"Your Honor, we must remember who the parties are in this case. The prosecuting party is the State of Israel—"

"But, Mister Tamir, the State is not bringing this case on its own behalf, but rather on behalf of Doctor Kasztner," Judge Halevi said.

"Doctor Kasztner is a symbol of the State, Your Honor."

"Are you suggesting that the State is on trial, Mister Tamir?"

"I am suggesting precisely that, Your Honor," the defense lawyer said.

The judge leaned forward. "The State becomes the defendant in a case it has brought as the plaintiff," he intoned. "An interesting legal concept. Mister Tamir, have you any case authority? Perhaps Mister Levin can assist us."

Dov Levin, the legal encyclopedia, rose shyly in the court's presence. He was a student of the law for the law's sake, not a trial lawyer. Nevertheless, he cited the court to precedent in several countries where the defense posture was to put the offense on trial. "This is particularly true in the context of a civil libel case, Your Honor. The plaintiff's reputation is always in issue, particularly when the trier of fact considers an award of damages. This is true in Israel as well, Your Honor," he said, citing a string of civil cases as precedent. "While I cannot recall an instance in Israel where the state brought a *criminal* libel action, the analogy could not be clearer. The State assumes the position of the plaintiff. Thus it is the *State's* reputation that is in issue, and if that reputation is anything but scrupulously clean, that is a matter the court must consider in assessing any kind of penalty against the defendant."

"That makes sense, Mister Levin. Thank you," the court said respectfully. "The court commends your argument. Perhaps you might come to court more often. It would raise the scholarly standards of practice."

Dov Levin blushed furiously and sat down.

"Well, Mister Cohen? Mister Tell?"

"Your Honor," Attorney General Cohen said, "There must come a time when we stop berating ourselves for the choices we make, and we must go on. We don't need to be constantly reminded and re-reminded of what went on. The evidence has no probative value. This is nineteen fifty-four, not nineteen forty-four. For better or for worse, we must have the confidence of our people and we cannot have that confidence if we sit here and stir up the old ashes of a dead fire that can, if aroused, burn all of us."

"Anything else, gentlemen?" Judge Halevi asked.

Neither side said anything and both sides submitted the question to the court.

"Very well," the court said impassively. "The motion to strike this afternoon's testimony of Mister Bader on cross-examination as it relates to Rabbi Weissmandel is granted. Rabbi Weissmandel's letter will remain in evidence. Court is in recess until tomorrow morning."

Judge Halevi rose swiftly before either counsel could react, turned on his heel, and walked out the door and into his chambers, where he poured himself a neat shot of Scotch whisky.

30

The two lovers stood huddled at the bus stop, waiting for the Number Five bus back to University housing. They'd eaten at "their" restaurant, which they considered lucky. The sun was setting in the west. The sky was suffused with the roseate glow of late spring. "Can't you come to the library and be with me when I study, darling?" Ephraim asked. "Two hours, three at most. Then it's time for love."

"All the more reason for me to go home first, Ephraim. A nice, warm shower in a place that has dependable hot water, not a dorm shower where you get freezing sticks of ice one moment and scalding fire the next. I'll have some time to speak with my father, which I haven't done since we've been together. Three hours just to take a little time for myself."

"Well—" he said, grinning one of those rare grins reserved for her.

"Listen, darling, I promise you this. If you get home so much as one minute after ten tonight, you'll find your bed nice and warm 'cause I'll be in it. Now give me a quick kiss and be on your way," she said, as she saw the bus approach.

He kissed her, but it wasn't a quick smack. It was warm and tender, then passionate, then sweet, and she was trembling when it was over. "Be on your way, my love," she said huskily.

As the bus moved off, she waved, knowing this was the night she'd talk to her father about the serious plans she and Ephraim had discussed two nights ago. Gabriel was gone, forgotten. It would delight her father to know she had found someone very special, someone whose background was similar to theirs. She knew it would bring him peace, just as the conduct of the trial seemed to be vindicating his honor.

She felt the explosion before she saw it. One moment, the Eged bus was rolling down the busy boulevard. The next, there was a loud WHUMPH that shook the entire street, a ball of bright orange and black, the sounds of a hundred screams. Ephraim had just reached his seat when the bus exploded. He instinctively tried to jump up and run. But he had no legs left to do so. And within another minute, he was no more.

Tamir stayed with her, held her, waited for her wracking sobs to stop. Then he said, in the gentlest voice, "Ariana, I'm so sorry. Ephraim's dead. He was my friend, too. I grieve for his soul and yours. But there were millions more who were taken before their time and we're trying to speak for them. For God's sake and Ephraim's, please, dear Ariana, please try, over the next days, to pull yourself together. I know your life seems like it's over, but it's not. I swear to you it's not."

He held her as one would hold a small child, while the last of the sobs coursed through her body. He'd always known her as a strong, brave woman, but now, collapsed, she'd somehow become smaller, compressed, fragile. When she looked up at him, her face was tear-streaked and splotchy. "We've been through this before, haven't we, Sam?" Her words were incongruous, yet they were the only sounds that made sense at this moment.

"Yes," he said softly.

"Tell me something, Sam, will you?"

"Anything, Ariana, if it will help."

"Did you ... did you feel this way when you heard about Hanna?"

He bit down on his lip, hard enough to draw blood. "Ariana," he croaked. "No one ever knew. No one ..."

In response, she squeezed his hand. "Don't worry, my friend. I swear I'll never tell anybody."

"How did you ... how did you know? She was more than ten years older than you. You can't have been more than a child."

"Ssshh," she said, finding solace in the knowledge that she was desperately needed at this moment. "Sometimes little girls see things they shouldn't, hear things they mustn't."

"When did you—?"

"Long ago. I thought nothing of it at the time. I didn't really know either of you then. Now we've come full circle, haven't we, Sam?"

"Yes, Ariana."

"Are you as happy with Ruth as you would have been with Hanna?"

"Yes, Ariana, I am. That's why I was able to tell you you'll live again, God willing you'll love again, and I pray you'll know the happiness I've found."

"Thank God you're with me tonight."

"Would that it had been on a happier occasion, my friend." He held her again. A few moments later, he took her hand, gently walked her to his car, and drove her to her father's house. They talked into the night, and none of them got much sleep.

The newspapers screamed the story of the bombing the next day. Terrorist attacks had made the situation more tense than ever. Israel was in an uproar. Arieh Marinsky telephoned Judge Halevi's chambers and the prosecutor's office first thing in the morning and explained what had happened. Everyone might be at one another's throats during the bitter, vicious trial. But, for the next three days, they declared a truce in order to mourn the loss. All of them, Kasztner, Tell, Chaim Cohen, the court, and the entire defense team stood silently together as Ephraim Biran was laid to rest in a plain, pine box.

The following day, the Israeli press reported that eight Israeli fighter aircraft had bombed a suspected terrorist camp into oblivion. Nineteen known terrorists had been annihilated. At the bottom of the article, there was a small entry that fifty-two others, including women and children, had also been killed.

31

When the trial resumed, several witnesses from the Jewish Agency, the Ministry of Trade and Commerce, and the Israeli government came forth, each of whom related how Doctor Kasztner was an indefatigable worker, a hero, a man who put duty above self. Curiously, no one had had personal or social dealings with the man, and, on Tamir's brief cross-examination of each, he elicited that Kasztner was known as a political opportunist and a bit of a cold fish. But none of the witnesses could be shaken in their basic feeling of admiration, and Tamir's cross-examination was half-hearted and perfunctory.

Tamir's staff dared not comment on their boss's lethargy, believing they knew the reason for it. Tamir, himself, knew better. It was the lull before the storm.

Reuven Katznelson had arranged for a brief weekend retreat at Tiberias for the whole family. Although it was not the first time they'd been in the exquisite northeastern part of Israel, it was wonderfully relaxing. During the day, the lawyer and his wife hiked in the hills above green valleys and bathed in the warm waters of Lake Kinneret, which Christians called the Sea of Galilee, while his father and mother read, played classical music on the Victrola, and watched their grandchildren frolicking on the beach.

That evening, after the youngsters had gone to sleep, Reuven, Bat-Sheva, Sam and Ruth sat around the table on their balcony overlooking the lights around the lake. "Looks to me like Tell's just about to wrap up his case," Reuven said. "He's put on fifteen witnesses and they've said just about everything that could be said."

"Mmm-hmm," Tamir nodded.

"Arieh told me you've been sleepwalking through the last six witnesses and Halevi was yawning about halfway through the last week."

"True about the judge. As for sleepwalking, that's not accurate. I just didn't want to add to the judge's boredom by underlining the obvious."

"So what's your strategy?" Sam's mother asked.

"We've got two alternatives. Obviously the judge is only interested in four witnesses – Greenwald, Catherina Senesh, Kasztner himself, and Joel Brand."

"I've heard rumors in the Senate chambers," Bat-Sheva said. "Ugly rumors that Sharett and even Ben Gurion have threatened that if Brand testifies he could be in serious trouble."

"Oh?" Tamir was suddenly interested. "What did you hear?"

"Government aides threatened him with imprisonment if he did not testify in a certain way."

"Which aides?"

"They didn't know the details, Samuel. Rumor more than anything else."

"Isn't that what got my loving husband into this case in the first place?" Ruth said. Tamir looked at his wife's tanned arms and legs beneath her khaki shirt and shorts and thought she'd never looked so lovely.

"What do you think Tell will do?" Reuven asked his son.

"Most likely, he'll rest at this point. He's made a *prima facie* case. I'm concerned about how I fit Joel Brand in as a witness. The court's already ruled that the testimony concerning Weissmandel and the knowledge of the Jewish Agency might not be relevant. My best hope is that Tell will call Brand as a witness."

"How is the girl handling Biran's death?" Bat-Sheva asked.

"Better than I would have hoped, *Ema*. After we sat *Shiva* for the mourning period, she took a night job as a nurse at Charity Hospital. She's strong. I'm sure she'll survive."

"It's a shame, though," Ruth said. "Two bad experiences in so short a lifetime."

"I wouldn't say her experience with Biran was bad at all," Tamir responded. "It showed her she could love again, gave her hope in place of lamenting a lost love."

"Sound familiar?" She smiled and squeezed his hand. Ruth knew of her husband's past with Hanna Senesh. It didn't upset her, nor diminish her love and trust for Sam. Ruth herself had been pursued and admired by more than one man, and she'd had her share of suitors.

"What if Tell puts Kasztner back on the stand before he rests his case?" Tamir's mother asked.

"Not likely. The last I heard, he's still in New York on government business. My guess is they'll keep him there as long as they can get away with it."

It was one in the morning when a sleepy Rudolf Kasztner answered the transatlantic call from Israel. He recognized the voice of Prime Minister Moshe Sharett immediately.

"Rudy, we're just about at the end of the prosecution's case. I think it would be a good idea for you to get back within the next few days."

"Impossible," Kasztner replied. "The trade talks are at a critical point. I've been able to sway several members of the United States Congress toward tariff reductions and this week I've scheduled meetings with major fundraising organizations in New York."

"How long before you come back?" his caller asked impatiently.

"Sixty days at the very earliest."

"Two months?" Sharett exclaimed. "The trial could be over by then, and if you don't return the court could declare a mistrial."

Just fine with me, Kasztner thought. *It was a mistake to dredge all this garbage up in the first place. Let things die down quietly. All I want now is peace and quiet. Perhaps an assignment as a legation first secretary, or as consul-general in San Francisco. That's supposed to be a beautiful city.*

Out loud, he said, "Is there any reason we can't simply enter into a quiet settlement?"

"Yes, there is," Sharett fumed. "That goddamned Tamir has implicated the entire government. We've got no choice but to fight it out. It's gotten bigger than Rudolf Kasztner," the prime minister said. "We started this one for you. You've got to stand by us."

"And if I can't make it?"

"You don't understand, Kasztner. You don't have a choice. You're either on the team or you're not. If you decide to abandon your government, there's always the anti-collaborationist law ..."

"Back to mutual blackmail, are we?" Kasztner asked smoothly. "Wouldn't it be nice if our honorable Prime Minister had his chance to testify and subject his own honor to the tender mercies of Samuel Tamir?"

"Suppose we could arrange that you wouldn't have to face Tamir when you return?"

32

"Your Honor, subject to the conclusion of Mister Tamir's cross-examination of Doctor Kasztner, the state is almost ready to rest its case. I doubt if we will call more that two additional witnesses. Perhaps Ehud Avriel will be summoned to close our list of witnesses. Otherwise, I shall rest the state's case tomorrow."

Tamir arose, glanced around the room filled with reporters, and reacted immediately. "Your Honor, in the event Avriel is not summoned tomorrow, the defense asks permission to start its case immediately tomorrow morning. Our first witness will be Joel Brand."

Amnon Tell, already on his feet, shouted, "Your Honor, Mister Tamir has not yet completed his examination of Doctor Kasztner. That witness is still in New York, in the midst of serious trade talks. I suggest the trial be continued for thirty days to enable Doctor Kasztner to return. He is away on state's business, and under the Code that constitutes good grounds for continuance. Besides, we are approaching the Shavuot holiday. I assume the Court would not hold session during that week. So what is lost?"

"Joel Brand may be lost!" Tamir shot back.

"Your Honor," Tell said, nearly shouting, "this is just one more tactic in the defense's smear campaign. I demand Mister Tamir be censured and directed to apologize to the entire State of Israel for his veiled hint that something might happen to Brand. We have called Joel Brand as our own witness. We have fully intended to produce him all along."

"That's an out-and-out lie, Your Honor!" Tamir responded, equally angry. "Joel Brand is in constant peril. He is being shadowed. Various elements are doing their utmost to suppress this man's evidence. I believe he is in physical danger. Moreover, various documents of the highest importance have been stolen from him. I demand that Brand be summoned immediately!"

"That is a scandalous, filthy smear!" Tell roared. "We intend to take necessary measures to prevent the repetition of such outrageous statements!"

The judge did nothing to stop the vicious interchange between the two attorneys, which continued as each taunted the other, their voices as loud as clashing swords.

"Are you threatening that the government will attempt to silence me?" Tamir turned ninety degrees to face the court. "Your Honor, I request once again that Joel Brand be summoned immediately as the first witness for the defense. For the past five years, this man has not managed to find employment. He hasn't been able to earn a living. But last week he was offered a job which involved his boarding one of our marine maritime steamers and leaving the country."

The judge raised his eyebrows. "Is this true, Mister Tell?"

"I .... I don't know, Your Honor," blustered the prosecutor. "I have heard of no such offer."

"Very well, gentlemen, we will have the chance to find out relatively quickly. Mister Tell, I trust you can produce Mister Brand tomorrow morning at nine a.m., can you not?"

"I cannot say for certain, Your Honor."

"Perhaps not, but I can. I am ordering you to produce him tomorrow morning. Court is in recess until tomorrow morning."

Halevi got up and left the courtroom.

The following morning, as Tamir walked up the steps to the court-house, he saw more than a hundred people pushing and shoving through the door ahead of him. *Must be something important going on. Odd, I haven't seen anything out of the ordinary in the morning papers.* As he entered the building, briefcase in hand, he turned right and approached Courtroom Five, his daytime home for the past few months. Before he got there, Shlomo, Judge Halevi's bailiff, intercepted him.

"Court's been moved, Mister Tamir. We've been assigned to Courtroom One for the rest of the trial." The deputy pointed down the hall to where the crowd Tamir had seen outside the courthouse had gathered.

When the bailiff cleared a path for defense counsel to enter the largest courtroom in Israel, Arieh Marinsky met him at the door.

"Holy something-or-other, boss, this place is packed to the rafters. Must be three hundred people in there already. I don't know how the rest of the observers are going to make it in. They'll probably have to stagger 'em in shifts."

"Any idea why we got switched, Arieh?"

"Beats me, Sam. Most likely the P.J.'s call," he replied, referring to the Presiding Judge of the Jerusalem court.

Twenty minutes later, Judge Halevi entered, agreed to postpone the morning's proceedings for five minutes while the press photographers finished taking their shots, then greeted the huge assembly politely. "Ladies, gentlemen, as you can see, we've been moved to somewhat more ostentatious quarters. Whether we are in Courtroom Five, Courtroom One, or on the beach in Tel Aviv makes no difference. We are here to do justice with dignity and respect for the rights of the litigants and the witnesses."

Judge Halevi looked toward the back of the courtroom and couldn't suppress a smile and a nod in the direction of the last row. His wife, their three grown children, and their respective romantic interests, filled a good section of the last row. Ruth Tamir noticed this and whispered to her husband, "His family's here. That may mean they're planning to take off early for the Shavuot holiday."

"Or maybe he's brought them here to watch the fireworks," Tamir whispered back.

Ruth resumed her seat next to Ariana Greenwald in the first row of observers.

"Mister Tell?" the court asked. "Have you produced Mister Brand?"

"We have, Your Honor," Tell said, pointing to a stocky blond man sitting across the aisle from Ruth and Ariana in the front row.

The prosecutor looked as though he'd had a very hard night. Tamir noticed a five o'clock shadow on his face, as if he'd been up very early and shaved several hours ago. "Your Honor," Tell continued, "having produced and identified the witness, we would now ask for a thirty day continuance."

"Well, now, Mister Tell," the judge said. "It seems like the prosecution's gone through a lot of trouble to make sure Mister Brand was in court today. Why don't we hear what he has to say?"

"But, Your Honor ...?"

"Mister Tell, you indicated to me yesterday you intended to call Mister Brand as the prosecution's witness, didn't you?"

"Yes, but I thought —"

"We all have our thoughts, Mister Tell. And I have not yet made up my mind about your request for a continuance. Mister Brand, why don't you come forward to the witness stand and I'll let the lawyers have a little chat with you?"

"Your Honor, if that's the court's decision, the prosecution demands that defense counsel not leave the courtroom or speak with the witness before we've had a chance to question him."

"I see nothing wrong with that request. Mister Tamir?"

"I have no need to speak with Mister Brand at this time."

"Very well. Mister Brand, come forward and be sworn."

At that moment, Chaim Cohen entered the courtroom and strode to the prosecution counsel's table. There was frantic whispering between them. Cohen wrote notes to his subordinate. Tell nodded, shrugged his shoulders, stood, and addressed the witness.

"Mister Brand, were you a member of the Budapest Rescue Committee?

"I was."

"How old are you?"

"I am forty-eight years old."

"I have no further questions."

There was angry grumbling throughout the courtroom. Ben Hecht's voice, ever voluble, could be heard over the crowd. "That's the cheapest shot I ever heard of in my life."

Brand started to leave the witness box.

Tamir stood, raised his hand to stop him from leaving, and addressed the judge.

"Your Honor will no doubt recall what I said yesterday about my fears for Mister Brand's life and his safety. The prosecution said it intended to use Mister Brand as its witness. If this is all the prosecution intends to elicit from Mister Brand, it is a fraud on the court, and I demand that Mister Tell be censured for it. What Mister Brand has to tell is one of the most shocking stories in the annals of Jewish history. It is critical that the court hears it. It is critical that the State of Israel hears it. It is even more critical that the world hears it.

"Yet, the prosecution comes forth, asks two questions so that the scope of cross examination will be limited to one irrelevant fact and leaves the court in a position of ignorance. Justice is blind, but justice is not stupid, Your Honor. Mister Tell's actions make a mockery of this courtroom."

"It would seem that way, wouldn't it?" the judge remarked, not at all angry. "Mister Tell, would you care to explain why all the uproar of the past couple days if this is all you wanted to extract from the witness?"

"Your Honor ... " Prosecutor Tell's face and neck were scarlet, this time not from anger but from embarrassment. He tried to recover, cleared his throat, coughed to clear it again. "Your Honor, we do not deny the defense its right to examine Mister Brand at the appropriate time. We just thought that right before the Shavuot break —"

"What about the Shavuot break, Mister Tell?"

"We thought Mister Tamir would have a better opportunity to question the witness more completely if he were given time to speak with him."

"I see. Mister Brand," the Court said, turning toward the witness. "I understand you have been out of work for some time?"

"That's correct, Your Honor," Brand said.

"Mister Tamir said something to the effect that the government offered you a job very recently?"

"That's also true, Your Honor."

"What kind of job, sir?"

"I've been offered a job as a customs clearance agent on the ship *Shiloah*. It leaves tonight for Rio de Janeiro, then Cape Town, then Sydney."

"How long is it expected to be gone?"

"Nine months, Your Honor."

Judge Halevi glared at Amnon Tell, who'd already sat down when Brand answered the judge's questions. "Mister Tell, I believe Mister Tamir's suggestion of censure, perhaps even of contempt of court, may be very well taken, but I don't intend to discuss that with you at this moment. Mister Tamir, I am going to allow you to take Mister Brand as your own witness, out of order, and I'm going to let you question him to the full extent that he has relevant testimony to give. You will not be limited to the scope of direct examination.

"However, Mister Tell has indicated to me that the government did not want you to converse with Mister Brand in advance of the prosecution's questioning. The prosecution has now completed that questioning and I'll afford you a reasonable time to visit with Mister Brand if you wish."

Tamir smiled at Arieh Marinsky, sitting next to him at counsel's table and gave a thumb's up sign. He rose, pushed back a shock of sandy hair that had fallen over his forehead, and spoke.

"Your Honor, in order to avoid misunderstanding, I respectfully inform the court that Joel Brand and I have met seven or eight times during the past fortnight. At our very first meeting two months ago, I asked him, in the presence of a third person, whether he had been summoned to testify by the prosecution. I specifically stressed that if such were the case, I had no right to contact him. Mister Brand told me he had not been approached by the prosecution. Hence, I considered myself free to discuss the matter with him and obtain whatever information he could provide. At my request, Mr. Brand consented to show me various documents, a number of which he placed at my disposal. These have been in my keeping until today. I am willing to return them to the witness at any time."

Chaim Cohen was on his feet by the time Tamir finished. "Your Honor, the State of Israel has the absolute right to know exactly what Mister Brand and Mister Tamir discussed. We demand that this court stand in recess until we have had the opportunity to do so."

"Mister Cohen," the court responded. "The prosecution has had its opportunity to speak with Mister Brand. Mister Tell was the one who advised me yesterday that the prosecution intended to use Mister Brand as its witness. I trust you were present to observe the travesty that took place a few minutes ago.

"It seems highly irregular that the prosecution first says Mister Tamir cannot speak with the witness, then, when Mister Tamir reveals he has spoken with the witness, the government tries to preview what the witness is going to say. Frankly, Mister Cohen, I find the government's position offensive and I do not intend to tolerate it. The prosecution's request is denied. Mister Tamir, you may proceed."

APRIL – JUNE 1944

BUDAPEST, ISTANBUL, ALEPPO

33

Joel Brand entered the Majestic Hotel, the *Kommandatur* head-quarters at 11:00 a.m. He was ushered immediately into a large, comfortable room, and told to sit opposite a desk occupied by a taller man, whose demeasor displayed arrogant urbanity.

"'Do you know who I am?' he asked Brand.

"Yes, Colonel Eichmann," Brand responded.

Eichmann continued, "I carried out the actions in Germany, Austria, Poland and Slovakia. My next task is Hungary. I have checked up on whether your Joint Distribution Committee are capable of getting things done. I want to make a deal with you.

""Blood for Cargo, Cargo for Blood!" the tall man remarked. "Tell me who you want to salvage – women who can bear children? Men in their prime? The aged? The young? Speak up!"

Joel Brand sat, listening nervously. A young woman sat behind the desk in the German's luxurious hotel suite, pencil in hand, ready to take notes. After a few moments, he answered carefully. "It's not for me to decide whom you are to murder, Colonel Eichmann. I would like to save everybody. I don't understand this deal. Where are we supposed to get the cargo? You have confiscated everything. The local Jews and our friends abroad may perhaps gather some money if lives are to be saved."

"Go to Switzerland, Turkey, Spain, wherever you please, so long as you produce the cargo."

"What sort of cargo?"

"A million Jews for ten thousand trucks and one thousand tons each of tea, coffee and soap."

"Do you believe anyone on earth will treat this offer seriously?"

"I am willing to offer you one hundred thousand Jews in advance. When I receive what I want, I will release the remainder in the same proportion. To show my good faith, I will cease the deportations and exterminations while the negotiations are going on."

"Have you talked to the Chairman of the Jewish Agency Rescue Committee about this, Colonel?" Brand asked.

"I have found Doctor Kasztner to be most cooperative."

"When do you expect me to accomplish all of this?"

"You must set out no later than May eighteenth, one month from now. On that date, we will begin to deport twelve thousand Hungarian Jews a day. None of them will be exterminated during the negotiations, but you, Herr Brand, must return within two weeks after you leave. If negotiations demand more time, we'll be considerate. If you return with the verbal acceptance of my offer, I will cease the gassing and lay down the advance payment of one hundred thousand Jews."

No sooner did Brand leave the Majestic Hotel, he went directly to the headquarters of the Hungarian Jewish Rescue Committee. Doctor Rudolf Kasztner, the chairman of the committee, greeted Joel Brand, and immediately escorted him into a conference room, where the entire Committee membership was awaiting his return.

The Chairman, spoke first. "I'm surprised Obersturmbahnführer Eichmann chose to speak with you when he knew I was chairman, but, of course, he is entitled to his choice."

"He is well aware of that, Rezső."

They discussed what Eichman had proposed for the next three hours. Although the assembly was almost equally divided, Doctor Kasztner cast the deciding vote.

"Gentlemen, let us assume that none of us trust the *Boches*. They've publicly given us no reason to do so. But I've met with Colonel Eichmann. I believe that no matter how unpleasant his mannerisms, he has been honest with me. Besides, what do we have to lose if the deportations stop during the talks?"

Brand realized he was only a junior delegate, a small cog in the gears, and that Doctor Kasztner spoke from a position of authority and familiarity with the Nazis. Thus, he deferred to Doctor Kasztner's impressive arguments.

Three days later, Brand entered Eichmann's office-suite once again. The S.S. Obersturmbahnführer remained seated. He smiled thinly as Joel Brand took the same chair in which he had sat the first time they'd met.

"I trust your talks with your comrades went well, Mister Brand?"

"So far as I know, Colonel Eichmann,"

"So Doctor Kasztner told me when we had dinner the other night. To seal our understanding, you are to set out now. If you come back within two weeks with an acceptance from your people, I will release one hundred thousand immediately."

The Junkers JU-52 diplomatic plane carrying Brand arrived at Istanbul's Yeşilköy Airport, fifteen kilometers south of Pera, at eight the following morning. No one had come to meet him. *Probably delayed in traffic, although the cable from the Agency specifically said I'd be met.* After a short delay to straighten out his entry visa, Brand and the man who'd accompanied him from Budapest made their way into the European section of the sprawling city. No sooner had Brand checked into his room at the city's most elegant hotel, the Pera Palas, than there was a sharp rap on his door.

When he opened the door, he stood facing a tall man of his own age with slicked-back dark hair and an open smile, wearing casual slacks and an open-necked shirt.

"Joel Brand?"

"Yes,"

"I'm Venia Pomerantz, Palestine Rescue Committee. The committee is waiting downstairs. Have you eaten yet?"

"No."

"Just as well. They've set up a buffet in the meeting room."

During the next hour-and-a-half, Brand reported the details of his meetings with Eichmann and the approval of his misson by the Budapest committee. He concluded by saying, "Time is the most critical factor. If I'm not back within two weeks, everything will be lost. Gentlemen, I need to return with my answer on the next diplomatic plane."

"Which leaves next Tuesday," Pomerantz replied.

After spirited discussion, the Istanbul committee decided to summon Moishe Shertok — "he's adopted the name Moshe Sharett" — to Istanbul.

At the conclusion of the meeting, Chaim Barlas, acting chairman, addressed the committee. "Gentlemen, are we agreed that under no circumstances should we inform the British of this offer? That would queer everything. Venia will set out for Palestine and see to it that Sharett comes to Istanbul by the fastest means. I'll approach Larry Steinhardt, the American ambassador in Ankara. He's Jewish so I know he'll be sympathetic. Mister Brand, hopefully you'll be able return to Hungary on next week's diplomatic plane."

There was unanimous affirmation of Barlas' remarks.

"Chaim, who in hell is responsible for this royal fuckup?"

"Calm down, Joel, I'm sure it'll be straightened out immediately," Barlas replied.

"While eight hundred thousand Jews ride the trains to their deaths? I told you guys Eichmann gave me two weeks. You know how the Germans are about rules. Every day I'm still here costs us twelve thousand Jews!"

"We're doing everything we can —"

"Fuckup number one," Brand continued angrily. "No travel papers to Ankara for a week. Menachem Bader was not the greatest baby sitter in the world. Fuckup number two, the Agency rescue officials draft a tentative agreement accepting Eichmann's offer, but Sharett doesn't come 'cause he doesn't have a visa. Fuckup number three, worst of all, the Agency tells me the Brits are preventing Sharett from coming. How did the goddamn limeys find out about this operation when we unanimously agreed not to tell them a thing?"

"That didn't come from our end," Barlas said defensively. "Maybe the Palestinian committee? Look, Joel, why don't you set out for the Turkish-Syrian border and meet Sharett there? You can be back in Istanbul within a few days."

"I'd rather go to the German consulate and arrange for my immediate return to Budapest. There's no way I'm going to step onto British soil at Aleppo. I've already got a copy of the draft agreement we drew up."

"And I give you my word you have nothing to worry about. I can promise you you'll be back in Istanbul in a day or two, and you can return to Budapest immediately."

"Your word as Chairman of the Istanbul Rescue Committee?"

"Of course."

"One or two days, Barlas said. We've been on this train that long, just you and me sharing a compartment, and I still have no idea how close we are to the border, Ehud. I only signed on for this trip because you, Bader, and Chaim had authority to speak for the Agency. Wasn't there supposed to be a Turkish Jew aboard to shepherd us through?"

"Not that I know of," Ehud Avriel replied.

"I for one am scared shitless. I should have listened to those two guys who boarded the train in Ankara and warned me not to go on. They told me British agents are waiting in Aleppo to arrest me."

"Stop worrying, Joel," Avriel replied. "Those guys are from splinter groups that have no clout. Why would you even consider taking their word over the assurance of the largest Jewish Agency in the world. Moshe Sharett will be there to meet us."

Shortly afterward, the conductor knocked on the door of their compartment.

"Gentlemen, we're two hours from the frontier. I suggest you have your papers in order when we arrive at Islahiye."

As soon as the conductor departed, Avriel said, "Should anything happen to you Joel, should we be separated and you get arrested, don't speak with the British unless somebody from the Agency is present."

"What the hell are you talking about, Ehud? You told me everything was all arranged."

"As far as I know it is. I'm just saying *if* something happens."

"Thanks for those comforting words," Brand said sourly.

"Alright, Mister Sharett, why don't you explain to me how this happened? The minute we crossed the Syrian border, the British arrested me and put me in their barracks for a day before they brought me here. Now, you and I get to talk, but with British officers listening to our every word and a stenographer taking this all down. I trust Venia Pomerantz told you the whole story?"

"He did."

"So you know exactly how desperate this mission is and you know my timetable. Do I tell Eichmann we have a deal or not?"

"Well, Mister Brand, that could take some time."

"What do you mean that could take some time? Twelve thousand Jews a day are going to the ovens in Auschwitz-Birkenau. Yes or no?"

"Well —"

"*Yes or no, Mister Sharett?*"

"As I said, that could take some time."

"Bullshit doubletalk, Mister Sharett, and you know it. Tell my 'hosts' to cut me loose and I'll be on my way back to Istanbul. Let those deaths be on your head, not mine."

"I'm afraid that can't happen, Mister Brand. You won't be able to return north, you'll have to go south."

1954

JERUSALEM DISTRICT COURT

COURTROOM ONE

34

Pandemonium erupted in the courtroom when the audience heard about what had occurred at the meeting between Sharett and Joel Brand. Judge Halevi banged the gavel several times before order was restored. Tamir continued quietly.

"What was your reaction to this, Mister Brand?"

"I was completely taken aback. I shouted that Sharett was signing a death warrant for a million Jews. He said there was no other alternative. I was taken to Cairo, where I was confined in a villa which was nothing more than a private prison. I remember listening to a report about my mission on the BBC, which was transmitted to Cairo."

"When was that?"

"June, 1944."

"Mister Brand, I am going to show you a full transcript of a broadcast made June 20, 1944, over the BBC. I ask whether this refreshes your recollection as to what you heard?"

Tamir showed the witness the document. Brand paled momentarily, then practically shouted, "That's it! That's exactly what they said!"

"Defense requests this transcript be admitted into evidence," Tamir said, passing a copy of the transcript to the judge and one to the prosecution.

The judge read the small script:

"'Two emissaries of the Hungarian government arrived in Turkey to present the allied representatives with an offer from the Hungarian government: all Jews remaining alive in Hungary will receive exit permits in return for a certain quantity of medical supplies and transport trucks from England and America. The promise was also made that these materials would not be used on the western front.

"'At this time, the names of the emissaries cannot be revealed. Authoritative British circles consider this offer as a crude attempt to weaken the allies, whose sympathy for the Hungarian Jews is well known, and to create dissension among the allies. There is not the slightest possibility that the British and American governments will agree to enter into any negotiations of this sort, although they would like to help the Hungarian Jews.'"

The judge turned to Brand. "Is this report accurate, sir?"

"Absolutely not, Your Honor. The offer was made by the Germans, not the Hungarians, and I was the only emissary sent out to the world Jews. I was never sent to the Allies. We specifically voted to keep the news away from the British."

"Did the British help the Hungarian Jews as they stated they wanted to do, Mister Brand?" the Judge asked.

"No, Your Honor, to the contrary. By the time this transcript was broadcast I had been in British custody for over two weeks. The English knew every detail of the offer. By that time, it was too late to do anything."

"Mister Tell, have you any objection to my admitting this document into evidence?"

"Yes, Your Honor. The document is hearsay and irrelevant."

"Mister Tamir?"

"Withdraw the request to admit the document."

The judge permitted himself a small smile. There was no way he intended to forget what the British had done.

"Mister Brand," Tamir continued, "did anything unusual happen during the English interrogation in Cairo?"

"Yes. After the tenth day, I went on a hunger strike. On the seventeenth day of that strike, a British officer handed me a note from Avriel, who urged me not to make difficulties. The note said everything was being done to insure the success of my mission."

"Did you write to the Jewish Agency while you were being held in Cairo?"

"Yes."

"Did you keep a copy of the letter you wrote?"

"I did." Brand extracted a piece of paper which he passed via the bailiff to the Judge. Brand continued, "I wasn't a prisoner in the sense that I was held behind bars. It was a house arrest. I could meet with Jewish Agency leaders. I did so on at least ten occasions, after which I was driven back to the villa where I was housed."

"How long did the British hold you in Cairo?"

"Four-and-a-half months. Then they said I could go back to Palestine, but not to Hungary."

"What happened when you arrived in Israel?"

"It was mid-October by that time. I immediately tried to reach Doctor Weizmann. I tried, time after time, to make an appointment with him. I left letter after letter in his office. I came by at least twice a week, sometimes waiting hours at a time. With each letter I sent, I begged him to help those Jews in Hungary who were still alive. I enclosed a full copy of Eichmann's offer. I pointed out that although we had lost a hundred thousand Jews by that time, Eichmann would still most likely accept the deal and we could bring the last surviving Jews out of the death camps."

Chaim Cohen was on his feet. Smoothly, urbanely, he stated, "Your Honor, I move to strike the last part of his testimony. These are all fabrications of a deranged mind. I challenge the witness to come forth with so much as one shred of paper showing he tried to send any such letters."

"You know that's a lie!" Brand exploded. "The originals of those documents were stolen from me a few days ago. I told Mister Tell they had mysteriously disappeared and he said he'd try and help me find them."

"Pity," Cohen continued. "Still, Your Honor, the motion to strike stands. Without documentary corroboration, there is nothing to implicate the Jewish Agency."

"I think I can solve the problem, Your Honor," Tamir said. He opened one of his three-hole trial notebooks and extracted six pieces of paper. Then he opened another notebook and took out a seventh. He passed them to opposing counsel. "Mister Brand allowed me to make photostats of all of the documents he describes, before they disappeared. I have them available to present to the Court. I ask that they be marked, identified, and admitted into evidence with the same force and effect as though they were the originals."

Tell was immediately on his feet, blazing, "Your Honor, I object to the introduction of any of these documents. I ask again that Mister Tamir be cited for gross misconduct. Since Mister Brand was called as a government witness, Mister Tamir committed an unethical act by meeting with Brand in the first place. Now he compounds that offense by filching documents from the witness."

"He did not filch anything from me," Brand said angrily. "I voluntarily gave them to him to copy."

"Gentlemen, gentlemen," the Court admonished. "I have already passed on the issue of the propriety of Mr. Tamir's acts in speaking with the witness prior to the State listing him as a witness three days ago. The Court will not revisit that issue. May I see those documents, please?" It took only a moment before Judge Halevi said, "These documents are admitted as Defendant's next in order. Continue your questions, Mr. Tamir."

"Did you ever hear back from Doctor Weizmann?"

"Yes, more than two months later."

"I would like to read the seventh document into the record, Your Honor."

"Objection. Document speaks for itself," from the prosecution.

"Overruled. You may read this document into the record, Mister Tamir."

"'Rehovoth, 29 December 1944. To Mister Joel Brand, Tel Aviv. Dear Mister Brand: I beg you to forgive me for having delayed in answering your letter. As you may have seen from the press, I have been traveling a good deal and generally did not have a free moment since my arrival here. I have read both your letter and your memorandum and shall be happy to see you some time the week after next, about the tenth of January. My secretary, Miss Itin, will get in touch with you to set up an appointment. With kind regards. Yours very sincerely, Chaim Weizmann.'"

"Mister Brand, did you find anything unusual about this reply?"

"Yes, Mister Tamir. During that time, more than a thousand Jews a day were being butchered. The Jewish Agency had known about the Eichmann offer for at least half a year. The killings were going on. And Doctor Weizmann, after ignoring my pleas for more than two months, put me off for another twelve days, letting thousands more Jews go to their deaths. It was the last straw."

On redirect examination, the prosecution attempted to undermine Joel Brand's testimony by asking whether it was not true that Brand had publicly condemned the government of Israel on several occasions.

"That is absolutely true, Mister Tell," Brand responded. "I have cursed Jewry's official leaders ever since Doctor Weizmann's letter. If you had lived through Avriel's betrayal, Barlas' betrayal, Sharett's betrayal, and this final insulting letter from Chaim Weizmann, I suggest you would feel exactly the same way I do."

"Mister Brand," Judge Halevi said, "the Court is going to use its discretion to question you for a few moments. Both counsel have suggested there was foul play in obtaining your presence here, and there exists the possibility of highly unethical conduct. I remind you that you are still under oath. Sir, has either the prosecution or the defense attempted in any way to influence what you were going to say in Court?"

"Yes, Sir."

"Which side was that?"

"The State, Your Honor."

"In what way?"

"Object!"

"Sit down, Mister Tell, and remain seated until I ask for your comments! Mister Brand, how did the State attempt to influence you?"

"I was approached by Mister Sharett's aides. They warned me that if I knew what was good for me, I'd best not mention Sharett or Chaim Weizmann at all. I was asked to falsify my testimony and perjure myself.

When I refused to give in to their demands, they said I could be imprisoned and committed to an asylum if I persisted in giving testimony."

"Did Mister Tell or Mister Cohen participate in these threats, Mister Brand?"

"No, Your Honor, not to my knowledge."

"Did you ever mention either to Mister Tell, Mister Cohen, or Mister Tamir that you had been threatened?"

"Only to Mister Tamir."

"What was his response, Mister Brand?"

"He said that if I told the whole truth and only the truth, I would have much less to remember. He asked me to testify, but he said that whatever I elected to say was a matter between me and my conscience."

"Gentlemen," the Court said, "I find no evidence sufficient to implicate any of you in wrongdoing. However, I have just been advised that I am being sent as the official delegate of the Israeli Judiciary to the World Judicial Conference in The Hague. This pretty much takes the prosecution's request for a continuance out of my hands. Trial is continued to June 1, 1954. The Court is in recess to that time. I wish each of you a Happy Shavuot, *Chag Sameach*."

35

Ruth pushed open the door to Tamir's office and gasped. Files were strewn all over the floor, steel case cabinets had been upended; deep gouges, apparently made by a claw hammer, striped her husband's desk. Chair legs lay broken and ink saturated and soiled the carpets, upholstery, and many of the files.

Whoever had done this had ripped Samuel's diplomas from their frames and printed ugly slogans in black and red throughout to offices – "Only thus, you Irgun asshole!," "Shame on you, you courtroom shit!" They had painted a crude, black swastika on the inside entry door, and oil-soaked rags had been spread throughout the suite. The smell of wet paint and oil filled the room.

Her hands shook as she phoned her husband. After speaking with him, she called the local police station and spoke at length with the watch commander. He indicated it was a holiday and he was sorry but he couldn't send an investigator until the following day.

"Sergeant," Ruth said, her voice dangerously low-pitched, "this is getting us nowhere. I demand to speak to your captain immediately."

"I'm sorry, ma'am, but he won't be back until nine o'clock tomorrow morning."

"Very well, then. I will remain here for another half hour. If, by that time, an inspector has not come to take a report and make a full inspection and inventory of this office suite, I will telephone two people. I will call my friend, the Minister of Justice, at his home, and I will call my husband's mother, Senator Katznelson. You may rest assured that if I do so, your next assignment will be guarding the entryway to Gaza City or the entryway to King Solomon's Caves in the Negev Desert. Do I make myself clear?"

Within half an hour, two inspectors, suitably apologetic and attentive, had thoroughly checked out the suite and made copious notes.

"Do you intend to furnish us with protection and to investigate this serious crime further?" Ruth asked. When the two officers ducked these questions, Ruth lost her patience and snapped, "Cut the doubletalk. Exactly what do you intend to do?"

"We intend to process the report in accordance with standard operating procedure," one of the officers remarked.

"Which means precisely what?" Ruth had not been married to a trial lawyer for the past seven years without learning something about how bureaucracy worked.

"That depends on what the captain says, ma'am."

"Gentlemen, I'm going to cut this conversation short. I want you to write in your report that the offices of Senator Katznelson's son were vandalized and his furniture destroyed. I want you to write in your report that my husband, Samuel Tamir, would be very concerned if the police were not doing their job correctly, and he would not hesitate to apply to the courts for damages, something I don't think would sit well with the Minister of Justice. I intend to pick up a copy of your report at five o'clock this afternoon and make damned well sure that it is one hundred percent accurate. I don't know if you inspectors have been paying much attention to the daily newspapers, but I can tell you my husband has been on the front page for the last several weeks and the papers will be happier than ever to print a copy of your report. Do I make myself clear?"

"Are you threatening us, Mrs. Tamir?" the older of the two officers asked, chewing his lip rapidly.

"Not at all, Inspector." She smiled sweetly. "I'm telling you what I intend to do."

Within hours, Samuel had gathered his staff together.

"Thank God, we've gotten most of the documents we needed into evidence, and a lot of the documents have been stored at my parents' home," he said. "I suggest we go through everything having to do with the Kasztner file and inventory what's been destroyed and what's missing. We could probably get Chaim Cohen to loan us some of the documents. Neither he nor Amnon is a bad guy when it comes to this sort of thing."

Within the next two hours, Tamir's team had ascertained that about fifty critical documents were missing or destroyed.

"Unfortunately, there's nothing we can do about these documents because, for the most part, the prosecution doesn't know we've got them. Pity, 'cause they really would have helped our case."

"Uh … boss?"

"Yes, Arieh."

"Could you show me a list of the documents that are gone or destroyed?"

"Of course, for whatever good that would do."

Marinsky read the list for several moments, then turned to his associate.

"Uh … boss?"

"I'm delighted at the expansion of your vocabulary, Arieh. What pearls of wisdom do you have to add to the expression 'uh?'"

"I may have pissed you off, but then again I may not."

"Go ahead."

"Since I don't have the memory of Dov Levin, I took it upon myself to photostat a bunch of papers every night after work and take copies home."

"How many papers?"

"The whole damn file."

"Oh, really?"

"Really."

"Mister Marinsky," Tamir said, grinning broadly. "Who the hell paid for the copies?"

"The Tamir law office."

"Any reason I shouldn't fire you on the spot and sue you for the cost of the paper?"

"None, I guess. If you want to use those sheets you have, be my guest."

"Smartass," an obviously relieved Samuel Tamir said. "You're fired, you're rehired, and the cost to me of the copies you made should equal the raise I just gave you.

"And to think I even came in early to listen to this lecture," Marinsky replied. "I almost forgot, the A-G himself called just after I got in. You might want to give him a call."

Tamir gazed at the window thermometer, which registered seventy-six degrees Fahrenheit and climbing, even at this early hour.

"He said he wanted to speak with you privately if you could spare him a few minutes. Curious, I know Cohen's office number by heart. He gave me an entirely different one this morning, neither a Jerusalem nor a Tel Aviv number."

"I'll let our esteemed Attorney General stew for a little while," Tamir said. "I should attend to paying clients first."

By the time Tamir dialed the number Arieh had given him, it was ten o'clock and eighty-nine degrees. Chaim Cohen answered the phone on the second ring. "Sam?"

"Here."

"Thanks for calling back. You're no doubt aware you've dialed a number in Caesaria?"

"I hadn't given it a thought one way or the other."

"I wanted to express my sympathy on your misfortune, Sam. I swear to you that what happened had nothing to do with the Kasztner trial."

Yeah, right, Tamir thought.

"Listen, my friend," Cohen said. "A telephone is no place to discuss these kinds of matters. I was wondering if you could see me some time today, in private."

"Where shall we meet?"

"You name it."

"Petah Tikvah? Halfway between Jerusalem and Caesaria. *Ema Sarah* off Tel Aviv Road, two hours from now?" Tamir rejoined. "As they say in the American cinema, 'High noon at the O.K. Corral.'"

There was a brief, appreciative chuckle at the other end of the line. "Thanks, Sam."

Ema Sarah's was a square, whitewashed building set back some fifty feet from the main Tel Aviv-Jerusalem Road. Its thick adobe walls kept the place bearable in the hundred degree heat, and there was a lovely green arbor in back, where people came from miles around to dine in the cool of the evening.

Sam had never seen Chaim Cohen in anything but an expensive business suit or his black silk gown, so he was somewhat surprised to see the Attorney General in a pair of khaki pants, a lightweight, open-necked sport shirt, and a safari hat. The man must have weighed close to two hundred fifty pounds and he was perspiring profusely, but he gave Tamir a hearty smile and a firm handshake.

As they entered the restaurant, a heavyset, motherly-looking woman in late middle age showed them to a quiet booth toward the back of the room. Without waiting for them to order, she brought them a carafe of red wine and two large glasses.

"*L'Chaim!*" the Attorney General toasted. "No reflection on my name," he said, grinning. Tamir had not often seen the large man smile. The defense lawyer returned the toast.

The woman, Mother Sarah, returned with a basket of freshly baked hot pita bread and a saucer of yogurt.

"No question you've kicked Amnon and me around the courtroom the last couple of months," Cohen said. "He wasn't expecting it and, to tell you the truth, neither was I. The press is celebrating the number of papers they're selling."

Tamir picked up a half-round of pita, filled the pocket with yogurt, and started munching. He closed his eyes momentarily, savoring the first tart bite. "Thanks for the compliment, Chaim, but I'd hardly say the trial is over."

Cohen scratched at his cheek, took out a handkerchief, and wiped off the top of his bald head. "You know, Sam, everyone thinks being the Attorney General is a great honor: riding around the country in a big car, addressing B'nai B'rith and Hadassah conventions, flying to Europe for conferences. Sounds wonderful, but it's not all it's advertised to be.

"Take your case, for example. You're in the middle of a trial against the State. It's anything but your typical criminal trial, but it's still no big deal."

Ema Sarah set a giant tray loaded with a huge tureen of vegetable soup, a hearty lamb-and-potato stew, a bowl full of fried potatoes, and another filled with Greek salad, on the table. Tamir ladled out a bowl of soup for Cohen and one for himself.

"Interesting, Chaim. That's the first time I've heard you refer to it as the Kasztner trial. Up 'til now, we've thought of it as the State of Israel versus Malchiel Greenwald. More recently, I've begun to think of it as Greenwald versus the State of Israel."

They stopped talking long enough to dive into their bowls of soup. Chaim Cohen slurped as he ate, and some of the hot, tasty liquid spilled on his shirt front. Samuel dipped his still-warm pita bread into his soup, draining the broth so that when he spooned it, he got a spoonful of fresh vegetables.

The conversation was not going as Cohen had hoped. He filled his soup bowl again and breathed deeply to allow him to expand his capacity for more food. "Actually, Sam, that's not why I asked you to come here."

By this time, Tamir had loaded his own plate with lamb stew and signaled *Ema* Sarah to bring more pita bread. "Why, then?"

"The State wants to cut a deal with you."

"On the Kasztner case?"

"And on the damages at your office."

"A little late to make an offer, isn't it, Chaim?"

"You of all people know it's never too late."

Tamir smiled at that statement. "Better than the deal that's on the table now?"

"Significantly better." Cohen ladled a large helping of lamb stew onto his plate and grabbed a handful of fried potatoes. He ate rapidly and spoke with his mouth half full. "Much better indeed. I'll speak to you about it after lunch and in private, if you don't mind."

"Fine with me."

Afterward, they went back out to the gravel parking lot. The temperature was well over a hundred degrees and their full bellies made the heat even more unbearable.

"Follow me," Cohen said. "A friend is letting us use his place this afternoon."

Ten minutes later, they arrived at a small, elegant villa. The flat had the latest in American air conditioning and the temperature stood at a comfortable seventy-five. Cohen showed his guest to the library, where the windows were covered with heavy curtains. They sat in plush upholstered rocking chairs. Cohen poured a snifter of brandy for himself. Tamir declined the brandy, but accepted a bottle of Pellegrino water.

"All right, Chaim, what's your deal?"

"Rather direct, aren't you?"

"I don't need to drag out the niceties."

"Very well, I'll be equally direct. We exonerate Greenwald, dismiss the criminal complaint with prejudice, and double his pension. Although we're not prepared to admit to any liability for what happened to you, the State will reimburse the insurance company every cent they've laid out for repair and replacement of your office."

"Interesting, Chaim. Very tempting. I trust the State will insist on a confidentiality clause?"

"Absolutely. With the tightest penalty provisions."

"And the newspapers will allow the story simply to fade away?"

"Correct."

"How much time will you give me to respond?"

"All the time you need, Sam. How much time do you think you'll need?"

"About ten seconds."

The Attorney General colored slightly, but remained outwardly calm. He felt a great ball of gas well up inside him. "I'm listening."

"I thank you and the State for your offer, Chaim, which is indeed generous. It's the most attractive offer I've had in my professional career. As to the Kasztner case, I will recommend in the strongest possible terms that Mister Greenwald decline your offer."

"I appreciate your candor, Sam," Cohen said, the smile now gone from his face. "I don't know that I consider your response to be in your client's best interests, but that is his decision and yours, not mine. So we do battle to the end?"

"It looks that way, Mister Attorney General."

"Very well. I respect you as an adversary. My comments at lunch were sincere."

"You'll be taking over from Amnon?"

"Yes."

Tamir smiled. "In that case, it really is Greenwald versus the State of Israel."

"Or vice versa," Cohen said smoothly. "A toast between warriors before the final battle is joined?" he said, handing Tamir another bottle of mineral water.

"*L'chaim*, Mister Attorney General," Tamir said. "Whatever happens, I wish you a long and healthy life."

36

If the government had hoped to stem the press's interest in the case, it was obvious from the packed courtroom when the trial resumed that its efforts had been unsuccessful.

"Good morning, gentlemen," Judge Halevi said. "I notice that Mr. Tell is absent this morning. Is there some reason for that?"

"There is, Your Honor," Chaim Cohen responded. "Due to the press of business, Mr. Tell is unable to continue with this case. The Attorney General has decided to take over the prosecution on the State's behalf."

"Very well, Mister Cohen. You may proceed."

"Thank you, Your Honor. The prosecution calls Ehud Avriel as its final witness."

Avriel, a middle-aged man with dark hair and piercing brown eyes, readily admitted he had met Joel Brand in Istanbul and ridden with him to the Syrian border. However, he vigorously denied that either he or the Jewish Agency had advised the British of Brand's mission. He confirmed that even after the English had detained him, Brand was allowed to speak freely with executives of the Jewish Agency.

Tamir's cross-examination struck hard rock.

"Joel Brand said you warned him what to do if the British arrested him, an hour before the train crossed the Syrian border."

"That's correct, Mister Tamir."

"Why would you do such a thing if you had no knowledge that the British knew of Brand's mission?"

"First, it was standard procedure that we warn any incoming Jew of possible British arrest. In your own experience as an Irgun detainee, Mister Tamir, you know how many refugees the English sent back to Cyprus after the war. Second, the British carefully screened passports. Joel Brand was traveling with a German passport, not the passport of *a* belligerent nation, but the passport of *the* belligerent nation. What explanation could he give that the one country determined to rid itself of all Jews had somehow given him a German diplomatic passport? Third, there was always the possibility that the Germans themselves leaked the nature of Brand's mission to the English through intermediaries."

Everywhere Tamir poked and prodded for a weakness, he could find none. Cohen clearly had prepared Avriel for the toughest cross-examination Tamir was able to mount. What was worse, where Brand had been emotional and Kasztner had been skittish, Avriel looked everyone in the eye, the judge, lawyers, and the press alike. He made no facial gestures of any kind. He answered simply, directly, without the slightest hint of doubletalk or guile. And his testimony was deadly.

On redirect examination, Avriel answered, over Tamir's objection, that Kasztner had a spotless reputation among the rescuers. "He was known as the hardest working, most effective rescuer we had."

Cohen played his hand very well, anticipating any subsequent cross examination. "Mister Avriel, didn't you find it offensive that Kasztner was consorting with the enemy?"

"Mister Cohen, I'd hardly call it 'consorting.' It was more like a lawyer who represents an unpopular client, but who argues so persuasively that the court believes him. Would you accuse such a lawyer of 'consorting' with the court? You must not forget, Mister Cohen, that at that time and in that place, the Germans were judge, jury, and executioner. The fact that they even listened to Kasztner at all was a miracle."

"Mister Avriel, are you aware of the article written and distributed by Mister Greenwald?"

"I am, Sir."

"What was your reaction to that article?"

"At first I was shocked. It completely departed from my personal knowledge of Doctor Kasztner's reputation."

"Did you believe any part of Mister Greenwald's article could be true?"

The witness shifted in his chair uncomfortably. "Let me say this, Mister Cohen. I consider myself a balanced man, willing to give a fair hearing to anyone. I would be the first to agree that he doesn't develop deep friendships. I was willing to consider possible adverse things he might have done. I was willing to listen to all the evidence."

"Did you question in your own mind whether Doctor Kasztner could have done these horrid things of which Mister Greenwald accused him?"

"I did."

"What do you feel today?"

"I don't really know. It's hard to say. Do I believe the article? Not without more proof. Am I more cautious in my dealings with Doctor Kasztner? Absolutely. If for some reason, he is guilty of what Mister Greenwald says in his newsletter, then I would certainly not want to associate with such a man."

Tamir continued. "Mister Avriel," he said, extracting a document from the exhibit pile. "I show you documents that have been admitted into evidence demonstrating that Doctor Kasztner gave affidavits favorable to Kurt Becher after the war."

"Yes, I have seen them, Mister Tamir."

"Do these affidavits change your opinion of Doctor Kasztner?"

"Not at all, Mister Tamir. If Kurt Becher had truly been responsible for slowing down the carnage, for trading Jews to Kasztner for whatever reason, for directly participating in the salvation of two thousand Jews, I, too, would have written such an affidavit. Not to have done so would have been an affront to the humanity and moral forgiveness of which we Jews have always been proud."

Tamir conferred briefly with Arieh Marinsky, who said took a sip of water, then said quietly to his senior associate, "Quit now, before you dig yourself any deeper."

"No further questions, Your Honor," Tamir said.

Ehud Avriel left the courtroom, unbowed, and unbloodied.

"Well, you can't win every battle," Tamir told his associates. "It's an entirely different war with Chaim Cohen on the other side. He rolls with the punches, he doesn't come unglued like Tell. He prepares his witnesses thoroughly, as each of you saw today."

"You think he'll have Kasztner prepared?" Dan asked.

"To the degree the good doctor can be prepared," Tamir responded, smiling. "Once an animal has attacked you and drawn serious blood, you approach that animal with far more caution the next time around."

37

Tamir riffled through a stack of papers for a few moments, the staccato sound serving as the drumroll before the opening notes of a grand symphony. "Time for a little drama," he whispered to Ruth. The press, aware that something momentous was about to occur, suddenly listened with great interest as Tamir, questioning his next witness, Professor Benjamin Aktzin, focused the spotlight on Hungary.

"Did the Wehrmacht come into Hungary in large numbers?"

"No, Mister Tamir. The war was going badly on both the Eastern and Western fronts. Hungary was very much a backwater, and the Germans could spare only a few thousand troops there." The witness coughed, tugged at his tie, took a deep breath, and continued. "The anti-Nazi Hungarians and the two hundred fifty thousand Jews in Budapest alone would have easily been able to overcome this token force. The Nazis were concerned with how they'd be able to capture and deport eight hundred thousand Jews to Auschwitz with only one hundred fifty S.S. foremen and five thousand Hungarian gendarmes."

"Yet the Germans were able to incinerate the eight hundred thousand?"

The learned historian sat back for a moment, as though thinking of his answer. The court was so silent that the loudest sound in the room was clock ticking. When he answered, his voice measured and quiet, his words rang throughout the courtroom. "Unfortunately, yes, Mister Tamir."

"How could that have happened, Professor?"

"The only possible way of getting Hungary's Jews to Auschwitz on schedule was to keep them ignorant of their fate and to do everything possible to spread the delusion among them that the Germans in Admiral Horthy's Hungary had no intent to murder them."

The witness looked down at his shoes for a moment, as if thinking through his answer, then continued, the drama belied by the measured, dry cadence of his voice. "The S.S. Colonels did not want a repetition of the Warsaw Ghetto uprising, where an incredibly small number of Jews had stood with pistols and clubs and broken bottles in their hands, against German tanks, cannon, machine guns, and the Luftwaffe, and miraculously held the Germans at bay for twenty-seven days.

"Things were not the same a year later in Budapest. The Germans couldn't afford another Warsaw Ghetto situation. They had no armored divisions to spare for battling Jews. That Nazis had suffered major defeats in Stalingrad and in Africa, the Allies were in Italy, Tito's forces were not far from Hungary's borders, and British and American planes were dropping bombs on Germany day and night."

Professor Aktzin rose from his chair, scratched the top of his head, then patted the witness chair and sat down again. "It was essential to the Germans that no word get out about the new Zyklon-B death chambers waiting in Auschwitz. The eight hundred thousand Jews must be speeded to their end, filled with the delusion that pleasant employment lay before them in various farming and industrial centers. The single most important strategy was that the Germans' true intention be hidden from the Jews."

"Was there another reason things had to be kept so secret?"

The witness smiled ironically before he answered. When he spoke, his voice was a trifle louder than it had been before. "Yes, Mister Tamir. Unlike Poland, Hungary was not a German territory. It was a semi-independent country that housed five neutral embassies, a Papal delegate, and a special mission of the International Red Cross. All eyes were watching what was going on. There were almost a million Jews in Hungary who had not been starved or tortured. Indeed," he continued, reaching into his breast pocket and extracting a single sheet of paper, "a group of Budapest Jews printed and distributed this leaflet."

Tamir took the piece of paper from Professor Aktzin and read the words out loud with no interruption:

"Fellow Hungarians: In the last hours of our tragedy, we, the Hungarian Jews, ask for help from you, our Hungarian Christian brothers and Sisters. We turn to you with whom we have shared good and bad in the Land which holds the graves of our ancestors.

"Death trains are leaving from every part of the country. A half million persons have been deported: old, young, sick, babies, pregnant women, cripples, all beaten and driven into freight cars. They do not ride off to work but to annihilation. The Christians of Hungary have no idea what is going on, There is no mention of atrocities in the press.

"Friends, should this appeal for our lives be in vain, we ask only one thing: spare us the horrors of deportation and end our suffering here, so at least we can be buried in our native land."

Tamir continued. "Was this handbill distributed widely, Professor Aktzin?"

"We have no records of how many of these were printed. We do know that the Nazis considered its publication to be a crime. They arrested those responsible for the printing and tortured and executed them."

Suddenly, there was a loud moan in the courtroom. Malchiel Greenwald, who up to this time had been a silent, orderly observer of the proceedings, rose from his seat and started banging his fists against his forehead. He swayed back and forth, shouting incomprehensible utterances, and Judge Halevi's pleas for order were in vain.

The judge banged his gavel down again and again. Finally, he addressed the bailiff.

"Mister Bailiff, would you please remove Mister Greenwald from the courtroom? Obviously something serious has caused him to lose control, but this Court must proceed in an orderly manner. Miss Greenwald," he said, turning to Greenwald's daughter, who had put her arms around her father. "Could you please assist your father and try to find out what is wrong?"

Ariana nodded her head and, in the bailiff's company, gently escorted the old man out the door. She returned to the courtroom momentarily. There was hurried whispering between Ariana and Tamir.

When order had been restored, the judge, more concerned than angry, said "Counsel, I could not hold Mister Greenwald in contempt. Do you know why your client committed this outburst in the middle of court proceedings? Is he ill? If this trial has been too much for him, perhaps counsel might wish to come into chambers and discuss this?"

"No, Your Honor," Tamir said quietly. "There is no reason to stop the trial although, had I known about it earlier, I would have requested that Mister Greenwald absent himself from this part of the testimony."

"Why is that, counsel? Miss Greenwald, do you have something to say which might shed some light on this?" the court asked. "I note you were standing and trying to signal the court."

"Yes, thank you, Your Honor," Ariana said. "I apologize to the court for my father's outburst, but it could not be helped. You see, Your Honor, there were three men in particular who were caught in connection with the publication of this letter. They were not only brutally tortured, but they were executed in a slow, particularly horrendous manner. They were Rabbi Fabian Herschkowitz, Rabbi Miklas Pennes, and the Director of the Jewish Museum in Budapest, Professor Phillip Greenwald."

"Greenwald?" the court said. "Was he related to …?"

"He was, Your Honor. He was my father's only brother, his baby brother."

"Professor Aktzin, is it true that the Joint Distribution Committee and the Jewish Agency suppressed the news of the extermination in the United States through 1944?"

"Yes," the scholar replied. Tamir noticed that a thin sheen of perspiration made Professor Aktzin's forehead glisten.

"Why was it so critically important to the Germans that what they had in store for the Hungarian Jews be kept secret?"

"The Jews of Budapest were well-connected in the spring of nineteen forty-four. There was an active Jewish Agency Relief Committee functioning in Hungary at the time."

"Who was the head of that committee?"

"Doctor Rudolf Kasztner."

"Do you have an opinion, Professor Aktzin, as to whether or not the Jewish Agency Relief Committee in Hungary aided the Germans in keeping secret the plans to round up the Jews of Hungary and ship them to Auschwitz for extermination?"

"I do."

"What is your opinion?"

Chaim Cohen immediately stood. "Objection, Your Honor. Any opinion by this witness would be based on hearsay."

Tamir rose to respond, but the Judge motioned him to sit down. "Gentlemen," Judge Halevi said, "while the Court is cognizant of the witness' vast and extraordinary background, the moral force of his integrity, his knowledge, and his unassailable credibility, we are dealing with a very specific alleged wrong and a very specific set of facts and circumstances. While we have all heard an almost Biblical account of our people's greatest tragedy in history, it is not relevant to these specific facts and circumstances. Accordingly, Professor Aktzin's testimony, except the statement that the Jewish Agency refrained from publishing news about the Jewish massacre in the American press, will be stricken."

Samuel Tamir turned white with shock. For one of the few times in his life, Tamir had attempted to play politics by bringing forth a known entity, and an expensive one. And it had backfired in his face. The defense lawyer sat heavily in his chair. He was thinking very hard and very fast. Perhaps, just perhaps, there might be a way to get Professor Aktzin's testimony in, but not just yet.

"Your Honor," he said, "Might the defense ask that the objection be sustained without prejudice, so that if the defense presents legally admissible evidence that supports Professor Aktzin's opinion the Court would be willing to revisit and reconsider its ruling?"

"That's a fair request, Mister Tamir. Objection sustained without prejudice." The court stands adjourned until tomorrow."

MAY 1944

CLUJ-KOLOZSVÁR-

KLOIZNBURG

HUNGARY

Three miles from the Romanian Frontier

38

THURSDAY, 18 MAY 1944, 11:00 P.M.
FELEAC HILL

Nine of them gathered in Emil Haţieganu's home. The sixty-five year-old former Minister of Labor and Social Security in the Mironescu government had retired from political life after his failed protest against the cession of Northern Transylvania to Hungary. Although he'd remained in quiet repose during the war years, he made no secret that he was alarmed by the recent concentration of Cluj's Jews into the Iris ghetto during the past month.

The renowned Romanian painter and journalist, Raoul Şorban, half Haţieganu's age, had fled Cluj for London after being held in custody by Hungarian authorities from March to October 1942. But now, back in favor and longing for his homeland, he'd driven two hundred seventy-eight miles from the capital to Cluj, a ten-hour trip, in his six-year-old Renault Juvaquatre, for this meeting earlier in the week, and had been ensconced in a small apartment adjacent to the older man's residence for the past two nights.

Four Jewish partisans, one each from the High Tatras in Poland, from Budapest, from Belgrade, and from Bucharest, had arrived five hours before, as had a Turkish Jew from Istanbul and an Irgunik from Palestine. The youngest of the group, barely out of his teens and known only as Alexandru, had joined the rest an hour ago.

After a late dinner, Şorban tapped lightly on a wineglass and addressed the gathering. "Gentlemen, the Nazis have tightened the noose and they're acting like it's Poland all over again."

"There are significant differences," the partisan from Yugoslavia, Kulic, said. "They've lost the Ploeşti oilfields, the Soviets are knocking at the door, and Broz has been kicking the shit out of them from our end. Gabor," he said, turning to the Hungarian, "you've heard the details of the Eichmann deal?"

"I have," the group's mole at the Hungarian Jewish Rescue Agency, a clerk in Komoly's office, said. "The *boches* are running short on a lot of things, including the manpower necessary to bring off this latest threat against our people."

"Add to that," Haţieganu said, "Romania has become disgusted with our present 'allies.' They haven't paid for the grain, the oil, or anything else they've 'bought' from us in the last year. Antonescu's government is skating on very thin ice and talk in the low level bureaucracy is that King Michael's about to mount a coup and align us with Moscow. I believe the time is ripe for what we propose to do."

"Is that why you brought us here tonight, Minister Haţieganu?" This from the Polish emissary.

"It is, Pan Krakowski. Within the past two weeks, the Jews have been concentrated in the old Iris brickyard. Hauptsturmführer Wisliceny's in charge of the ghetto. The head of the *Judenrat*, the Jewish council, Doctor Fisher, is Chairman Kasztner's mentor and father-in-law. There are two hundred *Sicherheitsdienst* troops —*two hundred armed men, total* —guarding eighteen *thousand* Jews. Those Jews are living in shacks with no water, electricity, or facilities *three miles from the Romanian border. Three miles!* The Jewish Rescue Agency, which has *got* to know those numbers, is cooperating with the Nazis. It seems incredulous to me that they'd even think to do so.

"Let's say the Jews broke out of the ghetto and marched *en masse* three miles into Romania. Let's say we'd lose two hundred, maybe even five hundred, God forbid. That means more than 17,500 men, women, and children would make it across the frontier to safety in Romania. If that many from Kolozsvár made it out, think of the signal that would send to the other 750,000 Jews living in Hungary. As well-uniformed and well-armed as they are, two hundred against eighteen thousand are impossible odds, even for their S.S. I assume our *landsmen* could be supplied with enough arms to make it more than a fair fight."

"How does that explain why we're here tonight?"

Raoul Şorban took up narrative. "We're going to try a test to see if Minister Haţieganu's idea has practical applications. Six of you are resistance fighters. Alexandru's a native of Kolozsvár. He knows every hill, bush, body of water, and rock in these parts. He has several confederates between here and Romania proper. Before dawn tomorrow, each of you will meet his associates and learn just how easy —or difficult —it would be to escape and make it into Romania ..."

19 MAY 1944. 3:40 A.M.

The slight breeze ruffled the low brush on the south side of Feleac Hill. Miroslav Kulic lay on his stomach at the top of the rise, wrapped in an overcoat and muffler, a dark cap covering his blond hair, a Hungarian Gepisztoly M43 machine pistol on a leather strap within his immediate reach. For the past half hour, he'd been surveying the whole of the internment camp through a pair of J3 Colt binoculars.

Even though it was mid-May, the damp from the wet earth chilled him to the bone, but there was nothing he could do about it. Below him, at the foot of the hill, two ghetto guards, a pale glow on their helmets from the last of the waning moonlight, rifles slung over their shoulders, were sharing a cigarette and talking in low voices, the harsh, guttural German sounds, *sch* and *kuh*, drifting up the hillsides.

Alexandru, lying next to Kulic, stared angrily at the *schleuh* below him. These were *his* hills, these noncommissioned troops, S.S. Unterscharführer by their insignia, were intruders, and he would, in time, settle with them. He raised his right hand a few inches, a signal to Kulic to be patient.

Kulic gritted his teeth as the wet grass slowly soaked his clothing. Ten minutes later, a lean, hard man a decade older than Alexandru appeared, bearing a bottle of *Vişinată*, local rotgut, undoubtedly home-brewed, which he insisted on opening and sharing with Alexandru and Kulic. He was thirty minutes late, but didn't seem the least bit disturbed by this.

"It's O.K.," Alexandru remarked in a low voice, which he knew would be harder for the enemy to hear than had he been whispering, "Jan worked at the brickworks in 'thirty-nine, when Kolozsvár was still *Romanian* Cluj. He knows all of the entries and exits where the guards will least likely patrol."

Below them, the German noncoms had themselves a final laugh, then parted, heading back into the ghetto by different routes.

Jan, the man who'd joined them, waited several minutes, then whispered, "We'll go down the hill now. Stay low to the ground and remain close to the perimeter of the camp."

While Alexandru remained on the rise, Jan and Kulic rose and scrambled down the hill, Kulic holding the machine pistol close to his side. Kulic was shocked at how stiff he'd gotten just lying on the damp earth for less than an hour.

At the foot of the hill, Jan took his shoes off, tied them at the laces, hung them around his neck, then stuffed his socks in his pockets. Kulic followed his lead, turning up his trouser cuffs as far as the knee. Jan stepped a stream just outside the perimeter of the camp. Kulic was right behind him. The cold water flowing toward a larger river beyond could not have been more than a foot-and-a-half deep. The sharp gravel of a midstream island provided relief for several yards before the water became knee-deep. At last, they reached the far bank, some twenty feet across from where they'd entered.

Jan sat in the grass and put his shoes and socks back on. Kulic followed suit. Then they ran up and and over a low rise until they found themselves inside the ghetto. Hunched over, the two men shuffled along the edge of the encampment until they reached an abandoned gate that seemed to lead to nowhere. As there were no guards or anyone else in the vicinity at this hour, Jan led his ward through the gate, onto a no-man's-land between the brickworks and the larger river.

They stayed close to the banks of the *Someşul Mic,* heading south and west, until they reached the southern extremities of the city, where they met another of Alexandru's friends, an attractive, young woman, olive-skinned, wearing a headscarf, and no more than five feet tall.

"Miroslav, Ana will be your guide for the final leg of the journey. She's from one of the Gilău villages that remained Romanian after the Germans gave most of Cluj County to Hungary."

Within a very short time, Ana led him into the forests of the Turda Gorges, where, even in late spring, he saw hundreds of men, women, and children wearing everything from peasant garb to the slacks and sweaters favored by city dwellers, busily picking barely matured berries on the limitless hillsides. *How easy it would be for hundreds of people to hide from a couple hundred troops guarding Kolozsvár,* he thought.

"How far is it to Romania?" he asked her.

"You're already *in* Romania," she replied.

"But the border guards? The formalities?"

"The closest official border crossing is in Turda, eighteen miles from Cluj. The borders themselves are not clearly defined, except by the people who live in Romania or Hungary. More than four out of every five people who live southeast of Cluj are Romanians and the Hungarians know enough not to challenge us."

Less than an hour later, they reached Someşu Cald in Gilău subprovince of Romania, where a sleepy-looking, hefty woman between fifty-five and sixty, whom they located at the village prefecture, waved them out the door without even checking their papers.

❧

Back at Haţieganu's home, all six of the men who'd been led into Romania and back related similar experiences: no apparent problems exiting Cluj, limitless opportunities to hide once they'd entered the Turda Gorges, and Romanian authorities who turned a blind eye toward their arrival.

"Gabor," Haţieganu addressed the man from Budapest. "How hard would it be to let the Rescue Committee know about our experiment?"

"If it were just Komoly and me, it would be easy. Unfortunately, Kasztner's the one in charge, and he's not the easiest man to approach. He seems very much taken with his own ideas of what's right and what's wrong. He most likely has his own plans for the best way to handle this situation."

1954

JERUSALEM DISTRICT COURT

COURTROOM ONE

39

Next morning, there was a visible change in the courtroom. Doctor Kasztner, who'd been absent for more than two months, arrived looking rested and fit. Gone was the frightened, cowering man who'd left Judge Halevi's court in nervous silence at the beginning of March. This Rudolf Kasztner came to court confidently, relying on the fact that Chaim Cohen was now in command. Under Cohen's astute training, Ehud Avriel had demolished the pesky Joel Brand, and Kasztner was armed with the knowledge that Cohen had kept out Dean Aktzin's testimony.

During the next several days, Samuel Tamir, relying on Judge Halevi's promise to reconsider his ruling should the defense establish grounds for the justification of Professor Aktzin's opinion, painted a vivid tableau of nineteen forty-four Hungary, filled with living characters.

"The defense calls Jacob Freifeld."

A short man, hardly more than five feet tall, came stiffly, painfully to the stand. He seemed to be about seventy. Tamir quickly established that Freifeld had lived in Jerusalem since July 1948, that he was forty-six years old, the same as Kasztner, that he'd been born in the Ukraine, and had emigrated to Cluj in 1934.

"How long did you live in Cluj, Mr. Freifeld?"

"Ten years."

"What happened then?"

"All the Jews of Cluj were rounded up and moved into concentrated areas of the city. The gendarmes told us it was just a temporary thing."

"What did you do when you were moved?"

"I contacted a friend of mine, Hillel Danzig. We had worked together in Ukraine before we left for Hungary. I asked him what this was all about. Hillel told me the Hungarians and Germans had created a new area where they intended to move all the Jews, a large farming community called *Kenyermeze*. This was to be an all-Jewish commune where we'd elect our own officials and issue our own money. We'd be a semi-autonomous country within a country. He told me the first trains would start leaving for Kenyermeze within the week, and I should sign up for an early train, because the first people at the new farm community would get the best housing and the best jobs."

"Did you believe him?"

"I'm not sure."

"What do you mean?"

"Mister Tamir, I didn't even graduate high school, but I work very well with wood. I'd always been able to make a good living as a furniture maker. I heard several rumors while I was in Cluj, I knew Jews were unpopular in Hungary. I'd heard stories about the German death camps in Poland, and I'd received a letter from a friend in Ukraine describing the German atrocities there. Nothing I heard was encouraging."

"So why were you willing to believe the stories about Kenyermeze?"

"My friends and I relied on the Jewish Agency Rescue Committee as the spokesman for us all. It was the only voice we had. Doctor Kasztner was one of ours. He had come from Cluj. We were proud that he'd risen through the ranks."

"Were you present when the first train left for Kenyermeze?"

"Not when the train actually left, but the night before. ..."

LATE MAY 1944

CLUJ-KOLOZSVÁR-KLOIZNBURG

HUNGARY

40

The meeting hall in the Kolozsvár Ghetto was filled to bursting on the evening of May 28, 1944. The walls were lined with huge black-and-white photographs of lush fields of wheat flanked by sunflowers, with obviously happy farmers in yarmulkes and *payess* — earlocks — waving at the photographer from the seats of modern tractors in the foreground. There were numerous shots of a modern synagogue, wide streets, cafés, and well-equipped game rooms and gyms, all filled with smiling, waving Jews. Had one taken the time to look carefully at the greatly enlarged pictures, one might have noticed that the village looked remarkably— *exactly*—like a place nearly three hundred miles to the west, a place forty miles north of Prague called Theresienstadt. As for the lush fields, those photos had been taken in central Turkey, with pictures of happy farmers in *Palestine* superimposed on the Turkish fields.

The celebration had started at seven in the evening with a huge and lavish buffet dinner of all the old favorites: roast brisket of beef, potato *latkes*, sweet-and-sour stuffed cabbage, as well as copious amounts of wine, *schnapps*, and *slivovitz* to lubricate the evening. A few S.S. officers, present when the festivities started, left within an hour or so.

Professor Joszef Fisher, head of the *Judenrat*, wore his full finery, including award medals from Cluj County. A number of Jewish representatives, including Doctor Rudolf Kasztner, Chairman of the Hungarian

Jewish Rescue Committee, had come down from Budapest with small gifts for those who were fortunate enough to be going to be on the first train to Kenyermeze the following morning.

Thirty-five year-old master carpenter Jacob Freifeld was part of the crowd in the meeting hall that evening. Early on, he recognized Hillel Danzig, a journalist he'd met a few times when they'd worked together on Zionist projects in Cluj. Now, Danzig had been elevated to a position on the Rescue Committee, but since this was a night for a happy look into the future, Freifeld came up to the other man, greeted him, and said, "This is almost like old times, eh, Hillel? The Germans must have mellowed once they'd come to Hungary."

"It seems that way," Danzig responded briefly. "Do you mind if I excuse myself for a few moments? Doctor Kasztner's about to speak and I want to make sure I get this story for the record."

An enthusiastic, immaculately dressed Rudolf Kasztner strode to the podium. "Good evening, my friends," he began. "I do not want to interfere with your celebration in any way, so my remarks will be mercifully brief. Most of you will be starting a new life tomorrow. I simply wanted you to know that I congratulate you and wish you only the best in your new destination. Please don't forget, you must be on the station platform no later than seven tomorrow morning. The train is on an extremely tight schedule and you will not be allowed to come to the station after the train leaves. *Mazel tov!*" As hearty applause rang out, he stepped down and yielded the floor to the next speaker.

There were many more speeches and toasts that night. By one o'clock the next morning, when the party finally wound down, Freifeld, like everyone else, was exhausted.

Jacob Freifeld arose at nine the next morning. The events of the night before had left him somewhat bleary-eyed and perhaps a bit hungover, but he was curious enough about the upshot of last night's festivities to make it over to the train station by ten thirty, more than three hours after the Kenyermeze express had been scheduled to leave.

When Freifeld arrived, there were thirty people milling about. He was surprised to see about twenty S.S. men, fifty Hungarian gendarmes, and a dozen police dogs on the platform. Several piles of suitcases were stacked neatly by the terminal and blood smears appeared close to the tracks.

Freifeld suddenly felt very nervous. Baruch Kohani, one of Kasztner's assistants, and Hillel Danzig came up him. Doctor Kasztner was present on the platform as well, but stood away from the group. Kohani spoke first.

"Gentlemen, I've just received a letter written to the Jewish Agency from Dovid Levitan in Kenyermeze. Some of you probably know the family." He waved a single page at the crowd, making sure he was far enough away that no one could read the handwriting.

"'Dear Doctor Kaztner: I cannot thank you enough for arranging for us to go to Kenyermeze. My whole family is working at good jobs, we're all in good health, and we're being well cared for as we adjust to our new lives.'"

A man of forty, about medium height, with his hair slicked back asked, "Mister Kohani, what's with the stacked suitcases, the blood on the platform, and the police dogs?"

"A slight problem," Kohani answered smoothly. "We misjudged the actual number of people going from Cluj to Kenyermeze. The luggage will be sent on the next train."

"What about the police? The blood?" the man continued.

"Ah, that is regrettable indeed," Kohano said. "The police were here to make sure there was order, but in their great rush to get out of the ghetto and into the new community, several passengers fell and bloodied themselves. Fortunately, the railway doctor said they could keep boarding and they'd be treated in the hospital car on the way to Kenyermeze."

After Kohani and Doctor Kaztner departed, Friefeld remained on the platform and addressed his acquaintance, Danzig. "Hillel, is the letter Kohani read us the truth?"

"I don't know. But I suggest you see if there's room on tomorrow's train and sign up. The ones who get there first will get the best jobs and the best housing."

"What about you?"

"I'm scheduled to go next Tuesday. If you make it on time, I'll see you there."

1954

JERUSALEM DISTRICT COURT

COURTROOM ONE

41

"What happened then, Mister Freifeld?"

"When my family and I came to the platform at seven the next morning, the train was waiting, all right. So were the S.S., the gendarmes, and the police dogs. No sooner had everyone got there, the guards took our suitcases from us, we were herded into line, and were shoved, pushed, and pummeled into cattle cars, eighty of us to a car."

"How long did it take you to get to Kenyermeze?"

There was a pause as Freifeld grasped for a glass of water on the counter adjacent to the witness stand. The courtroom was so quiet that the soft whir of the slowly spinning fan was magnified until it sounded almost like a train itself. When Freifeld finally answered, it was in an almost animal growl of hatred, recalled pain, and ultimate betrayal.

"*Kenyermeze? Kenyermeze, Mister Tamir? There was no Kenyermeze. It was all a sham, a fraud! I only realized that after they slammed the door of the cattle car!*"

"Where were you taken, Mister Freifeld?"

"To Auschwitz," he answered quietly.

"Did Hillel Danzig go to Auschwitz?"

"No, of course not. He was a member of the Jewish Council, working hard with the clique, so he remained safe. My whole family, ten people, were exterminated."

Chaim Cohen wisely refrained from cross-examination. However, Judge Halevi was intensely interested in what this camp survivor had to say. He pursued his own line of questioning.

"Do you believe your friend intentionally sent you to your death and was responsible for killing your whole family?"

"As hard as it is to believe such a thing, that is what he did. They all did it – Kasztner, Kohani, the whole lot of them, in order to save themselves."

"Ultimately what happened, Mister Friefeld?"

"I escaped. I'd prefer not to go into details, Your Honor. My entire family was incinerated."

Tamir amplified the tale told by Freifeld through the testimony of the next several witnesses.

Yechiel Shmueli, a native of Cluj, now an official in an Israeli army camp, dark-haired and calm, testified that he was moved to the Cluj ghetto on May 23, 1944, that he had no knowledge at that time that Jews were being exterminated in Auschwitz, and that he did not offer any resistance when he was put on the train because he, like others, had been told they were being taken to Kenyermeze. The Jews in charge of the ghetto had addressed them as brothers and told them they would remain in Kenyermeze until the end of the war. There was no Kenyermeze. They were taken directly to Auschwitz.

Doctor Kasztner had come to Cluj and showed the Cluj Jews postcards from people he said had relocated to Kenyermeze. He told them Kenyermeze was the best hope any of them had to survive the war.

Levi Blum testified that he attended a celebration for Doctor Kasztner in Tel Aviv in nineteen forty-eight, which was organized by the people he'd rescued who'd gone to Switzerland. Everyone there was saying what a heroic Jew-rescuer Doctor Kasztner had been. When Blum couldn't stand it anymore, he jumped up and shouted, "You people are making a big mistake about Kasztner! He was a close friend of Eichmann and his Nazis. He was to blame for the Jews of Hungary going to Auschwitz! He knew what the Germans were doing to them and he kept his mouth shut!" Kasztner refused to respond and when Blum asked who sent the postcards from Kenyermeze, Kasztner said, "That's none of your business. I don't have to explain what I did."

David Rozner, a steel mill owner from Cluj, testified that when he returned to Cluj after the war, what few survivors there were wanted to lynch Rudolf Kasztner. He was the man who misled the Jews into believing that the Germans had every good intention of resettling the Jews in the fictional Kenyermeze.

The parade of witnesses continued — short, pointed, and devastating. Doctor Kasztner, who'd come into court so fresh looking and relaxed earlier that morning was now shaking, sweaty, and pasty-faced when court recessed that afternoon. He was totally alone.

42

"Gentlemen," the Court announced the following morning. "This trial has been somewhat irregular to say the least. All of the prosecution witnesses have called the defense witnesses liars, and all of the defense witnesses have called the prosecution witnesses perjurers. Defense witness Freifeld brought a new name into the picture, Hillel Danzig of the Jewish agency in Cluj. As both counsel know, Mr. Danzig is one of Israel's leading journalists. Neither side listed Mister Danzig as a witness.

"Yesterday afternoon, the Court received a totally unsolicited letter from Mister Danzig in which he states, 'I am shocked and amazed that a witness named Jacob Freifeld made mention of me and described certain alleged incidents in his testimony this morning. I categorically state that I do not know a man named Freifeld and I can remember no such incidents as he describes. I demand the right to redeem my good name.' Gentlemen, do either of you have any desire to call Mister Danzig as a witness?"

Neither lawyer responded.

"Do either of you have any objection to the Court calling Mister Danzig as its own witness?"

Neither side objected, but Tamir said, "Your Honor, I feel that since Mister Freifeld's credibility has been placed in issue, he should have the right to be present when Mister Danzig testifies and, if necessary, to subject himself to further examination"

"I think that's a good idea, counsel. Court will be in recess until this afternoon. The bailiff is directed to summon Mr. Danzig to attend at the Court's specific request."

Hillel Danzig was as short and peppery as his letter. Jacob Freifeld was also present in court. The two men glared at each other.

Judge Halevi asked Freifeld to stand. "Mister Freifeld, I remind you that you are still under oath. Is the man named Hillel Danzig whom you knew in Cluj in this courtroom?"

"He is, Your Honor," Freifeld said. He pointed directly at Danzig. "That is the Hillel Danzig I knew in Cluj."

Judge Halenvi invited Danzig to the witness box and began his own questioning. "Mister Danzig, do you know Jacob Freifeld? Can you identify him as the man you knew in Cluj?"

Danzig paused as he faced the man who accused him of helping murder his family of ten to save his own skin. He glanced sideways at Freifeld, then quickly withdrew his gaze. Judge Halevi as well as Tamir noticed that he never made eye contact with Freifeld.

"Well, Mister Danzig?" the court said, sounding a note of impatience. "Do you or do you not recognize this man?"

Danzig answered cautiously. "I never knew him in Cluj and I don't remember any such name, but now that I see him I remember him as one of the men with me in the labor camp in the Soviet Union."

"Your letter denies the truth of his testimony."

"I can only repeat what I said in my letter. Freifeld's charge that I hurried him and his family to their deaths is utterly preposterous."

"Any questions from counsel? Mister Cohen?"

"None, Your Honor."

"Mister Tamir?"

"Mister Danzig, Freifeld said you definitely told him that the trains got to Kenyermeze."

"That is a lie."

"What reason would Freifeld have to lie?"

"The circumstances under which he came to give his testimony require clarification. I don't think he decided to testify of his own free will."

"I see. What do you assume, Mister Danzig? Are you saying he was bought? That he was bribed with money?"

"I don't know."

"I put it to you that Freifeld has told these facts about Cluj and about you to his friends throughout Israel for the past six years."

"How does it happen that such talk did not reach me?"

"You have refused to hear many things, Mister Danzig."

"How dare you say that, Mr. Tamir? Are you calling me a liar?"

Tamir ignored Danzig's jibe and kept boring in on this antagonistic witness.

"Mister Danzig, were you by any chance one of the people Doctor Kasztner arranged to send to a safe place on August 6, 1944?"

"I don't know who arranged it."

"Did you leave Cluj after the trains started transporting Jews to Auschwitz, but before August 6, 1944?"

"I did."

"Where did you go when you left Cluj?"

"I went to Budapest. I had important work to do for the Jewish Agency Rescue Committee."

"Did you leave Budapest on August 6, 1944?"

"It was some time in early August, yes."

"Where did you go when you left Budapest?"

"We stopped at Bergen-Belsen for a very short time. Then we went to Geneva."

"Did the train contain regulation passenger cars?"

"It did."

"And everyone had comfortable seats?"

"We did."

"How many others were on the train with you?"

"I don't know. Over three hundred."

"Were any of Doctor Kasztner's relatives on that train?"

"I believe so."

"How many?"

"I don't know. Offhand, I'd say eighteen or twenty. Certainly no more than thirty."

"Mister Danzig, isn't it a fact that you knew you were going to a safe place?"

"Yes, Doctor Kasztner had told me as much."

"At the time you were in Cluj, did you know that people like Freifeld were being taken to a place much worse than Switzerland?"

There was an angry murmur among the representatives of the press. It started to swell as Danzig looked about, to his left and to his right. "Your Honor," he pleaded, "this really has nothing to do with the trial or this caustic assault on my reputation."

"Mister Danzig," Judge Halevi intoned impassively, "you were the one who demanded the right to come to court and vindicate your reputation. You were the one who wrote a letter condemning these proceedings. You are a sophisticated, experienced reporter, and you, as well as anyone, know that when you demand to come to court and testify, you subject yourself to cross-examination. The Court finds that the question is relevant to the issue you yourself raised, and the Court directs you to answer this very simple question. *Did you or did you not know at the time you were in Cluj in nineteen forty-four that people like Freifeld were being taken to a place much worse than Switzerland?*"

The witness hesitated, looked around, paused, then said, in a barely audible voice, "Yes, I did."

The silence in the courtroom was so profound that when Tamir dropped a small paperclip on his table, the sound reverberated around the room. He waited several seconds before he resumed his cross-examination.

"You met Kasztner when he came to Cluj, correct?"

"Yes."

"Did he tell you the Jews who were boarding the trains were going to the gas chambers of Auschwitz?"

"I don't recall."

"Mister Danzig, I put it to you that one of two mutually incon-sistent things happened: either Doctor Kasztner knew what was going to happen to the Jews and didn't tell you, or you knew what was happening to the Jews and you kept it from them. Which of these answers is true?"

"I … I … I don't know. I don't recall."

"Thank you, Mister Danzig. Nothing further."

As the trial entered its thirtieth day, the press smelled blood. And it was not Malchiel Greenwald's blood they smelled.

43

"Mr. Palgi, what is your current profession?" Tamir asked.

"I am a lieutenant colonel in the Israel Air Defense Force,"

"Did you know Hanna Senesh?"

"Yes."

"Did she parachute into Yugoslavia with you?"

"Yes. Hanna, Peretz Goldstein, and I landed in Yugoslavia in March nineteen forty-four. Our mission was to enter Hungary and bring as many Jews as possible to Romania. From there, it would be easy to get them to freedom in Turkey."

"Was it a long distance from Hungary to Romania?"

"No. From Cluj, it was less than three miles."

"What happened when you landed in Yugoslavia?"

"We found that the Germans were already in Budapest. I suggested we gather more information before we went into Hungary."

"Did Hanna agree with you?"

"No. She said that every hour we delayed was a betrayal of our mission. The rescue of Jews must begin at once. Peretz and I agreed to stay for a few days, but Hanna Senesh said goodbye and we never saw her again."

"Did you and Peretz ultimately get to Budapest?"

"We did."

"What did you do then?"

"We reported to Doctor Rudolf Kasztner, our base commander in Hungary."

"Had you known Doctor Kasztner before?"

"Yes. Peretz and I were from Cluj. Hanna Senesh was from Budapest. Doctor Kasztner had been our Zionist youth leader in Cluj."

"What happened after you made contact with Doctor Kasztner?"

"He suggested that Peretz and I come out of hiding and meet with the German Gestapo Chief Klages. He assured us we'd immediately be granted clemency and that the German and Hungarian authorities would allow us to join him in saving Jews. We trusted Doctor Kasztner implicitly and turned ourselves in, fully expecting we'd be released in a matter of a few hours."

"Did that eventuate?"

"No. We were arrested and tortured. The Germans and Hungarians told us that if we testified against Hanna Senesh we would be set free. We refused, of course. They held us in confinement for several months. In November 1944, they placed Peretz and me in a sealed cattle car with eighty others. When the train was forced onto a siding while a military train went by, I leapt from the cattle car and escaped. I never saw Peretz again."

The Attorney General rose and began his cross-exaimnation.

"Colonel Palgi, I very much regret what happened to you, as does Doctor Kasztner. Do you have any information that would show that Doctor Kasztner was not duped just like you by the Germans and Hungarians?"

Palgi considered the question for a few moments, then answered carefully. "Yes, counselor, I believe he knew exactly what he was doing and what effect it would have on us."

"What makes you say that, Colonel?"

"We were in jail for more than five months. Neither Doctor Kasztner nor anyone from the Jewish Agency visited us once during that time, nor did they provide us with any food or clothing. We wrote several letters to him and never received an answer."

"Isn't it possible that your captors simply kept the letters from him?"

"Anything is possible, Mister Cohen, but it's not bloody likely, is it? After all, Kasztner himself promised us what would happen if we turned ourselves in. You'd think he'd be the first one to know of any irregularity."

44

Summer came to Israel with a vengeance. The country broiled in its sixteenth straight day of one hundred degree temperatures.

The young, "hep" Israelis joined their American counterparts in humming "Istanbul," "Hernando's Hideway," "Mister Sandman," and "Three Coins in the Fountain." Saturday evening is celebration time around the world. Nowhere, however, is it quite the same as in Israel, whether on Tel Aviv's Dizengoff Street, Ben Yehuda Street in Jerusalem, or on the waterfront at Netanya. Israel entered its somnolent state each Friday night and exploded with a regeneration of life as soon as the sun went down twenty-four hours later.

Samuel Tamir arrived early enough at Café Mexico to get a side-walk table right on Dizengoff itself, close enough to the large floor fan to make things tolerably comfortable. He was joined momentarily by a tall, suave man of proud but indeterminate golden age, immaculately dressed in the latest western fashion.

"Rather a different Bedouin sheikh this evening," Tamir remarked, laughing. It was not the first time he'd seen Rashid so bedecked, but it never ceased to amaze him how profoundly western accouterments changed his appearance. His entire demeanor, the way he walked, the way he smiled, and the set of his face and body bespoke an entire metamorphosis.

"If I want to leer at some of your beautiful young ladies, or offer them to become one of my wives, it's best that I at least look affluent," Rashid responded. "Speaking of beauty, how is the Greenwald child?"

"Surviving. This trial and her closeness with her father have kept her going."

"But you're worried for her."

"The trial will come to an end in a very few days. Even though the man seems healthy, he's no longer young. The whole situation has put a strain on him in ways he might never fathom."

"That's true. Ah, yes, I will have Turkish coffee, please," Rashid said, nodding to a young waiter in a white apron who'd just come to their table.

"Hot tea, please, with milk," Tamir said.

"Your British years?" the Bedouin remarked.

"Some habits don't change. I see you're still able to appreciate feminine beauty with your eyes," Tamir said.

"Some habits don't change," the Arab repeated, his face crinkling into a smile. "My word, would you look at that!"

Tamir glanced over to where his friend pointed. Between the cars parked on both sides of Dizengoff and the chockablock traffic jam, everything had come to a halt. A dozen young men and women scampered over the cars, their sandaled feet leaving marks on hoods, roofs, and trunks. The drivers shouted furiously at the energetic adolescents, but it made no difference. Two policemen standing nearby simply shrugged their shoulders.

"Ah, the Israelis bring culture and western civilization to the backward Arab race," Rashid said, chuckling.

Soon, another twenty revelers, seeing the fun their comrades were having, joined the human Chinese checkers game. The policemen, now agitated, started blowing whistles, trying to unsnarl what had become the Dizengoff parking lot. It took several minutes, with Rashid and Tamir enjoying their ringside seat. Eventually, with the help of reinforcements, traffic was moving once again.

"So how goes the trial?"

"In confidence?"

"Of course."

"The State offered me everything except Kasztner's head on a platter and full restitution for my own damages and injuries."

The waiter reappeared with their drinks. When he left, Rashid said, "Confirming your original opinion that the State was behind the so-called 'accident.'"

"Absolutely."

"But that's not what you want?"

"Am I wrong to want Kasztner to be tried by the State?"

Rashid did not immediately respond. When he did, it was circuitous. "Samuel, every man starts his life believing he's on the side of good. I'm sure Doctor Kasztner believed that as vehemently as anyone else. When you're young, it's easy to know exactly what's right and what's wrong. But as you grow older, the borders of good and evil start to blur. Charged up as you are with the desire to find truth — as you define it — at any cost, this may be hard for you to comprehend.

"The real world is a place where you do what you must to survive as best you can. In Doctor Kasztner's case, he looked at reality as he perceived it in the Hungary of nineteen forty-four. I have no doubt he may have been motivated by the need for self-importance, but do you question that his first desire was to save as many Jews as he could?"

"I never thought about it one way or the other, Rashid."

"Perhaps before you come down too hard on the man, you should. Let's say he wants to save all the Jews, eight hundred thousand. Then reality takes hold. Suppose he can only save four hundred thousand, maybe a mere one hundred thousand. You know why, in the Jewish religion, you need ten men to have a *minyan*, the minimum necessary for a complete group prayer."

"Of course. In the time of the ancient city of Sodom, God told Lot that He intended to destroy the city. Lot bargained with God. 'If I can find a hundred good men, will you spare the city?' God agreed, but Lot could not find a hundred. Ultimately, Lot goaded God into a commitment that if Lot could find fifty, forty, thirty, twenty, finally ten good men in the city, Sodom wouldn't be destroyed. Since that time, recalling God's bargain, the Jews have required the same number as would have convinced God to save that ancient place. Excuse me, Rashid, but could you look me in the eye while I'm talking."

"If you want someone to look at you, haul out a mirror. As for me, how do you expect me to take my eyes off that marvelous pair of —" he cupped his hands in front of his chest and stared fixedly at the ends of his fingers — "fingernails sashaying down the street?"

Tamir blushed, then turned away. Sometimes his Arab friend was a bit too direct for the lawyer's sensitivities. A taunting female giggle surrounded him. Then she was gone in the swish of a short skirt, leaving a trail of sultry perfume behind her.

Rashid sipped his sweet, syrupy Turkish coffee again. "Let's say Kasztner bargained with the Nazi god. If he couldn't save a hundred thousand, what about fifty, forty, even two thousand Jews out of eight hundred thousand. Wasn't that better than nothing at all?"

"Perhaps, but Lot never asked God to kill the ten good men. He asked God to spare the entire city because the ten good men may have existed. That, my friend, is the fundamental difference between Rudolf Kasztner and Lot. *Kasztner was willing to sacrifice seven hundred ninety-eight thousand 'good men' innocent Jewish men, women, and children in order to save two thousand.*"

"So you don't accept my proposition that the lines between good and evil blur as you become older and, presumably, wiser?"

"I don't say that, Rashid," Tamir said, noisily slurping at his tea, which was scalding despite his attempt to blow it cool. "It's just that I refuse to acknowledge that if enough people tell me black is white I must believe it."

"Do you feel if Kasztner were tried he'd be convicted?"

"Most likely not. He'd probably plead no contest to a much lesser charge, get a few weeks of house arrest— "

"And his political career would be ruined. That's what you really want, isn't it?"

Now Tamir found himself on the defensive, albeit not uncomfortably so. "I guess it is, Rashid. I'm not naïve enough to believe the government of Israel is somehow more perfect, less capable of making human mistakes than any other government in the world. But if I can remove one bad example I will, at least, have done my small part to help society."

"What if Kasztner came to you and asked you to defend him? Are your morals so high that you'd refuse him? Particularly when, by your own oath to the Bar of Justice and your reputation, you swore to defend any and all citizens?"

"You pose a most difficult question, Rashid."

"You know, Samuel," the older man said, "once, just once, I'd like you to pull me off the pedestal of being your all-wise advisor, your pain-in-the-arse conscience, and simply have a fun night out. Waiter!" he shouted good-naturedly. "We've had enough of this horse piss you call coffee and tea. Do you have any decent Arak?"

"Of course, sir!" the young man said smartly. He dashed into the back of the restaurant and returned with two glasses of the clear liquid. "Tiger's milk?" he asked, lifting a large carafe of water.

"Of course, my good man."

As the waiter poured water into the three-quarters-filled glasses, the clear Arak turned milky white. "All right, lawyer boy," Rashid said, puffing out his chest. "Last one to bolt this down pays for it. *L'chaim!*"

"*Sherefenize!*" Tamir returned the toast in the Turkish his Bedouin friend had used decades ago.

Rashid winked. The two men drank one, then another, and several minutes later, all hope of serious talk forgotten, they sang some folk song or another — in a very poor attempt at harmony.

45

A distraught Rudolf Kasztner, his tan rapidly fading, had demanded a meeting with his old Jewish Agency associate. He'd also requested that David Ben Gurion attend the meeting, but that old political warrior remained in seclusion at Sde Boker.

"Moshe, this has got to stop. You've got to do something!"

"Just what do you expect me to do?" an angry Sharett fumed. "This entire fiasco was your idea. Didn't you learn your lesson when you brought a libel trial in forty-eight in the Jewish Agency Honor Court and the result was a stand-off?"

"What if I simply don't show up tomorrow and let the trial go on without me?"

"Tamir's demanding you be tried under the anti-collaborationist law, a capital offense, and now the goddamned press is starting to pick up that story."

"If that happens, Moshe, we're all in danger, you, me, Ben Gurion, the whole lot of us. The last thing we need is an old memory that no one can do anything about eating us from within. Our national security is at stake."

"Let's call a spade a shit shovel, Rudy, *your* security is at stake."

"I don't consider your heavy-handed attempt at humor funny at all, Moshe. This is not a question of rats deserting a sinking ship. Israel is the ship and if the crew deserts the whole ship sinks. I don't intend to be the scapegoat for the whole pack of us."

The Prime Minister walked over to the library window, lit another cigarette, the third one he'd smoked in the last twenty minutes, then turned back to Kasztner. "Suppose I could work things out with Chaim, even with the judge, that you plead no contest to a lesser included offense, say involuntary manslaughter or negligence, something like that. Two months in a light labor camp in the Negev and you're free."

"And my political career is ruined? There's no way I would even consider that. For God's sake, man, I don't know how I can get it into the Mapai's collective thick head. I saved Jews. I didn't do anything wrong. What does it take to convince you people? I'm one of you. I've been one of the most ardent Zionists for over twenty years."

"Would you consider an honorable retirement on a state pension, provided you left the country and retired to Switzerland?"

"Banishment?" Kasztner's voice rose. "Are you crazy, Moshe? *Banishment? Me?* After all I've done to help you people out?" Suddenly, Kasztner's anger broke. He was no longer nervous. The Prime Minister may have unwittingly given him his opportunity.

"Moshe," he said smoothly, "suppose in lieu of trial, in lieu of retirement, you appointed me ambassador to a foreign country? It doesn't have to be the United States or England. South Africa is supposed to be an incredibly wealthy and beautiful country."

The Prime Minister thought for several moments. Kasztner's idea certainly had merit. Although Sharett had never voiced it publicly, and certainly not to the other man, Kasztner was fast becoming a political liability. A foreign service post, away from the country for a few years … Memories fade, new scandals make the front page, presidents and prime ministers retire. On the other hand, Kasztner's suggestion had more immediate, darker implications. The country's newspapers and *Kol Yisrael*, the national and international radio service of Israel, were interested enough — and angry enough — at the Kasztner revelations to keep the heat on everyone concerned. If Kasztner suddenly disappeared and the trial became moot because of diplomatic immunity, the glare of an angry spotlight would undoubtedly refocus on the Prime Minister's chair.

"Listen, Rudy, there's always the chance that Benjamin Halevi will rule in your favor. After all, he's still one of us. I could hint at a Supreme Court appointment. Your foreign service suggestion is interesting and I'll certainly consider it. We can use it as a last resort if need be. Do me a personal favor and finish this trial. If anything goes wrong, I promise you we'll file an immediate appeal. You know how close we are to our friends on the Supreme Court. There'll be plenty of time to consider all our options then."

"You're telling me, you're not asking me," Kasztner said.

"Perhaps, but one hand washes the other. I assure you the ship of state won't sink."

Samuel Tamir put Malchiel Greenwald through a blistering rehearsal for Cohen's anticipated cross-examination, designed to shock, humiliate, and break the old man. Despite the most vicious browbeating of which Tamir was capable, Greenwald reacted the same to each question. His answers were slow, plodding, dry, devoid of doubletalk, boring, and entirely credible. If his answer to a given question made him admit a damaging fact, he did it with a straight face and without the evasive pleading for understanding that was typical of Kasztner's testimony.

By ten thirty that morning, Tamir had concluded his questioning. Greenwald asked, "Do any of you mind if I light up a cigar?"

"Mister Greenwald," Tamir said, smiling, "I don't want to challenge the fates by telling you how well you've done, but I'll light your cigar for you." He extracted a box of wooden matches from his desk drawer, struck one, cupped his hands. Even in the absence of a breeze, Israeli matches were notorious for going out immediately.

"Thank you. Do you want me to do anything differently, Mister Tamir?"

"Not at all. I would like to ask how you managed to remember so much."

"What's to remember? I simply told the truth. That means there's nothing to remember."

"Mr. Greenwald. I had planned to work through the entire afternoon with you, but I see there's no need."

"Then why shouldn't we take a walk around my Jerusalem?" Greenwald said.

"Aside from the fact that it's over ninety degrees today, why would you want to do that?"

"To show you why it's so important to me that Eretz Israel's leaders remain loyal to a higher standard than other governments. It'll take an hour of your time and you'll make an old man happy."

"How about the rest of you?" Samuel asked.

Ruth and Ariana agreed. The others happily made excuses: family commitments, researching the law, preserving a garden. There were as many excuses as employees.

They drove up Jericho Road, turned right at the Church of All Nations, turned right again just before the Church of the Eleona, and parked at the new Intercontinental Hotel. From there, it was a short walk to the summit of the Mount of Olives.

"Let's look around us for a moment," Greenwald said. "I came to the top of this mountain the first day I came to Jerusalem. There wasn't an Intercontinental Hotel back then. There was hardly anything back then. Can you see *Nebi Samwil*?" he asked.

"Barely," Tamir replied, looking toward a high mountain beyond the Dome of the Rock.

"When I first came, there were hardly any buildings in the Kidron Valley, only olive trees all the way to the far mountain. Richard the Lion Heart called it the Mount of Joy because he got his first view of Jerusalem from there. But I prefer this mountain for two reasons: first, you can see the heights of Mount Olivet from any part of the city, and, second, you can see the entire city from here. Look!" he said, pointing into the Kidron Valley. "There's the old hotel we bought when we first came here."

They descended down Gesthemane Road past the Church of Mary Magdalene, then cut sharply left into the old City of David. Fortunately, the walk was downhill all the way. Despite the heat, the women wore scarves on their heads. Both Greenwald and Tamir wore wide-brimmed hats to avid the broiling sun.

Like many of the world's most beautiful cities, Jerusalem was a contrast of hills and alternating valleys. The rolling landscape descended into the Judean desert. "My Bedouin friend Rashid told me that unlike the Sinai Desert, the Judean Desert has always been able to sustain wandering tribes. In the lean years the desperate desert tribesmen often attacked the city, so King David built thick, heavily fortified walls and the city prospered so that it soon outgrew its walls."

"Anyone for cooling off?" Ruth asked.

"If you mean Hezekiah's tunnel, I hope you brought a flashlight," Ariana said.

Just south of Silwan School, they came to Gihon Spring and carefully walked underground to a dark path which King Hezekiah of Judah had hewn out of hard rock three thousand years before. That ancient monarch had decided to bring the waters of Gihon into the city and store them in the Pool of Shiloah to ensure a steady supply of water during siege or war. He sealed the opening to the spring so it could not be used to enter the city.

As they descended, the temperature dropped by twenty degrees. Soon, they found themselves calf-deep in cool, running water. Ruth took the lead and the others followed as the tunnel wound a torturous six hundred yards until they came out three quarters of an hour later at what had been, in Biblical times, the southwest edge of the City.

"All right, my friends," Tamir said. "In a few moments we'll be just as hot as we were, we're soaked, and it's uphill all the way back to the Intercontinental."

At that moment, they spotted a large Eged city bus stop just across the road. Greenwald was the first to spot the number 42 bus approaching. "I feel wealthy this afternoon," the old man said. "I passed the hospital physical two days ago, my Ariana is with me, and my two friends told me this morning that I did well. I'll pay for the bus trip back up the hill for all of us."

He did, and within twenty minutes they were sipping tea on the veranda of the Intercontinental Hotel, overlooking all of Jerusalem, and promising one another they'd retire early and get a good night's rest for what promised to be the last, and most critical, week of the trial.

46

The following day, Tamir called Malchiel Greenwald as his first witness. The old man testified as to his background and his experience as a reporter of sorts in Vienna, Budapest, and, most recently, in Israel. He admitted writing the article in question and distributing it to his five hundred friends in the Mizrachi, a right wing Israeli splinter party. When asked whether he believed the truth of what he wrote, he affirmed that he did. If he was nervous he did not display it. He gestured with his hands and arms when making a point, looked directly at his counsel and at the judge, and seemed to treat the entire examination as an animated conversation. Tamir finished in less than two hours.

The court took a ten minute recess. Greenwald went to the restroom. On his return, Tamir spoke softly with him. "You're doing a great job, Mister Greenwald, but now comes the difficult part. Remember what I told you. Take your time, don't let Cohen rush you, count to three in your head before you answer any question, to give me a chance to object. It's likely I won't object to anything because I want the judge to see you in an entirely natural light. Do you have any questions?"

"No, Mister Tamir, except I want to thank you from the bottom of my heart for everything you've done. Whether we win or lose, there is only the truth to be told, and I feel I have made a friend for life." He squeezed the lawyer's hand warmly, then resumed his place in the witness box.

Chaim Cohen experienced a rare moment of nervousness on his own. Judge Halevi was courtly and stern. To come at the witness full bore, as was his fashion, might be difficult with the aged, obviously likable Greenwald. Slashing cross-examination was Tamir's way. Cohen had to admit that the arrogant Doctor Kasztner lent himself to such treatment. But Malchiel Greenwald was a different sort. Cohen began gently.

"Tell me, Mister Greenwald, in your article you stated, '*We* demand an impartial investigation.' Who was the 'we,' Sir?"

"Just me at the time I wrote the article. However, I hoped to interest others."

"In other words, you wanted to incite others to action by your demand?"

Tamir nearly rose to object but held his seat nervously.

"That's true."

"What kind of action, Mister Greenwald?"

"To see that justice is done."

"You mean take the law into your own hands?"

"No, Mister Cohen," Greenwald answered politely. "I was hoping that anyone who read the article might try to contact the Attorney General."

"And you couldn't ask the Attorney General for help on your own?"

"I don't think that would have worked, Mister Cohen."

"What makes you say that? Surely you trust in Israeli Justice?" the Attorney General said, his voice turning into a mild sneer for the first time.

"Mister Cohen, I understand Mister Tamir asked you to prosecute Doctor Kasztner under the anti-collaborationist law some time ago. I haven't seen any hint of an indictment or even a criminal investigation. Now, if a famous lawyer like Mister Tamir couldn't get the Attorney-General's attention, what makes you think someone like me could?"

"You say, 'We shall keep this on our agenda until the evil is ended!' What agenda, Mister Greenwald?"

"A very simple agenda, counselor. I intended — and I still intend — to do everything I can to find out the truth about Doctor Kasztner or any other Jew who collaborated with the Nazis."

"So you fancy yourself a Simon Wiesenthal?" the Attorney General asked. He had meant his tone to be heavily sarcastic. Instead, it was simply heavily bombastic.

"No, Mister Cohen, I do not," Greenwald answered. "I don't have Mister Wiesenthal's youth or his vigor. I don't know to what degree he has money, but I know I have none. I couldn't even afford to pay my lawyer the cost of defending this suit, Mister Cohen. But even a little *nochschlepper* like me has the right to demand right and justice, even if the Attorney General ignores my request, and even if I have to fight the whole State to get that justice."

"Move to strike! Move to strike!" Cohen yelled, glaring murderously at the witness.

"Motion denied, counsel!" Judge Halevi said, a shade louder than he had to. "I find your motion to be frivolous. If I hear such a motion one more time I will order sanctions."

Cohen conferred with his client, Kasztner. After a vicious series of loud whispers and exchanges, Cohen announced, "No further questions of this witness, Your Honor."

"Mister Tamir?"

"Nothing further, Your Honor," Samuel Tamir responded.

"Very well, gentlemen, we'll take our noon recess. The witness is excused. Thank you, Mister Greenwald."

47

That afternoon, Chaim Cohen brought Doctor Kasztner back to the witness stand for redirect examination. After an hour on the stand, Doctor Kasztner felt he had nothing to fear. Chaim Cohen was on his side. So were all the solid leaders of Israel.

"I don't think I phrased my testimony in the most truthful manner," he offered. "If, under the pressure of a rather savage cross-examination, I said a few things for which I am truly sorry today, it doesn't change my basic attitude in this matter."

"Let's return to the affidavit you made," Cohen said. "If you had been asked to give this affidavit today, would you have given it or not?"

"Yes, I would have given it, but I would have made it in my own name. I would not have made it in the name of the Jewish Agency."

"Do you think it is the duty of any honorable man, under the same circumstances, to do what you did?"

"Yes, Mister Cohen. Every honorable man would have done the same as I did."

It was three o'clock in the afternoon by the time Tamir's turn came to speak with Doctor Kasztner. As Tamir stood to address the witness, Kasztner exhibited a noticeable tic. He grabbed the lapels of his suit jacket and drew the garment tighter around him.

"Doctor Kasztner, what department did Kurt Becher work in?" Tamir began.

"The Economic Department of the Waffen S.S."

"Are you aware that the Waffen S.S. used to appropriate the clothes and belongings of the exterminated Jews?"

A mere two questions into the cross-examination, Kasztner lost his composure. He shouted, "I never heard of that! As a systematic procedure that is absolutely untrue!"

"Isn't it a fact that the people of the Economic Department plucked out the gold-filled teeth of the murdered Jews?"

"You are an ignoramus!" Kasztner blazed, clearly on the defensive, "That is an absolute lie!"

"I have an affidavit from the Nuremberg Trials that your friend Becher received suitcases containing two million dollars' worth of jewelry and cash. Do you have any reason to disbelieve this affidavit?"

"I know of no such thing. I cannot admit or deny. It was not my concern."

"Are you aware that Becher personally shook down the Manfred Weiss family, the richest Jewish family in Hungary?"

"I know of no such thing. How dare you keep trying to impugn my honesty by throwing out things I know nothing about! Why can't you simply stick to the facts? Get to the real testimony, Mister Tamir!" Kasztner flailed wildly about, his color gone to high red. "Get to the point of how many Jews I saved! Get to the point of your client's vicious libel, how he tried to destroy a good man and everything he stood for! What in the hell is the matter with you anyway? Don't you have any respect for the law?"

"Mister Kasztner," the judge said, banging his gavel for order. Both Chaim Cohen and Samuel Tamir noticed that the court had now dropped the honorific *Doctor* Kasztner. "Given the latitude which this Court has allowed both sides, Mister Tamir's questioning is well within the bounds of his rights. If your counsel believes a question is improper, he may make the appropriate objection and I will rule on it. Otherwise you must answer, and the Court will thank you not to make comments of a personal nature during your testimony."

"Doctor Kasztner," Tamir continued, "isn't it a fact that the Economic Department of the Waffen S.S. was charged with extracting anything of value from Jews who perished in the camps — hair, gold teeth, jewelry, money, books, clothes — anything useful?"

"I do not know that to be a fact," the witness mumbled.

"Are you saying that you, the Chairman of the Jewish Agency Rescue Committee in Hungary, had no knowledge of what the Economic Department was all about?"

"I didn't say that! You are twisting my words and making them come out wrong."

"Please feel free to correct me, Doctor Kasztner. What, in your opinion, was the role of the Economic Department?"

"To deal in financial matters."

"What kind of financial matters, sir? The making of a budget? Issuing a profit and loss statement for the Hungarian government? For the Waffen S.S.?"

"Objection, compound," the Attorney General said, but his voice was lackluster.

"Sustained," the judge said, to his apparent surprise.

"What kind of financial matters did the Economic Department of the Waffen S.S. deal in, Doctor Kasztner?"

"I don't know. It had something to do with the management of Jewish assets."

"The management of Jewish assets." Tamir made it as a statement, not a question, so that the entire courtroom could hear. "And just what kind of assets did the Jews have left to manage, Doctor Kasztner?"

"Object, Your Honor," Cohen said, rising to his feet wearily. "Counsel is badgering the witness again."

"Objection overruled."

"You may answer the question, Doctor Kasztner," Tamir said.

"I don't know," the witness answered shakily.

"Did Colonel Eichmann tell you in the latter part of April, nineteen forty-four, that he wished to avoid a second Warsaw uprising?"

"Yes."

"Isn't it a fact that the S.S. began their work in Hungary by setting up a ghetto in your home town of Cluj?"

"I don't know that to be a fact."

"Do you know of any other towns where ghettoes were set up before Cluj?"

"No."

"How many Jews lived in Cluj in May, nineteen forty-four?"

"Twenty thousand, thirty thousand, I don't know the precise number."

"Did any of your S.S. friends tell you anything about a place called Kenyermeze?"

"Yes."

"What did they tell you?"

"That the Jews were going to be taken to a German occupied area called Kenyermeze. They would be given jobs. Every Jew would be permitted to take his entire family with him. They explained to me that their new leniency toward Jews was a matter of practicality; they'd learned from experience that a Jew would work harder and produce more if he had his family around him."

"Did the Germans ask you to explain about Kenyermeze to the Jews of Cluj?"

"They did."

"And did you agree to do that?"

"Yes."

"Why?"

"Why?" the witness repeated, now looking like a boxer who'd been thrown against the ropes once too often.

"Yes, why, Doctor Kasztner? You knew you were in a position of authority with the Jewish Agency?"

"Yes."

"You were a native of Cluj?"

"Yes."

"So you knew you were a hero to the locals?"

"I don't know how they viewed me," Kasztner answered weakly.

"You knew they would believe your word over that of the Germans?"

"I did not know that for a fact."

"Doctor Kasztner, do you think that maybe the Jews of Cluj *might* have believed you a little more than they would have believed the Nazis who occupied Hungary?"

"I don't know, Mister Tamir. How many times do you intend to torture me with the same question?"

"Only until you answer it, Doctor Kasztner," Tamir replied softly.

"Your Honor, might I request a break in the questioning?" the witness asked, his skin now a sickly gray color, perspiration running freely down his brow.

"Court is in recess for fifteen minutes," Judge Halevi announced curtly.

"Had you ever been invited to see Kenyermeze with your own eyes, Doctor Kasztner?" the defense counsel prodded.

"No."

"Were you present when the first train left for Kenyermeze, Doctor Kasztner?"

"I was."

"How long was it before the Germans turned over postcards and letters from Kenyermeze to you?"

"A week, ten days."

"What did the Germans give you?"

"Postcards and brief letters. The cards and letters all said Kenyermeze was a fine place, the work, food, and lodging were fine, they sent love to all."

"Did you recognize the handwriting on any of the postcards or letters?"

"No, but they were mostly written in Yiddish."

"Were these postcards and letters addressed specifically to anyone?"

"No. To the Jewish Agency Rescue Committee, but I cannot remember any names."

"Did you ever wonder why, if these cards and letters had been *mailed* to the Jewish Agency Rescue Committee, they were *handed* to you by Waffen S.S. officers?"

"Yes, I thought about that."

"Did you ask any of the S.S. representatives?"

"No."

"Why not?"

"I don't know. I just didn't."

"Did you subsequently learn that the letters were forgeries?"

The witness stood for a moment, inhaled deeply, and resumed his seat. His voice was so low as to be barely discernible as he answered, "Yes."

"When?"

"I don't recall. Later that year."

"Do you know where the first train went?"

"No, I don't."

"I put it to you, Doctor Kasztner, that the first, and every other train supposedly destined for Kenyermeze, went directly to Auschwitz."

"That's your statement!" Kasztner flared, but it was the false light of a dead flame.

"Did you ever ask to go to Kenyermeze to see if any Jews arrived there?"

"I did not."

"Why not?"

"Because the Germans advised me not to go there."

"The Germans authorized you to use a car, correct?"

"Yes."

"They allowed you to drive anywhere you wanted?"

"They never stopped me, if that's what you mean."

"You had a German passport?"

"Yes."

"They allowed you to go to Switzerland frequently?"

"Yes, but only in the company of German officers."

"They allowed you to go to Berlin?"

"Again, only in the presence of the S.S."

"Isn't it a fact that you never even asked to go to Kenyermeze?"

"That is a fact."

"Now, Doctor Kasztner, you had an automobile of your own all during 1944-45?"

"Yes."

"You had telephones in your home and in your office?"

"I did."

"You could telephone Palestine if you wanted?"

"Yes, and I did."

"You could telephone anywhere in the world you wanted, isn't that a fact?"

"Only if I paid my telephone bill." The attempt at humor fell absolutely flat. There wasn't a sound in the courtroom.

"You had freedom to travel anywhere in Hungary any time you wanted."

"That is so."

Tamir extracted a letter not previously introduced into evidence. He handed a copy to Cohen, a copy of it to the bailiff, and a copy to the witness. By this time, Kasztner's hands were shaking so hard he had difficulty focusing on the words. "Doctor Kasztner, is this your signature?"

"It ... it looks like it. Yes, I suppose it is."

"Do you recall this as a letter you wrote to the Jewish Agency in nineteen forty-four after Herr Vezenmayer had arranged for your release?"

"I don't know. I wrote several letters. I could have written it."

Judge Halevi looked at the letter, read the contents, and made notes.

"We now believe that if Eichmann helps, if he does us small favors, if Hitler's personal representative Vezenmayer intervenes for us with the Hungarian government, it is certain they do not do it on their own decision. It must be they are obeying higher German authority. It is obvious that we, the Rescue Committee, have a place in their plans."

Tamir saw no need to belabor the point. He was looking for harsher truths.

"In May 1944, did Krumey, Eichmann, and von Wisliczeny tell you that you could pick out three hundred Jews from Budapest and three hundred from the outlying towns to be sent out of German-occupied countries?"

"Yes."

"Doctor Kasztner," Tamir said sharply, "isn't it a fact that instead of picking Jews from outlying towns, you picked precisely 388 Jews from Cluj alone?"

"I don't know the precise number. A large number of Jews that escaped to safety happened to live in Cluj."

"And Cluj just happened to be your home town?"

"That is true." Now Kasztner had started to hyperventilate.

"And the Jews who were chosen to go were all members of Zionist groups?"

"No, not all of them."

"Isn't it a fact, Doctor Kasztner, that the only rescued Jews from Cluj who were not members of Zionist groups were members of your own family?"

"You are distorting the truth again!" Kasztner said, and now tears were openly rolling down his face. "That is not the truth and you know it."

"Mister Kasztner," the Court said quietly, "how many members of your family were among the escapees?"

"I don't know, Your Honor. Maybe ten, maybe twenty, I don't recall."

The judge raised his eyebrows. It seemed apparent to him that the witness was bluffing, trying to cover up the ugly truth. "Mister Kasztner, how many members of the Zionist groups were on the August train that escaped to Switzerland?"

"I have no idea."

"More than three hundred?" the judge asked.

"I don't know whose names were on the manifest, Your Honor, but I would say three hundred or more were on the train."

"Out of three hundred eighty-eight?"

"Yes, sir."

"Then it would seem to me, Mister Kasztner, that Mister Tamir's suggestions are not totally out of line."

"But Your Honor," the witness said in a whiny voice, "his questions are designed to distort the facts."

"How, Mister Kasztner?" the Court asked quietly.

"Well, they just distort the facts, that's all. You had to have been there to know the difficulties under which we labored."

"You may continue, Mister Tamir," the judge said equably.

"Thank you, Your Honor. Doctor Kasztner, isn't it a fact that when you came to Cluj you knew that the deportation of the Jews to Auschwtiz was about to begin?"

"Yes."

"You knew there were no trains to Kenyermeze?"

"I did not know that."

"You spoke with Colonel Krumey before you went to Cluj, did you not?"

"Yes."

"He told you that Cluj's twenty thousand Jews were restive, did he not?"

"He did."

"He asked you to calm them down, did he not?"

"Yes."

"Doctor Kasztner, how far was Cluj from the Romanian border?"

"About three miles."

"How many troops were guarding the Cluj ghetto?"

"I don't recall there being any troops."

"Doctor Kasztner," Tamir said softly, "I put it to you that there were only twenty Hungarian gendarmes and one German S.S. officer guarding the twenty thousand people in the Cluj ghetto, which was only three miles from safety."

"I don't know that. I never counted."

"Did you have representatives in Cluj?"

"Of course."

"Were they living in the ghetto?"

"Yes."

"Do you think they might have been able to tell you that there were only twenty policemen and one German officer guarding the ghetto?"

"I don't know, Mister Tamir. I didn't ask them their thoughts and they never volunteered that information to me."

"Who was the leader of the Cluj Zionist organization?"

"Doctor Joseph Fisher."

"Your wife's father?"

The answer was barely a hoarse whisper. "Yes."

"Did you tell Doctor Fisher he was going to a better place than the rest of Cluj's Jews?"

"Yes." Kasztner choked on the word.

"Doctor Kasztner, during your speeches to the Jews of Cluj, isn't it a fact that you urged them not to resist the Germans?"

"The Germans were an occupying force. Resistance would have been futile."

"I see. But going to the ovens in Auschwitz would not have been?"

"Objection!" Cohen roared. "That is a scandalous question and is designed for no reason other than to prejudice the Court."

"Yes," the judge said mildly. "The question is somewhat argumentative. I'll sustain the objection. Gentlemen, I see that it's ten past five. I think that's enough for today. Court is in recess."

48

The next day, Tamir continued. "Doctor Kaszner, do you recall that in 1946, at the Zionist Congress, you were accused by a Hungarian activist of having sacrificed Hungarian Jews for your own personal safety?"

"I don't know what you're talking about."

"Did you not bring a libel suit against your accuser in the Zionist Congress?"

"I only remember that the panel asked me to account for all my wartime activities in Hungary, and I wrote a lengthy report to them."

"Isn't it a fact that your accuser was found innocent of libel."

"That is not so," Kasztner snapped.

"What was the result, then?"

"The panel concluded it did not have enough evidence to reach a conclusion."

"Is it true that you were interrogated by the Israeli police about the Cluj ghetto three years ago, Doctor Kasztner?"

"Yes."

"Why did the police ask you about Cluj?"

The witness gasped at the lapels of his sports jacket and tugged at them, as though they would provide protection from Tamir's onslaught. "I wasn't interested enough in it to ask them their reason."

"Are you aware that the anti-collaboration law had been passed less than a month before the police questioned you?"

"I knew such a law had been enacted."

"Did you think there might be a connection between the new law and the police interrogation of your activities in Cluj?"

"I wasn't at all interested in that subject."

"Precisely what did the police ask you about?"

"They asked me if I knew what had happened in the Cluj ghetto, and why some people thought there was a connection between the deportation of the Jewish community of Cluj and the rescue of three hundred eighty-eight Zionists."

"Isn't it fact, sir, that while 20,000 Jews of Cluj were being shipped to the gas chambers, your Committee was compiling its list of the 388 who would be saved?"

"That is true."

"Did you know at the time the true significance of the deportation to Auschwitz?"

"I knew," the witness whispered.

"When you talked to the leader of the Jewish Rescue Committee in Cluj, did you advise him to organize resistance?"

"No, I did not."

"How do you account for the fact that more people from Cluj were selected to be rescued than from any other Hungarian town?"

"That had nothing to do with me."

"Did you specifically request favoritism for your people in Cluj from Eichmann."

"Yes, I asked it specifically."

"You had 'nothing to do with that,' and yet you 'asked it specifically' Doctor Kasztner?"

The inconsistency was so obvious that one would have had to be an idiot not to pick it up, and Judge Halevi was anything but an idiot. Tamir let the question hang in the air and the witness frantically hoped it would simply float away.

"Was there a branch of your Rescue Committee in Cluj, Doctor Kasztner?"

"Not formally, but a few people were active."

"What were their names?"

"I remember Doctor Marton and Hillel Danzig."

"They were under your guidance?"

"Yes. All the local Rescue Committees were under my jurisdiction."

"Where else except Cluj was there such a committee?"

"The committee in Cluj was the only one in Hungary."

"Did your Budapest committee contact other towns on the telephone?"

"I didn't personally. There was a subcommittee that dealt with these matters."

"A subcommittee. Do you know the names of any of its members?"

"No, Mister Tamir. This was ten years ago."

"Are you telling me that no one from your Committee tried to telephone the other Hungarian towns from which half a million Jews were about to be deported?"

"Maybe some other members of my committee were able to telephone other towns. I don't know."

"Did your subcommittee in Budapest report to you on their activities?"

"Yes, of course."

"Was the subcomittee's telephone at your disposal?"

"What for?"

"I want to know if you could talk to the towns and villages of Hungary?"

"I could have done so."

"Did you talk to any town other than Cluj?"

"No, I could not do everything myself, so I concentrated on Cluj for obvious reasons. There simply wasn't time enough to contact all these towns."

"If you were so busy with your political activities, why didn't you assign the task to another rescue worker less busy than yourself?"

"That was impossible."

"Let's sum this all up: you had the opportunity to communicate with all the towns in Hungary?"

"Yes."

"You do not know if any of your assistants tried to warn the Jews of Hungary?"

Kasztner screamed wildly, "I can't remember!"

The court stepped into the fray. "Do you not feel well, Doctor Kasztner?"

"I'm … I'm nervous, Your Honor."

"Very well. Court will be in recess for thirty minutes."

When the hearing resumed, the Judge instructed the bailiff to fetch a chair for the witness. "You may proceed with your questioning, Mister Tamir."

"How many times did you visit Cluj, Doctor Kasztner?"

"Twice."

"Could you not have gone to other towns if you were able to go twice to Cluj."

"A Jew was not allowed to travel."

"But you told us earlier that *you* were allowed to travel anywhere you wanted in Hungary, and in your own car."

Kasztner mumbled some halfhearted answer. Tamir knew when to leave a question hanging in the air, and he did so again.

"Is it not true, Doctor Kasztner, that some people in Budapest warned you that all your negotiations with Colonel Eichmann were only for the purpose of distracting the Jews from the knowledge of their extermination?"

"There were such opinions expressed. I also felt the same thing in my heart."

Slowly and distinctly, Judge Halevi asked, "*Mister Kasztner, did you tell anybody in Cluj what you knew about the extermination that was going on in Auschwitz?*"

Kasztner turned pale. His throat was dry as he answered. "I beg the Court's permission to explain. I cannot answer in one word. Those whom

I contacted heard me say what the Germans were doing to Jews in Poland and Russia."

Judge Halevi stared directly at the witness and spoke sternly. *"That was not my question. Did you tell anyone that the Germans were preparing the deportation of Hungary's Jews to Auschwitz?"*

"I had no definite knowledge. I heard rumors in Budapest spread by Germans and Hungarians about resettling the Jews in Kenyermeze. We all tried to check these rumors."

"But," the judge pressed on, *"you, yourself said that at the end of April you knew that the gas chambers and crematoria were ready in Auschwitz and that the train schedule for deportation from Hungary to Auschwitz had already been fixed."*

"I couldn't check all the rumors," the sweating witness replied shakily.

"But Joel Brand, who left Budapest on May seventeenth, told everybody in Istanbul that twelve thousand Jews a day were being deported from Hungary to Auschwitz," the Court said.

"I don't know on what he based that statement, Your Honor."

"It was based on what Colonel Eichmann had told him at their meeting, after which you met Brand."

"But Eichmann said he would wait two weeks for Brand's answer," Kasztner replied evasively.

Judge Halevi was not to be deterred. "And then he would start the extermination after two weeks at the rate of twelve thousand a day?"

"Yes, Your Honor. I don't know whether he knew the rate."

"He testified in Court that he knew it and that you knew it as well."

The witness coughed and wiped his forehead. "My hopes were dashed only at the end of May. Until then I thought maybe not … maybe not so many."

"A train left every day after the middle of May, a sealed train that went to Auschwitz. *Did you know that?"* the Judge asked.

"Yes. After the middle of May I knew that as a fact."

This was Kasztner's second admission to shake Israel. Kasztner had admitted that he knew. Judge Halevi took a deep breath and carefully phrased the ominous question.

"Why didn't you inform the Jews of Cluj what you knew, Doctor Kasztner?"

When Kasztner finally answered, it was in a faint, tremulous voice. "I told them everything I knew when I was in contact with them. Later, I was in contact only with my father-in-law and I dared give only one clear hint. He had to know that deportation and extermination would follow."

"Then why didn't the Jews of Cluj know about all of that?"

"Your Honor asks me ..." Kasztner stopped before the monstrous question. The judge had asked Kasztner in no uncertain terms whether Kasztner was an evil man, a Jew who helped the Nazis slaughter his own people. He turned to the judge. There were tears in his eyes. Finally, slowly, he answered. *"Your Honor, I think that my colleagues in Cluj, including my father-in-law, did not do all in their power... did not do all that could have been done. On the other hand, Your Honor, I am sorry to say that the witnesses from Cluj who testified here ... in my opinion, I don't think they represent the true Jewry of Cluj. For it is not a coincidence that there was not one single important figure among those who testified against me in this trial."*

Judge Halevi sat in shocked disbelief at the unspeakable arrogance of this man. Caught in a trap from which he could not possibly extricate himself, he resorted to the dishonest —and dishonorable —charade of blaming others for his own misdeeds.

But much more incredible, and important, Doctor Rudolf Kasztner had, in the moment of his greatest weakness, displayed what the defense had argued all along: *the only Jews entitled to escape the Holocaust in the eyes of the Chief of the Jewish Agency Rescue Committee of Hungary were <u>the right kind of Jews</u>.*

49

On the sixth day of cross-examination, Tamir switched to a different subject altogether.

"Doctor Kasztner," he began, "what did you do to help Hanna Senesh?"

The courtroom suddenly became so silent that one would have thought the audience was attending a funeral. The press corps sat up in rapt attention. For Hanna Senesh was revered in Israel as the greatest heroine since Biblical times.

"We held committee meetings over what steps to take. We decided to find out from the Hungarian authorities if it was possible to release her. We decided to raise money for a lawyer to defend her."

"Was she defended? Did you get her a lawyer?"

"Yes, some young Hungarian military man, I don't remember his name."

"Did this lawyer get in touch with Hanna Senesh?"

"I don't know."

"You weren't interested?"

"I think Offenbach, a member of our Committee, told me he was handling the matter."

"Did the lawyer visit Hanna Senesh in jail?"

"I don't know."

"Did you ask whether Hanna had tried to send any messages to you through this lawyer?"

"No."

"Did you inquire whether she'd had any food in prison?"

"I did not."

"Did you inquire whether she was being tortured?"

"No."

"I put it to you, Doctor Kasztner, you were not interested in the fate of Hanna Senesh."

"That is not true!"

"I put it to you that you never looked for a lawyer for Hanna Senesh."

"You are wrong!"

"I put it to you that your aides advised Hanna's mother not to get a lawyer."

"That is not true!"

"Did you meet Hanna's mother?"

"No."

"Did her mother ever ask to meet you?"

"To the best of my knowledge, never."

"Was Hanna Senesh a British officer in addition to being an emissary of the Jewish Agency?"

"Yes."

"Were British interests in Hungary represented by the Swiss Consulate?"

"Yes."

"Did you notify the Swiss Consulate that a British prisoner of war was being held by the Hungarians?"

"No."

"Why not?"

"I think I had my reasons."

A sweating Kasztner waited for the all-out assault on his Hanna Senesh lies. In the eyes of the Israeli public, this was Kasztner's worst crime, for Hanna was no vague, dead Jewess lost in a mountain of corpses. Her poems were widely read and her memory was as alive as if she had died only a day ago.

Knowing that he had previewed the greatest coming attraction of the trial, and knowing his quarry was swaying on the ropes like a boxer who'd been hit once too often, Tamir switched gears again, digging on and on, extracting dazed but damning responses to virtually every question. Kasztner testified that in his travels he was accompanied by S.S. high officers. He was escorted to Switzerland and allowed to meet with Allied officials, but he never betrayed any significant information about the German war machine, or what was happening to the Jews, to them. His Nazi friends paid his fare from Switzerland back to Vienna so he could continue to save Jews.

"Doctor Kasztner, where did you stay when you went to Vienna?"

"At the Grand Hotel."

"In a room or in a suite?"

"In a suite."

"Who paid for the suite?"

"I'm not sure. Either the committee or Becher. I think it was Becher."

"And you had dinner each night with Krumey and his mistress, Eva Kosytorz?"

"Not every night. Some evenings."

"How many Jews did you save while you were in Vienna, Doctor Kasztner?"

"I, personally? I don't know. I was in continuous negotiations for the release of Jews. I left the day-to-day work to my Committee back in Budapest."

"How far is Budapest from Vienna?"

"One-hundred fifty miles."

"A five hour journey by car?"

"About that, yes."

"Yet in all the time you were in Vienna, you never once drove there?"

"That's true."

"And you never once telephoned your Committee in Budapest?"

"I don't know that to be a fact. Do you have the telephone records or are you simply fabricating that statement like so many other of your lies?"

"Mister Kasztner," the court said, not unkindly, "please try and restrict your comments to answering Mister Tamir's questions. You need not editorialize."

Tamir continued. "In your report to Jewish Agency official Eleazar Kaplan, you described Kurt Becher as the liaison officer between Reichsführer Himmler and yourself."

"I don't deny that."

"You say in your report that Himmler issued an order to stop the exterminations on a certain date. Would you agree with me that this was not the result of your talks with Becher, but rather because the Russian, American, and British armies had surrounded him?"

"No, I don't agree."

"Let me get this straight. Your meetings with Becher were more important for the Jews than the strategic situation of Germany toward the end of the War?"

"Yes. I have no doubts in making that statement."

"Becher helped you save Jews?"

"Yes."

"And Himmler helped you save Jews?"

"Yes."

"Did you meet with Colonel Hoess in Budapest in nineteen forty-four?"

"I did."

"That is the same Colonel Hoess who testified at Nuremberg that he personally supervised the murder of 2,500,684 Jews?"

"Yes."

"What was Colonel Hoess's job?"

"He was the commandant of Auschwitz."

"Did you speak with him in nineteen forty-five about the death march of the Jews from Hungary to Austria?"

"I did."

"And what did he say?"

"He thought what had happened was swinish and that he would take immediate steps to have the death march stopped."

The judge looked in silence at Kasztner. For a long time he said nothing while Kasztner looked back at him. Finally, Kaszter himself broke the silence. Apropos absolutely nothing, he said, "Strange and tragic and comic as it may seem, it is true."

Tamir, realizing that his quarry was now over the edge, continued his questioning in a more quiet tone.

"Would you agree with me, Doctor Kasztner, that those who died did so more of exposure than anything else? That food and clothing would have kept them alive?"

"Yes, that is true."

"Isn't it a fact that even in May 1945, Jews were still being exterminated?"

"I heard that."

"Doctor Kasztner, once you had gone from Switzerland back to Vienna, you never returned to Budapest, correct?"

"Correct."

"Where did you go from Vienna?"

"To Berlin."

"Did you stay there in April, 1945?"

"Yes."

"Where were you living?"

"In Becher's aide's apartment. I was only there for four or five days."

"What did you do while you were in Berlin?"

"I was waiting to meet with Himmler and Becher."

"Doctor Kasztner, can you recall even one instance where the Jewish Agency rescued anyone after October, 1944?"

"Of course. The Jewish Agency rescue operation in Bratislava in April 1945."

"Dunand, the Red Cross representative, states in his published book that when the Gestapo left Bratislava at the end of March 1945 and the Russians were about to enter it any minute, you were searching through the caves outside the city, collecting Jews to transfer to Switzerland. Is that true?"

"Yes."

"Why would you be doing that, Doctor Kasztner?"

"Because the Allies were already bombing the outskirts and I still had my rescue work to complete."

"How many Jews did you rescue from Bratislava?"

"I took twenty-six or twenty-seven Jews out of there."

"Doctor Kasztner, the Germans had already left. Why would it be so important for you to hunt up twenty-six or twenty-seven Jews and take them to Switzerland?"

"It was very important."

"In his book, Dunand says these Jews wanted to remain in Bratislava after the Russians came, but you persuaded them to go to Switzerland with you. You told them it wasn't a matter of rescue, but that they would be able to enjoy a convalescent rest in Switzerland, after which they could come back to Bratislava as they wished."

"That is true."

"Doctor Kasztner, I put it to you that you needed twenty-six or twenty-seven Jews to take along when you got to the Swiss border with Krumey. You needed them as an alibi for him as well as for yourself, and you were ready to dig Jews up from anywhere you could find them to furnish you with that alibi."

"That's a lie!" Kaztner burst out. "It is not true! Never! Not true!"

"I have no further questions of this witness," Tamir said quietly.

Judge Halevi waited a few moments for the explosive mood in the courtroom to cool down. Then he asked, "Do you have anything to correct or add to your testimony, Doctor Kasztner? If you have forgotten anything important, or if you were mistaken as to anything you said, I give you the opportunity to say so now."

"Your Honor," the witness said. "Will you give me some time to think?"

"Of course," said the Judge, whose face betrayed no emotion.

Kasztner requested a ballpoint pen and a notepad. He wrote for several minutes. Finally, he stopped writing and asked to dictate his notes to Judge Halevi's secretary. It took more than an hour. When he was finished, Judge Halevi asked, "Is that all?"

"Your Honor," Kasztner said. "I cannot refrain from expressing again my sorrow over the impression which may have been made in some people regarding the phrasing of my testimony about Becher and the result of it. Neither I nor my friends have anything to hide in this whole affair. We do not regret that we acted in accordance with our conscience, despite all that has been done to us in this trial."

And with that, a wobbly Kasztner, holding onto a rail at the side of the courtroom, ended his testimony and slowly made his way to the back of the room and out the door.

Not one person sought to assist him or speak with him.

50

"Your Honor, the defense calls as its final witness Mrs. Catherina Senesh."

The witness entered the courtroom. Tall, poised, and handsome, she spoke calmly, proudly from the witness box. After his preliminary questions elicited that she was the housemother of a girls' school in Tel Aviv, Tamir went directly to the heart of the issue.

"Mrs. Senesh, before you came here today, did anyone threaten you?"

"Yes, Mister Tamir. For the past three months, government officials have asked me not to testify. A deputy minister in the Department of Education warned me that I might lose my job if I appeared as a witness."

"Nevertheless, you chose to come here voluntarily, of your own accord?"

"I did."

Under the gentle questioning of Samuel Tamir, with every eye in the courtroom respectfully on this dignified woman, Catherina Senesh brought alive the story of her daughter.

"Hanna was born in Budapest in July, nineteen twenty-one. She was executed by a Hungarian firing squad at midnight in October nineteen forty-four. My husband and I owned a silverware and jewelry shop, but business was a minor issue in our lives. Bela, my late husband, was a writer and critic. He died in nineteen twenty-nine when Hanna was eight."

"Was Judaism important in your family when Hanna was young?"

"Not really, Mister Tamir. That's why I was so surprised when Hanna suddenly announced, a few days after she turned seventeen, that she was a Zionist. This was nineteen thirty-eight, and things were starting to fray around the edges for Hungarian Jews. Not that we were worried, because we were well-to-do people, but Hanna surprised me when she emigrated to Palestine a year later."

"Did you stay in Budapest?"

"I did. It was home. All my friends were here. But young people always want to see the world outside their door, and I couldn't, and really didn't want to, stop my Hanna from flying from the nest."

"Did you and Hanna keep up a correspondence?"

"Oh yes, regularly…"

PALESTINE – YUGOSLAVIA

NOVEMBER 1943 - MARCH 1944

51

17 NOVEMBER 1943
CAESARIA

"Dear Mama,

"I can't tell you how happy I've been since I came to Palestine. Who would have thought that a city girl from Budapest could find the true meaning of life digging soil, scrubbing floors in the kibbutz, and milking a herd of stubborn nanny goats? I've even started writing some poetry, not very good I'm afraid, but my girlfriend Elena said one of them, A Walk to Caesarea, might even be able to get published one day. … There's a young Irgun fighter, Shmuel Katznelson, who's taken an interest in me. Who knows where that could lead?

"Mama, I'm worried for your safety. I fear that with the Arrow Cross gaining power and the Germans on Hungary's doorstep, things won't remain the same for long. Please, please, please come to Palestine. It's a <u>much</u> safer place for Jews. Love, Hanna"

28 DECEMBER 1943
BUDAPEST

"Darling Hanna,

"Your letter of 1 December arrived yesterday. Your poem is lovely, as I'm sure you must know. You sounded somehow moody and a bit sad. Don't forget, I'm your mother. You can always share things with me, and I'd be there to comfort you in a moment. Where's the chin-up girl I've always known?

"I know how much you love Palestine, but that's a country for the young. In spite of the war, Europe needs a contining Jewish presence, since we Jews have always been in the forefront of keeping European culture alive. I believe things will get better rather than worse. Thank God, I think a noose is beginning to tighten around Hitler's neck. Skorzeny barely managed to save Mussolini. His new Fascist Republic of Northern Italy is nothing more than a puppet, propped up by the Führer. The Duce is a virtual prisoner, a tiger without teeth or claws. The Soviets have now kicked the Boches out of Russia. The fronts are showing signs of collapse everywhere. Despite the Arrow Cross, Admiral Horthy still holds the reins of power. The Germans have not crossed the border, and life remains stable.

Perhaps if you came for a brief visit, you might see with your own eyes that I'm alright, and there's nothing to worry about. Your loving mother."

JANUARY 1944, CANNOT DISCLOSE WHERE

"Oh, Mama!!!

"You won't believe what's happened these last two months!!! Neither can I. In early December, I said to myself, 'I can't sit around and do nothing while Europe continues to go to hell in a handbasket.'

"Later that month, a recruiter from the MI6 came by our kibbutz and spoke to us about working with the British underground

in the Occupied territories. I didn't sleep at all that night, and I was the first one in our kibbutz to sign up for the British Women's Auxiliary Air Force as an Aircraftwoman Second Class. A few days later, I was approached by a representative of the Special Operations Executive (SOE) to apply to become a parachutist.

"Thirty-five of us applied. Seventeen were chosen. I was the only woman. Next thing I knew, they sent me to a secret location for training. Two weeks ago, I passed the course! I'm enclosing a picture of me in my British uniform. Pretty impressive, eh? Here's another snapshot of our 'home in the air,' an Armstrong-Whitworth Albemarle, which was a medium bomber before it became a paratroop transport. I wish you could have seen me jumping out of that plane from 12,000 feet up when it was flying along at 170 miles per hour! I lost count of the number of times I jumped after 25. The idea was much scarier than the actual jumps, once we started. Mama, I imagine what your next letter will say. Just know that I'm happier than I've ever been because soon it will be time for me to go to war!

"All my love, Hanna"

MARCH 12, 1944
MALTA

The three Jewish paratroopers, Joel Palgi, Peretz Goldstein, Hanna Senesh, and an equal number of Brits, Captain Giles Newkirk, Flight Lieutenant Clive Adaire, and Sergeant Henry Laycock, the navigator, met at RAF Luqa, for final prebriefing three days prior to the mission.

Captain Newkirk stood, crushed his half-smoked cigarette in a nearby glass ashtray, and addressed the group. "Assuming weather along the route is acceptable, 'Go' date is 14 March at 1830 hours. We'll be flying at one-five thousand feet. Drop point is just south of Great Bečkerek, Yugoslavia. From there, it's twenty-eight miles to the Hungarian frontier. "With drop tanks, the Albemarle will have plenty of fuel to make it back to Belgrade."

"What kind of greeting can we expect from the population?" Palgi asked.

"It's been a German stronghold since 1941, but there's been an active Communist underground that's gotten stronger each year. Our latest intelligence puts a large contingent from the Soviet Union in control of southeastern Vojvodina, where you'll be landing."

"How long will we be in the air, Captain? Hanna asked.

"Six hours, Miss Senesh. Most of the way you'll fly in under cover of darkness. The reception committee will have triangulated the landing area. You, Mister Palgi, and Mister Goldstein, will be on your own from there."

"Is there a contingency plan, Captain?"

"Belgrade is reasonably safe for now, Miss Senesh."

"And Budapest?"

"Too close a question to call. As of this date, our Soviet allies are spearheading a drive from the east. The closest German salient is in Bratislava, just across the border from Hungary, two-and-a-half hours from Budapest."

"Not very comforting," Palgi said.

"If things don't go as expected, stay out of Hungary and turn south toward Belgrade. You'll find Tito's partisans just about any place along the route. Each of you will have radio transmitter/receivers. Clive, do you foresee any major problems enroute?"

"Not really, Captain. The Jerries are bottled up north of the destination, so it should be clear sailing if the weather cooperates."

MARCH 14-15, 1944,
FORTY MILES SOUTHEAST OF MOHÁCS

Bogdan Stojanovič, the short, barrel-chested captain of a small tug that plied the river between Hungary and Yugoslavia, had been a partisan since Tito's rise two years before. Stojanovič's cell had been told the approximate time the RAF Albemarle would be dropping three paratroopers into the no-man's land between Novi Sad and Subotica. Earlier that day, he and his fifteen-year-old son Dragan had docked at Novi Sad to pick up a barge loaded with industrial pipe bound for Budapest.

They'd spent the next few hours of the blustery March afternoon in a small taverna in Bačka Topola, a partisan stronghold southwest of Subotica, with two of Stojanovič's associates, Rodavan Miloje, a robust farmer in late middle age, and Andrej Zivko, a striking blond-haired Communist in his early twenties, who'd captured the allegiance of political adherents and what was between the legs of several nubile east Serbian women, single, widowed, or married during his three years in the province.

"Is the landing area properly secured?" Stojanovič asked.

"Of course," Miloje replied, brandishing a serviceable pistol which had been in his family since the turn of the century.

"And when they land?"

"We'll provide for them, Bogdan."

"What news to the north?"

"Not good. The *schleuh* are supposed to march into our northern neighbor from Bratislava later this evening."

"Maybe not so bad," Stojanovič shrugged. The *boches* may think they're still in control, but who knows how many days or weeks they have left? Once the Soviets cross the Prut, Hungary'll be the last loyal barrier between the Thousand-year Reich and annihilation."

At that, Andrej rose, grabbed a bottle of *slivovica* from the makeshift bar, and poured a generous draft into each man's glass, which, after they toasted the future, was emptied in one massive gulp. "Gentlemen, time to visit our landing strip."

At that, they rose as one, mounted the horses Miloje had brought, and cantered to a flat meadow circled by birch trees, which were far enough removed from the touch-down area to be safe, yet close enough to furnish protection from the wind blowing off the Carpathians.

From a hundred yards away, the quadrangle of sticks piled around the landing site looked like nothing so much as ordinary haystacks. The parachutists were expected to be clothed in black, so they'd be virtually invisible as they hit the ground. The fire at each corner of the quadrangle, which would be bright enough for the British aircraft to see from eight thousand feet above them, would be banked as soon as the Albemarle discharged its payload, to minimize the visibility from the ground of anyone who might be a spy or an insomniac wandering around the area within an hour or two after midnight. Of course, if such a person became a bit too interested, the farmer and his Communist associate were sufficiently armed.

1:00 a.m. the following morning.

As the *Tisza*, Stojanovič's vessel, chugged slowly upriver, its thirty-year-old boiler belchng a combination of soot and steam from the branches of soft wood which lined both banks of the Dunav, its forty-two year-old captain and his son looked toward the darkness to the east. His hearing sharpened by his years on the river, he could barely make out the soft rumble of a large aircraft far beyond his sight.

"Any moment now, Dragan," Bogdan murmured.

What seemed like longer, but was probably less than two minutes later, they heard the sound of the aircraft descending, its engines cutting back, as it approached the landing area. No lights could be seen.

Through a maze of static, Stojanovič heard a recognizable voice. "Three have landed, one a woman. Going to ground 'til daybreak. You are?"

"Two north of Vukovar."

Stojanovič shut down his radio transmitter after the brief interchange. He was well aware that an Opel Blitz 2.5, a workhorse of both the Wehrmacht and the Italian fascist army, would meet the *Tisza* in a hidden cove between Apatin and Iiberopolis after twilight had turned to darkness twenty hours from now. After discharging its real cargo, south of Mohács in Hungary, Bogdan's job would be complete. From there, it was up to the British paratroopers to find their way north and east to their ultimate destination.

52

"I don't think we should attempt this," Palgi said, as they ate a breakfast of black bread, hard cheese, and olives, and quaffed mugs of chicory after they'd awakened the next morning. "The B.B.C. reported that the Germans occupied Hungary last night."

"All the more reason to go in now," Hanna replied. "The confusion between Admiral Horthy's government, the Arrow Cross, and the new 'visitors' will give us the cover we need to go to ground quickly."

"Hanna, I don't mean to pour cold water on the mission, but I agree with Joel," Peretz Goldstein counseled. "I know you want this with all your heart, but while there might be some leeway in Budapest, our Nazi friends will make sure the first place they seal will be Hungary's borders with Yugoslavia and Romania, which they view as dynamite dumps about to explode."

"You don't understand!" Hanna's nerves were taut with exhaustion and frustration. This mission meant *everything* to her, she would not, she *could* not, let it fail. "Pan Zivko, you of all of us know the political as well as the military implications. Moscow knows how valuable this mission is." She brushed a wisp of hair from her forehead, a nervous habit, without being conscious she was doing so.

The communist cell leader watched the interchange impassively. His answer, when it came, was measured. He lit a Carpați cigarette, took two puffs, holding it underhand in the way of Romanians, and held the pack out to her. Senesh shook her head. "Well?" she asked.

"Miss Senesh, you're well aware of our commitment to the cause. Practically speaking, although the mission may have political and certainly public relations implications, the military effect will really be quite minimal. If anything, I'm sure that both the British and their American allies value a single human life more than a small military disturbance, no matter how important it may seem. Without in any way downplaying your immense courage and your emotional investment, I suggest perhaps the wisest course would be for you to retire to Bucharest for a short while and live to fight another day."

"Am I the only one who gives a damn about this project?" Hanna responded hotly. "Don't you understand? The Nazi occupation makes it more important than ever that we throw a lifeline to the Jews to hold onto. If this mission aborts, the entire Zionist cause will be viewed as a sham. Hundreds, thousand of Jews will perish and they won't blame Hitler, they'll blame us. And justifiably so." By the time she finished speaking, her face was red with anger and she was breathing harshly.

"Let's consider the benefits of what we propose to do," Goldstein offered.

"Cut the bullshit!" Hanna said angrily. "Are you or aren't you willing to stand up for your principles?"

Palgi and Goldstein looked down at the ground.

"Maybe a couple of days to think it through," Joel Palgi temporized.

"As if that would make an ounce of difference," Hanna said, spitting on the floor to emphasize her disdain. "Very well, boys," she continued. "You've made up your mind and I've made up mine. Mister Miloje, are you willing to do your part in this?"

"Yes'm" the farmer replied. "Of course, I'm not the one going into Hungary. Once I drop you off at the loading point, it's on your head."

"I'm aware of that and I accept it. When do we start out?"

"Two o'clock this afternoon. That will give us sufficient time, allowing for the side roads and rutted paths, to make the cove. Perhaps you should rest up if you're determined to go."

"I am sufficiently rested for what needs to be done, Pan Miloje. And I thank you for your commitment. I will review the plans and meet you here at two."

Shortly after noon, Hanna was eating a hearty midday meal of yogurt, red peppers, and tinned fish when she heard a sharp knock on the front door. The taller of the two shawled women, a rawboned matron who Hanna guessed to be in her mid-thirties, went to the entryway, which was beyond her line of vision. Momentarily, she heard a low-voiced discussion. When the woman reentered, she was accompanied by a man of indeterminate middle age, his dark hair combed back on his head, and another, younger fellow, who couldn't have been more than five-and-a-half feet tall, with eyes hooded but intense.

"Miss Hanna, these are Jewish Partisans, Gediminas Ruibys, originally from Lithuania," the tall woman said, indicating the older of the two, "and Ariel Yechupetz, from somewhere southeast of Bucharest."

"Gentlemen," Hanna said courteously.

"Pana Senesh," Ruibys said, "we've heard the parachutists who accompanied you have decided to take a safe alternative."

"So it seems," she answered, not without a bitter irony in her tone. "How, may I ask, did you find out?"

"We are a small group, but tightly-knit, and word goes around. A woman should not risk going into the devil's jaws alone," the younger man offered.

"Have you any suggestions, Mister Yechupetz?"

"Yes'm," the shorter man said. "We propose to go with you into Hungary."

Hanna brightened at this reaffirmation of her own commitment. "You really mean that?"

They both lowered their heads, a combination of a nod and a stiff bow.

"We understand you'll be leaving with Rodavan Miloje within the hour. The Opel normally carries eight troops, all standing, but there's no reason we can't look the part of stupid peasants coming along to help our farmer friend."

"May God bless your courage," was all the stunned Hanna Senesh could say.

At precisely two o'clock, the ten-year-old Opel Blitz 2.5 pulled noisily up to the small house where Hanna, Ruibys, and Yechupetz were waiting impatiently. Miloje proudly told his passengers, "This old girl was built in the Adam Opel factory in Rüsselsheim the year before General Motors' German subsidiary built its new factory in Brandenburg. She's a real hand-me-down, went from the Wehrmacht to the Italians, to the Romanians before I bought it in Iaşi as army surplus three years ago. It's ticked over 150,000 kilometers, but I've managed to keep it running and it's still the most dependable vehicle I've ever owned."

Hanna commented on its camouflage brown, gray, and green color scheme and the similarly colored canvas top which enclosed the rear bed.

"I painted out any military symbols or other marks that might identify it with any country, and I've kept it on the farm, so it's managed to avoid strafing from the Brits and the Americans. It'll take anything the sorry excuses for roads in this part of the world can throw at us. Enough talk. Hop in. Enjoy the hay. If I stop for any reason, you'll have to figure a way to bury yourself in it or act like my dumb-ass assistants. If anyone asks, we're hauling this stuff to Sombor, where we'll trade it for some old farm machinery to sell at Iiberpolis. There's always a shitload of traffic running up to Hungary or down to Belgrade and tractors, blades, or anything else can always be sold for profit on the river."

Without another word, the three invaders climbed into the truck's bed and sat on conveniently placed bales of hay.

Miloje shifted into the lowest of the ten gears and the four cylinder, sixty-eight horsepower vehicle pulled out over the tamped gravel which led to the macadamized side road from Bačka Topola toward Sombor. Once on the road, travel slowed to a crawl, hampered by bomb craters.

As they crossed a railroad bridge over a narrow river, Miloje waved to a train conductor he knew, a man of old-fashioned manners and grave demeanor, with a droopy mustache, a conductor's hat one size too large, and a limp from wounds he'd received when his small local train had been dive-bombed in the early days of the war.

West of Bačka Topola there was no war, only a rainy March afternoon, a strip of pale sky on the horizon, bare fields not yet planted, birch groves, and tiny streams. The air smelled of damp earth and signaled the oncoming rebirth of the land.

Farther along, the road intersected a train track. When he heard the short blast of a whistle, Miloje pulled over to a side road to allow the local train, which was propelled by an old wood-fired engine, to pass the crossing. This wasn't merely a courtesy. The Serbian farmer had experienced four years of war and knew the Luftwaffe pilots would occasionally deliberately attack these small trains for no other reason than to relieve their boredom with easy targets. Now that the Luftwaffe had, for the most part, disappeared from the skies over Serbia, Croatia, and Romania, Miloje knew that when these isolated attacks came they were the result of frustration that the once invincible German air force no longer ruled the skies.

Moments later, the farmer's intuition proved prescient as he first heard, then saw, a flight of Dornier DO-17 bombers in an unbalanced *V* formation, headed a little east of due north. That meant they'd been working one of the industrial cities to the southwest, maybe Niŝ, and were on their way home, their bomb bays hopefully empty, to an airfield in Slovakia or the General Gouvernement area, formerly Poland.

"Nothing for you down here," Miloje murmured quietly. "It's just a little train puffing through the fields. Harmless."

The Dorniers droned on. Below and behind them, a fighter escort of the best the Luftwaffe had to offer during the early days of the war, Messerschmitt Bf-109s. The pilots' job had little to do with skill or daring. They were nursemaids. From the wing position, one of the Messerschmitts sideslipped away from the formation, swooped down a sharp angle in a long, steep dive, flattened out in a strafing attitude, and prepared to aim at the small locomotive which was chugging along as if it didn't have a care in the world.

It appeared that the innocent, unknowing little train had an inescapable rendezvous with death when, seemingly from out of nowhere, a dozen Spitfires descended on the Germans. The Messerschmitt preparing to liquidate the train was blasted out of the sky in seconds. The remaining Nazi aircraft were obliterated in short order. Hanna and the two Jewish Partisans, who'd looked out the back of the truck when they heard the first noises, cheered as the enemy aircraft were destroyed.

"Should we see if there are any wounded?" Yechupetz called out to the driver.

"Hell, no!" Miloje shouted back, as he pulled the truck out from where it had been hidden and accelerated as fast as the Opel could.

As they approached the outskirts of Bajsa, they were barely able to make fifteen kilometers per hour without destroying the axles or risking a number of flat tires. Miloje turned north, off the road and onto a rutted track.

"Time for a rest stop and to figure out where we go next," he said, bringing the truck to a stop in the middle of a beet field.

The three passengers, stiff and sore from the bone-jarring half-hour they'd just passed in the wldly gyrating Opel, stepped gingerly out the back of the bed. Without a word being said, Hanna went to the right side of the cab, squatted, and relieved herself, and the men went to the left rear corner of the Blitz to take similar care of their needs. The driver extracted a jug of *slivovica* and two tin cups from the cab, and offered each of the troopers a slug of the stuff. Hanna declined, but accepted a third tin cup of warm, but refreshing, water.

"We can go one of two ways," the farmer said. "North to Krivaja, then turn southwest toward Gornja Rogatica, or south in the direction of Panonija and northwest."

"Which one do you suggest, Rodavan?" Ruibys asked.

"Neither," the older man said wryly. "All of those towns change hands twice a week. The last thing we need is somebody who decides to commandeer this lorry, and then we're out on our asses in the middle of nowhere."

"What then?"

"Make a straight run through fields and foothills to Telecka, which is reasonably safe and where we can fill the tank with petrol, then do the same thing 'til we get to Sombor."

"Won't that delay us?" Hanna asked.

"It will, but not as much as if we got caught up in some little war-lords' power grab. This way, we'll look like we're part of a farm wherever we go."

After they returned to their places, the truck descended gently into the steppes west of the Carpathians. Treeless, empty, sometimes a few thatched huts around a well and a tiny dirt road that ran off into the endless distance. Now and then a village, a log station house for local trains, but here it was mostly the small railroad track and the wind.

It was 6:30 and the sun was setting when they came to the outskirts of *Zombor*, as the city had been called since the Axis powers had annexed it to Hungary in 1941. When the Opel pulled over to a gasoline station beyond the city limits, the passengers emerged to relieve themselves once again.

"You said we're going to exchange the hay for machinery," Hanna said. "Are you sure it's safe to do so?"

Miloje noticed the dark circles that had formed under the young woman's eyes.

"That may have been the original plan," he responded. "But that was days ago and it was as plausible a story as any to tell you. We are most definitely *not* going into Sombor. Even now, there are vicious battles between the Russkies and the Krauts for control of the city. We'll wait for nightfall, then take the byroads to the cove where we're supposed to meet up with Stojanovic."

"The cargo —?"

"That'll be you and the two boys," the farmer said.

"And then?"

"You wanted to get to Hungary. I imagine Captain Stojanovič will drop you off south of Mohács, most likely in some hidden landing near Bèda Karapancsa, and you'll be on your own from there. I trust you have maps of the area?"

"No, but I'm familiar with the route from Mohács to the capital."

"Best avoid Mohács, Miss Senesh. It's the closest border station to Yugoslavia and it'll be swarming with Hungarian Gendarmes and their new friends, particularly for the next few nights, as the *Boches*'ll want to make an impressive show of force. I suggest you lay low in the woods or the marshes and work your way northeast through the most uninhabited area you can find."

Once they were rolling again, Hanna pulled out her British issue Galvin SCR-536 walkie talkie from under the hay where it had been hidden and tested it to make sure it had a live signal. She'd learned from her trainers that a radio transmitter / receiver this small and light would have been unthinkable even three years ago. The unit, which incorporated five vacuum tubes in a waterproof case, had no separate power switch. Instead the radio turned on when the antenna was pulled out, and off when it was retracted. The SCR-536 weighed only five pounds with batteries. Its range was one mile over land, and 3 miles over water. It was her lifeline to her British allies and she must protect it at all costs.

Shortly after nine that night, the truck came to a gradual stop in total darkness. Miloje came around to the back and spoke in a low voice, knowing that the sound of a whispter would carry farther than ordinary conversational tone.

"Time to get out and be off," he said cheerfully.

As they stepped out of the truck, they shivered in the cold of the night air. Wherever they'd stopped, the place was deserted — only the sigh of the wind, moths fluttering in the Opel's headlights, and the splash of water.

"Where are we?" Hanna asked.

"Alive and safe," Miloje said.

They heard the sound of a wooden structure, Stojanović's tug, banging softly against a jetty, its lone barge trailing behind it.

"Right on time, Bogdan," Miloje said. "Dragan with you?"

"Of course. He's monitoring the engine so it's not too noisy. Are these the three that landed last night?"

"No, Pan Stojanovič," Hanna volunteered. "Mister Palgi and Mister Goldstein, who accompanied me on the way down, decided they had ... safer ... things to do. These two brave men," she said," indicating Ruibys and Yechupetz, "were kind enough or brave enough, or foolhardy enough to take their places."

"So they'll be going with us into *Magyarország?*"

"That's so," Ruibys answered. "Gediminas Ruibys," he continued, holding out his right hand. "My associate is Ariel Yechupetz," he said, indicating the shorter man.

"Very well, lady, gentlemen. Welcome aboard the *Tisza*.."

As they crossed the frontier into Hungary and the Dunav became the *Duna* the following day, Stojanovič's seasoned eye quickly became alert to the fact that there were more Kriegsmarine vessels on the Danube than there had been since the Wehrmacht's access to the Romanian oilfields and the means of upriver transport of this critical commodity had been destroyed the year before.

"A show of force to impress the locals," he grumbled. "We'll most likely be subject to more bloody inspections than ever," he continued.

The hastily-convened group, the captain, his son, and their three "guests" spoke in hushed voices as they considered the options, none of them particularly promising, for the two Partisans and their female leader.

"Do you have papers?" Stojanovič asked Hanna.

"A three-year-old Budapest residence permit," she responded. "And, of course, anyone who hears me speak would recognize my native accent."

"Not good enough," Dragan Stojanovič volunteered. "The Hungarians have always been sticklers for formality. They were the petty bureaucrats of Austria-Hungary and their Gestapo successors are even worse."

"What then?" Hanna asked the captain, her voice betraying nervous fear overriding her zealot's passion for the first time.

"Probably best to appear as normal as we can, even move a bit slower than usual, putting in at small ports along the river, staying well below Mohács until after nightfall."

He lit up a cigarette and passed a pack around.

"I see you've switched from Carpați to Trommler since we crossed the frontier," Ruibys remarked.

"When in Rome, and all that," Stojanovič responded. "Dependng on where we are or who checks my identity, I carry several brands. Carpați, naturally, since it's easy to identify me as a Balkan mongrel. Lucky Strikes if there are Brits or Americans anywhere on the river. I'm sure the new Nazi overlords of our Hungarian hosts would feel more comfortable around me if I offered them the one brand the Führer sanctions. By the way," he continued, switching subjects, "I'd get rid of the walkie-talkie if I were you, Miss Senesh. It pretty well identifies your loyalties should you be stopped by anyone."

"Can't do that, Captain," Hanna remarked curtly.

"Can't or won't?"

"Take your choice, Pan Stojanovič. It's my safety net."

"Safety net or prison cell?"

"How else could I keep in contact with my friends who could help me?"

"Seriously, Miss Senesh, aren't you pretty much on your own here? I haven't noticed any Allied military in this area to speak of. If I might be so bold as to ask, why did you volunteer for this job in the first place? To help the Brits or for other purposes?"

Hanna ignored the question. "If I can save even one Jew, I've saved the world," she replied. "You think it's best to drop us off at nighttime?"

"I know it's your best chance."

During the next week, Senesh and her associates kept well away from places of habitation as they skirted Szeksztárd, Paks, Dunaujváros, and Erd enroute to their destination, Budapest. Once in the capital, she hoped to present herself at the headquarters of the Zionist Federation of Hungary, where she'd been told to ask for Doctor Ottó Komoly.

Unfortunately, the day after she arrived in Budapest, Hanna happened to ask a friendly-looking local traffic policeman where she could find the Zionist Federation offices on Erzsébet Boulevard. Fate takes strange paths. The policeman, a member of the Arrow Cross, not only gave her directions, but offered to walk with her the several blocks to the address. Immediately after she thanked him and entered the building, he reported this event to his immediate Arrow Cross superior.

As she left the building half an hour later, three Hungarian gendarmes approached her. "Excuse me, Miss," the senior of the police officers said courteously. "May we please see your identification papers?"

BUDAPEST

MAY – OCTOBER 1944

LATE MAY 1944

53

Hanna lay on a cot in a cell somewhere in Budapest, face up on the iron cot, the legs of which were embedded in a concrete floor. The room's whitewashed walls, stained and musty, barely concealed the odor of carbolic acid, sweat, and urine. Apart from a thin soiled mattress and a rolled up towel under her head, the bed contained no other linen. Two heavy leather straps secured her ankles, two more her thighs and wrists. A single strap pinned her chest down. She was barely conscious, breathing deeply and irregularly.

Her face had been bathed clean of blood, the ear and scalp sutured. A patch of adhesive gauze spanned her broken nose. She felt, rather than saw, the stumps of two broken front teeth.

Through a haze of pain and semiconsciousness, she saw and heard a man in a white coat straighten up and replace a stethoscope in his bag.

"What did you hit her with, an express train?" he asked the others in the room.

"Never mind, doctor. What's the damage?"

"Fracture of the right wrist, lacerated left ear and scalp, a broken nose, and two broken teeth. Multiple cuts and bruises, internal hemorrhaging, which could get worse and kill her. What worries me is the head.

There's a concussion for sure, although there don't seem to be any signs of a skull fracture. But the concussion could get worse if she's not left alone."

"We need to get answers to certain questions," a man adjacent to the doctor observed.

"If you start questioning this woman with your methods before she's recovered, she'll either die or become a raving lunatic."

The man listened to the doctor's bitter prediction without moving a muscle. "How long?" he asked.

"Impossible to say. She may regain consciousness tomorrow or not for days. Even then, she will not be medically fit for questioning for at least two weeks."

"There are certain drugs," murmured the man.

"Yes, there are. There's no way I'll prescribe them. You probably can get them, but not from me. Nothing she could tell you now would make the slightest sense. Her mind is scrambled. It may clear, it may not, but it must happen in its own time. Mind-bending drugs would simply produce an idiot, no use to you or anyone else. You'll just have to wait." The doctor turned and walked away, out of her sight.

But the doctor was wrong. Hanna opened her eyes two days later. The same day she had her first and only session with the interrogators.

The room was silent except for the sound of heavy, controlled breathing from the three men behind the table and the rasping rattle from the woman strapped to the heavy oak chair in front of it. There was only one pool of light, from a standard table lamp, but its bulb was of great brightness, adding to the stifling heat of the room. The bulb shone straight at the chair six feet away.

Hanna could not see the torsos and shoulders of the three men behind the table. The only way she could have seen her questioners would have been to leave her chair and move to the side, so that the indirect glow from the light would pick out their silhouettes, but that she could not do. Padded straps pinned her ankles firmly against the legs of the chair. From each of these legs, front and back, an L-shaped steel bracket was bolted into the floor. Hanna's wrists were secured to the arms of the chair by padded straps. The padding of each strap was drenched in sweat.

The top of the table was almost bare. Its only decoration was a slit bordered in brass and marked along one side with figures. A narrow brass arm with a knob protruded from the slit. Next to the slit there was an on/off switch. Two wires fell beneath the table, one from the switch and the other from the current control, toward an electric transformer lying on the floor near the feet of the chief interrogator.

In the far corner of the room, behind the questioners, a man sat at a wooden table, face to the wall, taking notes in shorthand. Apart from the breathing, the silence of the room was deafening. All three questioners were in shirtsleeves, rolled up high, and damp with sweat. The odor was overpowering, a stench of sweat, metal, stale smoke, and human vomit. Even the vomit, pungent though it was, was overwhelmed by the unmistakable reek of fear and pain.

The man in the center spoke at last, his voice civil, gentle, coaxing. "Listen Fräulein Senesh, you are going to tell us. Not now, perhaps, but eventually. You are an extraordinarily brave young woman, but even you cannot hold out much longer. You think your associates, Herr Palgi and Herr Goldstein would forbid you if they were here? They would order you to tell us. They know about these things. They would tell us themselves, to spare you discomfort. You must know, Fräulein Senesh, they always talk in the end. No one can go on and on and on. So why not now Fräulein Senesh? Then back to bed and blessed sleep, and no one will disturb you."

The woman in the chair raised a battered face, glistening with sweat, into the light. Her eyes were closed, whether by the great blue bruises or by the light, it didn't matter which. Her mouth opened and she tried to speak. A small gobbet of puke emerged and dribbled down her chest to the pool of vomit in her lap. Her head sagged back until the chin touched her chest again. She shook her head from side to side in answer.

The voice from behind the table began again. "You are a hard woman, Fräulein Senesh. We all recognize that. Even you can't go on. But we can, Fräulein Senesh, we can. If we have to keep you alive and conscious for days, even for weeks … There is no merciful oblivion. So why not talk? We know about pain, but the little crabs, they just don't understand. They just go on and on … electrodes … you own body tearing itself to shreds … Now tell us, Fräulein Senesh, what is the code word that enables you to communicate with your controllers?"

Hanna's head shook slowly from side to side. Little copper crabs grabbed the nipples of her breasts. A crab with serrated teeth held her clitoris in its relentless grip. The man nearest the slit in the table moved the toggle switch from two to three.

The little metal crabs fixed to the woman in the chair appeared to come alive with a slight buzzing. The figure in the chair rose as if propelled by a fist. Her legs and wrists bulged outwards against the straps until it seemed that even with the padding the leather must cut clean through the flesh and bone. Hanna's eyes, which were medically unable to see clearly through the puffed flesh around them, started outwards, bulging into vision and staring at the ceiling. Her mouth opened, as if in surprise. It took half a second before the demonic screams came out of her lungs. When they came, they went on without stop…

Catherina Senesh saw rather than heard the arrival of the khaki-colored Type 82 *Kübelwagen*, one of the gifts from the newly-arrived Germans to their Hungarian hosts, as it parked in front of her two-story home. Two Hungarian gendarmes got out of the cruiser and knocked on her door. When she answered, they requested, quite politely, that she accompany them to the central gendarmerie. Not knowing what to expect, but nervous and mistrustful, she had no option but to accede to what she took as an order.

When they arrived at headquarters, the commandant addressed her by her formal married name. "*Szensné* Catherina, we've requested your presence because your daughter has been arrested."

"You must be mistaken, Captain," Catherina Senesh replied. She maintained her dignified demeanor, despite an undertone of fear. "You are undoubtedly aware that she emigrated legally to Palestine four years ago."

"I'm afraid you're wrong, Madame Senesh," the officer responded. "She was seized five days ago and is suspected as a spy and an *agent provocateur*. It appears she parachuted into Serbian Yugoslavia and proceeded to Budapest, where she was caught as she exited the offices of the Hungarian Jewish Agency on Erzsébet Boulevard."

"What do you want from me?" Catherina said.

"We're hoping you can talk sensibly to her as a responsible mother."

"Meaning?"

"We've know that two accomplices parachuted into Yugoslavia with her. We have tried to persuade her, unsuccessfully so far, to reveal information about the others and about her mission."

"Why bring me in? You know I must have access to a lawyer."

"That's not necessary, Madame Senesh. You are neither a suspect nor have you been implicated in any way so far." The man's stressing the last two words was not lost on the pereceptive middle-aged woman. "We have no reason to believe you have any information to share with us. We simply ask that you speak with your daughter and exercise your maternal influence."

"Commander, if you have young adult children of your own, you must know the last thing they want is advice from their parents."

"Perhaps, perhaps not," he said, looking down at his left hand and rubbing an inkspot that had appeared there with his right forefinger. "At the very least, you should see and speak with her for a little while." Again an order, not a request.

Although she trembled uncontrollably, it was all she could do to stifle a horrified scream. The derelict hulk who sat in front of her, chained to a cheap iron chair, with broken front teeth, the left side of her face yellow and swollen, her eyes black and swelled shut, her hair a greasy tangle, couldn't possibly be her lovely young daughter. The woman handcuffed to the straight-backed seat looked like someone in the midst of a thirty-year nightmare.

Catherina looked frantically about her surroundings, trying desperately to escape the sight directly in front of her. An eight-by-eight-foot cell with a low-wattage lightbulb suspended from the ceiling. A single bucket, the sole depository for water and waste. A cot with metal springs and a thin, soiled blanket. No mattress. Dark. Three walls and a fourth side composed of bars and a small, locked door.

Inexorably, her eyes were drawn back toward her horridly tortured, disfigured, and abused twenty-two year-old daughter. A ragged voice issued from a parched throat.

"I'm sorry you had to see me like this, Mama. I did it for you."

Catherina choked back hot tears with all the strength she could muster. She would not let the two bastards standing immediately outside the cell see her break down.

She and Hanna spoke in soft tones.

"Did you …?"

"No, Mama, I didn't tell the names and I didn't tell the codes."

"But they could …?"

"Torture me more? Pull my fingernails out? Beat the bottom of my feet again?"

"Kill you."

"They could. But then they'd gain nothing. Does anyone on the outside except you know?"

"I don't think so, darling."

"They should."

"They will. I promise."

Without a word, one of the prison guards unlocked the cell door, roughly grabbed Catherina's arm, and propelled her out of Hanna's presence.

"Am I to understand you don't intend to cooperate?" The commandant had lost all semblance of civility.

Catherina remained silent as a stone and turned her back to him.

"Did you hear me, Szens*né* Catherina?"

From the stoic matron, nothing.

"Very well, then, for failure to cooperate with duly constituted authority, you may stay in the cell next to your daughter until you become more … compliant."

During the next several nights, Catherina Senesh, who was allowed no outside contact with anyone, struggled in vain to get even a few hours of sleep as she lay in pain on a cot exactly like Hanna's, in the cell adjacent to her daughter. A guard patrolled the immediate area, ensuring that there was little, if any, communication between Hanna and her mother. Grunts, nods, meaningful eye contact.

Each night, at various times, Hanna was taken from her cell. Minutes later, Catherina heard loud smacking and punching noises and Hanna's ceaseless screams. Catherina kept count of her time in prison by biting her finger and pressing it against a wall of her cell until a droplet of blood made a mark. This went on for ten days.

At the end of that period, she was once again taken to the commandant's office.

"Well, Szens*né* Catherina, have you had enough?"

Silence.

"You know, of course that we've told your daughter that it's your recalcitrance that has brought about more enhanced 'correctional methods' for her." A statement, not a question.

Once again, Catherina turned her back on the prison warden.

His temper on the verge of breaking, the commandant slapped Catherina's face, not hard enough to break the skin, but enough to inflict pain.

Catherina Senesh remained still and silent as a stone.

"I don't know how you managed to do this," the warden said angrily, "but we have received word from one of Admiral Horthy's delegates that you are to be released. Of course, your actions will be carefully monitored, and you will be allowed two visits with your treasonous spy-daughter before her trial. You heard me correctly. She will be tried by the Twelfth District Provisional Military Court and will most likely be sentenced to death."

Gyula Grossman, a minor functionary at the Jewish Rescue Agency, looked impatiently at the dignified middle-aged woman sitting in front of him. Grossman had awakened earlier that morning to an embittered scolding by his wife over some perceived misdemeanor. Breakfast had consisted of a thin gruel-like porridge and a cup consisting of half a teaspoon of tasteless chicory — ersatz coffee — in a cup of tepid, sugarless water. The woman who'd come in two minutes ago was the first of what would be a replication of every other day at the agency: a continual parade of supplicants and petitioners seeking aid which they didn't realize he had little, if any, power or authority to give them.

Grossman glanced at the name on the woman's thin dossier: Szensné Catherina, Mrs. Catherina Senesh.

"Yes?" he asked without preamble.

"I need the Agency to find me a lawyer."

"Madame, there are hundreds of lawyers in the city. The Agency simply does not have the funds to pay for a private lawyer for any given person."

"You don't understand, Mister Grossman," she said, reading from the nameplate in front of the balding mid-fiftyish man with pencil-thin mustache. "My daughter is Hanna Senesh."

"Yes?" Grossman answered, seemingly not comprehending. He pressed a buzzer on his telephone and picked up the receiver. "Sarah, do we have a file on a Hanna Senesh?" He waited a few moments, then said, "Bring it in, please."

A small woman in her late thirties entered the room, nodded deferentially, and, when Grossman crooked his finger beckoning her to enter, handed him a slim folder. Grossman lit a cigarette, drew in a few puffs, considered the dossier, then faced Mrs. Senesh.

"Ah, yes," he said. "Arrested as a spy for the English. We're aware of the case. Why do you need a lawyer?"

"She's to be tried for treason, Mister Grossman. I have scoured Budapest for an advocate to defend her. No Christian attorney will defend a Jew and an accused spy. The Arrow Cross has made sure of that. I have not been able to find a single Jewish lawyer allowed to practice in the Hungarian military courts. My daughter conveyed to me that she was arrested as she left the Jewish Agency offices three months ago."

Grossman offered Mrs. Senesh a cigarette from his pack, which she declined.

After a few more minutes and two or three telephone calls, he scribbled a few notes on the paper in front of him, looked up, and addressed her. "There's no need for a lawyer. We have everything under control. Go home. Your daughter should arrive at your doorstep within a few hours."

"How can you say that?" Catherina said, not believing her ears.

"The Jewish Agency has several connections most people don't even know about," he said. "Our chairman is in regular communication with the Germans, who, as I'm sure you are aware, have certain, shall we say, *influence* over their Hungarian brothers."

54

Two weeks later, Catherina welcomed three people she'd not met before, two men and a woman, to her home on an unseasonably hot late September afternoon, made muggier and more uncomfortable by a rain shower which had abated only an hour before. After they'd enjoyed tea and Mrs. Senesh's homemade *palatschinken*, crepes stuffed with apricot jam, the older man addressed her. "Imre Plotkin told me you wanted to see us?"

"I do, and thank you so much for coming on such short notice."

"You're Hanna Senesh's mother. How could we *not* have come? More to the point, how can we help you?"

"A fortnight ago a functionary at the Jewish Agency, Mister Grossman —"

"Ah, Julius Grossman, who calls himself Gyula in the Hungarian style. As useless a petty bureaucrat as the Agency ever hired ..." the man said.

"Whoever he was, he told me that Hanna had been released and was coming home. It turned out to be untrue."

"Of course," the woman said. "It makes the small functionaries feel important if they can make someone feel better for five minutes. Unless you go to the top, you'll get no real action."

"I've heard that Doctor Kaztner —"

"*If* you can get to see him. If you're from Kolozsvár or if you're a big-shot Zionist, it might be easier. Budapest, not so easy," the woman continued.

"They say Doctor Kasztner's the only Jew allowed to see imprisoned Jews whenever he wants," the younger of the two men said. "He's allowed to bring them food, clothing, and anything else they might need. I don't how he manages it, but he drives his own car around the city. There's a rumor that he was able to get thousands of Jews diverted from the camps and sent to this new farm community, Kenyermeze, and he got more than fifteen hundred Jews from Kolozsvár to Switzerland."

"Do you think he's heard of my Hanna?" Catherina asked hopefully.

"How could he *not* have heard of her?" the older man asked.

The woman who answered the door was in her mid-thirties, attractive, and seemed much more competent than Grossman.

"How did you get Doctor Kasztner's home address?" she asked Catherina.

"Sol Levinthal gave it to me. I asked Julius Grossman for his address last week, but Mister Grossman told me it was impossible to see Doctor Kasztner, since he was too busy. When I asked for Doctor Kasztner's address, Grossman told me he could not give it to me. Fortunately, Mister Levinthal was more forthcoming. Might I ask your name, Miss … Mrs. …"

"Hansi. Hansi Brand."

"I'm Catherina Senesh. I've heard that Doctor Kasztner is the only one who can help. My daughter is Hanna — "

"Hanna Senesh," Mrs. Brand finished the sentence. "One of the parachutists from Palestine. We know of the case. I understand Doctor Kasztner intends to see her in the next few days, as soon as he returns from Geneva. I'll give you Doctor Kasztner's private office address," she said, writing something on sheet of paper, which she handed to Mrs. Senesh.

"Not the Erzsébet Boulevard address?" Catherina asked, looking down at what Mrs. Brand had written.

"No. Erzsébet is the Agency's public office. This address is limited to those with special needs. You can talk to his secretary there. She'll arrange for you to meet with Doctor Kasztner. Might I suggest that if you have anything you want him to give your daughter, a food package, clothing, whatever, you take it to his secretary."

"Thank you, Mrs. Brand. You've been very kind."

On October 12, 1944. Catherina, now beyond desperation, entered Doctor Kasztner's outer office and confronted his secretary.

"Mrs. Blum, I've now come to this office every day for the past sixteen days. Each day you've told me a different story. Doctor Kasztner's in Zurich, Doctor Kasztner's in Vienna, Doctor Kasztner's everywhere but in Budapest."

Kasztner's secretary, in her early forties and obviously harried, replied curtly, "Mrs. Senesh, there are over a hundred thousand people who need to see Doctor Kasztner today, and there'll be another hundred thousand tomorrow. He can't see everyone. No human being could. I'm simply telling you that when he returns you'll be one of the first he sees. We know your daughter's case is important to you."

"Mrs. Blum, I understand all of that. All I want to know whether or not Hanna received the ten packages I left with you?"

"I'm sure they're in the qeue to be delivered."

"Please cut the doubletalk, Mrs. Blum," Catherina said impatiently, her voice rising.

"You don't need to shout. Madame," the secretary responded. "I can assure you that addressing me in such a disrespectful manner will not hasten the delivery of goods to your daughter or anyone else."

"Thank you very much," Catherina said icily. She slammed the door on her way out and made it halfway down the hall before she sat down on the nearest bench and burst into tears.

Catherina Senesh had no idea how long she'd been weeping in the hallway when a gentle man in his mid-fifties offered her a glass of water and invited her to sit in his office while she composed herself. When she sat in a scarred and faded, but comfortable leather chair, the man brought her a fresh handkerchief to dry her eyes and a small glass of red wine, then sat in a chair next to her, holding her hand and saying nothing.

Momentarily, when she felt she'd regained control, she said, "I cannot thank you enough for your kindness, Mister —?"

"Komoly," the man replied. "Please call me Ottó."

She smiled for the first time all day. "You are Doctor Komoly of the Jewish Agency?"

"I am."

"My daughter mentioned your name. She said she had come to see you but you were not at the Agency on the day she came. She was arrested by the Hungarian gendarmes as she left the Agency building."

"And her name?"

"Hanna. Hanna Senesh. Perhaps if I told you more …"

"But that is inexcusable! Criminal!" Komoly said angrily when Catherina had told him her story. "Why was I never informed? I used to be the Chairman of the Agency until a year ago. You would think I would be made aware of these things. I have not even heard that Hanna was in Budapest. We must get her a lawyer, right now, today!" he exclaimed, fishing in his desk drawer and extracting a small notebook filled with names, addresses, and telephone numbers. Within the hour, Doctor Komoly had located a Jewish advocate, who gave Catherina an appointment for 9:00 a.m. the following morning.

The same day Catherina Senesh was frantically making her rounds, Hanna, who'd been removed tom a general cell to await her trial for treason, addressed the two children, ages 12 and 10, who were her cellmates.

"Ephraim, what have you learned during the past week?"

"Nothing of importance," the twelve-year-old boy mumbled.

"Why do you say that? I'm so proud of the way you've excelled in studying for your Bar Mitzvah."

"Why are we kidding ourselves? I won't be alive for my Bar Mitzvah anyway, so why bother?"

"Don't say that, my Ephraim," she said, hugging him gently to her breast. "You are the future of our people and you must never give up hope."

"It's been eight months since my family was killed in Ukraine," the boy said. "Running and hiding for the last three years, caught eight months ago for smuggling. What have I got to live for, even if I survive?"

"You are tomorrow's hope, Ephraim, and every day you're still alive is one more day that the Jewish people will survive."

"Aren't you frightened, Miss Senesh? They say you'll be tried and executed any day."

"Of course I'm frightened, Ephraim, more so than I've ever been in my life. But the minute I give up hope is the minute that there will never be a new life, or a Jew left to carry on after five thousand years of history. So as long as I'm breathing, I believe in the goodness of the all-knowing God and I believe in the basic decency of human beings."

She placed her left forefinger between her nose and her upper lip. With her right hands, she made a slashing movement across her throat. The children grinned.

"You really think the monster will be dead one day?" the younger child, a girl named D'vora, said, smiling.

"I do, sweet girl," Hanna said. "And you, darling child, with God's help, will be alive long after he's gone.

"When I saw my friend Baruch in the yard, he told me you've been spreading rumors throughout the prison, flashing mirror signals, and holding up Hebrew letters in your window, but then they put you in a cell without a window," Ephraim said.

"That's right," Hanna replied. "If somehow I don't survive, promise me you'll do the same thing."

"We promise," the two of them said solemnly. In unison.

"That's outrageous!" Morechai Levi, the attorney Doctor Komoly had found for her, said. "They've disobeyed every section of the criminal code and violated every right afforded the accused in any civilized society! They've held her for seven months without bail or even preferring charges!"

"That's easy for us to say, Counselor. But we're on the outside. How could you even go about finding if a date has been set for her trial?"

"They say Doctor Kasztner knows everything there is to know about everything having to do with Jews in this country. I'm sure if I give his office a call, I'll found out immediately."

The advocate displayed a grim face when he saw Catherina later that afternoon.

"His secretary says he's still in Vienna. She doesn't know when he'll return. I told her she could surely telephone him and tell him how urgent this situation has become."

"A lot of good that would do," Catherina said angrily. "I got the same story for more than two weeks."

"But I'm one of the few Jewish lawyers still allowed to practice in

Budapest and one of only three accredited to the Jewish Agency. Hertha Blum knows that. I'm also sure she knows exactly where Rudolf Kasztner is and how to reach him. Either she's covering up and lying for him, which I doubt, or he's dodging the call because it's political dynamite, something he wants to avoid at all costs."

"Have you tried Doctor Komoly?"

"Of course. He was the first one I tried. He's the only one at the Agency who gives a damn about anyone. He told me that since he was pushed out of the Chairmanship it's like he's not even alive as far as the Hungarians and the Nazis are concerned."

"So what do we do?"

"I've got a friend who has connections with Major General Janos Teleki. The general's a good man who is horrified at the treatment the Jews have received since the Germans came to town and the Arrow Cross took over," Levi said. He looked at his wristwatch. "Damn! My friend leaves at two every afternoon. I'll call him at home, but even then it'll be early tomorrow morning before he can reach General Teleki. Let's you and I plan to meet here at eight. Is that too early for you?"

"Of course not, Mister Levi," Catherina said. "I'm so grateful for anything you can do."

The following morning, promptly at eight, Catherina arrived at lawyer Levi's office to find her counselor deep in conversation with two men, one of whom looked older than seventy, but whose military dress and distinguished demeanor gave him an aura of confidence and power.

"Catherina," Levi said in what she perceived as a mournful and defeated tone. "Catherina ..." The lawyer's voice broke and he put his face in his hands.

The younger of the two strangers looked directly at Catherina Senesh, his eyes gentle, his voice even more so. "Mrs. Senesh," he said, "my name is Szekeley Ferenc – Franz Szekeley. I am the retired chairman of the Budapest Bar Association. At six o'clock this morning, I received a telephone call from General Janos Teleki, the man sitting next to you. I'm afraid it's too late for any of us to help Hanna."

"What do you mean too late?" she gasped, the monstrosity of what had happened hitting her like a fist to her stomach. "How can that be?"

General Teleki reached over, grasped Catherina's right hand in his, and said, "Madame Senesh, you must try to be strong. I have been in the Hungarian army for forty-five years, since just before the turn of the century, and in all that time I have never been as embarrassed and ashamed of what has become of that army as I am today."

Catherina Senesh felt rather than heard the general's next words, and she was already weeping when they came.

"Mister Szekeley reached me at my home at 8:30 last evening. I immediately called Colonel deVersecy at his residence, and he in turn telephoned everyone he knew in the prison system. He called me back at three this morning and relayed to me that your daughter had been taken from her cell at nine o'clock last night. She was tried and convicted by a military tribunal and executed at midnight."

Attorney Levi's office was silent, but for the loud ticking of a Regulator clock. Barrister Szekeley reached into a box of cigarettes on Levi's desk, thought the better of it, and closed the box. The general sat impassively, waiting for the gravity of his words to sink in. Catherina Senesh, her face white with shock, sat silent and still for several moments.

Incongruously, she reached into her purse, pulled out a wallet, and extracted three photographs of Hanna, one taken when she was eight years old, one taken of her working on a kibbutz in Palestine, and a third of her in her parachutist's uniform. She passed them around, then, when they were returned to her, clutched them to her breast.

"This is my Hanna," she said, half-sobbing. "She was such an obedient, beautiful child. When she left for Palestine …" the words hung in the air.

"She wrote some months ago that there was a young man interested in her." Catherina's words only deepened her sorrow as the clock kept ticking. "I never even knew his name. Now I never will. Excuse me, General Teleki, gentlemen. I think I would like to use the ladies' room." She rose stiffly and left the office.

When she returned, ten minutes later, her face was more composed, but General Teleki realized that was because deep shock had set in. He knew what must follow.

And when it came, it was the keening wail of centuries of mothers who had lost their children before their time. It was an entire world's misery and pain and broken hearts and hopelessness, rolled into one single cry, condemning the God who would let this happen. And it went on and on and on …

Attorney Levi and General Teleki drove her home and sat with her the rest of that day and into the evening. The general's personal physician came to the house and administered a sedative, which dulled the pain only a little, but somehow allowed her to sleep that night.

General Teleki's message to Catherina was brief, heartfelt, and to the point. "Words can never bring back your daughter. Your suffering will be with me 'til my dying day. If there is any good at all to come out of this disaster, it is that I managed to intercede with the highest echelons of military authority. Two Jewish children who'd been in Hanna's cell with her were released from prison on my recognizance. D'vora Raskin, ten years old, was released to the remnant of her family somewhere in the High Tatras. A twelve-year-old orphan boy, Ephraim Biran, was turned over to a Jewish partisan group in the same area."

At General Teleki's instigation, a Hungarian official approached Catherina Senesh the following day later. He said to her, "I must bow my head over your daughter's behavior before her death. Her last words were that she was very proud to be a Jew." General Teleki and the official, whose name Catherina never learned, proved to be the kindest and most knowledgeable men she met during this terrible ordeal. The official, in particular, told her everything he knew about what had happened. He was extraordinarily generous with his time and his sympathy.

Two days later, Mister Levi returned to her home, his face red with anger. Through a haze of despair, Catherina Senesh deciphered the reason for his fury.

"I saw Doctor Kasztner with Colonel Eichmann riding together in a chauffeur-driven Grosser Mercedes this morning. They stopped and Kasztner got out just outside the Agency headquarters. Can you believe it? When I called his secretary, Hertha Blum, an hour after I saw them, she had the nerve to tell me that Doctor Kasztner was still in Vienna, and was not expected back for three more days."

JERUSALEM DISTRICT COURT

1954

55

"Mrs. Senesh," Tamir asked quietly, "did you ever meet Doctor Kasztner before your daughter's execution?"

"No, never."

"Have you met Doctor Kasztner in Israel?"

"Yes, once. I was in Jerusalem taking care of some matters for my school. I went to a government office. Doctor Kasztner apparently heard I was there. He walked in quickly and greeted me. I said to him, 'Doctor Kasztner, I am not prepared to meet you.' He asked me why and I said, 'There were times when I tried desperately to meet you and I was not successful.'"

"Did Doctor Kasztner respond?"

"Yes. He said, 'Believe me, it was only in Switzerland the next year that I heard how often you had come looking for me.'

"I replied, 'How is it possible that in such a crucial time you had such an irresponsible secretary who failed to tell you I came to your office every day looking for you?'"

"Doctor Kasztner answered, 'What happened pains me more than it does anyone else.' I said, 'I believe it is painful to you *now*, Doctor Kasztner, but at that time, when something could have been done, you don't seem to have been the least bit pained.'

"He said, 'No, we did everything we could have done. One day, I shall tell you how much we did.'

"I said to him, 'I know that is not true. I don't say that you could have saved my daughter Hanna, but you didn't even *try.* It makes it harder for me that nothing was done.'"

"What was Doctor Kasztner's response?" Tamir asked.

"He kept giving me doubletalk about how his committee did everything they could, and he would tell me about it one day. He told me, 'As a veteran Zionist, I fully appreciate your daughter's heroic deeds.'

"I said, 'How is it possible if that is the case, that on October 13 I saw Doctor Komoly, your colleague, who didn't even know Hanna was a parachutist, or even that she was in Budapest? At that time, there was nothing to eat in prison. At least you could have sent a parcel of food to her. More than that, my daughter Hanna waited for a sign that someone outside was even thinking about her.'

"Doctor Kasztner said, 'I really don't understand how it happened that none of the food parcels I sent your daughter arrived.'

"I said, 'It is a little difficult to understand why the food parcels my friends sent arrived and yours did not, Doctor Kasztner.'"

"Mrs. Senesh, did you keep anything your daughter had written during that time?"

"Yes, Mister Tamir. Just prior to her execution, she wrote me a note that I keep framed next to my bed:

> "'Dearest Mother" I don't know what to say, only this:
> a million thanks, and forgive me if you can. You know
> well why words aren't necessary. With love forever.
> Your daughter, Hanna.'"

"She wrote one last poem in her cell, which I treasure as much:

> "One-two-three ... eight feet long.
> Two strides across, the rest is dark
> Life hangs over me like a question mark.

> "One-two-three ... maybe another week,
> Or next month may still find me here
> But death, I feel, is very near.

"I gambled on what mattered most
The dice were cast. I lost."

The absolute silence in the courtroom was interrupted only by soft weeping. The Judge turned to face the back of the wall. His shoulders were heaving.

Attorney General Cohen waived cross-examination. That night, no newspaper in Israel challenged Mrs. Senesh's testimony.

After the conclusion of Mrs. Senesh's testimony, both sides rested. The Court set Monday, September 20, 1954, for the beginning of final arguments.

Hanna Senesh had just turned twenty-three when she was executed.

56

After the court adjourned, Rudolf Kasztner and his wife flew to Paris for a much-needed rest. Margarethe Fisher Kasztner, who'd stayed away from court at her husband's insistence, noticed that her husband looked gray and haggard, and that his mind seemed unfocused and distant.

As they stood in line at customs, Margarethe said, "The trial does not go well, Rudy?"

He looked at her as if the words were having difficulty penetrating. Finally he said, "It will all be over soon. Then we must start all over again."

"What are you talking about, my poor Rudy?" she asked, smoothing the hair on the back of his head down in place. It had become unruly during his attempt to doze on the plane and the wind as they walked down the stairwell after disembarking from the Lockheed Constellation.

"Greta," he said, "how long have we lived in Israel?"

"Seven years."

"Do you truly love it?"

"We're Jews. There's no safer haven for us on earth."

He lit a Gauloise cigarette as they cleared customs and hailed a cab from the ranks outside the airport. "The Crillon," he told the driver, who held the rear door of the Citroën open for them as they entered. Once under way, he said, "It depends if you're the right kind of Jew."

"What do you mean, darling? You're certainly the right kind of Jew. You've done so well in the few years we've been there: publisher of a highly successful newspaper, spokesman for the Trade Ministry. We're financially secure, we're comfortable, what more could we possibly want?"

"Greta, your friends can become your enemies very quickly if they feel your association with them proves embarrassing."

"So it is the trial."

"I didn't say that," he snapped.

"No, you didn't. But we've been married for twenty-two years, Rudy. A wife knows these things. How much weight have you lost in the past four weeks? Fifteen pounds, twenty? You come home and you barricade yourself in the den. You've taken to chain smoking. I've never seen you so nervous, not even …"

"Not even in Budapest, is that what you want to say?" his voice rose.

"Yes, darling, not even in Budapest," she said, putting her fingers to his lips. "Let's wait 'til we get to our hotel room to talk about it, shall we? After all, we're in Paris, the weather is lovely, we've got tickets to Molière, and we've got each other."

Words were a burden and Kasztner was happy to put the weight down for awhile.

The Crillon, just off the Champs Elysee and adjacent to the Opera, was situated on an entire square block. It was a symbol of plush-carpeted, crystal-staircased elegance. They'd been coming here on holiday for the past three years and Henri, the ancient elevator attendant, had come to recognize them. The ascenseur lifted them swiftly, silently, to the eighth floor, where they alighted. When they got to their room, they found that the porter had already installed their suitcases and turned down the bed covers. There were foil-wrapped chocolates on each of their pillows and a small rose reposed in a bud vase on her side of the bed. A bottle of champagne sat in a raised ice bucket on his side of the bed.

Margarethe's mood had lifted and she tried to raise her husband's out of his doldrums as well. Rudolf Kasztner glanced at his wife. At forty-four, she had lost none of her seductive charm. He thought for the thousandth time that maybe they should have had children. Greta had certainly wanted them, but it had been a dangerous time and a dangerous place for Jews to bring new lives into the world. By the time the War had ended, she was thirty-five, not too late, but still …

"Ah, Paris has always made me feel alive," he said, taking her in his arms.

"But not now?" she asked, looking archly at him. Rudolf had never been a great lover and he was far from sexually aggressive, but he seemed more listless than even his usual cool self.

"Gretl," he said, "have you ever considered what it would be like to live in Pretoria? I hear South Africa's one of the most beautiful countries on the face of the earth. There's Table Mountain, the Garden Route, the Paarl Valley, the Kruger Game Reserve. That alone is bigger than the whole state of Israel."

"What are you talking about, Rudy? Our home's in Israel. Our family is there. Wasn't it hard enough moving from Hungary to Switzerland and then to Jerusalem? Three times in anyone's life is certainly enough."

"I don't know," he said, stepping away from her and sitting on the bed. "Israel's become an unfriendly place. I thought perhaps a new start, where no one knows us."

"I can't believe you'd say that," she replied. "Your whole life has been public for as long as I've known you. That's what drew me to you in the first place. You were such a brave man, Rudy, even in Cluj, even with the Germans breathing down your neck in Budapest every minute of the day. Somehow I knew that when I was with you everything would always be alright. You were my shelter from the storm, and you still are," she said, squeezing his arm.

"That's just the point, Gretl. There comes a time in every man's life when he can't simply be everyone's father, everyone's hero. I've been the Chairman of the Committee, the man everyone depended upon for their lives, for the past twenty years. God knows I've done my part. It's time for me to step down and hand the reins over to someone else."

"But Rudy, only last year you were talking about the Foreign Ministry, a stepping stone to who-knows-what? Have you suddenly changed your mind?"

"Yes, Greta, I think I have. Being in the public eye has its good points, but as a national figure anyone who wants can say anything they want about you, right or wrong, truth or lie, and because you're a public figure you can't fight back."

Margarethe cracked the venetian blinds open. The late afternoon sun gave the room a golden brightness. Rudolf sat on the bed, his head in his hands. He was weeping, a strange and foreign emotion for him, and she felt vaguely frightened.

"None of them understand," he sobbed. "How could they understand what it was like? They weren't there. They're saying I conspired with the Nazis to kill eight hundred thousand Jews, simply because I wasn't able to save the whole million. Is that logical?"

Kasztner's wife sat down beside him on the bed. She held him gently in her arms, rocking him, soothing him, rubbing her hand up and down his back. "No, my Rudy, it's not logical and it's not right. The young are always so restless, so eager to make snap judgments and change the whole world. Except for your efforts, thousands would have lost their lives. Those who you saved should come to that courthouse on their hands and knees to kiss your feet and beg the judge to listen to them. Do you want me to go there, my darling? Do you want me to tell them the real story of one of the greatest heroes of Israel?"

In response, her husband wept harder. "And subject you to the tender mercies of that bastard Tamir? Let you be ripped apart, violated, raped before my eyes? I'd sooner die. I'd sooner they found me guilty than let any harm come to you."

She kept rubbing his back softly. "You're not on trial, darling. Always remember that, it's not you."

"Try and tell that to the judge," he said bitterly. "Tamir's turned it around. Depending on what the decision is, the government could be backed into a corner where they'd feel they have to throw me to the wolves and put on a show trial to demonstrate that 'no one is above the law.' What an incredible mockery of justice that would be."

"Is that why you spoke of South Africa?"

"Sharett as much as promised me I could have a minor diplomatic post somewhere. He didn't say South Africa, but I'm sure I could talk him into it. We could always come back to Israel to retire in a few years when things cool down — "

"I'm your wife, Rudy. Whither thou goest I will also go, and willingly, if that's what you want."

Suddenly he felt the lightness of relief, happier than he had felt in months. Perhaps that was the answer. He thought, *It will be alright. A new life. Dear God, let it be alright.*

Dinner at the Tour d'Argent was lovely. The view over the Seine, the paté de foie gras followed by the pressed duck was exquisite, the house burgundy divine. Their lovemaking that afternoon had been better than in several months, and he felt relaxed and stronger than at any time since he'd returned from New York. He had the constant love of a good woman, a beautiful woman, his wife, and it didn't matter what the court did, they'd be off to South Africa or Southern Rhodesia or even Southwest Africa, and things would be just fine.

It was Shabbat, the Jewish Sabbath. For the first time in weeks, he did not search out a synagogue to attend services. He'd earned this night off and God would surely understand.

What to do about the trial? The court had closed the presentation of evidence, so he'd just have to stay on for the closing arguments. If he were lucky, the court would not hand down its ruling immediately, but would take its time, weeks, perhaps months. During that period, he could secure his position. So what if it wasn't everything he was expecting. He would have peace.

In five years he would be only fifty-three, well-positioned for his climb up the next rung of the ladder. Greta had helped clear his thoughts. He was certainly too young to give up politics. Maybe a dozen years from now, but his wife was right: he was a born leader.

If she became pregnant now and he became a father at forty-nine, he would still be a youthful sixty-seven when his son joined the army and started his own climb to greatness. He squeezed Greta's hand under the table and smiled. It was going to be a wonderful weekend after all.

57

Judge Halevi's courtroom was jammed. Loudspeakers had been set up around the courthouse. The government pulled two of its stenographers out of the Knesset to take over the reporting. It was the largest assembly to see a trial in the Jerusalem court since the days of the ancient Romans.

Since the burden of proof was with the prosecution, the Attorney General spoke first. Chaim Cohen's black silk gown was immaculately pressed. His bald head was uncharacteristically bewigged, English style. When he rose to address the court, it was as if he were a prophet of old, and, indeed, he spoke for several hours, pausing only for a brief lunch.

"Your Honor, I pray that the man I represent will not suffer because of my unworthiness. It is presumptuous of me to try with my dull words to do justice to this great hero, who stood as a holy guard during the most tragic hour to befall our people. My prosecution today will be more firm and grave than it has ever been before an Israeli court.

"Any Jew who collaborated with the Nazis during the extermination deserves to be hanged. No one can dispute that. But here, there is not one iota of proof that Rudolf Kasztner became such a collaborator. His honorable intentions never left him to the end.

"My learned friend Tamir says that the Germans played a vicious trick, using Kasztner to help them induce the masses of Jews to avoid resistance, to avoid escape.

"*What masses? Escape? Where to? Revolt? By whom?* These Jews had already lived through long years of persecution, torture, and endless suffering, jammed into brick factories without a pillow for their head, without food, and without decent clothing.

"These should escape? They had no place to run. They should revolt? They had no hands with which to fight. There was no spirit left in them. Even in the Warsaw ghetto, the revolt was waged by only a few extraordinary characters.

"I am willing to assume that Kurt Becher was a vicious criminal, a man not to deal with. Kasztner did not lie about Becher and there was no contradiction in what he said. But let us assume for a moment that he did lie. Supposing Kasztner forgot after a lapse of ten years to whom he gave testimony, the affidavit. This may justify my learned friend Tamir in claiming that Kasztner has a weak memory, and that one cannot rely on his testimony.

"The question of whether or not Kasznter tells the truth or has a reliable memory has no bearing on the accusation at issue here. Mister Tamir asked some of his witnesses, 'Would you have given a sworn affidavit in favor of a Nazi?' All of them answered in chorus, 'No.'

"There may well be a divergence of opinion between such people and Doctor Kasztner as to what is correct and what is incorrect. He who thinks it is a national obligation to help S.S. Lieutenant General Becher with an affidavit does not become a worse Jew or a traitor. If Doctor Kasztner thought his way was the right way, then it was right for him, and nobody has the right or authority to say to Doctor Kasztner, 'You had no right to testify for a Nazi.' There is no one who can sit in judgment on Doctor Kasztner but Doctor Kasztner's own conscience.

"No one has the right to invent standards by which to measure a man's sense of national responsibility. If Mister Tamir wants to teach this court or me a lesson in national responsibility, pardon me if I look for a teacher elsewhere.

"My friend attacks Kasztner because he gave an affidavit on behalf of Kurt Becher in the name of the Jewish Agency and the Jewish World

Congress. I don't understand the aim of this attack. If it is intended to prove that Kasztner pretended to a standing he didn't have, or if it wishes to prove that Kasztner used the name of respectable institutions in order to raise himself above anyone's criticism, be that as it may, I believe Doctor Kasztner's explanation for his act is reasonable and wise. And I need not go into the question whether he did or did not have such authority.

"But let us assume he did not have such power. Since he had the authority to negotiate with Kurt Becher in the past, why should he think he had no power to testify for Becher as he did?

"Perhaps Doctor Kasztner was being boastful, as he often seems inclined to be, because he likes to pose as a man of high standing. What does that prove, using the name of the Jewish Agency and the World Jewish Congress? I say that as a man who negotiated with Becher in the name of the Jewish Agency and found out that Becher's reaction was good and beneficial for those institutions and for the Jews, Doctor Kasztner had the right to do what he did. In fact, he was morally bound to do what he did.

"On the other hand, I think defendant Greenwald's crime is as grave as actual bloodshed. He took upon himself the right to put the Sign of Cain on the forehead of a man for whom neither the defendant nor his lawyer is authorized to express any legitimate opinion whatsoever.

"There is not one iota of proof that Doctor Kasztner became a collaborator. His good intentions never left him. Doctor Kasztner had in his heart only one thing, the service of his people.

"The only thing the defense could prove was that Doctor Kasztner did not receive Mrs. Catherina Senesh for an interview or send parcels to prison, and that he did not put himself out enough. What does that prove? It proves that because of Kasztner's great heavy workload and responsibility for the lives of thousands of Jews, he was not active enough on behalf of one Palestinian Jewess, even if that Jewess was someone as admittedly courageous and heroic as Hanna Senesh. According to Mister Tamir, that one act makes him a traitor and collaborator. Has Your Honor, has anyone listening to my words, has Mister Tamir, or have I ever, done something, anything, he would choose to do differently, or not to do at all, if he were given another chance? Does one error, one minor mishap occasioned by nothing more than an overload of work saving

Jews, make Doctor Kasztner a traitor? A collaborator? I hardly think so. No more than my friend Tamir's adventure in the Irgun marks him as a traitor to Israel.

"Mister Tamir says Kasztner was a guest in Berlin in a Nazi officer's apartment, put at his disposal by Becher. Where should he live in Berlin? In the embassy of the Jewish community? Kasztner went to Berlin on a mission. What is more natural than that Becher gives him sleeping quarters? There is another charge: that Kasztner lived in the Grand Hotel in Vienna, the headquarters of the Nazi officers. Where should he have spent his stay? There were no hotels in Berlin or Vienna for transients. The defense charges it was Kasztner's great pleasure to mingle with the Nazis. I do not envy Kasztner these 'pleasures,' nor do I believe that in his heart of hearts my friend Tamir can truthfully state that he envied Kasztner these 'pleasures.'

"In sum, there is not one scintilla of evidence, not even a breath of innuendo, that Doctor Kasztner did or thought a wrong thing, not so much as one single thought, in his great and heroic work of rescuing Jews from the Nazi hell.

"He who saves one life, it is as though he has saved the entire universe. Doctor Kasztner saved over one thousand, six hundred universes. Multiply that by the generations to come, generations who will silently thank Doctor Rudolf Kasztner for the gift of life every waking hour of their lives.

"In Israel today, we sing hosannas to a man named Oscar Schindler, an agnostic and a German, who saved Jews, a lesser number than were saved by Rudolf Kasztner, while at the same time, the defendant attempts to impugn the accomplishments of Doctor Kasztner for the simple reason that he didn't save more Jews than he did.

"Do not insult the memory of those who passed before us by turning your back on a man who managed to save what few he could. Do not insult the Israeli man or woman who tries to live out his or her life in the best way possible, given the horrors that came before. An Israeli citizen, a Jew, has the same right as any other human being to live a life free from shame, humiliation, obloquy, and defamation.

"My learned friend Tamir has tried to twist the facts, to tailor the facts to his own way of thinking, to put a great rescuer of the Jewish people on trial, to shift the eyes of the court away from the grievous wrong done by his own client. I beg the court not to be cheated, not to be fooled, not to be hoodwinked by a wolf masquerading as a sheep. What took place was nothing more nor less than a vicious, libelous, scandalous attempt to defame a man's name, to take his humanity from him, to trash him, and to flush him down a communal toilet. Is that the thanks Doctor Kasztner deserves for what he did? Should he have let the sixteen hundred die? Should he have turned his back on everyone he saved because some day someone was going to stab him in the back with a dagger and say, 'Because you didn't save enough, you stand condemned?'

"No, Sir, no, I say! This calumny cannot, this calumny will not, be tolerated in a court of Israel. I demand, indeed all Israel demands, that Mister Greenwald be punished and that the reputation of this poor man, this great man, this good man, Doctor Rudolf Kasztner, son, husband, brother, uncle, and savior, be exonerated by an award of substantial imprisonment and damage that will make every man, woman, and child in Israel think twice before he dares cast such foul excrement upon the waters as Greenwald has done here!

"I thank you, Your Honor. Indeed Israel thanks you, to have the courage of your conviction, to tear away the smokescreen so hastily erected by the defense, to find the truth, and to rule for the State and its hero, Doctor Kaszter, and against Malchiel Greenwald."

58

"Your Honor," Tamir began. "This is my only chance to argue on behalf of my client, and on behalf of what I view to be justice. My argument will be lengthier than Mister Cohen's, but that is because he has the privilege of speaking to you twice, while I am afforded but one opportunity. Thus I beg your patience and your indulgence.

"Your Honor, a cruel and inevitable duty has been imposed on us in this trial. Every step taken had to be made through Jewish blood. And now a great human, moral, and historic task commands me. Our nation raises its eyes to the high seat of justice and awaits the sound of truth from it.

"From the end of the Holocaust until a year ago, our land was given to forgetfulness. The bones of the slain millions at Auschwitz had been plowed into German soil or Polish soil, or the soil of other countries in Europe as fertilizer. The plowmen have regained their freedom and have become leaders of the new Germany. The murderers and their collaborators have returned to the bosom of human society.

"In payment for Jewish blood, the State of Israel has been offered and has accepted money. Memorial forests have been planted in our land in honor of the exterminated Jews of Europe. But memorial forests do not silence the voices of the slaughtered. The voices have finally entered a courtroom in Jerusalem and compelled us to open the book of extermination, to study it, and to seek its truth.

"I heard the Attorney General's cry in this courtroom, 'Who are we and what are we to judge public officials who worked in that hell of death?"

"I heard that question. I ask another. *Who are we and what are we who dare to avoid facing the truth in our souls, the truth of why and how catastrophe came to our people. Out of all the shames and agonies which smote us during the slaughter of Jews, there is one shame we can remove today, the shame of hiding the truth.*

"Let us review the evidence in this trial. Let us examine again the history we have re-lived and experienced during these several months.

"With the Jewish leaders properly drugged, the Germans started the Jew round-up carefully. Their objective was to concentrate batches of five to twenty thousand Jews in ghettoes within easy reach of the railroad line to Auschwitz.

"But the Germans smelled trouble ahead. Reports were coming in that Jewish groups were meeting in secret, trying to organize armed resistance. Some Jews were escaping across the borders to areas that offered haven for Jews. The exodus might grow. The S.S. Colonels Becher, Krumey, and Eichmann knew what was needed to make the final solution deportations possible. Germans alone could not keep the doomed ones from suspecting. The Nazis needed a more potent drug than their smiles and blandishments.

"The Nazis needed Jews. Important, highly connected, authoritative Jews, whose words could soothe Jewish fears. Enter here the answer to the German problem, Rudolf Kasztner.

"The S.S. Colonels in Budapest invite Doctor Kasztner to their headquarters. He arrives boldly, briskly, ready to make deals for the Jews. He bristles with authority. The Kasztner personality is definitely a plus in Nazi eyes. It can be utilized. But more important than who Kasztner is, is *what* he is. He is the representative of the Jewish Agency of Palestine and a member of Ben-Gurion's Mapai Party.

"The S.S. Colonels in Budapest, whatever their other cultural or moral shortcomings, are not ignorant of the activities of modern Jewry.

They know that the religious Jews of Hungary are a minority and that a much smaller minority are Zionists. Moreover, they know that only a minority of the Zionists belong to the Mapai Party. Yet, knowing these things, they select Rudolf Kasztner, who represents almost no Jews at all in Hungary, as the man with whom to deal.

"Their selection of Kasztner is one of the not too frequent evidences of German political brightness. Kasztner represents the party that controls Jewish Palestine, the Mapai.

"Head Rescuer Kasztner, selected by the Mapai chiefs and now also selected by the Nazis, will serve everybody as they wish except the eight hundred thousand Jews. He will continue the elitist policy of Chaim Weizmann and, after some modest protest, he will be satisfied with the rescue of a selected group of sixteen hundred.

"And so, in the eyes of Hungary's Jews, the Nazis succeed in creating a great Jewish leader by treating him as one. But another factor, independent of Nazi plotting, helps raise the little Kasztner of Cluj to the big Kasztner of Budapest. Hungary's assimilated Jews, the bulk of its Jewry, realize now that they are an isolated mass. They have no connections. But Doctor Kasztner and his Mapai forces have connections everywhere: chairmen, meeting halls, executive boards in Geneva, Istanbul, Jerusalem, London, and New York.

"Not dreaming that the Mapai and its Zionist connections will keep silent about their catastrophe, the Jewish leaders of Hungary step aside. They give their places to Doctor Kasztner.

"With Eichmann's approval, Doctor Kasztner alters the original deal. Instead of picking Jews from 'outlying areas,' he picks three hundred eighty-eight Jews from Cluj alone, the best, most important members of Cluj Jewry, mainly Zionists. Of course, he includes his own family.

"The news of Kasztner's first victory is hailed by the Jews. Kasztner has breached the wall of Nazi Jew hatred. He has liberated Jews! It is at this hour of triumph that the 'good' Kasztner begins to dim. Krumey sends Kasztner to Cluj on a mission to reassure and cheer the doomed ones. Rudolf Kasztner knows the truth about the death trains to 'Kenyermeze.' Kasztner knows the truth about the final solution, about the S.S.

plan to deport all eight hundred thousand Jews of Hungary to Auschwitz for cremation."

"That's a lie!" Kasztner shouted, unable to control himself, rising from his seat and angrily denouncing Tamir.

"Order," the judge calls out, banging down his gavel. "This is argument, Mister Kasztner. I will determine what is true and what is not true."

Kasztner sat down. Chaim Cohen gently patted him on the arm. Tamir continued.

"Colonel Krumey knows that Kasztner is aware of the S.S. program for deporting Hungary's Jews to Auschwitz for extermination. Krumey is aware that Kasztner knows that the twenty thousand Cluj Jews are headed for the Zyklon-B gas chambers and that the Jews of Cluj are cut off from telephone, transport, and all information.

"If Kasztner breathes a word of this truth to a single condemned Jew in Cluj, the entire final solution will be wrecked. The twenty thousand Jews of Cluj will knock over their handful of guards and escape to Romania, *three miles away*. Yet Colonel Krumey confidently sends Kasztner to Cluj to move among the twenty thousand doomed men, women, and children.

"Rudolf Kasztner comes to Cluj. What a welcome! For weeks, the Cluj people have been talking about 'their' Doctor Kasztner. He is their own, born in Cluj, and reared among them. If only he would come and tell them what is true and what is untrue, everybody can sleep better. The Cluj Jews are filled with hope. Rudolf Kasztner has not forgotten his own. Famous though he has become, he is here to help them!

"Kasztner walks among the twenty thousand Jews in the town. He sits among the old Hebrew scholars and their young students. He attends meetings and renews old friendships.

"There are only twenty Hungarian gendarmes and one German S.S. officer guarding the twenty thousand people in the ghetto, and there are thousands of able-bodied men among the condemned. The border and freedom are only *three miles away*. The hopeful Jews of Cluj have their great man back among them. Now, thank God, they will find out the truth.

"There is a little trouble hatching here and there in basements. Hotheads are talking resistance and escape to Romania. The Romanians are no longer occupied in slaughtering Jews. They are getting their own heads blown off on the Russian front. Escape is easy. There are only twenty-one guards to overcome.

"Doctor Kasztner, moving among the muscled young ones in Cluj, helps cool the troublemakers down. He has the Zionist Organization behind him. In Cluj, the Zionists are the leaders of Jewry and the head man of all the Cluj Zionists is Doctor Joseph Fisher, Rudolf Kasztner's father-in-law.

"Kasztner takes no chances on the Auschwitz death plan leaking out. He does not even confide it to his father-in-law. His eminent relatives assemble to help cheer the waiting ones. Kasztner tells this elite number that they have been selected to go to 'a better place' than the one to which the remaining 19,620 Jews are to be taken. Doctor Fisher and his select group might have alerted their townspeople to action, but Kasztner and the German strategists succeed. They fool them.

"Kasztner tells them there should be no resistance. 'We are your leaders. You have nothing to fear. Everything is under control. Do not listen to the hotheads. We, your leaders, are the only ones who can save your lives.'

"A remarkable monster of a Kasztner returns to Budapest. He has done what he had guessed, despairingly, the Nazis would try to make him do. He has helped exterminate the Jews. His silence in Cluj was the death sentence for twenty thousand, minus three hundred eighty. Yet Kasztner shows no despair, no guilt. He does not hang his head. He does not find it hard to sleep at night. He walks as briskly as ever. He is full of pride, for he is a greater man in Budapest than ever before. The Jews in Budapest shake his hand. They know nothing of their own future travels.

"In the palaces of Budapest, the German colonels and their Hungarian cronies sit and chat. Kasztner, the Jew, often sits at their side while the death brigades are roaming the Jewish quarter and egging on the death march. During the Budapest slaughter summer, the Jewish Agency bigwigs in Palestine sit until the Jews of Hungary are destroyed. Their tongues and their right arms remain useless, pledged to the Nazis in Budapest and the British in Jerusalem. There is only one exception to the do-nothing, say-nothing policy of official Zionism: Rabbi Michael Dov

Weissmandel, the Rabbi in the cave. And what answer does Rabbi Weiss-mandel receive?

"In answer to the outcry of twelve thousand Jews going daily to be murdered, what does the Organized Jewish Community reply? What action does it take? What answer is made to the ways of rescue listed by the Rabbi writing from his cave? *There are no answers. There are no deeds.* Because here, in Eretz Israel, the official institutions have submitted to the British government. They are not willing to endanger themselves. It is easier simply to abandon European Jewry as lost.

"It is far too easy for the organized Jewish Community in Palestine to say in 1944, 'The British don't want to permit rescue and immigra-tion.' In 1947, the Haganah knew well how to follow the Irgun and blow up bridges so that the British would be forced to permit it. *How is it that in 1944 they didn't come out and fight for opening the gates of Palestine to the victims of Hitler?* In 1944, the coming results of the War were clear. The Germans had to wage war on all fronts. For us, for all surviving Jews, the whole attention had to be concentrated on one matter only, the rescue of hundreds of thousands of remaining Jews.

"If Kasztner is guilty of atrocities, he is not the only one. The Jews already in Palestine, Ben Gurion, Sharett, Weizmann, the Mapai Party, Histadrut, and the Jewish Agency press, reveled in the glories of modern Israel. Local problems, strikes, the cost of living, and political quibbling all received full coverage. But what about the horrors and details of the extermination of Jews and the rescue problems? *There was hardly a word about the atrocities. There was no coverage of the slaughter. The Jewish lead-ers knew twelve thousand Jews a day were going to their death, but since they were not 'the right kind of Jews,' it made no difference! Not until July 10, 1944, when most of the deportations from Hungary were over and nearly a million Jews had fallen victim to the gas chambers, was there any substantive coverage in the organized Jewish press! Instead of blazoning it in headlines, instead of arousing the world's Jews and non-Jews to action there was nothing!*

"Apropos nothing, the Attorney General dared to ask, 'Where were those in the time of war who come now with accusations?' If such a ques-tion is asked by so high a dignitary, I owe an answer. The people about whom he inquired were, in those days, in the small huts of Latrun, in the prison of Acre, in the African detention camps, and hanging from British gallows in Cairo! They were busy fighting to open the ports of Palestine for those Jews of Europe not yet murdered!

"And why did Ben Gurion, Sharett, Weizmann, and all the official leaders of Jewry suppress the dreadful news of the slaughter of nineteen forty-four? Because had the masses in Palestine known what was happening in Hungary and known the stony hearts of their leaders, a storm would have risen in our land. They would have fallen from power, which, it seems, was more important to them. There is no other explanation.

"The Attorney General said, 'Nothing is proven, not a single fact, it is all a baseless series of charges, all ripped up for political reasons.' Your Honor, if our charges were so 'groundless,' why does such great anxiety seize the Attorney General and those he represents? Why did he rush to take over the prosecution from his assistant? Why did he start pleading for long recesses to bring his witnesses from abroad? And why did 'important' public figures like Avriel. Danzig, and Bader appear here and make themselves laughingstocks in their efforts to conceal what they knew?

"If the Attorney General's case is so pure, why is it so dirty? He cries out that the dirt is in my client's accusations. The dirt is not in them, Your Honor, but in what they have exposed! I have heard it said, 'Even if it is true, why expose it? Can it restore the dead? It can only damage us. Exploring these matters can only damage all the Jews of Israel and the world.'

"There is something more important than any temporary damage that may be done by exposing the truth, and I, for one, am not damaged by exposing the truth. There is a young generation in Israel who must know the full story of what happened to all of us. This young generation must know the full truth in order that it may have a true scale for its judgments!

"The Attorney General said in his summation, 'Either Kasztner should be sentenced to death if the allegations are true, or, if they are not, Greenwald should die by the hand of God.' I do not insist that Rudolf Kasztner is a born criminal or a man who is entirely black. I shall not say, 'Death to Kasztner!'

"I say this: Just as Kasztner's brothers were exterminated bodily in Auschwitz, his soul was destroyed in Budapest. He, too, was a Hitler victim. The defense has shown, Your Honor, how an idealistic Zionist youth like Kasztner deteriorated into a trusted chum of the Nazi leaders in 1944. In explaining Kasztner's activities, the prosecution offered many facts in *his* defense. But how dare anyone stand in this Court and say we are not to judge Kasztner? And what is more insulting, this statement is made by the Attorney General of Israel who, himself, has prosecuted scores of offenders under the anti-collaboration law. Why is it so insulting? Because the Attorney General always brought to justice the 'little people.' A Jewish policeman who had beaten a woman in a concentration camp in order to save his own life. The whole force of the State of Israel was mobilized against such small, pathetic offenders, and the Attorney General thundered for conviction.

"Are the legal nets of our country only for catching little fish? Are there big holes left in them for the escape of big sharks? The Attorney General's words shocked my heart because it was not a privately hired lawyer who spoke here. It was the representative of the government of Israel.

"The Attorney General said of Hungary's one million Jews, 'Revolt? By whom? They had no hands. They had no feet. There was no spite in them.' Moshe Sharett is okay, Rudolf Kasztner is okay, Hillel Danzig is okay, but the Jewish masses in Cluj, Nodvarod, Budapest, they were *not* okay, they had no spirit, no hands. They were without courage and reason. Therefore, they had to be slaughtered. It was Heaven's decision that they must go like sheep to the slaughter pens.

"The Attorney General said, 'Who is he and what is he who dares to defame public officials who worked in the Hell of death?'

"And I say, '*Who is he and what is he who dares defame our own good Jewry which was so badly smeared by the prosecution witnesses in this trial? Who is he and what is he who dares utter this defamation of the Jewry of Herzl, Nordau, Dov Gruner, Jacob Weiss, Michael Dov Weissmandel, Hanna Senesh, and all the heroes and martyrs who sacrificed their souls?*

"The defense in this trial defends not the accused alone. It defends every Jew who has been berated and cursed by ruthless men. It defends the Jews who have been called dust, called Jews without spirit or hands, called the frozen hearts, called the non-Zionists.

"I call upon Your Honor to decide that in the choice between the Hungarian Jews who went to their death and Kasztner and his clique, it was Hungarian Jewry that was fine and great and tragic. There was no reason on earth for these men, women, and children of Hungary to go like sheep to the German butchers. It is a sin against God and it is a sin against Jewish pride and human dignity to say that nearly a million Jews had to go to their deaths the way they went, and that it was impossible for them to do other than they did; that a man had to go with his wife, his children, and his parents like an animal to the slaughter.

"The German murderers are primarily guilty for the Jews' deaths. Next in guilt are the nations who aided the murders, actively or passively, Hungary on the one hand, England on the other. Next come those other great, civilized nations, whose acquiescence and indifference spurred on the slaughter. But none the less guilty are those small-souled members of the Jewish leadership who traded courage for the maintenance of their position and prestige.

"Who is the Attorney General of Israel representing, the citizens of the State of Israel or the private interests of some officials of the State?' It's not too difficult a question to answer.

"The Attorney General is not alone in covering up for Kasztner. Many institutions have done the same. In 1946, the Zionist Congress in Basel, the Haganah trial in the case of the parachutists, and the Israeli police in 1951 all took a look at Kasztner's activities, and promptly covered up what they saw.

"And when all the Jewish leaders and all the powers of government had covered up for Kasztner, one old man steps forward to reveal the truth. Why did the powerful government institutions leave this truth-telling to Malchiel Greenwald? Why did they knowingly cover up the collaboration of Kasztner with the Nazis? There is one answer. *They had no choice. They had to protect Kasztner for fear he would reveal all the facts known to him about another collaboration, the Jewish Agency collaboration with the British which sabotaged the rescue of Europe's Jews and contributed to their annihilation.*

"Our charge against Kasztner is this: a community of twenty thousand Jews was sacrificed in order to save three hundred eighty-eight of his own friends and relatives. These three hundred eighty-eight people, and we are all happy they remain alive, were not Kaszner's achievement, but the price for sacrificing many thousands!

"We charge that this cost was reckoned and this price paid with the same lack of conscience that the Attorney General described with such enthusiasm when he declared that the sacrificed Jews were 'without hands or spirits.' We charge that Kasztner deliberarely decided it was best to rescue the 'prominents.'

"Kaszstner was not a born criminal. It is foolish to say that he was even a bloodthirsty man. The defense has never said — and would not insult the intelligence of this Court by saying — that Kasztner was a traitor who did what he did simply to receive money or favors from the Nazis. He did not start with treason. He started with collaboration, which was what the Nazis preferred. The traitor is not the most efficient instrument for an enemy. A traitor hands over his regiment or his information and his job is finished. The traitor's way is one act of surrender. Collaboration is a more effective technique. You take an important figure from the other side and you help him play the drama in which he stars as the leader of his people. But the cost of these successes to these people is their destruction.

"Kaszstner the collaborator was worse than Seyss-Inquart or Petain or Quisling because Kasztner's collaboration didn't sacrifice honor and freedom alone. It accomplished the extermination of people! It is only human for a man to save himself and his family first. Had it been an ordinary man, exploiting his connections and running away with his family, who would dare criticize him? Who knows if any of us would behave differently?

"But this is not the case with Kasztner. Here we are dealing with a leader of rescue, a man who became a national leader. That is another story altogether. Is this the motto our Attorney General wants to give to every officer in the Israeli Army and Navy, 'When danger comes, run away first and save yourself and your own?'

"Of course in the beginning Kasztner was trapped by the German state. Eichmann told him, 'Everything is lost. Your accursed Jews must all die. There is no way out. No matter what you do, they will be annihilated.' Then he adds, 'Perhaps you can save a few. But in return for such a favor, you have to help me.' And here, Kasztner's eagerness to be a somebody made him lose his conscience. He grabbed at Eichmann's proposal. In exchange for the three hundred eighty-eight, he kept the rest of the Hungarian Jews from knowing their fate.

"No wonder Kasztner will never return to his home town of Cluj. At the beginning, the Germans talked to him about money he must pay them. We heard the true account of the Joel Brand fiasco. But soon, Kasztner found out that the Germans had no financial interest in Jews. Kasztner alone among the Jewish leaders did not give the Germans a great deal of money. He had something better to give them. He gave them Jewish lives.

"If we are to believe Kasztner, everyone wanted to help the Jews – Krumey, Becher, Eichmann, even Heinrich Himmler. No one wanted to exterminate the Jews. *If that's the case, who exterminated the Jews?*

"And what was Kasztner doing in Berlin at the end of the War? The Attorney General says he was doing his solemn and noble duty. Does the Attorney General seriously claim that in the spring of 1945 there was such a close mutual interest between the Third Reich and the Jews? Did this mutual interest perhaps bloom when hundreds of thousands of Jews were rotting in the camps, being murdered daily by the thousands, and being used in laboratories for inhumane experiments?

"In the last, most crucial four months of the War, Kasztner the Jew spent his time among the highest Nazi chieftains in Vienna and Berlin. His Nazi friends allowed him to go to Switzerland in time to meet the American representative and supply that representative with everything he knew about the Nazi crimes. Is there a deeper trust that Kasztner's Nazi friends could show than this? What else does the defense have to prove in this case but this alone? The Nazis would never put such trust in an Englishman or an American, but they put their faith in the representative of the Jewish Agency who had witnessed their worst crimes!

"I therefore say to this Court that which the defendant Greenwald did not say in his pamphlet. I say that in the last months of the War, Kasztner became the agent for the whole Nazi gang, the most effective Jewish agent in their ranks. For he was now one of them, their trusted ally and apologist."

"That is not true, you lying scum, and you know that is not true!" Kasztner screamed. "I never, never, never was an apologist or representative for the Nazis! You go on reinventing history to serve your own agenda and that of your barbarous Likud party! You are trying to tear down the State!" Kasztner was on his feet, Cohen was on his feet, and there was an uproar that lasted more than two minutes as Shlomo enlisted the aid of two other deputies from adjacent courtrooms to help restore peace.

"Gentlemen! Gentlemen!" the judge admonished in a voice that carried over the melee. "I will have no more of this in my court. Mister Cohen, if your client can't confine himself, I will have him forcibly removed from the Court. Mister Tamir, the Court well understands what you are trying to say. Please stick to the facts that were developed at trial as they affect this trial, and do not propagandize your political agenda in a Court of law. Do I make myself clear, gentlemen?"

"Absolutely," both lawyers said, chastened.

"How much longer, Mister Tamir?"

"Twenty minutes, thirty at most."

"Very well. I will hold you to that estimate, lest things get more out of hand than they already are. Mister Kasztner, if you believe you can tolerate this for another thirty minutes, that is up to you. If you think you must leave, then you may do so, and I assure you that your leaving at this late point in the proceedings, after all the evidence has been presented, will not influence the decision of this Court one iota. I am here to decide the law and the facts and nothing else."

There was a hushed discussion between Chaim Cohen and Rudolf Kasztner. At the end of that discussion, Cohen rose ponderously to his feet. "Your Honor, my client is feeling a bit ill. Would the court indulge him in allowing him to leave a bit early today?"

"Of course. Doctor Kasztner, I thank you for your time. I realize it has been most difficult for you and your counsel to sit here and listen to all this. I wish you only good luck, sir."

Kasztner departed the courtroom. Tamir, now freed of the constraint of politesse, lashed out once again, careful, however, to keep within the strict parameters set by the Court.

"Who was Kasztner's friend Kurt Becher? The head of the Economic Department of the Waffen S.S. The Economic Department meant concentration camps, gold teeth, bones for fertilizer, clothes, and Jewish fat for soap. And it was for this crime that the Americans held Becher in custody from 1945 to 1948.

"All the witnesses have testified that General Kurt Becher always had the last word, that he was responsible only to Himmler himself. He decided who would be deported in the notorious death march. Yet Kasztner dares to make affidavits at Nuremberg declaring that Becher saved Jews in Budapest. And today where is Becher? He is one of the most successful businessmen in the new Germany.

"Your Honor, the learned Attorney General has the gall to deny Kasztner's proven lies. The Attorney General was here when Kasztner arrogantly blamed others in the face of his own lies. At least let the Attorney General keep silent and not deny that they were lies. Let our Attorney General sit silent in the face of the evidence and spare the bathos that he feels it is his great privilege to defend the honor of this man, Rudolf Kasztner. The Attorney General uses an interesting turn of the phrase when he claims he is *defending* Kasztner. Am I fooling myself, or did Mister Kasztner commence this case as the *plaintiff?* We need prove nothing. The burden of proof rests entirely with the State, through Kasztner, as the *plaintiff,* Your Honor.

"Neither the rhetoric of the Attorney General nor the backing of the whole Israeli government will overcome the truth!

"Finally, the defense challenges this Honorable Court. to raise itself to a higher level. Faced with a decision like no other that has ever been made in the history of the Jewish State, I ask the Court to remove itself from any political considerations from whatever side they come. And although the burden is almost too heavy for a single human being to carry, we respectfully ask the court to pass judgment in view of the facts only, facts so clear that nothing can withstand them!"

As Samuel Tamir concluded his remarks, the courtroom was silent for some minutes. Then, as Judge Halevi announced he would take the entire matter under submission, there was a mass exodus from the room. The public spectacle had come to an end, six months after it had begun. The press corps, which was ten times larger than it had been at the beginning of the trial, knew they'd be able to hold the coveted headline spot in their newspapers for two or three more days, but after that it would be a never-ending search for the next new scandal, the next explosive world event. They also knew that absent any quick, dramatic decision, which no one expected would happen, the case of *State of Israel vs. Greenwald,* which had come to be known as "the Kasztner affair," would sleep for the next several weeks.

After the departure of the vast audience, Malchiel Greenwald sat at his lawyer's table with a slightly bemused look on his face. His lovely daughter walked up, linked her arm in his, and said, "Papa, it's almost *Shabbos.* It is time to give thanks for many things, but mostly that we survived this ordeal."

"Yes, daughter," he said, rising slowly. Looking around the now nearly empty courtroom, he noticed that Doctor Kasztner had returned to the Attorney General's counsel table. Kasztner sat alone, abandoned, and in silence. Malchiel Greenwald walked over to the other man and said, "Good *Shabbos,* Doctor Kasztner. We have caused each other great pain. Now is the time for forgiveness, wouldn't you agree?"

Kasztner looked away and said nothing. Before he turned, Ariana Greenwald noticed that his eyes were puffy and red.

59

The following Friday at noon, Ruth and Samuel left the children with his parents and drove four hours to the Galilee. Although it was only mid-September, there was already a nip in the air that heralded the coming of autumn to the high country. Mount Hermon, the highest peak in Israel, dominated the horizon. Now that the trial was over, they needed the spiritual and physical refreshment this place offered on so many levels.

For hundreds of years, Safat had guarded the sanctity of Judaism. Even today the old town refused to bend the old laws. It was a place that would have been at home in the sixteenth century. Until recently, Arab and Jew had existed side by side in this place since time out of mind. Even today, half a dozen years after twelve hundred stubborn Jews had held out against a force of twenty thousand Arabs, the old Rabbis refused to acknowledge the existence of the secular Israeli state. When God wanted to send the Messiah, then Israel would be redeemed, not before.

They unpacked, checked into their room, and napped for two hours. Then they showered and dressed for a 'night on the town.' Ruth wore a long dress, almost down to her ankles, with a high-collared black blouse, her hair bound by a scarf.

The tension of the past months started finally to break. Samuel, too, dressed in very conservative clothing. No matter what they might think of the ultraorthodox adherents of the old religion, it was only appropriate that they share and be part of this place.

When they departed their cottage, they left a small light on and the door unlocked and ajar, for the Bible proscribed any work, even so little as turning on a light, during the Sabbath. They'd parked less than a quarter mile from town, for they knew they would not be able to use their car during the Sabbath. They climbed the ancient stone stairs from *Keren Hayosod* Street to *Beit Yosaef* Street, hunting for their favorite small restaurant from years before. Samuel looked east to the old citadel that crowned Safat. Hundreds of years before, the Crusaders had built a castle-fortress here, which had been reduced to rubble. As they walked the steep staircase streets and alleys of this city out of the Middle Ages, Samuel felt a subtle tug at his sleeve.

"*Gut Shabbos, Reb Yiddene,*" a voice behind him grated in the guttural Yiddish of the Polish *shtetl.*"

"Good eve – " Tamir started to say automatically, then turned and gasped. "Rashid? *Rashid!* What are you doing here of all places, you old reprobate?"

"Your mother said the two of you could use a chaperone. She said to make sure you behave. She didn't say *how* you should behave. Besides, this old Arab can use the bracing mountain air and the smell of cedar after a hot summer playing Bedouin sheikh."

Much to the consternation and tongue-clucking of a crowd of Orthodox Jews headed to their synagogues, Ruth grabbed the older man by the waist and hugged him. "Of course you must join us for *Shabbat* dinner."

During the meal, Ruth, Samuel, and Rashid relived what had been the longest six months of the advocate's life. "So now that you've achieved victory, you've come to Safat to celebrate?" Rashid said slyly.

"No, my friend," Tamir said. "No one will win any victory in this trial unless it is the Israeli system of justice. Regardless of what decision the Court makes, Kasztner and Greenwald are the losers; Greenwald because who knows what this has done to his life, his health. He's an old man, Rashid, and regardless of his high spirits, I've seen the toll the trial has taken on him.

"As for Kasztner, I have difficulty believing he's an evil man, or that he did what he did. But it seems the evidence points to the fact that even a man with the highest intentions can be bought if the price is right. I don't say that Kasztner's price was money or fame or even power, although God knows he's always wanted that. No, I think it was an accident of circumstance. I might have told the court that no moral Jew in his right mind would have acted as Kasztner did, but the more I think about it, given the situation in which Rudolf Kasztner found himself, I wonder if I would have done things any differently."

"Sort of like Safat," Rashid murmured.

"Very much like that," Tamir replied. "A few stubborn Israelis beat back the Arabs and gave birth to a miracle, but in the end I wonder what we won. Arabs and Jews had lived together in Safat for centuries. No one hurt one another, no one killed one another. The wisdom of the combined cultures, Arab, Jewish, and Christian, gave this town balance and peace. Now it seems we have none. The Orthodox Jews fight with the modern Sabras, the Arab Quarter has become an 'art colony,' where we'll see an ever-growing number of tourists, and the Christians have deserted the place. Yes, there was a miracle at Safat, but at what cost? There's an old saying, 'Be careful what you wish for, you may receive it.'"

"How long to do you think it will be before the Judge hands down his decision?" Rashid asked.

"It could be months," Tamir replied. "Truthfully, I hope it will be. It will give Israel time to heal from the revelation that even though we're the 'Chosen People,' we're really no better nor worse than anyone else. We happen to suffer from the same disease as everyone else. We happen to be human."

Months went by without a decision in the case. Malchiel Greenwald sat home and read. Ariana's job kept her busy, but not too busy to call Tamir's office every few weeks to find out if he'd heard anything. Ruth always answered patiently and always said much the same thing. "Nothing yet, Ariana, but the longer Judge Halevi takes, the better it is. If the decision was going to be a bad one, we'd have known it by now."

In Kasztner's quarters, the feeling was the same. Chaim Cohen told his client that the court was waiting until all the furor had cooled down, at which time Judge Halevi would probably issue a short decision with no explanation, one both sides could live with.

Nevertheless, when, fourteen months after the trial had begun and eight and one-half months after he had taken the case under submission, Judge Halevi's clerk advised the lawyers that the Court was ready to hand down its decision on Tuesday, June 21, 1955, a tremor went through Israel.

Two men were never further apart as Jews and patriots than Tamir and Judge Halevi at the start of the trial. Tamir was a child of revolt. He loved his country completely. But Tamir's country did not consist only of the righteous few who ran it. Tamir considered most of the government men in power had gotten there on the dreams and on the backs of others.

Not so Judge Halevi. Most of those who ran Israel were his friends, and he knew them to be men and women of upright character. He believed in order, and he felt the rulers of the new Israel supported his beliefs. He had read and re-read the trial transcript a dozen times. It had taken Judge Halevi nearly nine months to write his verdict. He did it in the loneliness of his study.

60

When Judge Halevi entered the courtroom, he bore a single thick manuscript which contained his verdict. There had been no leaks, for Halevi had only completed it the night before and had not even discussed it with his family.

The courtroom was filled to capacity. In addition to reporters from every newspaper in Israel, Judge Halevi's entire family was present. Malchiel Greenwald sat staring grimly, his daughter Ariana on one side, Samuel Tamir on the other. The judge lifted his eyebrows as he looked toward the prosecution table. Neither Doctor Kasztner nor Attorney General Chaim Cohen was present. After ascertaining that neither intended to come, Judge Halevi commenced reading his verdict in a low voice that was almost a whisper. But under his quiet tone, a storm was audible.

"The Court finds that the masses of Jews from Hungary's ghettoes obediently boarded the deportation trains without knowing their fate. They were full of confidence that they were being transferred to Kenyermeze. The Nazis could not have misled the masses of Jews so conclusively had they not spread their false information through Jewish channels.

"The Jews of the ghettoes would not have trusted the Nazi or Hungarian rulers. But they trusted their Jewish leaders. Eichmann and others used this fact to mislead the Jews. They were able to deport the Jews to their extermination because of the false information spread by these Jewish leaders. Those Jews who tried to warn their friends of the truth were shouted down and belittled by the Jewish leaders in charge of the local rescue work.

"Twenty thousand Jews were guarded by twenty police and a single gestapo agent. Yet not a single Jews made any attempt to overpower these few guards and escape to nearby Romania. The Jewish leaders did everything in their power to soothe the Jews in the ghettoes and to prevent such resistance activities.

"The same Jewish leaders who did not warn their own people against the misleading statements, the same Jewish leaders who did not organize any resistance or sabotage of the deportations — these same leaders did not join the people of their community in their journey to Auschwitz, but were included in the rescue train.

"The Nazis permitted Rudolf Kasztner and the members of the Jewish Council in Budapest to save themselves, their relatives, and their friends. In short, the Nazis succeeded in bringing the Jewish leaders into collaboration with them at the time of the catastrophe."

Malchiel Greenwald stared at the judge, not really comprehending where what seemed like a lecture to him seemed to be going. He wheezed, coughed into his closed fist, and tried to comprehend the judge's words.

"The Nazis had learned a lesson from the Warsaw Ghetto uprising. Eichmann did not want a second Warsaw. For this reason, the Nazis had to mislead and bribe the Jewish leaders. Rudolf Kasztner's personality made him a convenient cat's paw for Eichmann and his clique to draw into collaboration and make their task easier.

"The Court finds that the question here is not, as stated by the Attorney General, whether members of the Jewish Rescue Committee were or were not capable of fulfilling their duty without the patronage of the S.S. leaders. It is obvious that without such S.S. Nazi patronage, the Jewish Rescue Committee could not have existed.

"*The question is, as put by the defense: Why were the Nazis interested in the Rescue Committee? Why did the S.S. chiefs make every effort to encourage its existence?*

"The Nazis' patronage of Kasztner and their agreement to let him save sixteen hundred prominent Jews were part of the plan to exterminate the Jews. The opportunity of rescuing prominent people appealed greatly to Rudolf Kasztner. He considered the rescue of the most important Jews as a great personal success as well as a success for Zionism.

"*The Court finds that when Rudolf Kasztner received this present from the Nazis he, like Faust, sold his soul to the German Satan.*

"The sacrifice of the majority of the Jews in order to rescue the prominents was the basic element of the agreement between Kasztner and the Nazis. The Jewish nation was divided into two unequal camps: a small fragment of prominents, whom the Nazis promised Kasztner to save, on the one hand, and the great majority of Hungarian Jews whom the Nazis designated for death, on the other. An imperative condition was that Kasztner would not interfere in the Nazis' action against the other camp and would not hamper them in the extermination of 'the other kind of Jew.'"

Malchiel Greenwald, aware that any sound be made would distract the court and, perhaps, be to his detriment, quietly printed a message on a legal pad, which he passed to his counsel. "Is this good or bad for us?"

Tamir nodded once, but said nothing. Meanwhile, the judge continued reading.

"Kasztner fulfilled this condition. He concentrated his efforts in the rescue of the prominents and treated the others as if they had already been wiped out from the book of the living.

"According to Kasztner, Himmler, Hoess, Becher and Krumey were all active in rescuing Jews. Just as the Nazi war criminals knew they needed an alibi and hoped to achieve it by the rescue of Jews at the eleventh hour, so Kasztner also needed an alibi. The collaboration between the Rescue Committee and the exterminators was solidified in Budapest, Vienna, and Berlin.

"The Court finds that Rudolf Kasztner knowingly perjured himself in his testimony before this Court when he denied that he had interceded on Becher's behalf. Moreover, he concealed that he interceded for Becher in the name of the Jewish Agency and the Jewish World Congress.

"As to the contents of Kasztner's affidavit, it was enough for the defense to prove Becher was a war criminal. It was up to the prosecution to remove Becher from this status if they wished to negate the affidavit. The Attorney General admitted that Becher was a war criminal.

"The lies in Kasztner's affidavit, the lies in his testimony concerning the document, Kasztner's knowing participation in the activities of Nazi war criminals, and his participation in the last-minute fake rescue activities all combine to show one overwhelming truth: that neither Rudolf Kasztner's affidavit nor his conduct before this Court was made in good faith."

For the first time, Greenwald let out a deep breath. The ghost of a smile started to form, but at a sharp glance from Tamir, the old man quickly suppressed it.

"Kasztner knew well, as he himself testified, that Becher had never stood up against the stream of Jewish extermination, as he stated in his affidavit. Neither Becher nor Himmler intended to save Jews. Rather, they intended to serve the Nazi regime. There is no truth in Kasztner's testimony that he never doubted for one moment the good intentions of Kurt Becher.

"Kasztner's recommendation was of decisive importance for Becher. Kasztner did not exaggerate when he said that Becher was released by the Allies because of his personal intervention. The lies in Kasztner's affidavit were sufficient to annul the value of his statements, and to prove there was no good faith in his testimony. Kasztner's affidavit in favor of Becher was willfully false, given in favor of a war criminal to save him from trial and punishment in Nuremberg.

"Therefore, the Court finds for the defendant, Malchiel Greenwald as regards the truth of his first, second, and fourth statements."

The judge paused, took out a white handkerchief, and mopped his brow. The bailiff poured a glass of water from a pitcher of water at his own table and handed it to the judge. Halevi coughed once, drank the water in a few gulps, and wiped his mouth with the handkerchief before he continued.

"However, the court does find by a preponderance of the evidence that Kasztner never actually personally collected money from the Nazis. On that account, and only on that account, the Court must regretfully find Mister Greenwald guilty of libel.

"Therefore, the Court orders, adjudges, and decrees that Malchiel Greenwald shall pay to the State of Israel for damages to Doctor Rudolf Kasztner the sum of one pound — fifty cents. Further, the Court orders the government of Israel to pay to Malchiel Greenwald the sum of ten thousand pounds in attorneys' fees and two hundred pounds as court costs. This Court is adjourned."

Judge Halevi stood, exhausted, and walked determinedly into his chambers. He refused to speak to anyone from the press.

The Minister of Justice of the State of Israel filed an appeal the following morning.

The Prime Minister's instruction to the Attorney General to lodge an appeal precipitated a cabinet crisis when the General Zionists refused to support the Government on a no-confidence motion.

The Kasztner case thus became a major issue in the election campaign of 1955. In a savage backlash of public fury, Sharett was voted out of office.

MARCH, 1957

TEL AVIV, ISRAEL

61

The city cast off its daytime cloak as the sun set in red-gold splendor over the Mediterranean. Soon the lights of Tel Aviv would burst forth in full array. From her small office beside the window, Ariana Greenwald could see the deepening shadows to the east, the line of bright lights created by the street lamps and the café-bound traffic on Dizengoff Street. Neon signs and stark white modernity proclaimed the presence of the waterfront's two newest monoliths, the Hilton and the Sheraton. Ariana glanced at her wristwatch. Five past six.

The man emerged five minutes later, smooth and suave as always. "Well, boys and girls," he said to the assembled staff of typists, secretaries, and junior clerks who were still working in the large central room. "I don't know about the rest of you, but I'm calling it a night."

As he passed each desk, the remarks of each staffer were delivered in perfunctory monotone, devoid of warmth or respect. Just before he opened the front door to leave, the Minister, apparently oblivious to the dispirited aura that pervaded the office, appeared in Ariana's doorway. "You're not coming out of your office to say goodnight to your superior?" he asked, his smile more of a leer than a paternal look.

She ignored him and started dictating into the Stenorette on her desk.

"More notes? For what, Ariana? Certainly it's time we let bygones be bygones. It is not beyond me to forgive and forget."

She glared at him wordlessly, then turned away.

"Very well," Kasztner said coolly. He turned on his heel and departed.

Rudolf Kasztner had had a busy day. He'd had conferences with various important government officials about the chances of his pending appeal to the Supreme Court and the possibility of a Kasztner trial. All was in order. The basic situation was unchanged. He knew the great leaders of Israel would stand behind him. They'd *better* stand behind him.

He'd noticed that the leaders had become a little cool toward him of late. They frowned and talked curtly in his presence. But Kasztner, a realist from way back, knew that into each life some rain must fall. Let them frown and snub him as much as they wanted. When the time came to fight for his honor and perhaps even for his life, the mighty state of Israel would rally to his side.

Kasztner drove over to the offices of *A Jovo*, the large and successful Hungarian newspaper he owned. By ten thirty that night, he'd finished his editorial work, straightened his desk, smoothed his hair with a pocket comb, and walked into the Tel Aviv night.

Two years ago, when the Cluj business and the Kurt Becher business and the parachutist business had come to Israel's attention, he might have felt nervous about walking down a dark street alone. But not tonight. On this night, the hotheads were off on other topics: the Gaza retreat and the business of Amos Ben-Gurion. This was a night of trouble for David Ben-Gurion, not Rudolf Kasztner.

Two months ago, the secret police guard which had been assigned to guard him since the announcement of the verdict had been relieved of their task. He was old news. Nobody cared about him any longer. An unruffled Kasztner stepped into his parked gray Chevrolet sedan and started for home. Twenty minutes later, he stepped out of his car in front of his residence at 6 Emmanuel Street. The air was balmy. The night glowed with starlight. Kasztner started across the pavement for his front door.

A young man stepped out of the shadows and asked, "Are you Doctor Kasztner?"

Kasztner answered politely, "Yes, I am."

The young man pulled a gun out of his pocket. Startled, Kasztner saw the weapon and started running. The young man fired a bullet, hitting his intended victim.

Kasztner felt a fire in his side. He yelled out in surprised pain and kept running. Two more bullets hit him in his head and body. He dropped and lay moaning in the street.

An ex-Haganah officer happened to be in the neighborhood. He'd been calling on his girlfriend and was just leaving on his motorcycle when the shooting started. He saw the assassin jump into a waiting Jeep and drive off.

After emergency surgery, Kasztner started to regain his health. Like the proverbial cat, the many-lived Kasztner appeared to have survived once again. But after ten days of continued improvement, Rudolf Kasztner took a sudden turn for the worse and died on March 15, 1957. There was an impressive funeral for the one-time rescuer of Jews. Doctor Rudolf Kasztner was buried with high honors and the government exhibited its grief.

Three men were arrested, tried, and convicted in connection with the crime. The actual confessed killer, Ze'ev Eckstein, had, until a few months before, been a paid undercover agent of the Israel Government Intelligence Service. The trial was brief and to the point. Eckstein was quickly convicted and sentenced to life imprisonment.

Eight months later he was quietly pardoned and exiled to Switzerland on full pension for the rest of his life.

On January 19, 1958 by a four-to-one vote, the Supreme Court of Israel reversed Judge Halevi's decision. All five Supreme Court Justices upheld Halevi's verdict in the 'criminally perjurious manner' in which Kasztner had saved Nazi war criminal Becher after the War. As a result of this judgment of partial reversal, Malchiel Greenwald was given a suspended sentence of one year and fined one Israeli pound — fifty cents, as court costs.

AFTERWORD

The trial, which government lawyers expected to last four days, lasted for two years, and resulted in 1955 in the acquittal of Malchiel Greenwald.

What ever happened to those involved, directly or by implication, after the trial?

Malchiel Greenwald died in 1958, shortly after the Supreme Court decision. Chaim Cohen (1911-2002), the Attorney General who prosecuted the case, was appointed to the Supreme Court in 1960, a position he held until his retirement in 1981.

Judge Benjamin Halevi (1910-1996) was also elevated to the Supreme Court in 1963. Halevi was one of three judges in the world-famous trial of Adolf Eichmann. In 1969, Halevi resigned from the court in order to enter politics. He was elected to three successive sessions of the Knesset, the Israeli parliament, serving from 1969 to 1983. During the Ninth Knesset he served as deputy speaker. He died in 1996 at the age of 86.

Samuel Tamir (1923-1987) had a notable career as a lawyer and conducted several famous political cases. He was elected to the Knesset, where he served from 1965 to 1980, rising to become Minister of Justice in the Menachem Begin government from 1977 until 1980. A larger-than-life character, Tamir's maverick politics finally led him into a party of one after several coalitions with nationalist parties. He resigned from the cabinet on August 5, 1980, when his party was frozen out of coalition decision-making. At the ensuing 1981 election he lost his seat. Soon afterwards he was chosen to head up the peace operation known as Operation Galilee that dealt with POWs after the war in southern Lebanon.

Finally, we touch briefly on the career of S.S. Obergruppenführer Kurt Becher (1909-1995), for whom Kasztner wrote his infamous affidavit.

In January 1945, Becher was appointed as special Reich Commissioner for all the concentration camps by Himmler. He was arrested in May 1945 by the Allies and imprisoned at Nuremberg, but was not prosecuted as a war criminal, serving only as a witness during the Nuremberg Trials, as a result of a statement provided on his behalf by Rudolf Kasztner. In his affidavit, Kasztner stated, "There can be no doubt that Becher belongs to the very few S.S. leaders having the courage to oppose the program of annihilation of the Jews, and trying to rescue human lives — that Kurt Becher did everything within the realm of possibilities to save innocent human beings from the blind fury of the Nazi leaders. I never doubted for one moment the good intentions of Kurt Becher."

After the war, Becher became a prosperous businessman in Bremen. He was the president of many corporations, including the Cologne-Handel Gesellschaft, which did extensive business with the Israeli government. By 1960, he was one of the wealthiest men in West Germany, with estimated assets of U.S. $30 million. He came to public attention once again in 1961, when he served as a witness for the prosecution during the trial in Jerusalem of S.S. Colonel Adolf Eichmann. He provided his testimony from his home in Germany, because he was unwilling to travel to Israel. He died a wealthy man in 1995.

Now, more than sixty-five years later, the dust has settled. Israel is beset from all sides with new problems, and peace, that most elusive of all dreams, continues to elude the Holy Land.

And as to those who cast such giant shadows in those pioneer years of toil, those building years, those critical years?

Mortui sunt omnes.

- THE END-

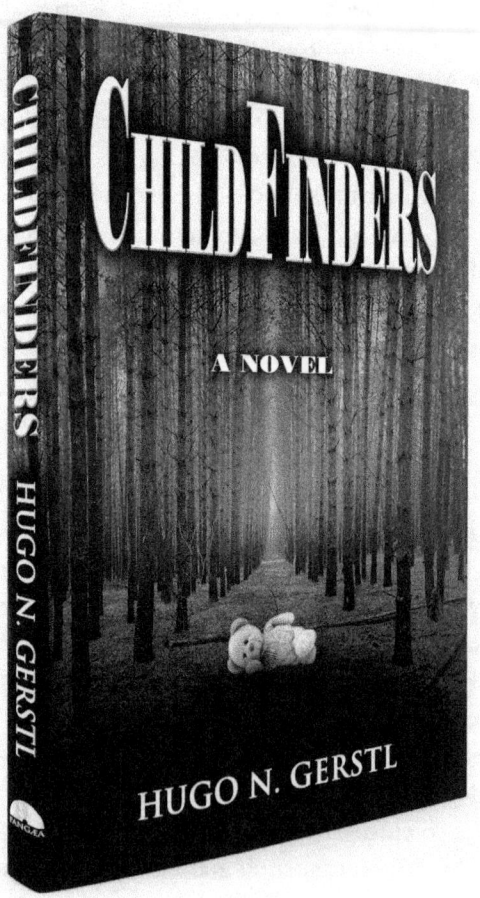

www.ingramcontent.com/pod-product-compliance
Lightning Source LLC
Chambersburg PA
CBHW072256020726

47501CB00002B/283